PRAISE FOR ARIEL LAWHON'S
FLIGHT OF DREAMS

"Mystery, romance—it is all here, told in a mesmerizing tale."   —Kate Alcott, *New York Times* bestselling author of *The Dressmaker*

"*Flight of Dreams* may be viewed as a *Titanic* of the skies. Lawhon's novel, however, needs no such comparison. It has ample emotional fuel to sail on its own, even knowing its spectacular end."   —The Associated Press

"A magnificent, tour de force story, *Flight of Dreams* will break your heart and satisfy every conspiracy theorist who's wondered what really happened to the *Hindenburg*. Simply spectacular. . . . Lawhon has written the book of the year. She's a writer to watch—now, and for many years to come."
—J. T. Ellison, author of *What Lies Behind*

"Difficult to put down."   —*BookPage*

"A spectacular page-turner of class and distinction. Intricately plotted and deftly characterized, this beautifully written novel is wonderfully satisfying—historical fiction at its best."   —Alex George, author of *A Good American*

"It's a sign of an extremely talented writer who can take a story that's been told before and tell it in a completely new, imaginative way that is so compelling and exciting."
—Charles Belfoure, author of *The Paris Architect*

"[A] wonderfully suspenseful, heart-wrenching account. . . . [Lawhon's] vision for the journey and the cause of the explosion is masterful."
— *The Free Lance-Star* (Fredericksburg, VA)

"Lawhon once again reimagines a front-page news event, filling in the entertaining backstory with passion, secrets, and nail-biting suspense." —*Publishers Weekly*

"The clever banter, elaborate plot twists, and period detail will be appreciated by lovers of historical fiction. Readers of Melanie Benjamin's *The Aviator's Wife* or Nancy Horan's *Under the Wide and Starry Sky* should find this entertaining." —*Library Journal*

ARIEL LAWHON
FLIGHT OF DREAMS

Ariel Lawhon is a critically acclaimed author of historical fiction. Her books have been translated into numerous languages and have been Library Reads, One Book One County, and Book of the Month Club selections. She is the cofounder of SheReads.org and lives in the rolling hills outside Nashville, Tennessee, with her husband, four sons, and a black Lab—who is, thankfully, a girl.

www.ariellawhon.com

FLIGHT

OF

DREAMS

A Novel

ARIEL LAWHON

ANCHOR BOOKS

A DIVISION OF PENGUIN RANDOM HOUSE LLC

NEW YORK

FIRST ANCHOR BOOKS EDITION, JANUARY 2016

The Library of Congress has cataloged the Doubleday edition
as follows:
Flight of dreams / by Ariel Lawhon. — First United States edition.
pages ; cm
1. Hindenburg (Airship) — Fiction.   2. Airships — Germany —
Fiction.   3. Aircraft accidents — New Jersey — Fiction.   I. Title.
PS3601.L447F58 2016   813'.6 — dc23   2015023339

Anchor Books Trade Paperback ISBN: 978-1-101-87392-2
eBook ISBN: 978-0-385-54003-2

www.anchorbooks.com

Printed in the United States of America
10 9 8 7 6 5 4 3 2 1

To love at all is to be vulnerable. Love anything, and your heart will certainly be wrung and possibly be broken.

— C. S. LEWIS, *THE FOUR LOVES*

FLIGHT

OF

DREAMS

Please inform the Zeppelin company in Frankfurt that they should open and search all mail before it is put on board prior to every flight of the Zeppelin *Hindenburg*. The Zeppelin is going to be destroyed by a time bomb during its flight to another country.

—*Letter from Kathie Rusch of Milwaukee to the German embassy in Washington, D.C., dated April 8, 1937*

This was not the first bomb threat, correct?" The man in the black glasses lifts the letter and waves it before the crowd. "Did anyone bother to *count* how many there were? Or, for God's sake, to *believe* them?"

Max thinks the man's last name is Schroeder, but he can't remember, and in truth he doesn't care. He's a fool if he believes that crazy woman from Milwaukee and her letter. Not that anyone else in the room is concerned with Max's quiet derision. People whisper and nod their heads like mindless puppets at the idea of sabotage. Search the mail, she said. There's a bomb on board, she said. It's a popular theory, especially now, with the wreckage still sprawled in the field outside. But no one cares about the truth. They prefer theatrics and conspiracy theories. And Schroeder is happy to provide them. He is ringmaster of this circus. He will make sure the mob is entertained.

Wilhelm Balla limps his way through the crowded hangar to stand next to Max. He escaped the crash with little more than a sprained ankle, but Max suspects he's exaggerating even that. He leans a bit hard to the left with each step, showing off. Letting the world know he's injured.

Balla searches Max's face for clues to his emotional state. "Emilie?" he asks.

"What about her?"

"She's prepared for the trip back to Germany?"

Max turns his attention to the spectacle at the front of the room. "I haven't asked."

"Let me know when she is. I'd like to say good-bye." Balla clears his throat. "They have me booked on the *Europa* with Werner on the fifteenth. How is she going home?"

"On the *Hamburg*. With the others. It sails in three days."

Wilhelm Balla is not a man who often displays emotion. It is up for debate whether he actually has a pulse. But this surprises him. "You aren't traveling with her?"

Max leans his head against the window. The cool glass feels good against his throbbing temple. He hasn't been able to shake this headache since the crash. No surprise, really, all things considered. "There are many things outside of my control, not the least of which is travel." He taps the envelope in his pocket with the pad of one finger and then draws his hand away. "I don't testify until the nineteenth. I'll take the *Bremen* the following day."

Balla gives him the long, appraising look that Max finds so aggravating. "How many times have you read Emilie's letter?"

"Once was enough." It's a lie. But he has no interest in confiding in Balla. Not after the trouble he caused.

From his position beside the window, Max can see the airfield and the charred skeleton that lies crumpled beside the mooring mast. He closes his eyes and tries to push the sight away, but to no avail. The images are there—will be there, he is certain, for the rest of his life; a single tongue of blue flame licking the *Hindenburg*'s spine, a fluttering of silver skin followed by the shudder of metallic bone, a flash, barely visible to those on the ground below. Bedlam. He is certain that the passengers close enough to see the explosion never heard it. They were simply consumed as the backbone of the great floating beast snapped in half. Thirty-four seconds of catastrophic billowing flames, followed by total, profound destruction. In half a minute the airship went from flying luxury hotel to smoking rubble—a skeleton lying crumpled in this New Jersey field, blacked by smoke and flame. No, these are things he will never forget.

Already the hearings have begun. There will be testimony. Reporters and flashbulbs. A different sort of pandemonium and a desperate attempt to understand *why*. There will be political conflagration. Headlines screaming out their theories in bold print, punctuated for emphasis. ACCIDENT! SABOTAGE! Fingers pointing in all directions and, of course, the subtle, insinuating whispers. The quiet placing of blame. Max wonders if their names and faces will be forgotten when the headlines are replaced by some new tragedy. Will anyone remember the particulars of those who fell from the sky a few short days ago? The vaudeville acrobat. The cabin boy. The journalists. An American heiress. The German cotton broker and the Jewish food distributor. A young family of German expatriates living in Mexico City. Chefs and mechanics. Photographers and navigators. The commander and his crew. A small army of stewards and Emilie, the only stewardess. Old men and young boys. Women past their prime and a fourteen-year-old girl who loved her father above all else. Will anyone remember them?

Bureaucrats measure loss with dollar signs and damage control. Already they have begun. There is standing room only in this hangar. But Max knows that to him, the cost will always be measured by lives lost. He also knows that in nine days, when his time comes to sit in that chair and give testimony, he will not tell them the truth. Instead he will look over Schroeder's shoulder at a point on the far wall and tell the lie he has already decided upon. It is the only way to protect Emilie. And the others. Max Zabel will swear before God and this committee that it was an uneventful flight.

DAY ONE

3 days, 6 hours, and 8 minutes until the explosion

Here is the goal of man's dream for many, many
generations. Not the airplane, not the hydroscope,
man has dreamed of a huge graceful ship that lifted
gently into the air and soared with ease. It is come, it is
completely successful, it is breathtakingly beautiful.

—Akron Beacon Journal

THE STEWARDESS

I t's a bad idea, don't you think?" Emilie asks, as she stands inside the kitchen door, propping it open with her foot. "Striking a match in here? You could blow us all to oblivion."

Xaver Maier is young for a head chef, only twenty-five, but he wears the pressed white uniform—a double-breasted jacket and checkered pants—with an air of authority. The starched apron is tied smartly at his waist, the toque fitted snuggly to his head. He gives her that careless, arrogant smirk that she has begrudgingly grown fond of and puts the cigarette to his lips. He inhales so deeply that she can see his chest expand, and then blows the smoke out the open galley window into the warm May evening. "Ventilation, love, it's all about proper ventilation."

The way he says the word, the way he holds his mouth, is clearly suggestive of other things, and she dismisses him with a laugh. Xaver Maier is much younger than Emilie and a great deal too impressed with himself. "At the moment, *love*, it's about aspirin. I need two. And a glass of water if you can summon the effort."

The kitchen is small but well ordered, and Xaver's assistant chefs are busy chopping, boiling, and basting in preparation for dinner. He stands in the center of the melee like a colonel directing his troops, an eye on every small movement.

"Faking a headache?" he asks. "Poor Max. I thought you'd finally come around. We've been taking bets, you know."

"Don't," she says, flinging a drawer open and shuffling through the contents. She has made it perfectly clear that all discussion of Max is off limits. She will make up her mind when she is good and ready. "I went to the dentist yesterday, and the left side of my jaw feels like it's about to fall off." She leaves the drawer open and moves on to another.

"Usually when a woman tells me her jaw is sore I apologize."

Emilie opens a third drawer. Then a fourth. Slams it. "I had a tooth filled." She's impatient now. And irritated. "*Aspirin?* I know you keep it around here somewhere."

He follows behind her, shoving the drawers shut. "Enough of that. You're as bad as the *verdammt* Gestapo."

"What?" She looks up.

Xaver reaches behind her head and lifts the door to a high, shallow cabinet attached to the ceiling. He pulls out a bottle of aspirin but doesn't hand it over. "I'm glad to hear you don't know *everything* that happens aboard this airship." He taps the bottle against the heel of his hand, making the pills inside rattle around with sharp little pings. "There's still the chance of keeping secrets."

"You can't keep secrets from me." She holds out her hand, palm up. "Two aspirin and a glass of water. What Gestapo?"

Xaver counts them out as though he's paying a debt. "They came because of the bomb threats. Fifteen of them in their *verdammte* gray uniforms."

"When?" She takes a glass from the drying board above the sink and fills it with tepid water. Emilie swallows her pills in one wild gulp.

"Yesterday. They searched the entire ship. Took almost three hours. I had to take the security officers down the lower keel walkway to the storage areas. The bastards opened every tin of caviar, every wheel of aged Camembert, and don't think they didn't sample everything they could find. Looking for explosives, they said. I was out half the night trying to find replacements. And," he pauses to take a long, calming drag on his cigarette, "you can be certain that frog-faced distributor in the Bockenheim district didn't take kindly to being woken at midnight to fill an order for goose liver pâté."

She has heard of the bomb threats, of course; they all have. Security measures have been tightened. Her bags were checked before she was allowed on the airfield that afternoon. But it seems so ridiculous, so impossible. Yet this is life in the new Germany, they say. A trigger-happy government. Suspicious of everyone, regardless of citizenship. No, not citizenship, she corrects herself, *race*.

Emilie looks out the galley windows at the empty tarmac. "Did you know they aren't letting anyone come for the send-off? All the passengers are waiting at a hotel in the city to be shuttled over by bus. No fanfare this time."

"Should be a fun flight."

"That," she says with a grin, "will have to wait until the return trip. We're fully booked. All those royalty-smitten Americans traveling over for King George's coronation."

"I'd take a smitten American. Preferably one from California. *Blondine.*"

Emilie rolls her eyes as he whistles and forms an hourglass figure with his hands.

"*Schwein*," she says, but she leans forward and gives him a kiss on the cheek anyway. "Thank you for the aspirin."

The kitchen smells of yeast and garlic and the clean, tangy scent of fresh melons. Emilie is hungry, but it will be some time before she gets the chance to eat. She is lamenting her inadequate early lunch when a low, good-humored voice speaks from the doorway.

"So that's all it takes to get a kiss from Fräulein Imhof?"

Max.

Emilie doesn't have to turn around to identify the voice. She is embarrassed that he has found her like this, flirting—albeit innocently—with the ship's resident lothario.

"I worked hard for that kiss. You should do so well," Xaver defends himself.

"I should like the opportunity to try."

The matter-of-fact way he says it unnerves her. Max looks dapper in his pressed navy-blue uniform. His hair is as dark and shiny as his shoes. The gray eyes do not look away. He waits patiently, as ever, for her to respond. How does he do that? she wonders. Max sees the bewilderment on her face, and a smile tugs at one corner of his mouth, hinting at a dimple, but he wrestles it into submission and turns to Xaver.

"Commander Pruss wants to know tonight's dinner menu. He will be dining with several of the American passengers and hopes the food will provide sufficient distraction."

Xaver bristles. "Commander Pruss will no longer notice his companions when my meal arrives. We will dine on poached salmon with a creamy spice sauce, château potatoes, green beans *à la princesse*, iced California melon, freshly baked French rolls, and a variety of cakes, all washed down with Turkish coffee and a sparkling 1928 Feist Brut." He says this, chin lifted, the stiff notes of dignity in his voice, as though citing the provenance of a painting and then squints at Max. "Should I write that down? I don't want him being told I'm cooking fish and vegetables for dinner."

Max repeats the details verbatim, and Xaver gives a begrudging nod of approval.

"Now, out of my kitchen. Both of you. I have work to do. Dinner is at ten sharp." He shuffles them into the keel corridor, then closes the door. Xaver might be an opportunist—he would gladly take a real kiss from Emilie if she were to offer one—but he knows of her budding affection, and he's more than willing to make room for it to bloom further.

Max leans against the wall. His smile is tentative, testing. "Hello, Emilie. I've missed you."

She's certain the chef is on the other side listening. She can smell cigarette smoke drifting through the crack around the door. He would like nothing better than to dish out a portion of gossip with the evening meal. And Emilie would love to tell Max that she has missed him as well in the months since their last passenger flight. She would love to tell him that she has very much looked forward to today. But she doesn't want to give Xaver the satisfaction. The moment passes into awkward silence.

"Listen . . ." Max reaches out his hand to brush one finger against her cheek when the air horn sounds with a thunderous bellow from the control car below them. The tension is broken and they shift away from each other. He shoves his hands in his pockets and stares at the ceiling. "That is such a hateful noise."

Emilie tugs at the cuff of her blouse, pulling it over the base of her thumb. She doesn't look at Max. "We're about to start boarding passengers."

"I really must see if they can do something about that. A whistle, maybe?"

"I should get out there and greet them."

"Emilie—"

But she's already backing away, coward that she is, on her way down the corridor to the gangway stairs.

THE JOURNALIST

Gertrud Adelt has no patience for fools. In her opinion, Americans fit the description almost categorically. The one sitting across from her now is drunk, leaning precariously into the aisle and singing out of tune. He shouts the words to some bawdy drinking song as if he were dancing on a bar instead of sitting in a bus filled with exhausted passengers. His voice is bombastic, loud and abrasive, and *mein Gott, please make him stop,* she thinks. She turns her pretty mouth to her husband's ear and quietly asks, "Can't you do something?"

Leonhard looks at his watch, then up at the heavily listing American. "He's been drinking since three o'clock. I'd say he's managing quite well, all things considered."

"He's obnoxious."

"He's happy to be leaving Deutschland. There's no crime in that." The look he gives her is tinged with understanding. Who wouldn't want to leave this country? Anyone but the two of them, most likely. As it stands, the thought makes her ache. Their son, little more than a year old, is in the care of Gertrud's mother at the insistence of a senior SS officer. Blackmail by way of separation. Return as promised, or else. In recent months, Germany has grown adept at making sure that valued citizens do not defect.

The Adelts have spent the better part of their day waiting in the lobby of Frankfurt's Hof Hotel. Waiting for lunch. Waiting for a telegram from Leonhard's publisher. Waiting for the government to change their minds and revoke permission for the trip altogether. At four o'clock the buses arrived to shuttle them to the Rhein-Main Flughafen. But then they waited while their luggage was searched and their papers checked and double-checked and triple-checked. The first indication that Gertrud was ready to snap came when her bag was weighed.

"I'm sorry, Frau Adelt," the customs officer informed her. "Your bag is fifteen kilos over the twenty-kilo limit. You will have to pay a fine of five marks for every extra kilo."

Gertrud looked around the bar, eyeing each of the men waiting to board the buses. She sniffed and rose to her full height. "Then it's a good thing I weigh twenty kilos less than the average passenger."

The customs officer was not amused, and Leonhard handed over the seventy-five marks before Gertrud could further complicate the process. By the time they were finally allowed on the bus and took their seats, she was exhausted and entirely without coping skills to deal with fellow passengers.

Now, the long muscles along her spine feel ready to snap. They are tight and aching, strained by her rigid posture over the last few hours. The American's voice grinds against her skull like mortar against pestle. The back of her eyes hurt. Gertrud fights the irrational urge to reach across the aisle and strike his face. She tucks her hands between her knees instead.

Something outside the window catches the American's attention and he drifts into silence. Gertrud sighs, squeezes her eyes shut, and leans her head against Leonhard's shoulder. The bus rumbles along steadily for a few moments, vibrations coming up through the floor and into their feet. They are jostled by the occasional pothole—the broad paved streets of Frankfurt have fallen into disrepair, but fixing them hardly seems a priority to anyone. They soon pass a sign with a white arrow directing them to the airfield. The bus veers to the left, and an excited murmur runs through the passengers. Somewhere, behind them, a child cheers. Gertrud feels a twinge of anger that some other child is allowed to make the voyage while hers is forced to stay behind. The American, however, is energized by their near arrival and belts out the second verse of his drinking song. He leans toward her, eyes crossed, chuckling, and she recoils from his sour breath.

Leonhard grabs her wrist just as she's about to lash out. "No," he says. "Be good." Her husband is twenty-two years older than she is, but time has not dulled his strength one iota. He puts two broad hands around her waist and lifts her up and over his lap. Leonhard deposits her neatly by the window, his body a wall between her and the American.

Gertrud offers a wry smile. "Good? You know that being *good* isn't part of my skill set."

"Now is not the time to talk about your many attributes, *Liebchen*. Humor me this once. Please?"

She can still hear the American, but she can no longer see him, and this is a great mercy. She gives Leonhard's hand a squeeze of gratitude, then leans her forehead against the cool glass of the window. She tries not to think of Egon and his chubby, dimpled fists. His bright blue eyes. The soft brown hair that is just starting to coil above his ears. Gertrud thinks instead of the career she has worked so hard to build and how it lies in rubble behind her. Her press card having been revoked by Hitler's Ministry of Propaganda. Troublemaker, that's what they have branded her. In reality she has simply been a question asker. She is a good journalist. But she has never been a good rule follower. Or a good girl, for that matter, despite Leonhard's admonition. Yet, even now, she cannot bring herself to regret the choices she has made this year.

A few minutes later the bus slows and turns onto the airfield. A great hangar looms in front of them, taller, wider, longer than any structure she has ever seen. And moored just outside is the D-LZ129 *Hindenburg*, almost sixteen stories tall and over eight hundred feet long. From their vantage point, Gertrud can barely make out the airship's name written aft of the bow in a blood-red Gothic font, and farther back, the massive tail fins emblazoned with their fifty-foot swastikas. The irony is not lost on her. They will make this trip, but only under a watchful Nazi eye.

"*Mein Gott,*" Leonhard whispers, placing one large, calloused hand on her knee.

The zeppelin floats several feet off the ground, moored on either side by thick, corded landing lines. The only parts of the actual structure that touch the ground are the landing wheels and a set of retractable gangway ladders that lead up and into the passenger decks. They will board there, directly into the behemoth's swollen silver belly. Gertrud stops herself from cracking jokes about Jonah and his infamous whale, but she does feel very much as though she's about to be swallowed whole.

The ground crew scurries around, preparing to cast off, while the flight crew stands in a long, neat line near the gangway waiting to greet them. The American chooses this moment to finish his drinking song with one last, raucous burst.

Gertrud is up and out of her seat like a shot. She climbs over Leonhard, knees the American in the shoulder, and rushes down the aisle without regard for any of the other passengers. "I'm sorry," she says by way of apology to the driver. "I'm feeling sick. I need fresh air." The bus is still rolling to a stop, but the driver swings the door open and Gertrud takes the steps two at a time, only pausing to breathe when her feet are planted firmly on the ground. She stands off to the side, waiting for Leonhard, while the other passengers unload and venture toward the ship, forming a line in front of the crew. She clenches her fists and inhales deeply through her nose. For the first time since early that afternoon she can neither see nor hear the American. Gertrud takes another deep, ragged breath and stands with her eyes closed in the middle of the tarmac, soaking in the fresh, cool evening air. She can feel the tension begin to lessen in her neck.

A bevy of ground crew come to collect the luggage stored in compartments beneath the bus, but Gertrud intercepts one of them and grabs a brown leather satchel. "I'll keep this with me," she says. "It's mine."

"Come along." Leonhard has their tickets in hand, and he steers her to the back of the line. In front of them is a family of five. Two young boys jump up and down, barely able to contain their excitement, while their teenage sister holds her father's hand and grins with unabashed delight.

"I can't do this," Gertrud whispers. "Egon—"

"Will be fine," he says, finishing her sentence with certainty. "Three months. We can do this for three months."

"He will think we have abandoned him."

"He will not even remember our absence." Leonhard sets his hands on her shoulders. He looks at her calmly, with a smile that does not reach his eyes. He appears lighthearted, jovial even. His voice, though, is low and measured and serious. "We will do what we have to do, *Liebchen*. And then we will return home to our son. Now, turn and give your papers to the steward. Do it with a smile if possible."

They are greeted at the base of the gangway by the chief steward. His name tag reads HEINRICH KUBIS—neat, square little letters as neat and square as the man himself. He takes their paperwork, scrutinizes it, then runs the stubby end of one finger along his clipboard. "Ah. You are in one of the staterooms on B-deck," he says. "Cabin nine, just aft of the smoking room. Your bags will be taken up, and you are free to board. If you follow these stairs all the way to the top you will have a lovely view of takeoff from the portside dining salon on A-deck."

"May I take your bag, Frau Adelt?" Gertrud hears the voice, recognizes it as female, but does not acknowledge it. She stares instead at the rectangle of light at the top of the gangway stairs.

"Frau Adelt?" Again that voice. She ignores it.

Leonhard pulls the satchel from her hands. "Yes. Please. My wife would like that very much."

"It will be with your things."

Leonhard leads his wife up the steps, but it is as though she's an automaton, stiff and leaden. "You were quite awful to that woman just now."

His voice registers. "What?"

"The stewardess. The one who took your bag. You didn't even look at her. You will have to watch that, *Liebchen*."

Gertrud looks over her shoulder and sees the back of a tall, slender woman dressed in uniform. Her hair is dark and wavy and falls neatly to her shoulders. One of the ship's officers approaches her, his hands tucked shyly in his pockets, and she laughs at something he says. The stewardess has the charming, musical sort of laugh that Gertrud has always envied in other women. She sniffs, irritated.

The gaze she levels at her husband borders on panic. "My mind is on other things right now. Yours should be as well."

THE NAVIGATOR

"You're staring at her again."

Max turns to find a slow, amused smile disrupting the sharp angles of Wilhelm Balla's usually stoic face. It looks ill-fitting on the steward, as though he has borrowed another man's coat.

"Wouldn't you?"

"I would go talk to her, not stand there like a pubescent boy with a secret crush."

"It's hardly a secret."

"Get on with it, then."

"Emilie is greeting passengers. And we've already said hello."

For a man with such a blunt personality, Wilhelm Balla has razor-sharp insight. "Can't have been much of a greeting. You didn't kiss her."

"How—"

The steward cuts him off by holding up his manifest—right between their faces—and reading from it. "It appears as though Frau Imhof is greeting the last of her passengers now. Journalists from Frankfurt. She will likely have a few scarce moments before boarding herself."

Max can't hear what Emilie says to the dismissive young woman, but she has to repeat herself. The journalist still doesn't respond, and her husband finally tugs a satchel from her hands and passes it to Emilie with an apologetic shrug. Emilie looks slightly embarrassed, and Max takes a strong and immediate dislike to the journalists.

"Did she tell you I didn't kiss her?" He clears his throat. "Did she want me to—"

"Go."

The steward gives Max one hard shove. He stumbles forward and tucks his hands in his pockets because he doesn't know what else to do with them. Emilie stands near the portside gangway holding the satchel and scowling at the couple as they whisper intently on their way up.

"Pay them no mind," he mutters low, over her shoulder, so that his breath tickles her ear. "People go crazy when they fly. I've seen decorated soldiers lose their *Scheiße*."

She laughs, loudly at first, and then lower, a gentle shaking of her shoulders. God, he loves her laugh.

"Are you going to commandeer every conversation I have over the next three days?"

"Are you going to kiss everyone but me?"

"I didn't kiss either of *them*."

"You kissed the cook."

"Chef. And you sound petty. I can kiss who I like."

He loves this about Emilie. How brassy and direct she is. They are well matched in spirit, if not height. Emilie is but an inch or two shorter than Max, and he constantly finds himself in the unusual position of facing her eye to eye depending on her footwear. He is tall; so is she, for a woman.

"Kiss whoever you like. As long as I'm the one you like the most." He lowers his voice. "You did promise me an answer on this flight. Have you forgotten?"

Emilie is about to respond when they are interrupted by screeching tires.

Max grabs Emilie by the arm and pulls her back a step as the careening taxi lurches to a stop beside the airship. A small, wiry man leaps from the backseat, followed by a dog so alarmingly white that Emilie gasps. The new arrival surveys the curious onlookers as though he has come onstage for an encore. Max half expects him to bow. Instead, the dog barks and things disintegrate into bedlam. Three security guards, two customs officials, and the chief steward all descend on the strange little man as though he's holding a detonator. But he fans his ticket and travel papers in front of his face without the least bit of concern.

"Joseph Späh!" he announces to no one in particular, and this time he does give a theatrical bow. He motions toward the dog. "And this is Ulla. We are so pleased to join everyone on this voyage."

The ground crew searches his bags, and Späh hangs back to watch, quietly mocking their curiosity. One of the soldiers finds a brightly wrapped package and tears off the paper. He lifts a doll from the pile of tissue and appears somewhat disappointed at the find.

"It's a girl, *Dummkopf*," Späh says when the officer turns it over to check beneath the ruffled skirt.

It takes no small amount of time to verify that Joseph Späh is a legitimate passenger on board the *Hindenburg*, that Ulla's presence and freight have been approved and paid for in advance, and to locate his cabin—which, as it turns out, is on A-deck near the dining room, much to Späh's satisfaction. He seems delighted at the prospect of maintaining his role as entertainer.

Max and Emilie watch the entire spectacle in bemused silence, and he takes immense pleasure in the fact that she does not draw her arm away from his hand. He can feel the warmth of her skin through the thin sleeve of her dress. Max soaks it in. He has never given her more than a glancing touch before. This is progress.

Max's reverie is broken by the guttural clearing of a throat. He turns to find Heinrich Kubis staring at his hand on Emilie's arm. The chief steward drops two bulging mailbags at Max's feet. "These are yours, I believe?"

He releases Emilie and lifts the bags. They are surprisingly heavy, but he's determined not to show it. "So there's the last of it. Commander Pruss said two more loads were coming on the bus."

Emilie nods at the bags. "What's this?"

"Max is our new postmaster," Kubis says. He glances at Max and Emilie as though an idea has just occurred to him. "He will attend to those duties in his off hours."

"His off hours? Meaning he won't *have* any hours off?"

"You will have precious few yourself, Fräulein Imhof. And I'd highly suggest that you not spend them fraternizing with an officer in full view of the passengers." He tips his head toward the control car. "Or the commander."

Max is absurdly pleased that Emilie looks disappointed at this news. Perhaps she had imagined ways of filling his spare time? He takes a step back and clicks his heels sharply. Nods. "If you will excuse me, I need to get these stored in the mailroom before we cast off."

Emilie is not pleased that their conversations seem to end on his terms, and he enjoys the lines of frustration that appear between her eyes. "Don't you want my answer?" she calls after him.

"Send it by post!"

She may have something left to say, but he doesn't wait to hear it. Max turns, a mailbag gripped tightly in each hand, and walks up the gangway. Instead of taking a sharp right and going up another set of stairs to A-deck, he turns left into the keel corridor and heads toward the front of the airship.

Max neatly sidesteps Wilhelm Balla. He has his hand on the elbow of a staggering American who is mumbling the words to some lewd drinking song, but the man slurs so badly Max catches only every other word.

"No. Your cabin is this way," Balla says. "Nothing to see down there."

Max offers the steward a cheerful smile. "Good luck with that."

Balla expertly holds up the American with one arm while

checking his manifest with the other. "The good news is that this *Arschloch*'s room isn't on A-deck. I probably couldn't get him up the stairs. The better news is that his cabin is right next to Kubis."

The chief steward is a teetotaler and not generally fond of anything originating from America, whether people or products. Watching these two interact over the next few days should be interesting. Balla, at least, is smiling at the prospect. He shuffles off with the American, wearing the impish grin of a schoolboy anticipating some minor disaster.

The mailroom is down the corridor, on the left, just before the officers' quarters, and Max has to drop the mailbags so he can unlock the door. All 17,000 pieces of mail were inspected by hand earlier that day in Frankfurt. The cutoff for letters to make this flight was three o'clock, and based on the weight of the last two bags, there was quite a last-minute rush. This is Max's first flight as postmaster, having inherited the position from Kurt Schönherr for this year's flight season, and he inspects the room carefully to make sure everything is in order.

The room smells of paper and ink and musty canvas, and in the dim light the piles of mail bear an uncomfortable resemblance to body bags. A bag marked KÖLN hangs on a hook by the door, waiting for the airdrop later that evening. In the corner is a squat, black, protective container. Metal. Locked. Fireproof. And off-limits to everyone but him. Inside are pieces of registered mail. And the items that require special care or discretion. The key to this lockbox is on the ring at Max's waist. Three hours ago he was given a small package, one hundred newly printed marks, and a promise that if the package is kept safe until their arrival in New Jersey, he would receive another hundred.

The parcel is inside the lockbox, and the box itself is, thankfully, still locked. Max scans the room one more time to make sure everything is in order. Then he pats the mailbag headed for Cologne and locks the door behind him.

THE AMERICAN

He isn't drunk. Not even close. It would take more than three watered-down gin and tonics to make him stumble. But he leans on the steward's arm just the same. A well-timed lurch, a garbled word here and there, and no one is the wiser. The easiest way to be dismissed is to appear inordinately pissed in public.

Before he's shuffled away by the steward, the American takes note of the key ring clipped to the officer's belt and which door leads to the mailroom. Its proximity to the control car is problematic — there will always be officers lurking about — but he can deal with that later. The keel corridor is long and narrow with walls that slant outward, and he and the steward have to stand aside to let others pass four times before they reach his stateroom. It wouldn't be appropriate to deposit a wasted Yankee in someone else's cabin, so the humorless steward checks his clipboard twice before shoving the door open and guiding him to the bed. The steward's name tag reads WILHELM BALLA, and his white jacket is perfectly pressed, as are the corners of his mouth. The American takes a perverse pride in the steward's disapproval.

"You've got the room to yourself, so there's no need to worry about inconveniencing anyone else while you sleep this off." The steward shrugs out from beneath one of the American's leaden arms. The American tips backward into the berth, seemingly incoherent. "Dinner is at ten. You'll be seated at Commander Pruss's table, I understand?" He waits for a beat and then continues, not bothering to hide the disdain in his voice. "I'll come collect you if you've not woken by then."

The American does not respond. He counts to five after the door clicks shut. Then he sits up and straightens his jacket. The room is larger than is typical for a cabin on board an airship. Eight feet wide by ten feet long. One berth that can sleep two instead of bunk beds. But it's the window that makes it worth the ticket price. Like the windows elsewhere on board, this one is long and narrow and set into the slanted wall. Unlike the observation windows on the promenade, however, this one does not open. The sink and writing desk are larger here than on A-deck—there's a bit of room to spread out. The small, narrow closet has enough room to hang a handful of shirts and trousers, but the rest of his clothing will need to be stowed beneath the bed. No trouble, he only checked two bags, and the item he is most eager to find isn't in either of them. The American stands in the middle of the room and turns in small quarter-circle increments, methodically taking note of every detail. The walls and ceiling are made of foam board, thin and covered with cloth. Sound will travel easily through them. A handy thing if one wants to listen in on the conversations of one's fellow passengers.

Where would it be? He tips his head to the side, pensive. Not in the closet. A quick search finds no hidden panels or packages. Neither is it in the mattress, pillowcases, or any of the bedding. The cabinets above and below the sink are empty, as is the light fixture attached to the ceiling. The American wonders for a brief moment if his request has been refused. He dismisses the idea out of hand. His requests are never refused. There is only one place in the room he has not checked, and he immediately feels a sense of disappointment. He thought the officer would have more imagination. Apparently not. He finds what he's looking for beneath the berth in the farthest, darkest corner: an olive-green military-issue canvas bag. He is pleased with the contents.

A note, folded in half, with three words scrawled in black ink by a hasty hand: *Make it clean.*

A dog tag strung on a rusted ball chain, once belonging to the man he has come to kill. And a pistol, a Luger with a fully loaded cartridge. But there is no name. He was promised a name. He lifts the tag and inspects the information stamped on its surface. They expect him to decipher this clue on his own. They have baited him.

The American slides the bag under his pillow and stretches out on the bed, his arms beneath his head. He's still lying there ten minutes later when the steward returns with his suitcases. They are tucked beneath the bed and once again he is alone. But not asleep. He is thinking about what he must do next. He is thinking about the mailroom and how he will get inside unnoticed before they reach Cologne later tonight. He is thinking about the letter that has to be delivered. The American creates a mental inventory of each action that needs to be taken over the next three days and how everything—absolutely everything—must go according to plan.

THE CABIN BOY

Werner Franz will not let them see him cry. He has smashed his knee into the edge of a large steamer trunk and the pain is so sharp and deep inside the bone that he can feel a howl building in his chest and he clamps his teeth shut so it won't come bellowing out. If he were at home or at school or anywhere but here with these men, he would allow himself the luxury of sobbing. But he will not prove himself a baby in front of his fellow crew members. He already takes enough ribbing as it is. So Werner steps aside and closes his eyes. Men pass him carrying trunks and luggage. He hears the shuffling of feet and the bark of a dog and a muttered curse, and he counts to ten silently, trying to compose himself. He lets out a long, deep breath, his scream subdued into silence, but he can't help glaring at the trunk. It's none the worse for wear, but he'll be bruised for weeks.

Werner spins around when a large hand grips his shoulder. He looks directly into a broad barrel chest, then up into the face of Ludwig Knorr. The man is a legend on this ship, and Werner is in awe of him. But it's the sort of awe that leads him to scuttle out of a room when Knorr enters, or to press himself against the corridor wall when they pass one another. A sort of reverence turned to abject terror, even though the man has never so much as spoken to him. Until now.

"If you're going to kick something," Knorr says, his voice a low rumble, "make sure it's the door and not that trunk." He points at the letters LV stamped in gold filigree across the leather. "It costs more than you'll make all year. Understand?"

Werner nods his head. Drops his eyes. "Yes, Herr Knorr."

Ludwig ruffles his hair. "And steer clear of Kubis for a while. He's in a rage today. It's the dogs. He hates dogs."

Heinrich Kubis checks the tag on the trunk next to Werner. Then he orders one of the riggers to take it to the cargo area instead of to the passenger quarters. He ticks a box on the clipboard in his hand and moves on to the next item. Beside Kubis is a large provisioning hatch that opens onto the tarmac below, where a pile of luggage is waiting to be lifted into the ship. The tricky part is determining whether the items go to the cabins or the cargo area. Kubis is unruffled, however, and gives orders without the slightest hesitation.

There is a frantic scrambling and clanging as the dogs are raised on the cargo platform. They spin and bark and whimper, making their wicker crates rattle. Werner knows the poor little beasts are terrified, but Kubis shows no sympathy. "To the cargo hold," he orders, and the cages are lifted by two riggers apiece and carted away through the cavernous interior of the ship.

"I will never understand," Kubis mutters, "why these fools insist on traveling with their pets."

After ten more minutes of Kubis griping about live cargo, all the luggage has been dispersed except for one leather satchel. This he hands to Werner. "Stateroom nine on B-deck. Set it neatly on the bed so Frau Adelt will see it upon entering. She is, apparently, quite particular about her things."

Werner takes the satchel and heads toward the passenger area. He is as familiar with the layout of this ship as he is with his parents' apartment in Frankfurt. He turns the corner near the gangway stairs a bit too fast, almost knocking a young woman to the ground. But she has great reflexes and an even better sense of humor. She dances out of the way with a smile.

"I'm so sorry, Fräulein." Werner blushes.

She ignores the apology. "Have you seen my brother?"

Werner is typically quick on his feet and quite affable. But this girl is *very* pretty. And she looks to be about his age. She's staring at him, waiting for an answer to her question. He can't seem to remember what she asked, so he stands there with the satchel clutched stupidly to his chest.

"My brother?" she asks again. "Have you seen him? He's eight and blond and I'm going to wring his neck when I find him. Mama is in a state looking for him."

"No." Werner clears his throat so his voice won't crack. "I've not seen him."

"Well, if you come across the little imp, would you send him to the observation deck?"

"Of course. What is his name?"

"Werner."

"That is my name also." He almost doesn't ask. It isn't technically appropriate. But the question is out before he can reel it back in. "What is yours?"

Her eyes widen a bit, but in surprise, he thinks, not objection. "Irene."

He's careful to give her a small subservient nod. "Nice to meet you."

Irene almost says something to this—her lips are parted slightly as though to reply—but she appears to change her mind. She pauses for a moment, then flounces off without another word. But when she turns to go up the stairs to A-deck, Werner can see a smile playing at the corners of her mouth, and she betrays herself by giving him a quick backward glance before she disappears. He stands there, watching her go, wondering why he wishes she would come back and make some other impertinent remark about her brother.

It has been almost two years since Werner was in school, and just as long since he has spent any significant amount of time around girls. So he is surprised by the heat in his cheeks and the smile on his face. He does not know what to make of the flipping in his stomach. Werner cannot identify the subtle shift that takes place within him as he carries the satchel through the open door and into the Adelts' stateroom. He places it carefully beside the pillow. It feels as though the wires in his mind have come alive all at once in a sudden rush of electrical current. There is a buzzing in his head. He knows what it's like to be afraid and to be exhausted and to be hungry, and even though this feels like a combination of all three, he is aware that it is something different. Something unique. Werner Franz makes his way to the observation deck to join the rest of the stewards, experiencing something very new indeed.

THE STEWARDESS

The promenade on A-deck is filled with passengers leaning over the slanted observation windows when Emilie enters, holding the hand of a tear-stained young boy who has lost his mother. She squats down next to him, his hand nestled in her palm, and points at a short, capable-looking woman who is stretched onto her tiptoes to see over the shoulders of the man in front of her. "See, there she is. I told you we wouldn't leave without her."

Matilde Doehner. Emilie pronounces the woman's name to herself three times—once in German, once in English, and once in Italian—to set the face in her mind. It had taken poor little Werner two minutes of rattled sobs to stutter her name. He'd managed to say his own name with a teakettle screech and a fresh batch of tears.

The child is eight years old and clinging to the last remnants of little boyhood. He pulls his hand from Emilie's, wipes his sleeve across his nose, then takes a deep breath that bears an uncanny resemblance to a hiccup. "Please don't tell my brother I cried. He'll think I'm a baby."

His little face is so earnest, so fearful that she has to suppress a laugh. "I won't say a word. I promise."

Werner's brother—Walter, she notes, again mentally, repeating the name in every language she knows—stands next to their mother, back turned. The bottom of one pant leg is tucked into his sock, and his shoes are unlaced. Emilie is certain that when push comes to shove—which it certainly will, they are boys after all—little Werner will be able to hold his own. "Off you go," she says, then gently nudges him toward his mother.

He squares his shoulders and joins his family as they jostle for position in front of the windows. He announces his arrival by giving Walter a pre-emptive elbow in the ribs. *I'm here,* that elbow says, *and I'm not afraid of you.* Emilie fights the ache she feels at the good-natured tussle.

"Neatly done, Fräulein Imhof."

It takes her one beat too long to recognize Colonel Fritz Erdmann. He's wearing civilian clothes instead of his Luftwaffe uniform. He hasn't shaved. And he looks haggard.

"Colonel Erdmann"—she dips her head slightly in respect—"how can I help you?"

Erdmann motions her to step aside with him. He lowers his head and his voice. "I need you to page my wife."

"But we're about to cast off—"

"Bring her to me. I need to say good-bye."

Erdmann has a strong Germanic brow ridge and bright, curious eyes. Emilie feels very much as though she's being skewered by his gaze. And she would like to ask if there is someone else who can perform this errand—she is in the middle of her duties, after all—but the look on Colonel Erdmann's face brooks no argument.

"Of course," she says. "Where should I bring her?"

He looks around the promenade as though the question has rendered him helpless. It seems as though every passenger is crowded around the windows pointing, laughing, eager. "Here will be fine, I suppose."

Emilie takes the stairs two at a time down to B-deck. She's not entirely certain there is time to fulfill Colonel Erdmann's request, although she does note that the ground crew has not raised the gangway stairs.

Willy Speck and Herbert Dowe startle when Emilie throws the

door back and steps into the radio room. They look at her as though she has materialized naked right in front of them, as though they've never seen a woman before. Both men are at their stations, headphones on, fingers hovering over a board filled with knobs and levers as they await orders for liftoff.

"You can't be in here," Willy says. The lame protest seems to be the only speech he's capable of, for he falls silent afterward.

"Yes I can." Emilie has never taken kindly to being told what she can and cannot do. Certainly not by a gap-toothed radioman with hygiene issues.

"But you're a . . . woman," he adds lamely.

"I'm a crew member. Same as you. With full access to the ship. Same as you. I also happen to be performing my duties, namely having a family member of one of our premier passengers paged to come aboard the ship. Excuse me," she says, pushing past the still-silent-therefore-clearly-more-intelligent Herbert Dowe and descending a ladder into the control car below. Her uniform makes the job delicate, but she's too angry now to care. If anyone below is peering up her skirt, let them see her garter belt, and her acrimony. But the officers below are gentlemen. They keep their eyes lowered until she has planted both feet firmly on the carpeted floor of the utility room.

Emilie meets the questioning glances of Commander Pruss and his crew without hesitation. "I'm sorry to interrupt your flight preparations, Commander, but Colonel Erdmann requested that I page his wife."

"Why?"

She doesn't intend to lie; the words simply form in her mouth before she has time to think about them. "He didn't say. But he's quite insistent."

The colonel said he wanted to tell his wife good-bye. That's what she's thinking while Pruss mulls the request. It was the strangled note in Erdmann's voice at the word *good-bye* that has Emilie lying so easily now. Her own husband never had the chance to say good-bye before he left her for good. Her fingers twitch, wanting to reach up and find the key that hangs between her breasts, the key that her husband gave her on their wedding night.

One of the things that puzzles Emilie most about Max Zabel is his timing. He finds her, always, in these moments when she is vulnerable. Emilie does not want to be rescued, and yet there he is. Max descends the ladder into the control car and steps forward to stand between her and Commander Pruss. The gesture is not so much protective as authoritative, as though he's certain that whatever the trouble might be he can resolve it.

"Is something wrong?" Max asks.

Emilie finds herself the object of Max's curious gaze. It is alarming, that gaze, how it can root her to the floor. How it can wipe her mind clean of every thought, every objection. How it can make her forget even her late husband. This is why she resists Max, why she hates him at times. Emilie does not want to forget.

They both look to Pruss for an answer.

"No," the commander says, but does not elaborate. Instead he stares at Emilie as though he is seeing her for the first time.

Many years of service aboard ocean liners and her tenure aboard the airship have taught Emilie that important men do not like to be pressed for time, answers, or decisions. Benevolence, although often required, is something they bestow on their own terms. In their own way. So she stands with her fingers laced in front of her, her face set pleasantly in expectation, her lips pressed together with the barest hint of a patient smile. *Hurry, hurry*, she thinks. *I'm the one who will have to serve Colonel Erdmann for the next three days, not you.* If Pruss refuses the colonel's request there is nothing she will be able to do about it. He is commander, after all, but she will be required to deliver the news.

"Max," Pruss finally orders, "get the bullhorn and instruct the ground crew to have Dorothea Erdmann brought up from the other hangar." He turns to Emilie. "You will collect her, I presume?"

"Yes, Commander."

Max gives Pruss a sharp, obedient nod and steps around a glass wall into the navigation room. She has never seen him in this envi-

ronment before; she has been in the control car only one time—
during her initial tour of the airship. Seeing Max surrounded by
his charts and navigational equipment makes sense. Another little
piece of the puzzle locks into place. He is a mystery that is slowly,
consistently being solved.

"Is there anything else, Fräulein Imhof?" There's the trace of
humor in Commander Pruss's voice.

She's staring at Max. *Damn it*, she thinks. *Everyone has noticed.
They'll pick him apart for that.* "No," she answers.

"You may return to your duties, then."

Emilie hears a distorted version of Max's deep voice echoing
through the bullhorn as she ascends the ladder. The pointed look
she gives the radiomen is very much an I-told-you-so rebuke. Once
the door is shut behind her she stops to compose herself.

The only jewelry that Emilie wears is a skeleton key on a silver chain around her neck. The chain is long and tucked beneath
her dress, hidden from view. She has not taken it off in the years
since Hans died, and the side that lies against her skin has grown
tarnished. It feels warm and heavy now, like a weight against her
heart, so she pulls it out and cradles the key in her palm. It is the
only thing she has left of her old life.

It is a life worth remembering, and Emilie struggles to keep Max
Zabel from invading it. She tucks the key back inside her uniform,
squares her shoulders, and goes to the gangway stairs to collect
Dorothea Erdmann.

THE JOURNALIST

Who is that woman, do you think?" Gertrud sets a slender fingertip against the window and points at a military jeep speed-
ing across the tarmac toward them. A woman sits in the front seat,
her hair blowing wildly around her face while she holds on to the
door with one hand.

"She was on the bus. I saw her," Leonhard says.

"Is she a passenger?"

"Apparently not."

The jeep parks directly below them, out of sight, and a few moments later the woman rushes into the promenade, followed closely by the stewardess, and throws herself into the arms of a man standing apart from the rest of the passengers. Some turn to watch the spectacle, but most seem oblivious, their attention held by the pre-flight operations below.

The moment the couple embraces, the stewardess backs away, leaving the room looking pale and unsettled. Gertrud puzzles at this as they embrace each other, as tight as two humans can, for well over a minute.

"You know," Leonhard whispers, "I've never seen a guest brought on board this close to takeoff before. They're quite serious about security. It's likely that only his rank made it possible."

The man's clothing is indistinguishable from that of the other civilian passengers, and Gertrud gives her husband a questioning glance. "Who is he?"

"Fritz Erdmann."

"You know him?"

"He's a Luftwaffe colonel. Kommandant at the Military Signal Communications School. He was appointed as a military observer to the *Hindenburg* earlier this year. It's not something he's thrilled about."

"You know this because . . . ?"

"He told me. During the first commercial flight to Rio de Janeiro in March."

Of course Leonhard would know this. Leonhard knows *everything* about Germany's airship program. It is this knowledge, and his journalism skills, that have them on this ridiculous flight to begin with. He has recently collaborated on the autobiography of Captain Ernst Lehmann, director of flight operations for the Deutsche Zeppelin-Reederei. This flight was provided gratis so Leonhard could meet with his U.S. publishers prior to the book's release next month. Gertrud's attendance, though unwilling, was required as well.

Colonel Erdmann and his wife finally separate and stand gazing at one another. He brushes his thumb along her cheekbone, perhaps to wipe away a tear—Gertrud cannot be certain—and then she steps away from him and quietly leaves the ship. It occurs to Gertrud as she watches the jeep carry Frau Erdmann back to the hangar that neither of them uttered a word the entire time.

The colonel looks despondent as he watches his wife leave, and Gertrud smells a story. She sets her hand on Leonhard's arm. "Darling," she says, "I think that man needs a drink."

Leonhard gives her the look, the one that says he recognizes the purr in her voice, and that he knows she's up to something, but she's just too damn clever for him to preempt whatever mischief she has planned. He won't try to stop her, though. He never does.

"You will behave yourself?" He takes a step toward the door.

"Where are you going?"

"To the bar."

"Why? The stewards are passing out champagne."

He clucks his tongue. "*Liebchen*, champagne is not going to give you what you're after."

"Who says I'm after anything?"

"I would be highly disappointed if you weren't."

This is why Gertrud married a widower twenty-two years her senior. Leonhard is the only man she has ever met who not only appreciates her gumption but encourages it. "Well, then, order the good colonel a Maybach 12 and one for me as well."

"Careful, *Liebchen. Alte Füchse gehen schwer in die Falle.*"

She laughs and pats his cheek. "He's not such an old fox as that. Younger than you by the looks of it. And my traps are well laid."

Leonhard lifts her hand and turns it palm up. He kisses it lightly. "I cannot argue that." He dips his mouth toward her ear. "Many things about you are well laid, *Liebchen*. Though I prefer that you not spread such tempting traps for him as you did for me."

"I hardly doubt you'll be gone long enough for that."

"If it's the Maybach 12 you're drinking tonight, you'll not have much time yourself before I'll have to carry *you* to bed."

"You'll hardly get the chance if you never get the drinks."

"Start slowly at least. You don't have the legs to hold much of that particular drink." Leonhard leaves her then and goes in search of the bar on B-deck and its famous cocktail, the recipe for which is known only to the bar steward, a secret that is guarded more closely than the *Hindenburg* itself.

Gertrud sniffs. They have established on more than one occasion that she is a lightweight when it comes to booze. Fine. She'll pace herself. But still, she waits a few moments to approach Colonel Erdmann. Waits to make sure that none of the other passengers will seek him out. He lingers apart from the cluster of people, his eyes glued to the hangar on the other side of the tarmac where his wife has disappeared once again.

She goes to stand beside him but does not draw attention to herself. After a moment she simply says, "Your wife is lovely."

He does not look at her when he responds, "You have no idea."

"You might be surprised. I'm a good judge of character."

"I'll grant that. Given your husband."

He is observant. She will have to be careful. "You know Leonhard?"

"As much as one man can know another from a few pleasant conversations."

"He thinks highly of you."

"I think not."

This takes her aback. "Oh?"

For the first time since he entered the promenade Colonel Erdmann grins. He turns to face her. "It will take more than one Maybach 12 to get me talking, Frau Adelt. I would hope Leonhard gives me more credit than that."

"So you heard our conversation?"

He shrugs. "I pay attention."

Observant *and* clever. Gertrud mentally recalculates her plan of attack. "Alas, I am responsible for that poor estimate. Forgive me? I tend to assume the Luftwaffe recruits only one kind of man."

He gives a lopsided grin. Waits for the punch line.

"Libertines."

"Guilty as charged."

She takes his laughter as a small victory and extends her hand with a smile. "Gertrud Adelt."

"Fritz Erdmann." He grasps her hand. Shakes it. "I see that you and Leonhard are very well matched."

Gertrud opens her mouth to answer but is interrupted by the return of her husband.

"I'll be damned if I wasn't going to get it right the second time around." Leonhard joins them at the window carrying three frosted glasses containing ice chips and a murky citrine liquid. The look he gives Gertrud is a mixture of astonishment and respect. He hands one of the glasses to the colonel. "You will join us for dinner? Unless my wife has revealed too much of her impetuous nature."

Gertrud takes a tiny sip of the Maybach 12 and can almost feel her hair blow back. The drink is everything, all at once, and she has an immediate appreciation for its reputation. She can taste the kirsch and the Benedictine in equal parts, along with a good dry gin, and something else she can't identify. "He means I'm an acquired taste."

"On the contrary, *Liebchen,*" Leonhard says. "It didn't take me long at all. One kiss, if I recall correctly."

The colonel is clearly enjoying their banter. "This may come as a surprise to you, Frau Adelt, but I prefer women who speak *and* drink freely."

"Why would that surprise me?"

"It's not the sort of thing you admit in polite society."

"Oh, I'm hardly polite."

"Neither is my wife."

Gertrud can't help but look at the rectangular hangar across the tarmac. She's trying to find the right thing to say when the colonel speaks again.

"Dorothea would have liked you very much."

"I would be honored to meet her. Perhaps when we return to Frankfurt?"

She offers her drink in toast, but he only clinks her glass half-heartedly. "Perhaps."

THE NAVIGATOR

She's down there," Willy Speck says when Max enters the radio room. He gives a pointed nod at the ladder that leads down to the control car.

"Who?"

"Your girl."

Their relationship seems to be an established fact for everyone but Emilie herself. Max can hear her then, asking Commander Pruss to have someone paged. He pushes past the radiomen and slides down the ladder as quickly as he can. Finding Emilie in the control car like this feels a bit like finding her in his bed. It's not unwelcome, just startling, as though she has made herself familiar with his things. The way a lover would. And, as he would most certainly feel in that situation, Max does not know what to do next. She hasn't ventured into the navigation room but stands patiently in the utility area waiting for Commander Pruss's decision.

She's good at this, he notes. Emilie does not push. She doesn't demand answers. And in the end Pruss asks him to call for Dorothea Erdmann. But Emilie does not escape the control car before revealing her own fascination with Max's domain. She watches him for an unguarded moment and is then dismissed by Commander Pruss. But Max does not watch her go. They will give him hell if he does.

"*Ruhe, bitte!*" Max warns, a slight growl in his voice, when he turns from the window, bullhorn in hand.

Pruss is standing in the doorway to the chart room, his cap so low on his forehead that Max can't tell whether he looks stern or amused. "Where were you?"

"Mail," he answers.

"Not chatting up the female employee again?"

Max snorts. No secrets indeed. He casts a derisive glance at the ladder as an answer. *How could he be chatting her up*, the look says, *when she was here with you?*

Pruss simply turns and without preamble gives the order to begin preparations for casting off. Max takes his position in the chart room amid his maps and logbook, his charts and his direction-finding instruments.

Commander Pruss may be in charge of the airship on this trip, but it is Captain Ernst Lehmann who usually flies it, and this is a privilege he considers sacred. To be at the helm is almost an act of worship for the director of flight operations. He's in the control car for castoff despite technically being an observer on this flight—a symbolic role while en route to America to prepare for a book tour promoting his biography, *Zeppelin*. His co-author—a journalist of some repute—is on board as well, though Max hasn't met him yet.

While Pruss prepares for liftoff, Lehmann stands with hands clasped behind his back, restraining himself from giving orders. He watches as they methodically go through the pre-flight checklist, as they check gauges and ballasts, wheels, rudders, and elevator lines. When all seems to be in order, Pruss takes the bullhorn from Max's table and leans out the open window. "*Zeppelin marsch!*"

Pruss's voice is strong and authoritative. Loud. Max hears the metallic clang of the gangway ladders being slammed into place, and there is an immediate, subtle shift beneath them. The passengers on B- and A-decks likely don't feel it at all. But the control car, only a few feet off the ground, vibrates with the movement.

The *Hindenburg*'s forward landing wheel is located directly beneath the chart room where Max stands. The wheel is accessed by a panel under his feet and is one of three points on which the airship can rest when on the ground, the other two being the gangway stairs and the rear landing wheel. Like the blade on an ice skate, each wheel is simply a point of contact on which the ship balances when moored to the ground. Operating this small but vital piece of machinery is Max's job during every takeoff and landing, regardless of time or day, regardless of shift. And while the mechanics of it are easy enough—he raises and lowers the wheel using a valve to direct the flow of compressed air and a detachable control to keep the wheel and its housing turned into the wind—it is, in actuality, a tricky task requiring a steady hand and no small amount of concentration.

Max slides the floor panel aside so he can raise the wheel. It lifts into the ship smoothly, without shudder or noise. He pulls the retractable control gears from the floor slot so the wheel can't drop again. Max checks the locking mechanism to make sure the wheel is secure within its casing, and the rest is a matter of waiting.

"Well done, Max," Pruss says.

He nods in response, pleased with himself, and stands aside to watch the ground crew take over below. Peering out the portside window in the control car, he watches the yaw ropes being held tightly in the hands of the ground crew. First one rope, then the other, stretches to its full length. Max can feel the portside ropes tighten with a subtle shift of the wind, and the *Hindenburg* is pushed starboard in response. The airship is held to the earth by little more than these ropes and the determination of a few men on the tarmac.

The *Hindenburg* shudders to life. Each of the four engines— separated from the main body of the airship by steel girders and a narrow catwalk—rumbles, then smoothes into a steady purr. Some of the ground crew grip the yaw lines and lean away from the ship's mass at exaggerated angles. They disconnect the ropes from the heavy anchors driven into the tarmac but keep the lines taut, straining against the wind. Other crewmen are lined beneath the engine gondolas, gripping the rails. Together they walk the *Hindenburg* away from the hangar, and she glides forward as though weightless, as if her great mass were nothing more than a breath.

The air horn, much louder now that Max is in the control car, gives a long and strident blast. The muscles in his neck and jaw seize in response. He makes a mental note to research alternative notification devices once they are back in Germany. The ground crew stops in unison, the muscles in their forearms straining to keep the airship under control. Pruss is still at the window, and he waits for a count of three before shouting, "*Schiff hoch!*" into the bull-horn. Up ship.

Max notes their departure time as 8:18 p.m. in his logbook.

The great web of handling lines are drawn into the ship at Pruss's command, and the crewmen beneath the gondolas give a heaving, upward push. There is a lift and a pull, and she hovers twenty feet off the ground for a moment as the crew cheers. Then Pruss gives the order for two tons of water to be released from ballasts on either side of the ship, and like a balloon no longer tethered to the hand of an impatient child, the great silver zeppelin rises into the rose-colored Frankfurt sky.

THE AMERICAN

The American has made himself presentable and is sitting alone at the far end of the narrow dining room. He picked this seat so that he could see the entire area, could monitor the comings and goings of everyone else. The American likes the sense of control this gives him. He's early, the other guests having gone back to their rooms to change before the late dinner. The only other passengers in sight are a teenage girl patiently watching her two younger broth-ers. They lean over the observation windows, their noses pressed against the glass as the airship floats over the darkened countryside. He watches the children with a growing sense of unease. They are wild and loud, and one of the small boys pounds his fist against the glass. The American fears the little cuss will discover the windows can be opened and that he'll tumble out and drop to his death below.

He balls his fists in his lap. Clamps his lips tight to restrain himself from scolding the child. What happens to the boy is no concern of his. He shouldn't care one way or another. But he does. The American had a brother of his own, and he remembers those moments when they played with abandon, unfettered by fear or consequence. But that was a long time ago. Long before the First World War stripped away the vestiges of their youthful innocence. He knows how the world works now. And that young boy stands no chance.

The child grows foolish now, showing off for his siblings as he tries to scramble up onto the windows themselves. His sister, tall and blond and rail thin, rises smoothly from her seat and cuffs his ear. The movement is so quick, so graceful that the boy does not see it coming.

"*Nein*," she says.

"You're not my mother," he howls. "You can't do that!"

"Go on, then. Tell *Mama*. See if she doesn't cuff you again. And for impudence this time."

The two boys rush off, intent on telling their version of events first, and the girl follows slowly behind, head high, back straight, secure in her position as eldest child. The boys can say what they like; their parents will believe her. She knows this and leaves the dining room without looking the least bit perturbed. The American is certain that she will not embellish what the child did. She will simply deliver the facts, perhaps with leniency even, and let them decide.

A-deck is made up almost entirely of passenger cabins. The staterooms below, on B-deck, are new, added early this year to help accommodate the growing demand for passage on the *Hindenburg*. But the primary quarters are up here. Twenty-five cabins with two berths each, a dining room and promenade on the port side, and on the starboard side, the lounge, reading room, and a second promenade. The only area on A-deck that is not accessible to passengers is a small serving pantry beside the dining room. No bigger than one of the cabins, it has two long counters with overhead cabinets filled with extra utensils, glassware, and linens. Along one wall is a dumbwaiter used to lift food from the kitchen below. It is too small to hold a grown man—a young child perhaps, but that does the American no good—and he has already ruled it out as a possible means of escape should he need to get out of sight quickly.

All of this he discovered when he entered the dining room ten minutes ago. He took a quick glance inside the pantry and then muttered an apology. Wilhelm Balla was inside folding napkins, and it was easy enough to convince the steward he was lost. More than anything Balla appeared relieved that he didn't have to come collect the drunkard. The American decided to let the sour-faced steward's opinion of him remain exactly as it stands. He wants to be dismissed. To be underestimated. At least for now.

Slowly the American is getting his bearings inside the airship. There isn't much territory to cover in the public areas—he will get to the off-limits sections later—but there are a number of players within those areas, and he has yet to put them into the appropriate slots. Ally. Threat. Hindrance. Unnecessary. There are so many options. This evening's dinner should help quite a bit with that. Or it will help with sorting out the passengers, at least. Nothing reveals a man's true character like the way he behaves when being served a meal. And the vantage point he has chosen will make this task easy enough. His seat, in the back corner, faces outward, and he can see not only every other table but the passing skyscape as well. At the moment there is nothing but the inky darkness of a spring evening outside the windows. The occasional star or wispy passing cloud. The moon is out, but it's hidden on the starboard side. Below them, the *Hindenburg*'s searchlight slides over small towns and villages, pastures, and here and there the glassy surface of a lake, briefly illuminating the microcosm of rural life.

The ambiance inside the dining room is, he has to admit, quite impressive. He flew aboard the *Graf Zeppelin* several years earlier, but it cannot compete with the opulence in which he finds himself. Hand-painted murals by Otto Arpke line all three walls, showing scenes of the landscape captured on one of the *Graf Zeppelin*'s flights between Friedrichshafen and Rio de Janeiro. Brightly winged birds in midflight. Green-tipped mountains. The graceful arc of a white-sand beach. A rushing waterfall. The tables are draped in pressed white napery and set with the Deutsche Zeppelin-Reederei silver and the china custom-made for the *Hindenburg*. In the center of each table is a thin stem of Austrian crystal with a single fresh flower. Tonight the flowers are lilies, bright and pink and fragrant. Tomorrow they will be something else. He reaches out one blunt fingertip and touches the thick, silky petal and can't help but wonder where the flowers are stored. The American looks at his place setting, the ridiculous array of silverware, and lifts the salad fork from its place. The fork is real silver, its metal soft, and he bends one tine back with the tip of his finger. He slips the fork into his pocket.

The American is perusing the wine list for the third time—its bold print smugly reads WEINKARTE and boasts an array of tasteful French Burgundies and expensive German Models—when the first of his dinner companions arrives. A small man, little more than five feet tall, with the buoyant walk of someone who is used to being watched. No, the American thinks, someone who *likes* being watched. Expects it, actually. Yes, an entertainer, he decides before the man has even reached the table.

"Joseph Späh"—he sticks his hand out, right in the American's face so he has no choice but to take it. "Acrobat. Filmmaker. Comedian. International *personality*. And you are?"

"American. Belligerent. Hungover."

Späh laughs and takes his seat. He pulls the wine list from the American's grasp. "I'd best catch up with you then."

"Competitive?"

"Thirsty."

He's muttering about whether to start with red or white when a lilting voice interrupts them. "Oh. I'm early. How gauche of me."

A single glance at the wealthy woman makes it clear that she is used to being noticed when she enters a room. She has the look of a woman whose beauty has long been enhanced by wealth and doesn't show any signs of deteriorating soon. Early to midfifties, he guesses. He and Joseph Späh rise to greet her. Späh pulls out her chair and settles her in. Then he introduces himself in the same absurdly confident way he had with the American just a few moments earlier.

"Margaret Mather. Heiress. Spinster. Inappropriate."

"I think we will be fast friends, Miss Mather," Späh says.

"And you?"

She's looking at the American, but Späh interjects, "Ah, this is a man of mystery. We know nothing of him other than that he drinks too much." He lifts a dark eyebrow in question. "Or is it that you can't *hold* your liquor?"

Margaret claps her hands. "Oh! I do like this. Let's make a game of it, shall we? We will try and guess who he is."

You would think the two of them had known one another all their lives the way they fall into this easy familiarity. Talking. Joking. Späh recommends a wine for her, but the quick flicker of his glance gives him away: he's guessing. He might be an entertainer, used to accommodating the wealthy, but he doesn't run in their circles. Not really. If Margaret Mather realizes this she doesn't let on. Despite her excessive wealth she is kind. The American notes all of these things, files them away, as he places his dinner companions into their proper slots.

Margaret is a woman of easy grace. She's comfortable in her own skin. Yet he notices that every few moments she brushes her fingertips along her bare collarbone, searching for something that is not there.

"Have you lost something, Miss Mather?" he asks.

"Oh. No. I'm sorry. Do excuse me. Force of habit, I'm afraid. As it turns out I had a rather inept maid this morning." She blushes at this confession, as though having a maid is something of which to be ashamed. "She packed all of my jewelry in my steamer trunk, and I feel rather naked without a bobble or two."

The American assures her that she looks lovely nonetheless, but he files this bit of information away for future use.

The dining room is full, most of the seats taken, when Commander Pruss enters. He greets the occasional passenger. Shaking hands. Welcoming people. And then he makes his way to the back table. He's too gracious to make it obvious, but he does not want to be here. The American can plainly see that the glad-handing is his least favorite part of the job.

No sooner has Commander Pruss taken his seat than the serving pantry grows busy. Dinner is ready. Chilled salmon in honor of the warm spring evening. Or the late castoff perhaps. Nonetheless it is delicious, and the four of them fall to it like they have not eaten in days. But while the American, Margaret, and Späh enjoy the *Weinkarte*'s better offerings, Commander Pruss drinks nothing but sparkling water, insisting that he will imbibe in the lounge after dinner. The others make plans to join him.

The meal is light and delicious. The salmon perfectly poached. The rolls are soft and bursting with steam as they are broken open. The meal is everything one would expect from a world-class airship. But as the American goes to eat his melon he summons Wilhelm Balla from where he stands against the wall.

"It seems I don't have a salad fork." He motions at the empty spot on the table.

Balla squints. "My apologies. I set the table myself."

He turns on his heel, but not before the American catches the look of suspicion in the steward's eyes. He feels a petty delight, certain that pestering Balla will be one of his most enjoyable forms of recreation over the next few days. The steward brings him a new salad fork moments later.

It is easy enough for the American to make his observations about the remaining passengers during dinner. The stewards have seated two Jewish men at a table together. They are the last to get their drinks. The last to get their meal. And yet both hold themselves with dignity and restraint, even when forced to repeat a request. They do not admonish their steward—an arrogant young man who seems to enjoy toying with them—or complain to anyone else. Counting the stewardess who lingers near the family with the children, there are eight women on board the airship. Only three of them are younger than fifty: the stewardess, the teenage girl, and the journalist from the Hof Hotel. She and her husband make an unusual and unnerving pair. He is clearly much older than she is. Tall. Broad. Entirely bald—the American guesses he shaves what little is left of his hair—and adorned with the small round glasses of an intellectual. Yet his wife is a different story. She oozes the brash sex appeal that has been the downfall of many a sedate, established man. Her hair is honey-colored and curly. Her eyes a bright and startling blue. When she smiles he can see every single tooth on top, all the way to the back of her mouth, and not a single one on bottom. There is a sharp, wicked, intelligent note to her laughter. Yet the thing that unsettles the American most about this pair is his certainty that he has seen them before. Not just on the bus and in the hotel but even further back. There is something important he must remember about them.

The American is puzzling over this when Margaret Mather turns the dinner conversation in an unexpected direction. "You don't really think," she says, spearing a sliver of salmon with her fork and looking at Commander Pruss with open curiosity, "that there's anything to the bomb threats, do you?"

"I think that bomb threats should always be taken seriously."

"I was raised by diplomats, Commander. I know politics when I hear it. What I'm interested in are *your* thoughts. Do you really think they could destroy this ship?" She looks around the dining room. Up at the ceiling. Considers the vastness of the structure that is floating six hundred feet off the ground and is carrying them through the darkness at over seventy miles an hour.

"They?"

She waves a hand dismissively. "Whoever."

"There are two answers to that question, *Frau* . . ." Pruss searches for her name.

"Fräulein."

Interesting that, the American notes, her clarification of the German designation of an unmarried woman. He wonders if perhaps the heiress is lonely. If she is looking for companionship on this voyage. Advertising her availability.

"*Fräulein* . . . Mather. First and most important is that we would not let anyone destroy this great airship. Every conceivable precaution has been taken. But speaking to the *possibility*?" And here he becomes the storyteller the American has heard him to be. "The *Hindenburg* has only one great weakness."

Margaret Mather and Joseph Späh lower their forks and lean forward, expectantly.

"Hydrogen." The American pre-empts.

Pruss nods. "It's flammable."

"It's combustible, you mean."

"Only when mixed with oxygen." Pruss tilts his head a few degrees to the side. Takes in the American now that he has been challenged twice. "You are American?"

He nods at the others. "We all are."

"I see," Pruss says, "then you might want to ask your government why they are hoarding the world's largest supplies of helium." He gives Margaret Mather a look that could be mistaken for an apology but is actually defensiveness. "This ship was designed to be lifted by helium. Which is not flammable."

"Combustible." The American corrects him again quietly.

"But your government," Pruss continues, "refused to sell us the gas. Regardless of our arguments and our generous offers. So we were forced to use hydrogen."

"But why wouldn't they sell Germany the helium?"

The American smiles. *Oh, Margaret,* he thinks, *you pretty fool.* "Our government," he says, "is not in the business of furthering Germany's military goals."

Pruss snorts. "This is a passenger ship."

"With swastikas emblazoned on the side. Flown by Luftwaffe pilots. And fitted for artillery. It may look like a floating luxury hotel, Miss Mather, but you are, in reality, traveling on a Nazi warship."

"That is a gross misrepresentation," Pruss says. The angrier he gets, the heavier his accent becomes, the more he fumbles with what is usually clear and precise English.

The American draws back now that he has brought the commander to the edge of rage. He puts his hands up—a show of surrender. "I do not mean to offend. I simply meant to help Miss Mather understand the politics at play. The underlying tensions, so to speak."

It's a cheap trick, using her as a shield, and Pruss is not fooled. "There is no tension." He smiles at Margaret, then looks at the American. His eyes tighten at the corners, but the anger slips from his face. Pruss makes a jab of his own. "You purchased a ticket for this flight. Why financially support this airship when you claim to be so offended by it?"

"I didn't pay for my ticket. The McCann Erickson company did." The American deflects the blow easily, then circles back to his point. "Regardless, a Nazi warship that flies over New York City fifteen times a year creates more than enough tension. Especially when safety is not always the primary concern of Zeppelin-Reederei."

"Do explain what you mean by that." Pruss leans back in his chair, arms crossed over his chest, scowling.

The American takes a long sip of his wine, swishing it around his mouth before answering. "The propaganda flight last year on behalf of Herr Goebbels? Didn't this airship sustain damage during takeoff? And all so you could drop election pamphlets for the Nazis in adverse weather conditions?" He looks at Margaret and gives her a grin. Easy. Jovial. Uncomplicated. "Whatever else this airship might be, it was first funded by the Nazis and used for their purposes."

While Pruss is formulating his answer, the American rises from the table and wipes his mouth with a linen napkin. "If you will excuse me, I need to use the restroom." Seeds are planted and germinating within the minds of the two most social passengers on board this airship. Joseph and Margaret will spread this message from person to person, meal to meal, over the next three days. And by the time they land, every one of them will look at this ship and its parent company with the appropriate level of misgiving. The American is certain of this, determined even, that it will be so.

The American leaves Commander Pruss behind to deal with his rhetoric. As he weaves his way through the dining room, he can hear Pruss dismissing the accusations offhand, the commander's accent growing heavier with each word. It is as he passes the lovely young journalist and her husband that he remembers where he has seen them.

Neue Mainzer Strasse 56. The Frankfurt branch of the Ministry of Propaganda. Fourth floor. Three months ago.

Yes, it is all coming back to him now, confirmed in the curious glance Gertrud Adelt—for that is her name, he's certain of it now—directs at him as he passes. He remembers her bellow of rage as she stood in the fourth-floor hallway before the Kulturstaatssekretär. It was loud enough to draw the American from his desk on the floor below and up the stairs into the hall. She handed over her press card with a shaking hand, but her voice was calm and firm as she uttered such a string of profanities that every man present stood with mouth agape. It had certainly made an impression on the American. He's quite certain that he had witnessed her inventing a new obscenity on the spot. And then her husband had deftly removed her from the building before she could be arrested. Had Leonhard Adelt not been a man of some import himself, the American is certain things would have gone quite differently for them that day.

The American debates whether to classify Gertrud as a threat or a hindrance as he leaves the dining room. She clearly has no love for the Nazis, but she is too curious for her own good. In the end he decides to label her as unknown. It will have to do until he can make a better assessment.

All of the passengers are either seated at the tables or in the promenade as he slips into the keel corridor. Most of the crew is either serving dinner or in the midst of flight operations, so he goes down the stairs, away from the restrooms, and into the corridor on B-deck without being seen. The American pulls the pilfered salad fork from his pocket and tucks it into his palm, the handle hidden in his sleeve, as he approaches the mailroom door.

The lock is harder to pick than he anticipated, and for one moment he fears the tine will break off, but the tumblers shift at the last moment and the door swings inward. When he pulls the fork out he notices that the sharpest point of the tine has indeed snapped inside the lock and is lodged within. No worry. He won't need to do this again.

The American shuts the door behind him but does not turn on the light. He is accustomed to the dark. The letter in his suit pocket is standard size, thin, and cased in a thick paper envelope. Stamped express mail. The address typewritten. The single sheet of paper within contains a single line of print, also typewritten: *On board. Collect load at Hof Hotel. Room* 218. *Will proceed as planned.* There is no light other than what seeps in beneath the door, and it takes his eyes a couple of moments to adjust. But he quickly finds the bag marked KÖLN hanging by the door and unties it. He tucks his letter inside and knots it again easily. The American is reaching for the door when he hears voices in the corridor outside. The doorknob jiggles. Someone curses. And he dives for the pile of mailbags on the floor.

THE STEWARDESS

By the time Emilie collapses into the banquette in the crew's mess she is limp from exhaustion and shaking with hunger. A table is tucked into each of the four corners, and padded seats run the length of two walls. The banquettes create distinct nooks where small groups of crew members can eat their meals in peace. Emilie sits at one on the far side with her back to the observation windows, ignoring the darkened scenery below. She's the only person in the mess, the rest of the crew having long since eaten their dinner. Emilie barely has a chance to settle into the upholstered cushions when Xaver Maier sets a plate of poached salmon in front of her. He arranges the utensils to accommodate her left hand.

"You remembered?" She wiggles her fingers and picks up the fork.

"It's my job." He shrugs. "The rolls were hot an hour ago."

"I wouldn't care if they were frozen. I'm starving."

Emilie falls to her food as though it's her last meal on earth, and Xaver watches like a hovering parent, making sure each item is sampled and appreciated.

"How is it," Max asks, standing in the doorway once again, "that this chef knows every important detail about you—the fact that you're left-handed, for instance—while I know so little?"

"She's not a chart, *Dummkopf*. Stop trying to read her," Xaver says, irritated, as he pushes against the swinging door that leads into the kitchen. He stops midstep and turns. "If you'd like coffee I'd be happy to make some."

Emilie shakes her head and waves him off. She glares at Max. Her mouth is full of roasted potatoes, and she has to chew quickly then swallow before she can speak. "How do you *do* that?"

Max grins. "Do what?"

"Magically appear in the doorway every time I'm in the middle of a conversation?"

"It's a gift, I suppose."

"It's obnoxious," Emilie says, but she's smiling anyway.

He settles into the seat across from her, arms on the table as though he's got nothing else to do.

"That's rude, you know, staring at people while they eat," she says around a mouthful of green beans.

"It's also rude to talk with your mouth full. Yet here we are." He waits a moment as though deciding whether to concede, and then adds, "I came to collect you. I thought it would be polite to let you finish dinner."

She growls softly and attacks her meal with renewed energy. Emilie is neither delicate nor discreet about the way she dispatches the rest of her meal. She's hungry, damn it, and she doesn't care if Max is horrified. Perhaps this will run him off. She can feel the taut thread of exhaustion in her spine begin to fray, ready to snap. With a job like this, each day brings a definite and complete end to her coping skills. She stabs at a loose green bean with the tines of her fork and watches it skitter off the edge of the plate and onto the table. She pinches it with two fingers and eats it anyway. Of *course* someone would need her the moment she finally has a chance to sit down and eat. Emilie catalogues the passengers she is responsible for on this flight, trying to guess which one might have paged her. It's a game she plays on every trip, and she's almost always correct. She once had a passenger on board the *Columbus* who insisted that Emilie clean beneath her toenails with a letter opener every night before bed. Emilie had the woman pegged as trouble the moment she walked up the gangway pinching her nostrils and complaining about the harbor stench.

"Was it good?" Max asks when she finally sets her fork down.

"I don't know. I didn't get the chance to taste it." She's immediately sorry for snapping at him. She softens her tone. "Haven't you eaten?"

"I'm still on duty." He shrugs. "The mail."

"Oh. I'm sorry."

Max waves the apology away and motions her toward the door. They step into the dim, empty corridor. She straightens her uniform, then takes a deep breath to gird herself for whatever distasteful task awaits. "Which one of the passengers paged me?"

"I never said a passenger needed you."

"You said you came to—"

"Collect you."

"For what?"

Max extends his hand, palm up, as though pleading. "There's something I'd like to show you."

A memory, sudden and Technicolor, rises to the surface: Hamburg, Germany, twenty years ago, a blue door, a red dress, and fingers fumbling at a zipper. Emilie leans against the corridor wall to steady herself as a sudden, unexpected burst of laughter erupts. Two minutes ago she wanted to stab Max with her fork, and now she can barely stand because she's laughing so hard.

"What's so funny?"

"I'm sorry. I can't help it. The last time a boy said those words to me, I was fifteen years old, and Frank Becker took me to the back of my father's shop and tried to show me his *Schwanz.*"

Max is dark. Black hair. Olive skin. Eyes like flint. But the color still begins to show in his face, and this makes her laugh even harder. She's doubled over now, arms wrapped around her ribs, leaning hard against the wall so she won't tip over.

"That's not what I ... I don't ... well, I mean I *do*, but ... *Scheiße*! I'll shut up."

Her breath comes in gasps. "Oh no, do keep going."

Max clears his throat. Tries to regain his dignity. To match her bawdiness. "Did he succeed, then, Frank Becker?"

"Almost. I left him there, balled up on the floor grabbing his crotch."

"Duly noted."

"Oh, I *was* curious." Emilie hiccups. "But I felt that I had to kick him on principle."

"No uninvited *Schwanz* flashing?"

"It simply won't do." She gives a curt shake of her head, making her curls bounce against her shoulders. "Besides, I was a good girl. And my father would have castrated Frank if he'd found out. A bloody mess that would have been, given that he worked with Frank's father."

"Pun intended?"

"Most definitely."

"And what did your father do for a living?"

"He was a butcher."

Now it's Max's turn to laugh. It occurs to Emilie that she likes the sound very much and that she doesn't hear it often enough.

"I am curious about something, Herr Zabel."

"Yes?"

"Why is it that I can't spend ten minutes in your company without laughing?"

There's something about the look on his face, like he's pleased with the whole world, like this is a private triumph. She wants to know what's behind that look, but she is also aware that Max has revealed a lot about his feelings for her, and that she has given him little in the way of reciprocation. So she isn't surprised when he brushes the question aside.

"If you're going to make a joke about my face, I'd like the chance to beg your mercy. My *Schwanz* has already shrunk an inch thanks to your last story. I'm not sure how much more of your honesty I can take."

Emilie sets a hand against his cheek. His skin is soft below the day's worth of stubble. "Well," she says, her voice just a notch above a whisper, "I've not been acquainted with the other, but I like your face just fine."

Max leans into her touch. The softness around his eyes and the curve of his mouth suggests he can't help himself. "This is where I prove myself to be smarter than young Herr Becker."

"It's not hard, but pray tell, how do you plan on doing that?"

"By keeping my trousers zipped."

There is an easiness in the way she relates to Max that Emilie finds alarming. Easy anger. Easy laughter. Easy companionship. It has been a long time since Emilie has felt these things, and she does not know how to surrender to them. She meets Max's steady gaze with all the bravery she can muster. "Now, what was it you wanted to show me?"

"Cologne," he says.

THE JOURNALIST

Damn German men and their cast-iron livers, Gertrud thinks, *damn them all*. Leonhard included. The more she drinks, the more she talks, and the more she needs to pee. But she's not the one who needs to talk, it's Colonel Erdmann, and he's zipped up tight, laughing at her with his eyes as he eats the last of his pastry.

"I'm going to the bar," she says abruptly. Gertrud pushes her plate away and stands up. She's wobbly, but she steadies herself easily enough by holding on to the back of her chair. Leonhard and the colonel jump to their feet out of courtesy, both startled. "And you're welcome to come with me."

"Where else would I go, *Liebchen*?" Leonhard asks. His tone is soft. Indulgent.

She can think of a number of ways to answer that question—all of them impudent—but she says none of them. It's one thing to be charming and pert and amusing in front of the colonel, but she will not be disrespectful to her husband. She won't shame him. She's tipsy, not stupid. Not only would it hurt Leonhard terribly—he is a man, after all, and his ego is nothing to toy with—but she would lose all the advantage she has built with Colonel Erdmann over dinner.

"You will join us, Colonel?" he asks. "I assure you my wife is quite entertaining when she's good and fully drunk."

"Entertaining? Or talkative?" The wry one-sided smirk suggests that the colonel is not as irritated by the prospect as he sounds.

"They are often one and the same."

"In that case I'd be honored."

Leonhard tucks Gertrud's hand beneath his arm. She leans into him, unstable, and he gives her a fond smile, but there is a warning glint in his eyes. *Do not push the colonel too far,* it says. *Play nice. Remember who you're dealing with.* Their marriage is young, just two years old, but they've learned to read each other remarkably well in that time. To speak with the slightest movements. To communicate with little more than a drumming finger or a long stare. It is a rare gift in marriages, one they capitalize on often.

Leonhard guides them out of the dining room, down the corridor, down the stairs, and onto B-deck. He pauses for a moment outside the toilets when Gertrud squeezes his arm to let him know she needs a moment of privacy.

"Forgive my wife," she hears Leonhard say as the door swings shut. "She has the bladder of a tiny bird."

The colonel follows with some rejoinder about his own wife, and she knows that they are fast becoming friends. The toilet is tiny, made of some shiny, lightweight metal, and cold enough to make her gasp. She finishes her business quickly and tidies up in front of the mirror. Another coat of red lipstick. She wipes the mascara smudges from beneath her eyes. Smoothes her hair. Something in the roundness of her eyes, the exhaustion written there, reminds her of Egon, the way he looks when she puts him to bed at night. She is struck with a pang so deep she struggles for breath. Gertrud has not thought of her son in two hours. Not once during dinner. Guilt. Sadness. Anger. All of these things are written on her face, on the brightness of her cheeks. Leonhard sees the emotion clearly when she joins them in the hallway, and he gives her hand a questioning squeeze. He won't ask her here, but she knows he has marked it mentally.

The corridor takes a sharp left and then an immediate right, depositing them directly in front of a heavy glass door. Leonhard raps on the door sharply with his knuckles and steps aside as a steward pushes it open. There is an immediate hiss of air and Gertrud's ears pop. The steward holds the door as they enter. It is ingenious the way they have designed this part of the airship. Safety, beauty, and practicality all rolled into one. The cramped antechamber into which they enter is in effect little more than an air lock monitored by the bar steward. To one side is a fully stocked bar, shaped like a banquette with room for one man to stand, but there are no chairs. No tables.

She doesn't catch the steward's first name when he shakes Leonhard's hand, but she hears his last: Schulze. "This room and the one beyond," he points at the door opposite, "are pressurized, you see. To prevent any trace amounts of hydrogen from entering. Otherwise no one would be allowed to smoke on board."

Schulze leads them to the opposite door, also glass, and into the smoking lounge. If the rest of the ship is luxurious, this room is opulent. *Priorities,* Gertrud thinks, *the Zeppelin-Reederei knows whom to indulge.* Leather benches and armchairs line the perfectly square room, leaving the center open. Hand-painted murals of early hot-air balloons decorate the walls. Small square tables are set with playing cards and poker chips. Carpet, such a dark blue that it looks like spilled ink, covers the floor. The place smells faintly of sweet pipe tobacco, and also the bitter smoke of cigarettes and cigars, though she can tell they've gone to great pains to air the room out. Wall sconces fill the space with warm yellow light. And then, of course, the starboard wall is an entire bank of windows. The same as elsewhere on the airship, slanted outward at waist height so you can lean over them and see the ground below. This is where she gravitates while Leonhard and the colonel choose a table. There is so little to see at this time of night that Gertrud is drawn to every prick of light. There the headlights of a vehicle. There the light in a farmhouse window. And on the horizon a luminous string, like a glowworm, hinting at some looming piece of civilization.

Schulze sets the cocktail menus on the table. "These rooms are open until three a.m.," he says. "You will find that we have all varieties of wine and alcohol on board. Cigars. And tobacco as well, though we do not provide the pipes. Our menu is generous, and I can make anything to order, though, if I might be so bold, I highly recommend the Maybach 12. It is a drink of my own invention and is excellent, if I may say so." He glances at Gertrud as if to measure her tolerance for alcohol. She must appear wanting, for he adds, "Though it is of considerable horsepower. I will be in the bar when you're ready to order."

They settle into a table near the window, and Leonhard and the colonel begin to discuss the finer points of some obscure brand of Scotch. In the end they both decide to try the LZ 129 Frosted Cocktail, some ridiculous concoction of gin and orange juice, so they can save the straight liquor for the end of the night when they are good and sauced and their taste buds have thrown in the towel for the day. Gertrud orders the Maybach 12 just to spite everyone. Leonhard dutifully delivers their order to the bar, and when her drink arrives several moments later it is completely devoid of spirits. So he's decided to enable her on this fool's errand after all? The man does surprise her. The look she gives him lasts no longer than a blink, and his answering shrug could be misconstrued as the shift of an aging man trying to get comfortable in his seat.

"We'll be approaching Cologne shortly," the colonel says, looking at Leonhard. "You are from there, correct?"

"Yes. My family moved from Dortmund to Cologne when I was seventeen."

"You make it sound so prosaic. Tell him why your family was forced to move." When Leonhard grins but does not speak she turns to the colonel. "My husband tried his hand at writing at a young age. He published his first novel at seventeen, and it caused such a stir that he lost his apprenticeship as a bookseller in Kleve. What did you title your book, darling?"

"*Werden.*"

"That doesn't sound so threatening," the colonel says. "There's nothing particularly obscene about willpower."

Gertrud laughs. "Perhaps it was the lack thereof that had the censors riled. Leonhard's book was filled with teenage sexual *experiences.*" She whispers this last word as though imparting a juicy bit of gossip.

Leonhard shrugs. "I was seventeen. And curious."

"Lucky for me you still are."

He pulls an ice cube from his glass and crushes it between his teeth. "It ended up being a good thing. I went to work for another bookseller once we got to Cologne, and then I started writing for the newspapers."

"A rather inauspicious beginning to a successful career," the colonel notes.

"And look at you." Gertrud cannot disguise the pride in her smile. "Thirty years later and you're still causing trouble."

The colonel settles into his chair and sets the rim of his glass against his lower lip. "Do you make it back to Cologne often?"

"Not directly. I only visit in letters these days."

"Well, you'll visit it tonight," the colonel says. "At least from the air. There it is now." He points out the window at the long, faint glow on the horizon.

They all look out the window for a moment and then fall into conversation. Gertrud flirts with her husband and with the colonel. She tells stories of her childhood. She gives a passionate account of the last few months and how the Nazis revoked her press card after she began to write unflattering articles about the Ministry of Propaganda. And by the time other passengers begin filtering into the smoking room, Colonel Erdmann is finally talking freely. Of his wife. Of his children. Of this flight and how he'd rather be home.

"And yet you're here. With us," she says.

His grimace is one of resignation. "Duty calls."

At this point Gertrud is well into her second virgin Maybach 12 and is the only person at the table who is not slurring. She speaks slowly to make up for it. "And all because of a few stupid bomb threats."

Finally, *finally* Colonel Erdmann leans across the table and gives her what she wants. He pokes the polished wood surface with his finger for emphasis. "No, Frau Adelt, I'm not here because of the bomb threats. I'm here because the bomb threats are *credible*."

THE NAVIGATOR

Cologne?" Emilie tilts her chin to the side, curious. Her eyes are warm and brown and curious, so light they are almost the color of rust.

"Trust me." Max takes her hand, laces his fingers through hers, and leads her brazenly down the keel corridor in full view of anyone who cares to watch. The corridor is empty, of course, it always is this time of night, but Emilie whips her head around anyway.

"No need to look so guilty, Fräulein Imhof."

She lifts their entwined hands. "This is against the rules."

"Which is exactly why it's fun."

They are getting perilously close to the door that leads into the officers' quarters when Max stops short at the mailroom door. He frees her hand to unlatch the key ring at his belt. The lock sticks and he has to jiggle the key several times before the tumblers catch and align.

"*Für'n Arsch!*" Bloody useless!

The room is dark and musty. He fumbles for the light switch. Everything should be just the way he left it, yet it seems wrong somehow. The smell and the shadows and the mailbags piled against the wall all seem out of place.

"What's that?" Emilie asks. She points at the lockbox.

"A protective case."

"For the mail?"

"For certified letters. Legal documents, mostly. Stuff that's more valuable than a postcard to your cousin back home. Correspondence that people have paid extra to keep safe."

The mailroom is quiet. Still. There's no sound except for the distant, faint hum of the exterior engines. This room, like most aboard the airship, is not heated or cooled, and there isn't even the gentle whoosh of moving air. Emilie turns in a small circle in the middle of the room. "Safe from what?"

"Prying eyes. No one is allowed in here but me." And Kurt Schönherr of course. He has the other set of keys. But Kurt won't interfere unless Max falls down on the job. And that won't happen unless Emilie becomes an insurmountable distraction.

She smiles at him as though able to read his mind. "Do your eyes *pry*, Max?"

He likes it when she's coy. "Depends on the company."

"Present company excluded?"

"Afraid not."

"Good." The smile she offers is filled with encouragement. Max considers it a wild leap forward on her part. "I'm breaking the rules, being here. Right?"

"I'm afraid so."

"You're a bad influence, Herr Zabel."

"I do my best."

"Don't get me wrong. This is all very interesting, but it doesn't look like Cologne to me."

"It wouldn't. Not in here." Max lifts a bag from the hook by the door and points at the label. The word is printed in white block letters on the green canvas bag. "Cologne is below us. We're flying over it right now."

Max slides one arm through the strap and hoists the bag off the hook so that he can swing it around his shoulder. He scans the room once more, then leads Emilie back out into the corridor. The lock is even less cooperative this time, and he curses again, testing the knob several times before he's sufficiently convinced that the door won't swing back open. Max nods at the radio room door across the corridor. "Would you open that for me?"

"They aren't exactly fond of me in there, you know."

"You don't mean to tell me that you're intimidated by Willy Speck?"

"I am intimidated by Commander Pruss who—"

"Is currently in the lounge nursing his second gin and orange juice. I think the bartender calls it the LZ 129 or something equally pretentious. The glasses are frosted, and so is the drinker after downing a few." Max gives her a gentle thump with the mailbag. "After you. I'd still like to show you the city."

He follows close behind as Emilie steps into the radio room. Willy Speck and Herbert Dowe take one look at her and turn back to their instruments without a word. Max drops the mail bag through the opening into the utility room below and then descends the ladder so he can help Emilie down.

"Mail drop," he announces to the skeleton crew in the control car. The car is crowded with officers and observers during the day but is almost vacant at this time of night, manned by those with the least seniority.

No one seems to care that Max has brought Emilie with him, or if they do they'll save their questions and complaints for later. She is still an anomaly on board, an ill omen. The leftover prejudice of old mariners who believe women to be bad luck on the open seas. No matter that they'll be sailing over them, not in them. Superstitions die hard.

Perhaps Emilie is ignoring the other officers, or maybe she really is enthralled by the sight below. Regardless, she stands at the portside windows, her palms and the tip of her nose pressed against the cool glass. A tiny cloud of fog gathers near her mouth each time she exhales and then fades away as she draws another breath. The baroque silhouette of Cologne's cathedral is clearly visible beneath them, its two great spires reaching up to embrace the airship.

Emilie's mouth is round with wonder. "I've never seen anything like it."

The *Hindenburg* usually flies at an altitude of six hundred feet, but they have made a slow descent and now hover a mere two hundred feet above the city. The buildings and streets take on a different dimension from above. Boxed out and rimmed with pale light from streetlamps, they look like aerial drawings done in pen and ink. It is well into the evening and the respectable citizens of Cologne have gone to sleep. Only hardy souls wander these streets tonight, and they can be seen furtively drifting in and out of the pooled light. These are the ones who make their living by darkness. An occasional face turns upward as the mechanical roar of the airship passes overhead, but most move farther into the shadows.

"How does it work?" Emilie nods at the mailbag that now rests on the floor at her feet. "The drop?"

"Watch," Max says.

"Airfield ahead," Christian Nielsen calls. He has replaced Max in the navigation room for third shift and already looks weary an hour into the job.

Max opens the mailbag and pulls out what appears to be a checkered silk parachute from an inside pocket. He attaches it to the canvas with a series of elaborate knots, then secures it with two carabiners just to be sure.

Max can feel the *Hindenburg* turn slightly starboard. It is amazing to him how this is the only place on ship where directional changes can be felt. Or perhaps he has become attuned to them over time. The Cologne airfield comes into view and is significantly better lit than most of the city itself. They begin a lazy circle toward the middle of the airfield.

Once they approach the massive, illuminated X on the tarmac, he asks, "Would you do the honors?"

"Of?"

"Opening the window."

It takes her a few seconds to figure out the latch and to slide the heavy plate of glass to the side, but as soon as she has it open, cool air rushes into the control car and blows her hair away from her face, revealing the high angles of her cheekbones and the length of her neck. He's grateful that her attention is on the ground below and that she does not notice him stare.

"Will it catch?" Emilie lifts the edge of the silk parachute.

"It usually does."

"And if it doesn't?"

"I saw a mailbag split open on the tarmac once. The impact sent letters flying in a hundred different directions. I imagine it was a hassle to collect them all again, but other than a bit of wasted time and dirty paper, no harm done."

"Well, then." Emilie grins. "Let's see if this little bird can fly."

He knew this would delight her. Emilie has always seemed the sort of woman who is fascinated by new things. And, as it turns out, the bird does fly. It's all in the technique, of course. Max drops the bag just right, allowing the parachute to catch and fill almost immediately. It floats to the ground and lands well within the perimeter of the X long before they have finished their orbit of the airfield and changed course. He and Emilie lean out the window together, shoulders pressed together for warmth, wind in their faces, as a military jeep drives out to collect the package.

"No wonder you volunteered for this job," she says as they finally pull back.

He slides the window shut and turns to lean against it.

"I knew you'd want to see this."

A wicked look crosses her face and she lifts one shoulder in an impish shrug. "Well, it doesn't compare to seeing your *Schwanz*, but it's a close second."

Emilie leaves Max in the control car, his fellow officers staring at him in astonishment, as she ascends the ladder back into the radio room.

THE AMERICAN

The American waits. He waits, buried under three canvas bags of international mail, as the navigator and his companion get the mail drop ready. He wonders at her identity. The American matches her voice against those he is already familiar with: the journalist, the heiress, the teenage girl, and a handful of other women he overheard at dinner. He has not heard this woman's voice before. She speaks easily in German, though he notices she tosses in the random English word for good measure. And occasionally one in Spanish or Italian. She's intelligent, clearly, and she doesn't seem uneasy in this room. A crew member, then. But there's only one of those that he has seen—a stewardess. Tall. Aloof. Pretty. So the navigator has himself a girl then? Yes. That will come in handy. By the time they leave the mailroom, the American is fully relaxed beneath his pile, quite content to have placed the stewardess in her slot.

He waits, breathing through his mouth to remain silent. He can feel the vibration from the engine gondolas faintly through the floor beneath him. A gentle hum through his cheek, chest, belly, thighs, each part of his body pressed against the floor by the weight of the mailbags. Still he waits.

Five minutes. Ten. Fifteen.

Finally the navigator and the stewardess exit the door opposite the mailroom. They wander off down the hall toward the passengers' quarters. Slowly, painfully, he pushes the mail aside to stand and stretch, allowing the circulation to return to his feet and to the tips of his fingers. The American is light-headed as the blood moves through his extremities again, but he does not lean against the wall or steady himself on anything. He simply closes his eyes, breathes evenly, and focuses on staying upright.

There will not be another mail drop during the flight, and it's a good thing. The navigator will likely have to get the doorknob replaced in New Jersey. Or at the very least after the return flight to Frankfurt. The lock is broken. That's his own fault, of course, but he is not concerned. One ruined lock is a small price to pay for having accomplished the first of his goals. Let the love-stricken navigator worry about how to protect his precious letters in the future.

The door closes behind him but barely latches. The tine has moved farther into the tumblers now. He does not hesitate in the hallway but moves off intently, as if he has every right to be here and will say so to anyone who questions him.

He's passing the dining room, on his way toward his cabin, when Joseph Späh steps in front of him holding a plate filled with dinner scraps. It's fish, mostly, but there are a couple of half-eaten rolls and bits of potato as well. The American stops abruptly so he won't run over the small man.

Späh lifts the plate. "I have a dog," he says matter-of-factly.

The American blinks but does not answer.

"You should come meet her."

"You mean the dog is on this ship?"

Späh looks at him like he has sprouted a second head. "Well, you didn't think this was for me?"

"I hadn't a clue what it was for."

"Good grief, man, where have you been? Didn't you catch my arrival? It caused quite a stir."

"I'm afraid I was rather indisposed. I hardly noted my own arrival. You could say I was quickly taken to my cabin and put out of the way."

"Ah. Your hangover."

The American shrugs but does not apologize. He's not the sort of man to apologize for anything.

They stare at one another awkwardly for a moment before Späh says, "Well?"

"What?"

"Are you going to come meet my dog or not? She's an honest-to-goodness European purebred Alsatian. Which is just a fancy way of saying German shepherd, but still, she's impressive. Her name is Ulla. I trained her to perform with me onstage. She has been all over Europe. I'm bringing her home as a gift for my daughter. It won't make up for missing her birthday, but at least she'll have bragging rights at school, and that is damn near good enough."

"Where is this mutt of yours? Surely they aren't letting you keep it in your cabin?"

"Hell no. They've got the poor bitch stored back in the freight room."

"And you're allowed back there?"

Joseph Späh is odd. He's the sort of man who is both insecure and absurdly arrogant. But he is also clever, manipulative, and fiercely intelligent. "It's either they let me back there at my leisure or they're the ones cleaning up dog shit twice a day."

The American laughs. "I think I would very much like to meet the dog that has the Zeppelin-Reederei crew breaking their precious rules." He looks at the plate, then around the empty corridor. "And we don't need an escort?"

Späh shrugs, sort of a hell-if-I-know movement, and heads off down the corridor to the steps leading to B-deck. The American follows quite happily behind.

If the Zeppelin-Reederei has spared no expense in making the passenger quarters a statement of luxury, they have spared no expense in this part of the ship on their engineering marvel. He follows Joseph Späh out of the passenger area, through a heavy door, and onto the keel catwalk, feeling every bit as though he is traversing the spine of a Leviathan. Gone are the residential trappings. Once they pass through the access door at the end of B-deck, clearly marked CREW ONLY, they enter into a world of duralumin and pipes. Air shafts and gas tanks. Catwalks. Girders. Valves. Bracing wires. Above them are countless massive fabric bladders filled with hydrogen gas and covered with thick cell netting. To him they look like giant inflated lungs. It is like taking a tour through the skeletal system of an automaton. The subtle creaking of welded joints is audible here in the absence of walls and doors and ceilings. But most amazing to the American is the skin of the airship itself. While the outside of the Hindenburg is a dazzling silver, the inside had been coated in a deep crimson thermite paint, giving life to the feeling that they are indeed traipsing through the belly of a sentient beast. The lights along the catwalk are spaced at intervals of twenty feet and are in tightly secured glass globes, but nonetheless their dim illumination amplifies the eerie, lifelike quality of the space.

They step around a massive T-shaped cruciform brace that must be one of the central supports, and then a short distance beyond that the spiral staircase that connects the keel catwalk to the axial catwalk eighty feet above them. The American has traveled aboard the *Graf Zeppelin* a number of times but has never been outside the passenger areas. This is to him a new and profound and disturbing experience.

"I halfway suspect I'll have nightmares tonight," Joseph Späh says.

The American answers this observation with a grunt. He will have nightmares tonight as well, but they will be about different things. His nightmares will tap into the most basic, primal fear he has: losing control. Behind his closed eyes he will see things falling apart. He will grasp after missed opportunities and misinformation. He will hear whispers in languages he does not know, and he will see faceless shapes slipping around corners and ducking through doors while he is exposed, frozen, unable to follow. His dreams will be all shadow and no substance.

The American shudders. Clears his mind. Marches behind Joseph Späh with a new determination.

Finally the small man points to a metal door marked FREIGHT. "She's in there."

At the sound of his voice a high, keening whine comes from the other side, followed by a bark. Then a second, deeper bark.

The freight room is cold and dark and smells of stale air and dog piss.

"Shit," Späh says. "I'm too late. Poor girl is probably scared stupid. Dogs piss on *everything* when they're scared."

So do men, the American thinks, but he does not say this out loud. He just stands back, watching.

Späh finds the light switch on the wall and a tepid glow fills the room. The cargo hold isn't very large. And apart from two dog crates it contains a number of steamer trunks, boxes, and what looks to be a large piece of furniture wrapped in a blanket.

Ulla sees her master and barks. She spins in a tight circle inside her crate, her tail thrashing against the wicker slats with a *thwap, thwap, thwap*.

"Who does that one belong to?" The American points at a second crate that holds a large, shivering mutt. It might be the half-breed bastard of something resembling a greyhound.

"I don't know." The American moves closer but Späh says, "Watch your step."

Three streams of urine trickle from a puddle in one corner of the mutt's crate. Späh gently lifts the latch on Ulla's crate. She pants. Presses her nose into the gap. Tries to force her way out.

"No," Späh says. "Sit."

The dog is reluctant and hungry but well trained. She drops her rump to the floor but cannot contain the frenzied thrashing of her tail. He sets the plate at his feet.

"Stay," he says.

The mutt whimpers, eyes locked on the plate of food.

Joseph Späh pulls the crate door open and steps backward. Ulla stays where she is, though with a great effort. The American can see her training wrestling with her instinct. The muscles in her forelegs spasm with little jerks as she forces herself to obey.

"Eat."

Ulla rushes forward at the command and inhales her dinner.

When observed coldly, the act is almost violent. She does not bite or chew but rather consumes with bared teeth and wild gulps. Alsatians are nearly indistinguishable from German shepherds, their temperaments fierce and protective, but Ulla has one great distinction. Instead of the traditional brown and black markings, she is completely white. Albino? he wonders. But no, her eyes are a deep black. In the scant light they look like bits of obsidian, reflecting his curiosity back at him. Joseph Späh has her well in hand, but the American does not doubt for a moment that this animal is intelligent. She is not to be trifled with.

"Shut up," Späh says to the mutt in the other cage as it throws itself against the slats, whining.

"It's hungry."

Späh frowns. "It is not my responsibility." But there is no hardness in his voice. Rather a faint thread of compassion.

Ulla licks the plate until it rattles against the floor. There isn't so much as a breadcrumb or ribbon of fish left when she's done. The expensive Nazi plate is delicate, with silver edging, and it's being licked by a dog. The American finds this very apropos, and the sight puts him in an inexplicably good mood.

As it turns out, Ulla proves to be worth whatever Späh has paid to transport her across the Atlantic. The tricks he has taught her are quite spectacular. She can stand on her hind legs or forelegs at a single command. She can do a back flip and speak her name. Ulla is almost human in the way she anticipates her master's needs, and the American quite enjoys the show Späh performs on his behalf.

"Good night, girl," Späh whispers as he rubs behind her ears and under her chin. "I'll be back tomorrow."

Until now the airship has felt incomplete to the American, as though he has seen only part of a map. But now, having walked the *Hindenburg* from one end to the other, he feels a greater sense of certainty in his mission. There are still closed doors, places he has not been, things he hasn't seen, but he will rectify that. He has been on board for a little over five hours, and the shape of the great airship is forming in his mind.

He bids Späh good night and thanks him for the chance to meet Ulla as they re-enter the passenger area.

"You should come with me again tomorrow. I think she likes you."

Foolish dog, the American thinks.

Späh claps him on the back. "I'll come get you in the morning."

"Not too early."

He peers at the ceiling as though trying to decide the time of day. "Don't worry, when I get home my days of sleeping in are over. I have three children. They wake up at the most ungodly hour every single day."

"Anytime after seven." He parts ways with Späh, who turns at the stairs to head up toward A-deck, and returns to his room.

The pistol is still there. He moved it to the bottom of his suitcase when he went to dinner. The American feels the reassuring weight of it in his hands. The clip is still loaded. His room has not been entered. He can tell this by the little clues he set in place before leaving: one corner of the pillowcase tucked underneath. The closet door closed but not latched. The sink set to a faint drip. The shirts folded at the top of his suitcase. He takes a deep, satisfied breath and begins to undress for bed. It will take some time to quiet his mind. It will take much longer to fall asleep.

He has just stretched out on the berth when the door to the next cabin opens. Laughter. A man's voice, and then a woman's. Whispers. The door closes with a loud click.

It is well past midnight now and the airship is eerily quiet. Too quiet for the woman to be speaking as loudly as she does.

"Do you think he's right?" she asks.

"Ssshhhh," her partner says, and then lower, "About what, *Liebchen?*"

"About the bomb."

The American sits up straight, every muscle tense, breath held, listening for whatever it is they will say next.

THE JOURNALIST

Ssshhhh." Leonhard stands behind her, his lips close to her ear. Warm. And his voice is little more than a whisper. "It's Colonel Erdmann's job to worry, not yours."

"But—"

"Quiet, *Liebchen.*"

"He said—"

"I know what he said."

Gertrud loves Leonhard's hands. He is bright and educated and easily the funniest man she has ever met, but his hands are not the soft, indolent hands of an academic. They are broad and strong and calloused. They are the hands of a man who has never known a sedentary day. And right now those hands snake around her waist, stroking, massaging until they find the top button of her skirt. He flicks it open with two fingers and the fabric at her waist relaxes. Gertrud is never more aware of how much older Leonhard is than when he touches her. It is startling how much skill he has acquired in those two extra decades.

"I know what you're doing," she says.

When Leonhard tugs at her skirt it falls a few inches to settle on her hips.

"I'd say it's fairly obvious."

"You're trying to distract me."

Gertrud's skirt drops to the floor, and Leonhard moves those nimble, calloused fingers to her blouse. One button. Two. Three. He spreads the collar open, revealing an elegant sweep of clavicle and the pale ivory of her camisole. Next he shifts his attention to the opening at the back of her slip as he unbuckles her garters from behind.

"You never did tell me what you were thinking," he whispers. Leonhard tugs lightly at her earlobe with his teeth.

It takes a beat too long for Gertrud to find her question. "When?"

"When you came out of the toilet after dinner. You looked sad and guilty, like you could cry but were too angry. Why?"

"Egon. I hadn't thought of him for hours."

"Ah. I thought so." He gently pulls her to him, her back pressing against his chest. Leonhard is warm and solid, and she settles against him. "Egon is at home with your mother, asleep. You should sleep as well."

"There's little chance of that."

"Oh?" One of those hands she loves so much drops between them and makes its way under her slip.

"It isn't going to work, you know."

"No?" The warmth of his palm high on the inside of her thigh. The stroke of one well-placed finger.

Gertrud clears her throat. "Absolutely not."

"We shall see about that." He nuzzles his nose into the soft spot beneath her left ear. Finds her pulse with the tip of his tongue.

"That's not fair." Her words come out in a rush.

"The rules of fair play do not apply in love or war."

"Don't you quote John Lyly to me."

He does not answer, simply continues his gentle stroking against the soft skin of her throat.

"Which is this, then?" she asks. "Love or war."

"Erotisch."

So much for fair play. "You didn't answer my question."

"Oh, but I did, *Liebchen*." Leonhard finishes unbuttoning her blouse. He slides it off her shoulders and down her arms with warm, long fingers.

This is how she found herself married to Leonhard in the first place. His single-minded, relentless ability to get what he wants. And for the last few years it appears that Gertrud is the only thing he wants. It started with a glass of wine after an editorial meeting. She hadn't wanted to go with him that afternoon—he intimidated her with his age and self-assurance—but he just seemed so certain that *he* wanted to go with *her*, so she relented. Then dinner a few nights later. It must have been excruciating for Leonhard to wait the appropriate amount of time before he could employ his more persuasive abilities. She has wondered since what he would have done had she rebuffed him before he could put them to good use. Alas, she never got the chance to find out. Leonhard Adelt is not the sort of man to let a prize slip through his fingers.

And those fingers are quite busy now hiking her slip higher and higher until it rests at the top of her thighs. "Stop thinking of Egon. He's fine," he whispers as he hooks his thumbs into the edge of her stockings. Tugs. The sheer silk slides down her legs. Leonhard kicks them toward the growing pile of clothing, then systematically dispatches her garters as well. Leonhard lifts her hands and slides the camisole up and over her head. Unhooks her bra with one hand and drops it to the floor.

"I'm not thinking about him. Not anymore."

"Liar." He sets his hands on her hips and slides them slowly up the slope of her belly, over her ribs, until he cups a breast in each hand.

Egon is not quite a year old, and one month ago she was still nursing him twice a day. The process of weaning him was rushed and unwilling and fraught with emotion on both their parts thanks to this trip. And it is only now, as her husband's strong and gentle hands massage her breasts, that she realizes how heavy they are, filled with a phantom ache.

"It's gone," she whispers, trying to reassure him, as she remembers the awkward pairing of motherhood and lovemaking. There is no polite way to escape the realities of biology when one has a child. Acceptance is the only real course of action. And good humor.

"It never bothered me, *Liebchen*. You know that." His attentions are methodical as he explores all the dips and hollows, the ridges and mounds of her body, with those expert hands. "But I was right, you do need to be distracted. You won't sleep otherwise."

If Leonhard was careful in the removal of her clothing, he is efficient when it comes to his own. In a matter of moments there is no fabric between them. He pushes her gently onto the bed.

"It won't work."

"You keep saying that," Leonhard says as he climbs in and hovers over her, "but there is so much you have to learn, *Liebchen*." He graces her with a patient smile.

"You've been a thorough teacher so far."

"Perhaps . . . *perhaps* I shall exhaust you so thoroughly that you will concede my point."

"I'd like to see you try."

He laughs. Then growls. Drops his mouth to her skin. Leonhard kisses the hollow where neck and shoulder meet. It takes only seconds for his ministrations to become more sensual.

Gertrud is not as crafty as her husband, but she's every bit as provocative and quite a bit faster. "No so fast," she whispers, pulling away slightly.

He shudders and his eyes take on a glassy, hungry look that only feeds her determination. He murmurs something desperate against her throat.

"Not this time, *Geliebter*," she whispers. "It's my turn to teach you a thing or two."

THE CABIN BOY

On his first trip aboard the *Hindenburg*, Werner Franz negotiated his position on the top bunk with an aplomb far beyond his age. One look at his indomitable cabin mate, Wilhelm Balla, convinced him that the best approach would be one of emotionless logic. So Werner had suggested that it would be easier for him to move in and out of the high, narrow berth due to the fact that he was younger, lighter, and smaller. Balla had looked at the boy and then the ladder that led to the bunk for a prolonged moment, shrugged, and tossed his bag on the lower mattress. They had never spoken of sleeping arrangements again. The truth of the situation, however, was that Werner desperately wanted the top. His reasons were immature, but he was too immature himself to recognize them: being the younger brother, he'd never gotten the top bunk at home, and he was willing to endure any amount of negotiation to make sure he acquired it now.

Balla isn't the most interesting cabin mate, but they get along well enough. And they've learned not to disturb one another as they come and go at different hours. So when Werner hears the door open, he assumes that Balla is turning in for the night. As cabin boy, Werner's primary job is to serve the officers, and his schedule accommodates theirs, stretching from early breakfast at six to evening coffee at nine-thirty. Balla tends the passengers and keeps to more traditional hours. Werner is almost asleep again when he realizes that a gentle snoring is coming from the bunk below. Balla is already in bed. Someone else has opened the door.

"Get up," a voice says, close to his ear. It is not Balla's.

Werner squeezes his eyes shut. He murmurs a feeble objection and pulls the heavy knit blanket over his head.

The blanket is stripped away. "If I have to turn on the light it will wake Balla and you'll likely get a beating from both of us. Up now. You have work to do."

It's well past midnight. Werner feels certain of this. He was in bed by eleven p.m. and has been sleeping soundly for some time. He runs through a quick mental checklist to ensure that he has done everything required of him this evening: he has served dinner to the officers, scrubbed down their dining area, and cleaned and put away the dishes; he has taken coffee to the control car for those working the night shift; he has made sure all of the officers' beds are made and their cabins tidy. His clothes are pressed and laid out for the next day. He has not missed anything. He never does.

"I will yank your scrawny carcass from this bed if you're not on the floor in three seconds." The voice is stern and all the more intimidating for its lack of volume.

Werner has an older brother and has long since learned to take such threats seriously. He's on the floor, hand gripping the ladder for balance, before he has even made the conscious decision to do so. There is a sharp twinge in his bruised knee and he winces at the pain.

It takes several seconds for him to recognize the severe face of Heinrich Kubis. The chief steward is standing with his back to the door, his face cast in deep, angled shadows, and he is holding a large basket of shoes in the crook of his arm. His short black mustache looks like a grim slash in the half-light, a mark of displeasure. Werner says the only words he can gather at this moment. "I don't understand."

"Come with me."

The boy looks at his faded flannel pajamas. "But—"

"No need to get dressed."

Werner grabs his pocket watch from the dressing table, then gently pulls the door shut and follows Kubis down the corridor. He is barefoot and rumpled and half-asleep, and the watch hangs heavy in his pocket. "Where are we going?"

Kubis turns the corner and stops before the gangway stairs. He tips his head to the side, thinks for a moment, and sets the basket down on the third step. "Here."

The cabin boy pretends to understand. He doesn't ask any questions, but rather looks at Kubis expectantly, as though awaiting instructions. Silence, when coming from a child, is usually interpreted by adults as understanding. Or, at worst, fear. It is a trick he has used every day since coming to work aboard the *Hindenburg*. He watches and listens and inevitably gets the answers he's looking for without ever having to ask.

Kubis points at the basket. "There's a brush and a rag and a tin of wax at the bottom. You will shine those shoes and you will do a damn good job. Understand?"

The boy doesn't trust his voice enough to say more than the minimum. "Yes."

Werner has worked on board the Hindenburg for seven months and never once has he been asked to perform this task. When Heinrich Kubis hired him last year this was not listed among his job duties. And yet here he is, pulled from a sound sleep and given the chief steward's work to do. If he were a man he would punch Kubis right in his knobby Adam's apple. But he's little more than a boy, so he blinks back tears instead.

Kubis is gone without so much as a word of further instruction. Not that Werner needs it, of course. He has been shining shoes for his father since he was three years old. He looks at the basket. It is brimming—probably ten pairs—and he slumps to the carpeted steps, defeated. His feet are cold, and, the longer he sits there, so is his rear end. The Franz men are not known for having a well-padded posterior, and he is no exception.

Werner winds the pocket watch and sets it on the step next to him. The gentle ticking is a comfort, and the tarnished face reminds him of his grandfather. It is neither gold nor silver but rich and heavy pewter, a family heirloom given to Werner by his father the night before his first voyage on the *Hindenburg*. The glass is scratched and clouded, but the numbers are clear and dark, written in the Roman style. He looks at the time and cringes.

Receiving the watch was a rite of passage, an acknowledgment that he had begun the journey toward manhood. It has traditionally passed from father to oldest son, but his brother insisted that Werner had earned the right to the watch when he gained his position on the *Hindenburg*. So they had gathered in the tiny apartment—his parents, grandfather, and brother—and eaten an elaborate meal they could not afford. His father presented the watch to him with great pomp and circumstance—and no small amount of pride—while his mother played Eddie Rosner on the record player, the trumpet vibrant and celebratory to mark the occasion. Werner has carried the watch with him on every flight since and set it beside him every time he feels lost or lonely or afraid. The watch gives him courage. He draws from it now.

Each pair of shoes has a paper tab tied to the laces indicating the deck and room number. Werner hasn't been given specific instructions, but he would guess it falls to him to return the shoes once they have been shined. He'd rather throw them in the trash and go back to bed than touch a single one of them. The first night of any voyage is always the hardest—so much excitement and adrenaline and so many things that need adjustment—and he feels the exhaustion most acutely in his shins. It's an odd place, granted, but he has been on his feet all day; he is still growing, and all of the strain in his body has settled into that one stretch of bone. When he makes such complaints to his mother she laughs and says he is afflicted with a galloping pain. "Today your wrist, tomorrow your leg," she says, but she always brings him warm milk with sugar and vanilla and rubs his back until his eyes are heavy and his muscles have relaxed. Werner is usually so caught up in this grand adventure—the travel and the work—that he does not miss his family. But he has such an acute longing to be back home with them at this moment that he has to compose himself by wiping tears and snot on the sleeve of his pajamas.

Werner looks at the watch and thinks of his father, sick and bedridden in their shabby one-bedroom flat in Frankfurt, a man who would give anything to be *able* to work, and reprimands himself for acting like a child. So what if the task costs him an hour or two of sleep? He's making a wage and he can help his family. His mother and father are sleeping all the better tonight because of this job. Werner shakes his head, growls a bit to clear his mind, then gets to work. Best to get the task over with.

Ten minutes later he has settled into something of a rhythm and is working on the second shoe in a pair of black cap-toed loafers—this one tagged for a passenger in cabin A4—when someone comes around the corner at a fast clip. It's that obnoxious American passenger. Werner pulls himself into the shadows because the last thing he needs is to be noticed and sent on some other random errand in the middle of the night. He sits perfectly still and absolutely quiet, waiting for the man to pass, when Max Zabel comes around the gangway stairs from the other direction. For a moment he is certain the American sees Max and that he will sidestep him, but then Werner notices something flash across the American's face—he can't exactly tell from this distance what sort of expression it is—and they collide. The force knocks Max sideways.

Werner is wondering where they are off to at this hour when Heinrich Kubis appears before him with a second basket. This time Werner cannot prevent a small complaint. "There's *more?*"

"I will be in the crew's mess if you need me."

Oh. Werner understands now. He has tried, and failed, on more than one occasion to join the late-night card game that takes place among the crew.

"Poker?"

Kubis sets this basket down beside the other. He shrugs. "You're a lucky boy," he says, "to have a job like this. You can help your family. See the world. It would be such a pity if you didn't pass your probationary period." He gives Werner a cold smile. "Come get me when you're finished."

THE AMERICAN

It is an awkward thing to listen to someone else's lovemaking. Even when you are alone. Even when they are trying to be quiet. The rustling and moans, the terms of endearment mingled with profanity, the occasional thump of a head against the wall, and the muffled laughter are enough to make a grown man lose his mind. This has happened to the American only twice before—both times during the First World War—and he's no better at dealing with it now than he was then. Perhaps worse. He was twenty and a virgin then and has since figured out what the fuss is all about. The American has been alone for many years now, and his lovers have been few and far between. And, based on what he hears on the other side of the thin fabric wall, his experiences have been completely unsatisfactory.

When, after ten minutes, the couple shows no signs of slowing down, he dresses and pulls a clean pair of shoes from his suitcase. While he has no love for the Zeppelin-Reederei overall, he cannot begrudge the world-class treatment of their passengers. Shoes left outside the cabins are collected at night, polished by the stewards, and returned before morning. They're offering the service, so he may as well take advantage of it. The American carefully opens the door so as not to be heard by his neighbors. Or rather so they will not know he has heard *them*. No sooner does he step into the corridor, however, than he comes face-to-face with Heinrich Kubis, the chief steward, standing outside the Adelts' door with a look that is perfectly split between hunger and horror. He grips a basket full of shoes in his hands.

The American cannot remember the last time he blushed, but he does so now. After he and the steward stare at one another for one long, awkward moment, he shrugs and sets his scuffed shoes in the basket with the others.

After a moment the steward clears his throat and stands to his full height. "The bar is open until three," he says, "should you need something to occupy your time this evening."

There is a burst of laughter and then whispered hushes on the other side of the Adelts' door.

"I think that would be a good idea."

"Down the corridor and to the left," Kubis says.

The American proceeds in that direction and turns the corner only to run directly into the navigator. They mumble apologies while trying to figure out how to pass one another in the narrow space. He does not know the man's name—he will have to find out tomorrow—but he remembers his face. They bid one another a good evening, and the American mentally sets him into place. He takes a few steps forward but then stops and turns to watch the navigator retreat down the corridor, toward the crew's quarters. But not the ones beyond the control car reserved for the officers. The navigator is headed toward the stewards' rooms. And there is only one person housed in this part of the ship that he would likely be interested in seeing after such a long shift: the lovely stewardess with the large breasts, the tiny waist, and the bright smile. So they will be spending more time together this evening? It is but another detail that the American files away for future use.

THE STEWARDESS

Emilie sets the makeup case on her bed and empties out the contents. Lotions. Perfumes. A variety of expensive cosmetics—she takes much better care of her skin now that she has gotten older—and the necessary products that accompany being a woman in this modern world: curlers and sanitary napkins, talcum powder and tweezers. She shoves all of this aside and presses her fingernails into the panel at the bottom of the case, exposing a compartment less than an inch deep. The panel lifts easily and she sighs. Emilie knew the documents would be there, but still it's a relief to see them. It took months to get everything together, and even longer to convert the Deutsche marks to American dollars, one small bill at a time. Anything more than a handful every other week would bring too much attention. But it's all here now, neatly stacked and bound with string. She counts it again, just to be sure. This is her insurance policy. And her indictment. These papers contain all but one of her most guarded secrets: her mother's maiden name.

Abramson.

It is a detail that has been obscured by time and marriage. But the names of her parents are plainly written on these documents, and it would take a curious mind very little time to discover the truth. It would be her ruin.

Funny how marriage can erase the person you used to be, she thinks. It happened for her mother. And it happened to her as well. When she married Hans Imhof all those years ago she went from being the daughter of a Jewish woman to being the wife of a German innkeeper. In a breath—no longer than the time it took to speak a vow—she was someone else.

The loss of her name never troubled her much. But she has never recovered from the loss of her husband.

Emilie pulls off her dress and stockings. She hangs them on the ladder that leads to the upper berth and allows herself to be comfortable for the first time that evening. A hesitant knock sounds on the door. The tension that only moments ago had subsided in her shoulders, the small of her back, and the arches of her feet returns with a lurch. She curses silently. There is no time to shove everything back in her case, so Emilie grabs the papers and the money and hides them in the closet. The knock sounds again, lighter this time. Emilie is at the door wearing nothing but a slip before she can properly think through her response.

"What?" She yanks the door open with a growl and immediately regrets it.

"I'm sorry. I didn't think you'd be in bed already. I just came to say good night."

It is a great credit to Max's sense of honor that he looks at nothing but her eyes.

"Just a moment."

Whether he takes a peek as she turns to get her robe she cannot say, but he is waiting calmly at the door, eyes on the carpet, when she returns a few seconds later. There is a decision to be made and she must do it quickly because they are standing in the corridor, in full view of anyone who should happen upon them.

"Come in," she whispers.

Max takes off his cap and steps into the room. It's identical to his own cabin, but he looks around anyway. Her clothes are hung neatly over the rungs of the ladder. Max reaches out to finger the collar of her uniform.

"I've never seen you not wearing this," he says.

"I do have other clothes."

He flicks a glance to the deep V of her satin robe. "So I see."

The twitching at the corner of his mouth makes Emilie wonder if he wasn't so noble with his gaze after all. It has been less than an hour since the mail drop over Cologne, but from the hunger in his gaze you would think he hadn't seen her in months.

"Is there something I can do for you, Herr Zabel?"

"Yes." He steps forward and the room shrinks considerably. "You can start calling me Max."

"I already do."

"Only sometimes."

"Are you suggesting that we are on a first-name basis now?"

"I should like to think so."

"And you don't think that perhaps you're taking liberties?"

"Not at all." Max seats himself on the edge of the bed and pats the space next to him. He seems unconcerned by the fact that her personal items are strewn all over the blanket. "Let me explain."

Damn it, she thinks, *how does he do that?* But she only hesitates for a moment before settling next to him on the heavy knit blanket. "This I need to hear."

"It's really quite simple," he says. "We've just spent the evening together—or some of it, at any rate. And now I'm sitting in your private quarters kissing you good night. I think that puts us on a permanent first-name basis."

She looks up at him in surprise. Max catches her face in his hands. He gives her a smile that is so mischievous, so pleased with himself, that she cannot help but return it.

It has been ten years since Emilie kissed her husband good-bye. Ten years since he left for work one morning and never returned. And in those years she has forgotten the profound, blood-warming pleasure of being kissed. *Of course he would be good at this*, she thinks. He begins with a tender brushing of his lips against hers, and when she tilts her head and softens beneath him he pulls her close and earnestly goes to work. There is no uncertainty with Max, and when her lips part he finds her tongue with his. He tastes of white wine and fresh melon, and she thinks that there is truly no better combination.

She is not ready for him to pull away, but he does anyway.

Max straightens his collar and smoothes his hair. Oh God, did I do that? she wonders briefly, and is certain that she did, in fact, twist her fingers through his hair. She cannot remember doing so. Ten years of widowhood and this is what one brief kiss does to her?

Emilie has no idea what expressions are running over her face in rapid succession, but Max laughs at her.

"You don't have to look so bereft," he says, bending closer and playing with the curls at the base of her neck. "I'm not ready to stop either. I just thought I'd better make sure you wanted to keep going."

"So *now* you ask my permission?"

"Easier to ask forgiveness."

"So you're sorry?"

"Not even a little bit."

Emilie is certain now that she did indeed muss his hair a moment ago. Because it's between her hands again and this time she notices how smoothly it slides between her fingers.

"*Mein Gott*, that feels good," he mutters against her lips. "Don't stop."

Max lays his palm against her neck. His hand is soft and warm, and she shivers just a bit as he slides it downward. It stops at the base of her throat when his fingers meet the chain that she wears around her neck. He pulls away to look at her and then at the chain. Max tucks one finger under the edge of her robe so that he can lift the chain out.

"A key?"

Slowly, *slowly* she realizes what is puddled in the palm of his hand and she jerks back, taking the necklace with her.

"I'm sorry. I didn't mean to—"

"My husband gave it to me," she says. "On our wedding night."

Max knows she is widowed. Everyone knows this. But the words have a corrosive effect nonetheless. The heat that charged the air only seconds ago vanishes completely, and they are left sitting on the bed staring at one another in silence.

After a few seconds he manages to speak. "And you still carry it?"

"It's all I have left of him."

"What was his name?" Max whispers.

"Hans."

"And you miss him?"

"Every day."

"You love him still?"

"I will *always* love him." The ferocity of this statement startles

Emilie. The key is gripped so tightly in her hand that it cuts into the tender skin of her palm.

"How did he die?"

"He drowned." It's her polite way of saying that Hans drove off a bridge and dropped sixty feet into the Main River. But she doesn't tell him this. She doesn't like to think of that long, horrifying fall or the churning water that waited for her husband at the bottom.

Max does not ask for these details. He merely sits there, hands folded in his lap, thinking.

Emilie wants to apologize for her reaction. She wants to explain everything. But she cannot find the words. *It's just a key*, she tells herself; *it can't bring Hans back*. But she holds it anyway.

Max nods at her fist. "What is it to?"

"The front door of the inn we owned. It was a dream. A wedding gift. And when he died I lost it. I lost everything."

"Except the key?"

She nods. "I took it with me when I went to work on the *Columbus*. I lied to the people who bought the inn. I told them I'd lost the key. I couldn't bear for them to have it."

Emile can see Max connecting the dots in his mind. A young widow forced to sell everything she owns. Forced to take a job serving wealthy passengers on an ocean liner. Ten years of drifting, never having a home, never working with anyone long enough to call them friend. She erupts in sudden fury at the sympathy she sees written across his face. "I don't want your pity!"

"I wasn't offering it."

"Then why are you here, Herr Zabel?"

"No." He catches her face in his hands again. Firm. But gentle. "You don't get to call me that anymore. Not after the way you just kissed me."

She tries to speak, but her voice cracks. Emilie clears her throat and tries again, but she manages little more than a whisper. "Why are you here?"

"To offer myself as a very willing and very eager substitute for the man you've lost."

"He can't be replaced."

Max takes her clenched fist in his palm. He pries her fingers open, pulls the key from her grasp. He dangles it six inches from her nose. "You don't have to torture yourself with this memory."

She owes him an answer. That's why he came here tonight. And he has forced her hand. Quite literally.

"Max . . ."

He lowers his head and brushes the corner of his mouth against hers. "That's much better."

This time when the knock sounds at the door it is hard and urgent and official.

Max doesn't speak aloud, but she can read his lips, and she is quite surprised at his creativity. She has never seen those words used in that particular combination before.

"Yes?" she calls, turning toward the door. Her voice sounds a bit too strangled for her liking, but it's the best response she can muster under the circumstances.

"You have been paged, Frau Imhof." The dry, impatient voice is that of Heinrich Kubis. "Margaret Mather requires your assistance."

Emilie mentally repeats the name in several languages until the face of the American heiress drifts into her mind.

"I will be right there."

"Very well."

She listens to Kubis's retreating footsteps. And now, another choice. Max cannot very well be seen following her from the room, especially with Kubis in the corridor. But if he stays here they will have to continue this conversation, and Emilie will have to finally give her answer. She sits there, looking at Max, one hand on the key and the other pressed lightly to her lips where he has just kissed her. "Will you wait here?" she whispers.

He gives a small, pleased smile. "Of course."

Max stands and lifts her dress from the ladder. "I am quite fond of that robe already, and what lies beneath it even more so, but I doubt Kubis would approve of your attending to Frau Mather in your slip."

"And you propose to help me dress?"

"I can turn to the wall, if you like."

As always, the decision is hers. Max Zabel truly is the most infuriating man she has ever met. But Emilie unties her robe and sets it on the top berth. She shrugs and raises her hands above her head like a little girl being dressed by her mother.

This time Max does look. But it's the barest whisper of a glance as he lowers the dress over her head. Somehow they do the buttoning and the belting in tandem. They do not speak. They do not look at one another. Max approaches the job very much the way she imagines he approaches his charts: with precision and delicacy. And it is now, even more so than during the kiss, that Emilie realizes how much she has missed being touched.

In the end he does turn to the wall when she pulls on her stockings. There is only so much intimacy she can handle for one night.

Max straightens her collar and with a warm hand slides the key back inside her slip. His knuckles brush against the swell of her breast but it does not linger. Seconds later he stands there, hands tucked into his pockets.

"I will be right back," she says.

"I will be right here."

THE NAVIGATOR

Max does not mean to find the documents. It happens by accident, the way everything with Emilie happens. Much like the way he has fallen in love with her. She should have been back by now. Of course, he thought that thirty minutes ago as well. Whatever help this Mather woman needs must be excessive and completely unnecessary. It has been over an hour now, and Max has not even begun to cool off. That's what set him pacing in the first place. And if he hadn't been pacing he wouldn't have gotten a little carried away and started swinging his arms in agitation. And if he hadn't been charging around the room like a damned horny monkey he wouldn't have run into the closet door, knocking it open. And he would not now be staring at a birth certificate, passport, five hundred American dollars, and immigration documents in the name of one Fräulein Emilie Imhof. Max scoops them up, takes one look, and then sits down roughly on the bed.

Emilie does not plan on returning to Germany.

The strangled sound he makes is one of despair. These are her private things, and he has no business riffling through them. He knows that. Emilie owes him nothing. But she kissed him back, damn it. He mutters this as he lifts the pale green satin robe from the bed. He buries his face in it, inhales her clean, sweet scent until it fills his head.

For over a year Max has wondered what it would be like to kiss Emilie. He has watched her from the day of their first flight. He has created opportunities to speak with her. Slowly, one trip at a time, he has lessened her resistance. He has reveled in her humor. Marveled at her defiance, her intelligence, her uncanny ability to anticipate the needs of others. And now he knows that her kiss is even sweeter than he imagined, that her skin is softer, and the feel of her breast beneath his hand—no matter how fleeting—reduces him to putty.

And Emilie Imhof is leaving him.

There are certain attributes that work better than others in the field of aviation, and for the most part Max has them in abundance. He is cautious. Patient. Thorough. Punctual. He has diligently applied these traits to his pursuit of Emilie. But at this moment he is also embarrassed. He is hurt. Sad. Volatile emotions that filter through a rapidly deteriorating fuse of anger. When that fuse burns dry he is past the point of reason.

Max jerks to his feet. He grabs his cap from the top berth and places it firmly on his head. He pulls a pen from the inside of his coat pocket and writes a note, a single line, on the envelope that holds her money, the nib digging so deeply into the paper that it almost tears. He looks at what he has written. It's blunt and acerbic, and he isn't sorry. He sets everything back in the closet where he found it. Then Max Zabel, navigator, postmaster, breaks his first promise to Emilie. He does not wait for her to return.

THE JOURNALIST

Leonhard is wrong. She cannot sleep. He lies beside her, on the outer edge of the berth, lost in the deep, contented slumber of a man who has just been soundly bedded. She spoke the truth to him earlier that day: being a good girl is not one of her talents. She has many others that he much prefers anyway.

He looks younger when he sleeps, boyish somehow. The deep lines on his brow smooth out, his mouth relaxes. She lifts the glasses gently from his face—she hadn't noticed that he'd left them on—and sets them on the ledge beside the bed. They will be the first thing he reaches for in the morning. He turns to the side and buries his face in the pillow while Gertrud pushes the sheet away and rolls around, unable to get comfortable. It's not that she doesn't want to sleep; she simply can't. Her mind is sharp and clear, every thought standing out in deeper contrast the longer she lies here. This is always what happens when she's on deadline. When a story has piqued her interest. When there is a trail to chase. But right now there are only worries to catalogue.

Egon. She tries to push that thought away but he only becomes clearer in her mind.

Colonel Erdmann.

The bomb threats. *Bomb threats*, for God's sake! And credible ones at that. How can a girl get an ounce of sleep with that on her mind? She balls her hand into a fist and pounds it against the mattress. Leonhard doesn't stir and she frowns in the dark, resenting this singular male ability to sleep like the dead after sex.

Gertrud thinks of the fact that at this very moment they are flying over the Atlantic Ocean in an aircraft lifted by combustible gas. *Of course a man would come up with this*, she thinks; you'd never find a woman inventing a floating bomb.

Her press card and its current location at the bottom of a desk drawer in Frankfurt. The thought makes her wince. And then cuss. *"Drecksau."* She spits the word out, not even bothering to whisper, but Leonhard doesn't so much as stir beside her.

That was easily the single worst day of her career. Leonhard had been so calm on the surface, so unperturbed, as he'd taken her arm and turned her back down the hallway after she'd insulted not only the Kulturstaatssekretär but the *Hure* fungus of a mother who brought him into the world. She regrets that last part. Gertrud hates the word, hates it entirely, and has made a point never to insult other women. For a woman who trades in words and wields them with precision, using such a word was inexcusable. And yet it came unbidden in her rage, and even Leonhard could not hide his astonishment.

The Frankfurt branch of the Ministry of Propaganda leases office space at Neue Mainzer Strasse 56. It's on the fourth floor and has an impressive view of the city. As do all the other floors, but they are empty except for a small sublet office on the third floor. She was told it is occupied by an American advertising company. Which would make sense. Many Germans aren't comfortable with the idea of doing business anywhere near the Ministry of Propaganda.

Something clicks in Gertrud's mind and she sits up so quickly the blood rushes to her head. She waits for the dizziness to subside, then picks the thought up. Turns it over. Examines it closely.

Neue Mainzer Strasse.

Her press card.

Americans.

"Oh shit."

Gertrud scrambles over Leonhard and stands stark naked in the middle of the room, thinking. She presses the heels of her hands against her temples, forcing her mind into submission. Forcing it to slow. Caution is not one of Gertrud's greater attributes, and she throws it to the wind now. She checks the watch on Leonhard's limp wrist. Two a.m. Her decision is made before she has time to stop and consider the consequences. She gathers her discarded clothing from the floor and dresses herself in the dark. Runs fingers through her hair. Pinches her cheeks.

Gertrud places a tender kiss on Leonhard's cheek and quietly slips out the door. The bathrooms are open at all hours and well lit. Thank goodness. So she's able to inspect her appearance with greater care before heading toward the bar. It will close in one hour, and she desperately needs a glass of wine and a good cigarette—something she hasn't enjoyed since becoming pregnant with Egon. The doctors told her she needn't quit, that smoking was a benign pleasure, but she had given it up anyway. The same way she'd given up coffee and drinking and a distinctly unladylike penchant for bicycling five miles a day.

"Oh. Back again?" the bartender asks. He takes in her wrinkled clothing, her disheveled hair with a curious tilt of his head.

Schulze. His name is Schulze, she thinks. "I couldn't sleep."

"And your husband?"

"That's not something he struggles with. Unfortunately."

"And what can I do for you, Frau . . ."

"Adelt."

"A nightcap perhaps? I make a fine hot toddy."

She had come for wine—Sauvignon blanc in particular—but something about the idea of whiskey and cinnamon, honey and lemon, cloves and a warm mug very much appeals to her right now. "That would be wonderful. And a pack of Chesterfields, if you have them."

"I do have them, but I can't give you a pack. I can bring you two to start with, and then more if needed. But the packs are not allowed out of the bar, and the cigarettes themselves stay in the smoking room. I'm sure you understand the need for this?"

"Yes. Of course."

"Follow me." Schulze motions toward the air-lock door.

There is only one other passenger in the room, and Gertrud stops short inside the door. His jacket is off. His tie is loose. And despite the fact that there are no fewer than five empty glasses on the table before him, his eyes are clear, quite different from how he looked on the bus that afternoon. The American has dark hair, parted down the middle, and a stray piece hangs across his forehead. It has been a long day for everyone, apparently. His mustache is neat and trimmed, but his lips are pursed. He is not happy to see her. The American slides something off the edge of the table—some sort of pendant on a ball chain—and tucks it in his suit pocket.

"Forgive me," Schulze says, "where are my manners? Frau Adelt, this is Edward Douglas. He's traveling home to visit family in America. Herr Douglas, this is Frau Adelt, a journalist, I believe?"

She nods when he looks at her in question.

Perhaps it's because her mind is already ticking along faster than she can control, but Gertrud makes the first move. "Pleased to meet you," she says, extending her hand.

The American takes it. "Charmed."

"Do you mind if I sit here?" Gertrud succeeds in summoning a perfectly guileless tone. "My husband is asleep, and I detest drinking alone."

"Of course." He stands and pulls out a chair from the table, the one farthest from him, she notes.

Having seen her neatly situated, Schulze returns to the bar to prepare her drink. Gertrud does not speak as she waits. Neither does the American. They simply survey one another, like two predators circling. Schulze returns with a tray and places it on the table, and she thanks him. Takes a sip of her hot toddy. Assures him that everything is to her liking.

The bartender lifts one of the cigarettes from the tray and pulls a pack of matches from his pocket. He is the keeper of flame on this airship. To Gertrud it appears as though he guards it with his life.

"May I?" Schulze asks.

"Please."

A sweet, pungent smoke drifts from the glowing end of her Chesterfield. She inhales once to show the bartender her gratitude but then waits until the air-lock door clicks shut behind him before she speaks. She looks at the American. "Who are you?"

"I could ask you the same thing."

"But I asked first."

"You heard the introduction. I'm American. I'm traveling home to visit my family in New Jersey."

"You're also a very, very good liar." She looks at the empty glasses on the table. Shakes her head.

"I've spoken nothing but the truth, Frau Adelt."

"Forgive me. You're a good *actor*, then."

He shrugs. "And you?"

"I'm a terrible actor."

"I'd imagine you're a damn good liar, though."

"I prefer the truth. I'm a journalist. But you already knew that, didn't you?"

"Yes," he says matter-of-factly. "I did."

"You were there that day in Frankfurt."

He nods.

"Why?"

"I work in the building."

"No one works in that building. Not unless they have a death wish."

"Cheap rent."

"You don't work for the Ministry of Propaganda?"

He snorts. "No."

"But you were in the hallway when it happened."

"You made quite a ruckus, Frau Adelt. It was hard to ignore."

"So curiosity brought you up those stairs?"

"It did rather sound as though you were being slaughtered."

"No. Not me. Just my career."

"It's one and the same where I come from," the American says.

This is why Gertrud pursued a career in journalism. She imagines it to be why people charge into battle or go on safari. There is nothing so addictive as the hunt. Her problem is that she likes it a little too much. Finds it too compelling. She swings her foot beneath the table, and her hands begin to tremble in anticipation, so she slowly raises the Chesterfield to her lips and pulls a mouthful of smoke into her lungs. Gertrud lets the cigarette sit there, burning, until her extremities settle.

"Just who the hell are you?" she asks.

DAY TWO

Out of the softening sunset came the airship; and the manner of its moving was beautiful. Few inanimate objects attain beauty in the pursuance of their courses, and yet, to me, at least, the flight of this ship was far lovelier than the swooping of a bird or the jumping of a horse. For it seemed to carry with it a calm dignity and consciousness of destiny which ranked it among the wonders of time itself.

—*From* The Zeppelin Reader,
"*Even the Birds: U.S.S.* Akron," *Anonymous*

THE STEWARDESS

Max's handwriting is exactly what you would expect from a man of charts and maps and letters. It is blunt and precise. He has a steady hand. No smudges or crooked letters. The harsh words are written with deep, straight lines, the strokes heavy and thick with ink. Each word makes Emilie wince. Their combined effect makes her angry and nauseous and ashamed.

You should have told me sooner.

She has a moment of heart-stuttering panic before she remembers that Max cannot have learned her heritage from those papers alone. If that were possible, the Zeppelin-Reederei would have done so long ago and she never would have been offered this job. Perhaps it was laziness on their part. She will never be certain. Regardless, knowing that the Nazis hired a Jewish woman as their first stewardess is a small, private triumph for Emilie.

It is her plan to defect that has angered Max, not her secret. He has written his note on the envelope that holds her life savings. She found it sitting on top of her travel papers when she got back to her empty room the night before. It had taken over an hour to get Margaret Mather out of her corset. The inept maid who had helped her into it in Frankfurt had double-knotted the laces at six points, leaving Emilie with no option but to cut the heiress out of her garment. Fräulein Mather had shown remarkably good humor during the ordeal. Emilie had done everything in her power to save the garment, and to untie the tangled knots first. But all to no avail. The heiress did not tell her what the contraption cost, but she winced visibly when it fell to the floor after being severed with a pair of Xaver's kitchen shears.

And all the time Emilie was gone the only thing she could think of was Max. The warmth of his hands. The way he looked at her beneath hooded lids. How she hungered to be kissed again. Only deeper and longer. By the time she slipped back into her cabin

Emilie had convinced herself that she wanted Max to stay. She was ready to give him the answer he desired. But the room was dark and silent, and she knew as soon as she shut the door behind her that he was no longer there. His absence was tangible.

It took Emilie several minutes to find the note. And when she read it a hundred tiny threads tethering her heart in place loosened and slipped away. She did not cry. Or rush after him. Emilie simply put her papers back in the bottom of her cosmetics case, stripped off her rumpled clothing, and crawled into bed. There was no transition between waking and sleeping. There was only the heavy, complete surrender to oblivion.

Sleep abandoned her just as suddenly a few moments ago, and now she lies wide-eyed in the dark. She is in the same position in which she fell asleep last night—on her back, fingers laced over her navel. She doubts that she even rolled over. It takes only a few breaths before she remembers the note.

You should have told me sooner.

Would it have changed anything? she wonders. Would he have decided not to waste his time? And what will he do now that he knows her plan? Betray her? She considers the possibility. No. Max would never do that.

Her shift begins in an hour, so she turns on the light and dresses in a clean uniform identical to the one she wore yesterday. Emilie looks wrong—disheveled and jumpy—and she feels wrong—flustered and restless—but she does not know what to fix. Or how to go about fixing it. It's as though she has taken a step sideways, outside herself, and can't get back in alignment. Emilie's hair is dark and her skin is light and her eyes are large, and the combination makes her look ghostly at this early hour. She brushes her hair until it crackles with static. She chooses the brightest shade of lipstick she owns—a deep ruby—and paints on a bit of mascara in the hope that it will make her eyes look bright instead of exhausted. It's not yet five-thirty but there is nothing else to be done, so she goes in search of food. Emilie will not make yesterday's mistakes. She will eat well. She will stay focused. She will avoid Max.

It is a good plan, but ill-fated. She has not reached the crew's mess before she finds herself face-to-face with the navigator. He is waiting for her in the keel corridor outside the kitchen. His eyes are the color of smoke this morning. They are bloodshot and rimmed with dark circles. Smoldering with anger. He didn't sleep well, and the exhaustion is evident despite his perfectly groomed appearance. Max has simply tried to put a good face on a bad night.

Emilie won't meet his gaze. She tries to step around him and into the kitchen, but he catches her elbow. "No."

"I'm hungry."

"You can wait."

When she tries to shake him off his grip tightens. "Let. Me. Go."

He takes a step forward, closing the gap between them. Max drops his mouth to her ear. "That's not going to happen, Emilie."

Most of the crew and passengers are still asleep, so there is no one to hear her complaints as Max pulls her back down the keel corridor, around the gangway stairs, and down the outer walkway beside the observation windows. Somewhere below them is the Atlantic Ocean, but all she can see is gaping, heavy darkness and her own guarded reflection in the glass.

"Where are you taking me?"

"Somewhere we can talk privately."

"I don't want to talk."

"I don't care."

"I thought you were a gentleman."

He snorts. "And I thought I could trust you."

"Trust?" Emilie yells just as Max opens the door to the public shower and pushes her inside. "*You* are lecturing *me* about trust?"

It's a small room, tiled floor to ceiling, and her voice ricochets the moment he closes the door behind them. It's the only shower on board the airship and is rarely used—most passengers prefer to wash in their rooms; the crew members who could most benefit from the luxury of a shower are discouraged from spending any time on the passenger decks. But she can tell someone has been here this morning. The showerhead is dripping, and rivulets of moisture are running down the tile walls. It smells of soap and humidity. Behind them is the steady, irritating drip of water.

"You went through my things!" Emilie's restraint vanishes, and she shoves Max against the wall, furious. Betrayed. Desperate. For a brief moment she thinks this display of emotion makes him smile. But she isn't sure. There's a single overhead light, and Max's face is obscured by the shadow of his cap.

"I wasn't trying to pry," Max says. "I knocked your closet door open. The papers were right there. It's not like I could miss them."

"You just knocked it open? That's convenient."

"I was restless. You stood me up."

"I didn't stand you up. I was—"

"I don't care what you were doing. You didn't come back. You said you would come back."

"I did. And you were gone when I got there."

"Did you expect me to wait all night? Or perhaps you'd like for me to wait even longer? Years, maybe, while you flounce around America?"

"That's not your business."

"It is now."

"What? You think I've promised you something? Just because we've *kissed*?"

"Do you treat kisses so lightly? Because I don't."

"It was just a kiss."

"It was a hell of a lot more than that, Emilie. And you know it." He seems to grow larger with every word, filling the bathroom until he's towering over her.

Emilie doesn't remember there being such a difference in their heights, but she feels very small right now. Somewhat ashamed. Afraid. She straightens her spine and meets his wounded gaze. "You read too much into it."

"You asked me to stay."

She winces a little at this. And then a new rage washes over her. "Well, you should have. I would have made it worth your while. That's what you want, right? My dress on the floor?"

Max places the tip of his right index finger in the middle of her breastbone. It feels like a poker, red-hot and searing. Her entire body feels anchored to that one spot. "I. Want. You."

"Then take me!"

"So you'd give me your body?" Max pulls away, slowly, in control of himself again. "And all the while you'd keep your heart locked away? I don't want one without the other."

"Oh, I think you do." Emilie takes a step forward. It's cruel, she knows, but she doesn't care. She's only inches away from him now. He inhales sharply as she rubs the tip of her nose along his jaw.

Max grabs her shoulders, and she can feel his arms tremble with restraint. He growls her name. And she is certain that he will kiss her. His head is tilting to the side to do just that. But he stops when Emilie begins to soften beneath him.

"No." A ragged breath. "We're not done talking."

"This conversation isn't urgent."

"Yes it is!" He shakes her a bit and lets go in alarm. Takes a deep breath. Steps back. "Don't you understand? *This* is urgent. Are you leaving?"

"Hush. Someone will hear you."

"I don't care."

"Well, I do, damn it," she whispers. "In case you haven't noticed, those papers aren't exactly public."

When he speaks the volume is gone but the rage is still there, bubbling below the surface. "Do you know what Captain Lehmann will do to you if he finds out? Commander Pruss? Have you even stopped to think about that?"

"Of course I have! Why do you think I hid them? I'm not stupid."

"They didn't look very hidden to me."

"I don't keep them in the closet, Max. I have a place. A compartment. I was looking at them last night when you came to my room. I wasn't expecting you."

"How long have you been planning this?"

"A while."

"So what was I? A distraction? Some toy that you played with to kill time?"

"Hey!" She shoves him again and tries to pull away, but there's no room in this tiny shower, and he's right there in front of her, no matter where she moves. "That's not fair and you know it. I didn't meet you until last year. I didn't *expect* you. You're just . . ." She waves her hands in front of her face as though trying to bat him away.

A glimmer of understanding crosses his face. "You were making up your mind last night, weren't you, when I knocked at the door?"

"I had already made my decision. But it was the wrong one."

Max looks as though he wants to touch her. To hold her. As though he wants to collect her in his arms and swallow her whole so that she can't run from him anymore. "How do you know?"

This crack in Emilie's defenses is a temporary thing. She pulls herself together right in front of him. Squares her shoulders. Sets her jaw. She controls every emotion with the same detached resolve that has enabled her to survive for the last decade. Her voice is cold when she finally speaks. "Because you weren't there when I got back."

"I'm here now," he says.

"Too late."

"Because I discovered your secret?"

"Are you going to tell?"

"Are you going to leave?"

"Yes."

"Why leave everything you've ever known? It makes no sense."

"My God, are you *blind*? *Deaf*? Do you not read the papers or listen to the radio? War is coming, Max."

"You don't know that."

"Hitler is trying to take Austria. Take it! Like a toy from another child. You think there won't be war?"

"I think a lot can happen between now and then."

"Then let me tell you what's happening *now*. In case that future threat is not enough." Emilie grows incensed but has no way to contain her trembling rage. "The Gestapo is more powerful than our court system. They are throwing people in prison just for criticizing Hitler."

Max flinches at this. He reaches out a finger and sets it on her lips to quiet her. They are on Hitler's prize airship after all.

Emilie continues in a whisper. "And the Jews? Where do I even begin with that?" She raises her hands and begins ticking offenses off with her fingers. "They are prohibited from all public and private employment. So they can't work. At all. They are not allowed in public buildings. Many families cannot even buy milk or medicine for their children. There are rumors that . . ." She cannot even speak it aloud, it is too insane. "This is the country we are returning to. And you want me to stay there and be consumed? There is nothing left for me in Germany." The diatribe leaves her breathless. Exhausted. To speak of her own people as *they*, as something *other*, to hide the fact that she is one of them leaves her ashamed, and she cannot meet Max's gaze.

He lifts her chin with one finger. "You have me."

"And you're a navigator. An officer aboard the *Hindenburg*. You will be gone the moment that first shot is fired, called away to fight another man's war, and I will be left again. Do you know what it's like to hear that knock on the door? To have a stranger tell you that you are a widow? Is that what you want for me? Because I don't. I am so tired of having things ripped from my hands. If you care anything for me at all, let me go. Please."

"So you'll do the leaving this time? The ripping? Without any concern for the state in which you're leaving *me*?"

"You're a man. It's different."

"And you're a fool if you believe that. I just hope you change your mind before we get off this damned ship on Thursday."

"I won't change my mind, Max. I can't." She lifts her palm and sets it gently against the smooth skin of his cheek.

"Do you have so little faith in me?"

"I have faith in nothing." She has never spoken the words aloud, but the admission leaves her gutted. For ten very long years this has been the truth. It is a jarring confession for a woman whose very identity is rooted in ancient faith.

"Give me the chance to restore it."

She shakes her head. No.

And then there is an urgent rapping of knuckles on the other side of the door. "Herr Zabel." The voice is young and male, and Emilie recognizes it as the cabin boy's.

Max does not answer. He reaches for Emilie's hand instead.

The cabin boy speaks again, his voice barely above a whisper, "There is an urgent message for you."

THE CABIN BOY

Werner sets the tray down beside the hatch that leads to the control car and yells, "Coffee!"

Usually before returning to the kitchen he waits beside the opening until one of the officers climbs the ladder to collect the tray. But this morning when Christian Nielsen pops his head out of the hatch he motions Werner forward. "Commander Pruss wants to see you," he says. There's less than an hour until Max replaces Nielsen at the navigation table, and he looks like a man eager to see his bed. Pallid skin. Tired eyes. And his breath isn't much to speak of either.

Werner blinks, startled. The commander has never summoned him before. Though it isn't uncommon for him to be called to help with the passengers occasionally, he is on this ship to serve the needs of the officers and crew. Werner joins Xaver Maier in the kitchen at 6:00 a.m. to clean any dishes used by the crew on the late shift. Plates and bowls and mugs are always strewn around the kitchen and mess areas, covered in bits of dried food. Xaver leaves out a variety of meats and cheeses and breads for them, and he is enraged every morning when he finds that none of the crew has gone to the trouble of rinsing their dishes in the sink. For his part, Werner doesn't know why the chef throws such a fit. He's not the one who has to wash them. It's part of the cabin boy's job, and he always does it without complaint. Once the kitchen is clean and prepped for breakfast, Werner takes coffee to the control car. A large silver carafe and six mugs. No cream. No sugar. No spoons. Werner has noticed that all of them sweeten their coffee when they have it in the officers' mess but they drink it black while on duty. For a long time he thought it had to do with wanting to stay alert. But he has known the men long enough now to realize they are simply competing with one another. It's stupid, he thinks, and when he's a man he'll drink his coffee however he wants and won't care if anyone thinks less of him for adding cream and sugar.

After an uncertain pause, Werner hands the tray to Nielsen and shimmies down the ladder after him. The control car is cold, at least a good ten to fifteen degrees colder than the rest of the airship, and all of these warm bodies in the chilly room have created a layer of condensation on the windows. They're foggy. Not that it would matter. Everything outside of them is gray mist anyway. He follows Nielsen through the utility area, into the navigation room, then to the bridge. Pruss stands at the rudder wheel, staring into the gloom.

"You need me, Commander?"

Pruss nods a greeting, then hands Werner a piece of paper folded in half. One word is scrawled on the outside in black ink, a surname. "I need you to deliver this right away," he says. He turns back to the rudder wheel without another word, but Werner can see his profile and he is struck, as he always is in the presence of the commander, that Pruss has the perpetual frown of a man lost in thought. The twin lines of concentration etched in his forehead are coupled with a determined mouth and a long, straight nose. This combination of features makes him appear formidable to Werner, almost unapproachable.

Werner waits until he has climbed the ladder and left the radio room to look at the name written on the paper. He doesn't want the other men to see him struggling to sound it out. He doesn't want them to know how difficult it is for him to read the simplest things.

To him, reading is a lesson in frustration. A reason to throw books and stomp his feet. Even though he has learned to control those childish urges, he still approaches the written word with dismay. Sometimes a page will blur around the edges, but most often the words will double when he tries to focus. He sees two Rs where there should be only one. But he is making progress, or at least that's what his mother says. She is the one who sits with him in the evenings and patiently, consistently teaches him to see the words through the pile of letters and symbols. Had she left it to the school he would never have learned to read at all. But there are things that even his mother cannot fix. She can't stop the letters from dancing or flipping over; a *d* becomes a *b* in the time it takes him to blink. Werner doesn't know whether that's the letter on the page or whether his mind has swapped it for something similar. He doesn't know whether he's reading about a ditch or a bitch.

Werner lifts the note and looks at the name. Breathes a sigh of relief. He knows this letter. Z. And because Werner has grown very used to guessing words instead of reading them, he assumes that the note in his hands is meant for Max Zabel.

Max is not in the officers' mess. Werner searches all of the passenger areas, the kitchen, and the corridors. He is starting to panic, to wonder what he will tell Commander Pruss if the navigator cannot be found, when he hears raised voices coming from the shower near the portside stairs. The boy has been taught not to eavesdrop, but he does so anyway, pushing aside the twinge of guilt that comes from knowing his mother would be disappointed. It takes only a few seconds to recognize Max's voice within. But he is clearly upset, and he's with a woman. Werner is scared to interrupt whatever is happening on the other side of the door.

Finally he reaches out and knocks. His fist sounds like a rabbit anxiously thumping its foot. "Herr Zabel," he says, his voice little more than a squeak.

There is no immediate answer from within.

He knocks again, louder this time. "There is an urgent message for you."

In the long seconds that follow Werner unclenches his hand and smoothes out the note. He looks at the name again, and this time Werner sounds it out carefully. His heart becomes a trip hammer. He had assumed that Pruss intended the note for Max. But he was wrong. It is meant for someone else.

Werner would usually never read a private communication from the commander, but he is terrified now. The message is two sentences long. Simple words. A direct command. And Werner makes his decision as the door swings outward. He will give the message to Max anyway.

THE NAVIGATOR

Max holds on to Emilie with one hand and fumbles the bathroom door open with the other. He pushes it out with such force that Werner Franz jumps back to avoid being hit. "What?"

"A message," he stutters. Werner blushes at the sight of their clasped hands and tries again. "I have a message for you. From the control car. It's important."

Before stepping into the corridor, Max turns back to Emilie. "This conversation isn't over."

She narrows her eyes, then shuts the door in his face to signify otherwise. Max takes a moment to smooth the scowl from his forehead and to straighten his cap and jacket. One measured breath helps him gain composure. Then he turns a gimlet eye on the cabin boy.

Werner Franz is only fourteen, a quiet boy known to work hard and rarely complain. Max feels guilty for being so gruff. But he isn't certain whether he will get another chance to talk sense into Emilie. She is water through his hands. Ungraspable. Elusive. And if he must frighten Werner to settle things with her, so be it.

The cabin boy hands him a square of paper, folded in half. Max reads the dispatch impassively. "How did you find me?"

"It wasn't hard. I'm surprised you didn't wake half the ship with all that shouting."

Some boys charge into adolescence as though it is something to be conquered with brute force. Others wake one day to find themselves unwilling participants, held hostage by their own bodies. Werner Franz is very much the latter. He often has the look of a boy who is surprised to find that his legs have grown longer overnight or that his voice has dropped an octave since breakfast. He is tall now and he'll be even taller as an adult, but he has not yet learned to manage this new length of bone with ease. He lopes instead of walks. He frequently runs into corners and knocks things over. He's at the stage in adolescence where feet and nose have outgrown the rest of his body. But once this clumsy phase has passed he will make a strong man. Werner has a pleasant face. High cheekbones and a strong nose with a slight arch that suggests Roman descent. His hair is cropped close to his skull at the sides but it hangs longer on top, flopping into his face. Werner smiles with his eyes and laughs with his entire body. It is hard not to like the kid, though Max isn't inclined to feel kindly toward him at this particular moment.

The lack of movement on Max's part clearly makes Werner nervous. "Commander Pruss sent me himself." He shifts back and forth, his eyes on a button in the middle of Max's shirt. "He wants you to go check the engine telegraph dial in gondola two. They aren't getting any response in the control car."

"*Scheiße!*" The dial in question transmits vital communications from the bridge to the engine gondolas, determining engine speed and power. "You'd best be getting back, then." Max heads for the security door without another word.

"Wait! I want to come with you."

"I'll be exiting the ship."

"I know."

"You don't have the clearance to leave ship while we're in transit."

"No. I don't. But I thought we might make some sort of arrangement."

Max growls a warning. He makes it six steps down the corridor before Werner calls out. "The stewardess!"

Max stops but doesn't turn. "What about her?"

"Crew members aren't allowed to fraternize."

"Do you even know what that word means?"

"No. But you were in the shower with Fräulein Imhof. And I'm pretty sure that's against the rules too. So take me out with you or I'll tell Commander Pruss what I saw."

"You're *blackmailing* me?"

"I am displaying ambition." Werner grins, impish and charming.

Max pauses long enough to hide his amusement and then says, "Come along, you *kleiner Scheißer.*"

Werner runs after Max, delighted. He steps through the security door with the look of a boy who has finally been allowed into his father's smoking club after years of begging. Max can see the boy's narrow rib cage expand with pride. Werner tries to hide his rapturous smile as he scans the cavernous belly of the airship, but the corners of his mouth quiver and Max turns away slightly so as not to embarrass him. He remembers what this feels like. It has not been so long for him either. Werner's unveiled sense of wonder has blunted his anger.

"It's okay if you stare for a bit," Max says. "I won't tell."

"They usually don't let me back here." Werner's head moves in small increments, slowly taking in the sight before him. "They treat me like a kid."

He is a kid. Max doesn't say this, however. Instead he pulls two pairs of felt boots with rubber soles from a set of hooks on the wall. He hands one pair to Werner. "Don't want to be treated like a kid? Respect is earned, not given. You can start by not blackmailing people. It's not typically considered an honorable trait."

"That's a one-time thing. Promise. I might not get another chance to go outside the ship." Werner takes the shoes and eyes them warily. "What are these for?"

Max pulls off one steel-toed boot, then the other. He sets them down gently beside the door. "These shoes were made to navigate the interior of this ship. There are no metal parts. They don't create static. So they won't make sparks."

Werner's dark eyes grow a little wider. "It's that dangerous?"

"I pity the idiot who is found back here without them."

Werner may be young and naive, but he is no coward. He slides the shoes over his long feet, lifts his chin, and marches after Max.

"Engine two is this way." Max nods down the keel catwalk.

The walkway runs the length of the ship, from nose to tail, and sits at the very bottom of the structure. Above them yawns an elaborate skeleton of carefully constructed girders and bracing forms. There are no guardrails on the narrow catwalk—only a rope on either side that would do little to break their fall. They go slowly, placing one foot carefully in front of the other. Should they lose their balance it would be a nasty fall to the fabric shell below. Werner seems cognizant of this and he doesn't try anything risky. No running or testing his balance. It occurs to Max that in order for Werner even to be working aboard the airship at such a young age he is quite a bit more mature than his peers.

Werner's thoughts must have been traveling the same course, for he speaks as he follows closely behind Max. "How do I earn their respect?"

"Work hard. Be honest. Stay out of trouble."

"Is that how you did it?"

Max nods his head, then asks, "How old are you?"

"Fourteen."

"I was seventeen when I went to work for the Hamburg American Line. I started out as an able seaman, which is a piss-poor job if you want to know the truth. And dirty too. Awful pay. But everyone starts somewhere. Usually at the bottom." He looks over his shoulder and gives Werner a wry smile. "Rather like a cabin boy."

"But you're a navigator now."

"I worked my way up. It took seven years, but by the time I was twenty-four I was second officer on the *Vogtland*. Three years in that position and then the Zeppelin Company came calling. I worked as a navigator on the *Graf Zeppelin* first. Then the *Hindenburg* was commissioned and here we are."

They walk silently for a few meters before Werner shares his thoughts. "Seems like such a long time."

Max stops in mid-step and turns to face his young charge. "Do you have anywhere else to be?"

The cabin boy shakes his head. "No."

"Then buck up and do your job. Besides, you have a three-year head start on me. You'll probably be a commander by the time you're my age."

This cheers Werner immensely and they continue the trek.

"So you've quit school, then?" Max asks.

"I'm not very good at sums."

"I don't believe you."

"I—"

"They don't let *dumm* boys work on ships like this. Complain all you want about them treating you like a child, but you did something right just to get here. And I'd wager it didn't happen by failing algebra."

There is a note of defiance and the slightest hint of anger when Werner replies. "*Mutter* said it was time for me to become a man."

"Ah. So how long has he been dead, then, your father?"

The voice that answers is feral. "He's not *dead*."

"Gone?"

"He's sick! Okay? Sick! We've all gone to work. *Mutter*. My brother. Me."

Max stops but doesn't turn this time. Neither does he apologize. He gives Werner all the privacy he needs to compose his face and check the tears that are threatening to take his voice hostage. "Well, there you have it. You've already earned some respect, my young friend. From me."

There is a long pause as Werner pulls himself together. Then he asks, "How much farther?"

"There. On the left." Max points to an access walkway that leads to a hatch in the side of the airship. A small rectangle is barely discernible against the exterior skin. "I hope you're not afraid of heights."

THE AMERICAN

He squats in front of the cage, face twisted into a scowl. The dog has been left to sit in its own mess. Less than twelve hours since he was here with Joseph Späh, and the mutt has still not been fed or walked. It is pressed into one corner, tail wrapped around its hind legs to avoid lying in the puddle of concentrated urine. Ulla is stretched out in her crate opposite, curious but content, her large dark eyes alert and her chin resting on her paws. The other dog, however, is quivering with pent-up energy. It's some odd mix of greyhound and Labrador and doesn't seem to know what to do with its body in such a small space.

The American sets his palm against the latch and the mutt rushes forward to sniff him. It is overeager. Spastic. Desperate for affection and exercise. Its small black nose is dry and rough against his palm. The dog is hungry and dirty and confused. The sight makes the American angry, and a small bead of heat gathers at the center of his chest.

"What's your name, mongrel?" he asks aloud.

If it was capable of answering, he is certain it would. The dog leans into his hand with such enthusiasm he's afraid it might bend the latch. There is no collar and no paperwork attached to the crate by which to identify it, and a cursory glance at its underbelly reveals no immediately distinguishing signs of gender. Only wet, matted clumps of hair. Given the mess, he isn't inclined to investigate further.

"Shit," he says, "now I have to kill two people on this damned ship."

The American unlatches the crate, then steps aside quickly as the dog bolts out. It rushes around his legs in frantic circles, tail lashing and tongue hanging out. "Thirsty? You poor bastard. I have nothing for you."

He hasn't come for the dog. And it's a distraction now that he's here. But he can't very well ignore it. For one thing the crate is positioned right in front of the steamer trunk he has come to search. For another, he isn't inclined to admit that the dog evokes his pity. That emotion is a weakness. One he cannot afford.

"Sit," he says, and it does.

"Stay." Again, it obeys, its tail whipping the floor with a single-minded desperation to please.

He slides the crate out of the way and stands, hands on his hips, as he inspects the stacked pile of steamer trunks. He can see his own, halfway down the right-hand stack, toward the bottom. It's rather battered and old and certainly not the nicest of the lot. Then again, he doesn't usually travel via luxury liners of any sort. He is far more at home in wet trenches, dark bars, and back alleys.

He doesn't have much time. And the trunk he wants is a row back, halfway down the pile. He can see the iconic logo embossed on its leather exterior. It's a bit scuffed now, after so much travel, but that only increases the charm. A woman who can afford such a trunk can also afford to travel. The trunk is holding together nicely, as is its owner. Expensive things always do. Margaret Mather is not the sort of woman who would settle for anything less than Louis Vuitton. To her credit, however, she has not indulged in excess. She has brought only the one trunk. Women in her position often bring ten.

The American shifts the contents of the pile around until he's able to slide out the designer trunk and wrestle it to the floor in front of him. There isn't much space to work in the small cargo area, so he has to open the lid and pull out the compartments carefully. He feels certain Margaret Mather would approve of his delicate handling of her belongings if not the indecency of his digging through them. He finds what he's looking for in the third drawer down. It's cliché, really, the amount of jewels, but she is an heiress after all. Although, from the time he spent with her the evening before it seems as though she really doesn't suit them. She's too humble for this lifestyle.

Three items catch his eye. He goes for the smaller, less obtrusive pieces, the things that won't be immediately missed. A diamond solitaire ring. A delicate gold choker with a ruby pendant. A pair of simple pearl earrings. Anything gaudier than this and he won't be able to trade them for the information he needs. If she misses them at all, it will take some time to detect their absence. He deposits the jewelry in his pocket, then restacks the freight exactly as it was before.

The cargo room is small, square, and unheated. Apart from the dog crates and the steamer trunks, there are some heavy cardboard shipping boxes and a large, wrapped piece of furniture but nothing else. In one corner of the room is a pile of packing blankets, and in the other a stack of old newspapers. They'll have to do. He cleans up the mess inside the crate as best he can using a handful of wadded papers, then lines the bottom of the crate with a few others. The American curses himself for the display of sympathy even as the dog throws itself at his feet in gratitude. He scratches between its ears and under its chin.

"Stupid mutt," he says as the dog submits itself completely and lies on its back, belly exposed, adoration pooling in its dark eyes. The American can't remember the last time anyone or anything trusted him so quickly or so completely. "Well, no wonder. You're a boy."

He has always maintained that female dogs are smarter. He wouldn't pick a male dog from a litter to save his life. They destroy everything. They piss on themselves and on everything around them. And they escape at the first sign of a bitch in heat. Not so different from many of the soldiers he has known, now that he thinks about it. But still, given the choice, he would pick a female every time.

"What are we going to do with you? Tragic little fucker. And unlucky too. No name. Shit owner."

He scoots the reluctant dog back into the crate with his foot, then wipes his fingers on his trousers. He doesn't want to smell like a kennel for the rest of the day. He has already showered and changed his clothes and has no interest in repeating the process. The airship has only one shower, and it doesn't offer much in the way of water pressure or warmth. It does feel good to be clean though, despite the fact that his hair is still damp and his scalp is starting to get cold in the unheated room.

When he locks the crate the dog looks at him as though it's being abandoned.

"You're not my problem," he says. But the American knows better. He points an accusatory finger at the dog. "Damn it. Pathetic lazy owner. I don't have time for this."

The dog presses its nose between the wicker slats and whines in response.

"Well, I can't look after a nameless mutt. What should I call you?" He mentally scrolls through every dog name he has ever heard, but they feel trite under the circumstances. So he studies the lean body. The narrow snout. The dappled gray coat. The huge floppy ears. Its keen, intelligent eyes. The way its muscles quiver with anticipation and the longing for freedom. "I bet you're fast," he mutters.

And then he has it.

"Owens," he says. "Can't do much better than that. Let's just hope you give these fucking Nazis as much trouble as your namesake. Yes? Good."

The dog appraises him solemnly.

"I'll make sure you get something to eat soon."

The American closes the door to the cargo hold and tries to ignore the plaintive whimpering within. He turns away with a whispered oath and begins the trek back to the passenger area. It's a straight shot, though dimly lit, and he can see the security door at the distant end of the keel catwalk, the light above it shining like a beacon. The next shift change won't happen for another thirty minutes, so there's a good chance he can get back to the passenger quarters without running into any of the midshipmen. But when he reaches the bank of crew quarters near the stern, he sees two figures maneuvering down the catwalk toward him. Dark shapes moving with purpose. One is clearly an officer—he can tell by the cap and the jacket and the confident stride—and the other is significantly shorter. Leaner. Gangly. A child maybe? No. That wouldn't be logical. He filters all the possible options until his mind settles on the cabin boy. Yes. What is his name? Werner something. Franz. Werner Franz. Fourteen years old. A toothy boy with the look of perpetual curiosity about him.

The American has two options. Continue forward and face the difficult task of explaining why he has been wandering around prohibited areas of the ship, or duck into one of the crew quarters and run the risk that it is occupied. He has stopped and is reaching his hand slowly toward the door of a cabin when the officer and cabin boy turn onto an access walkway and disappear behind a series of duralumin girders. He makes a quick decision and creeps forward along the catwalk. Closer now, he can see them approach a small exit hatch in the side of the ship. He recognizes the navigator, locates the name in his encyclopedic mind. Max Zabel.

Surely not.

Zabel pushes the lever upward, then pulls the door in. The air immediately shifts and grows colder. The American can hear the whistle of air and the roar of an engine. Slowly, steadily he creeps closer until he can almost hear their conversation, until he can see the look of poorly disguised terror on the cabin boy's face. Then Zabel steps outside the airship, followed hesitantly a few moments later by Werner. The American glimpses a minuscule patch of cloud when he finally comes level to the access walkway. He's fairly certain where the two have gone, though he can't imagine what would have necessitated a trip to an outboard engine.

His curiosity is too strong to let this chance pass. The American treads quickly down the walkway, then sticks his head out the open hatch. The engine gondola lies ten feet below. The access hatch into the gondola is shut. Zabel and Werner are somewhere within, doing God knows what inside the gondola. The American backs away from the hatch; even he is not bold enough to explore outside the ship.

No one sees him as he slips back through the security door and into the passenger area. He makes a quick pass through the lounge to make sure the chief steward is tending passengers and is not in his stateroom. Sometimes fate cooperates in his machinations, and being placed in a cabin next to Heinrich Kubis is fortunate indeed. Not that he has to act drunk and confused when he picks the lock and sneaks into the room—there's no one around to see him—but that is something he can fall back on should he be discovered.

The steward's cabin is identical to his with one exception: a small antechamber used to store shoes and polish. Beyond that there is a meticulously made bed and the usual accouterments of someone in the service profession: first-aid box, sewing kit, miscellaneous grooming paraphernalia. The American cares nothing about these things. He has come for the shipping manifest, and he finds it on the top shelf of Heinrich Kubis's closet. The information he wants is hidden deep within the book, and his body is strained tight as he searches for it. If Kubis returns he will have to hide beneath the bed. And if he is discovered there? Well. That's a choice he'd rather not make this early in the flight.

The dog's name is not shown on the manifest, only its owner's: Edward Douglas. He reads it several times and curses so vehemently he has to wipe spittle from the page. The name is written in black ink, along with everything else, and it takes a bit of creative penmanship for the American to alter this record.

THE NAVIGATOR

It is freezing outside the airship. Not quite dawn. And the elevation, combined with the speed at which the *Hindenburg* travels, has turned the scattered clouds into little specks of ice that pelt against his cheeks. Max braces himself against the brisk rush of

Atlantic air. It smells of ocean and frost and the oily hint of engine exhaust. The slipstream moves visibly along the structure like silver ribbons in the pre-dawn light. The sky is a perfect soft pewter gray, and the water beneath them matches as though one is reflecting the other—bands of stratus above, calm sea underneath. The ship glides elegantly between the two, its shadow a charcoal smudge on the gentle waves below.

The barrage of sound coming from the engines is enough to split Max's head wide open. His senses are at war with one another, sight and sound registering two different things: beauty and turbulence. To his left is the propeller, twenty feet long and spinning like a flywheel. One slip, one wrong move, and death will come in the most gruesome way.

Perhaps Werner will think twice before dabbling in blackmail again. His face is strained with the effort not to look juvenile or afraid. And yet he pulls away from the hatch.

"Too late for that now," Max yells into the wind. "This was your idea. So come along. But mind your step. I'm the one who will have to write your mother if you go tumbling off. We're six hundred feet up. So the fall will kill you. But we can't turn back for your body. Understand?"

Werner nods feebly, and his skin turns a sickly shade of puce.

Max wants to laugh but doesn't. No one has ever fallen from this airship. Or any other that he's aware of. The zeppelins rarely travel fast enough to blow anyone off the ladders. Eighty miles an hour at most. But a bit of fear would do the boy good. He backs out of the hatch and takes one step onto the ladder that leads down into the engine car. "Crook your elbows around the windward edge like this. See?" He nods at his arm, the way it's bent around the handrail. "It will keep you steady against the wind. Go slow. Watch your feet. And you'll be fine."

Again Werner nods, skeptical.

"Chin up, kid. It's loud as *Hölle* down there."

Max descends the ladder without further instructions and stomps twice on the hatch door below to announce their arrival. It slides to the side and he drops into the engine room. He already has a certain fondness for the kid, but when Max sees Werner's slender body turn and back out of the opening, he feels a pride that he can only describe as fatherly. Werner is afraid. And hesitant. That much is certain. But he has not said or done anything to give Max cause to regret bringing him along. The boy obeys without question. And he summons the courage when it counts.

"What's he doing here?" August Deutschle is one of three mechanics assigned to this engine and, thankfully, the friendliest of the lot. The look he gives Werner leans more toward curiosity than irritation.

"The little bastard blackmailed me."

"I like him already." August grins, quick and wide. "And I'd pay good money to know what he has on you."

"The day you have money for anything other than booze and gambling will be a miracle."

"I find it when I need it." Already the wicked glint is growing in his eyes. "Ten marks says I can get the boy to tell me."

The last thing he needs is Werner developing a taste for gambling or extortion. Besides, the truth is harmless enough. "Let's just say he caught me conversing off duty with a certain female crew member."

The mechanic slaps Max on the shoulder hard enough to rattle his teeth. "About damn time!"

He's about to explain that it wasn't *that* sort of conversation when Werner shimmies down the ladder and onto the gondola with only a minor amount of terror. He's sure-footed and well balanced. Once Werner's rubber-soled boots land on the outer hatch ledge August gives an approving nod. "He'll do."

Max moves aside to let Werner drop down beside him. He rewards the boy with a proud smile and a pat on the back, then returns his attention to August. "What's this with the engine telegraph dial?"

"So they finally figured it out? Good. I was afraid one of us would have to go in."

"I got here as quickly as I could."

"But why you? I thought they would send Ludwig Knorr or maybe German Zettel. He's handy in a pinch." August looks at his watch. "And on duty right now."

It's a good question, and one he should have stopped to consider sooner. Max pulls the message from his pocket. Unfolds it. Rereads the hastily scribbled surname. *Zettel*. The chief mechanic. He turns slowly to Werner and gives him a withering glare.

"*Why?*"

There's no point explaining the question. The boy clearly knows what Max is asking. "It was a mistake," Werner says. His eyes have grown wide, his back rounded into a defensive posture as though he might bolt. Yet there's nowhere to go but up, and he needs Max's help for that.

"I don't believe you."

"I'm telling the truth. Honest! I thought it said Zabel. At first. And then, while I was waiting for you outside the err . . . you know, while I was waiting for you and uh, *her* to be . . . done, I reread the note and saw my mistake. But I'd already interrupted you. And you were mad enough. So I gave it to you anyway."

"And?" He knows there is more. With Werner there is always more. Layer upon layer of motive.

"And German Zettel doesn't like me. There's no way he would have brought me along."

"I truly hope this"—he waves his arm around the thunderous engine gondola—"was worth it."

August laughs. "Clever little bastard, indeed. I'll keep him around. Unless you decide to kill him. In which case I'll help you throw the body overboard. He's probably heavier than he looks."

It has been a long time since Max navigated the turbulent waters of adolescence, but he remembers his own wild mood swings and those of his parents as they tried, without much success, to keep him out of trouble. So he's not entirely surprised that the pride he felt at Werner's courage a few moments ago has taken a drastic left turn and has been transformed into anger at the boy's idiocy. He says nothing but turns to the control panel and taps on a glass-covered dial. It sits toward the bottom, grouped with other similar meters. But this needle spins frenetically, never settling on a number.

"Can you hear it?" August asks. "The engine. I can't adjust it with that thing broken."

Max can hear the engine. And he can also feel a slight shudder in the floor beneath him. This engine is working out of sync with the others. The mechanics have the noisiest job aboard the airship, and Max has never quite known how they don't lose their hearing within a week. The cacophonous roar of the diesel engines drowns out everything but the loudest yell. It's an alarming sound and Werner has backed himself up against the wall, hands over his ears and face scrunched in concentration. Max suspects that this is a defensive position and that the boy is waiting for Max to cuff his ear. The thought is tempting.

All of the mechanics wear thick leather aviator caps and earplugs beneath the flaps, but he knows that they rely mostly on lip reading and a sign language of sorts—adapted shorthand for the temporarily deaf. Each of them is limited to short double shifts, two hours during the day and three hours at night. The downtime is supposed to provide a respite from the noise, but since their quarters are located near the stern, they never really escape the deafening clamor of the Daimler-Benz motors. Max knows that the mechanics often wake when the engines are shut down for midair repairs. The silence is startling to them. It's an odd job, this, and few men are well suited for it. Given Werner's response to the danger and the noise thus far, Max would guess the boy is not one of them. Not that Max can blame Werner. He would sooner quit aviation altogether than spend one full day in this engine gondola, dangling over the Atlantic Ocean, slowly going deaf, and—depending on their destination—either half-frozen or melting right out of his uniform. Max Zabel aspires to consistency, calmness, and, above all else, self-control. He is a man who avoids extremes at all costs.

THE CABIN BOY

Werner watches Max lean closer to the dial. Max thumps it with an index finger, and the glass case wobbles at his touch. "Oh," he says. "That explains it."

The face of the dial is thick glass rimmed with metal. Max spreads his palm across the surface, fixing each finger at a point around the edge. He gently rotates it, and removes the dial face. The needle stops spinning altogether.

"The face came loose," he offers by way of explanation, holding it up. "The needle won't read accurately unless it's pressurized."

It would never have occurred to the cabin boy that he could simply pluck off the face of the dial, but Max has done it without the slightest hesitation. Max rubs the cuff of his sleeve against the glass to wipe away his fingerprints and then carefully holds it by the metal rim and pops the face back onto the dial. The needle wobbles uncertainly for a moment and then begins a lazy rotation around the numbers until it quivers to a stop, the arrows at each end pointing directly at nine and three.

August Deutschle jumps into action, adjusting the engine speed to correspond with the dial reading. Within seconds the revving evens out around them. Less of a shudder and more of a hum. Werner drops his hands to his side and lets out a breath he didn't know he was holding.

"You," Max pokes Werner in the breastbone, hard, with one finger, "are damn lucky I actually knew what to do."

The reprimand hurts the boy's pride more than he would like to admit. Werner rubs the spot with his thumb, trying not to pout. It has been his experience that a pout can often lead to tears.

"That's it?" August asks.

"Trust me. Much better a loose bit of glass than a blown engine. Yes?" Max glances at his watch. "I'd best get young Herr Franz back to his duties before someone figures out that he's taken a stroll in midair."

Max hoists Werner upward so he can grab the first rung of the ladder, and then follows close behind. Max doesn't crowd him, but Werner has the impression that the navigator is staying close enough to catch him should he stumble. He keeps his eyes forward and his feet steady and is halfway to the hatch above in no time.

"You have good balance," Max says.

"It's not so different than climbing a fire escape. Except for the wind."

Werner feels Max's hand clamp onto his ankle like a vise. "Wait. Look," he says.

Below them is the long, sleek form of an ocean liner. Werner can make out clean white letters that read *Europa* just above the water line. The smokestacks puff like dragon lungs as the ship cuts a clean wake through the water. It looks like a horned, painted sea serpent.

"That's one of the nicer ones," Max says.

"Is it expensive to travel by boat?" Werner has never even paid cab fare. He cannot fathom what sort of riches it would take to buy passage on an ocean liner.

"It's not cheap. But not nearly as expensive as this—or as fun, if you want to know the truth. You could buy a car for the price of a ticket on the *Hindenburg*."

They've not quite come parallel with the ocean liner when the *Europa* sends out a friendly bellow of her horn, and they look down to see a handful of people on deck waving madly in greeting. Tiny faceless mites. From this height they look no bigger than grains of rice. Werner wonders what it's like for them to look up and see this colossus overhead. How strange it must be. Beasts of this size should be in the ocean, not over it.

They wait to finish climbing the ladder until the *Europa* has slipped a good distance behind, her massive bulk dutifully chugging along. The hatch door slides shut once they've made it safely back inside the main structure, and Max secures the interior fasteners and double-checks to make sure it is locked securely.

"Satisfied?"

Werner is flushed and windblown. He is so excited that his words turn into an unbroken stream of syllables. "That was incredible!"

Werner flashes a grateful smile and marches back toward the security door. He is just as enraptured by the inner workings of the *Hindenburg* on the return trip, peppering Max with questions about this support beam or that aluminum shaft. Max can answer most of the questions easily, but there are a few that stump him. What coating covers the hydrogen cells to prevent the gas from leaking out? Who designed the diesel fuel tanks? The navigator grows impatient—Werner can tell by the clipped tone of his voice—but he humors him anyway, answering as best he can.

After another five questions Max laughs. "Go ahead. Tell me again that you're no good at sums."

Werner is ahead of Max now, and he lifts the sharp points of his shoulder blades in a shrug. He doesn't look back. "I was top of my class."

"That's what I thought."

It is the truth. Technically. But the credit lies more with Werner's mother than with him. She is the one who helped him study for every test; the one who patiently taught him to pick through words until he found their meaning. No longer being in school is irrelevant to Werner. But no longer being under his mother's tutelage is starting to take its toll.

Their shoes hang by the security door where they left them, and it takes only a moment to make the exchange. Werner stands straighter when back inside the passenger area. He's about to say something to Max—to thank him—when they round a corner and nearly collide with Irene Doehner and her two little brothers. She is herding them toward the dining room but looks as though she'd rather still be in bed.

Max catches him staring. The girl *is* pretty after all. Her hair is neither blond nor brown but one of those soft shades in between.

Lips bright and soft like one of his mother's potted roses. Blue eyes. They mumble apologies but do not make eye contact. It takes only a moment for her to glide around them in the corridor, and then she moves along after her brothers.

Max nudges him with an elbow. "Five marks says you already know that girl's name."

"Irene." It's a noble attempt at nonchalance, but his cheeks are hot.

"Save yourself the trouble, kid." Max straightens the collar of Werner's white jacket. He assesses his appearance head to toe to make sure he's not sporting grease stains or tears in his clothing. His voice betrays no hint of sadness, but he wears a melancholy expression that Werner has never seen before. "She'll only break your heart."

He opens his mouth to defend himself, but Max interrupts. "You know what? Don't tell me. I have my own troubles."

"There you are. I've been looking for you."

Werner turns to find the American waiting patiently a few steps away, sober, showered, and dressed in a clean, pressed suit. It takes Werner a moment to realize that he isn't speaking to Max.

"Might I have a word with you?" the American says.

Werner looks at Max for approval.

"Go on. You don't need my permission." Then he glances at the passenger and tips his hat. "*Guten Morgen*."

The American gives a disinterested nod, barely shifting his gaze to Max in greeting. Werner can't help but feel that it's not an altogether friendly gaze.

THE AMERICAN

The American leads Werner into the dining room before he speaks. But it becomes immediately apparent that the young Doehner girl is a distraction. The cabin boy is watching her situate her brothers at the table nearest the observation windows. And she must know it because her chin is lifted at a coy angle and there is an exaggerated awareness in her movements. Women do learn early.

The American clears his throat. "What do you know about dogs?"

Werner tries to mask his confusion. "They stink."

"Sometimes. But more to the point, do you like them?"

"Well enough. My grandfather breeds Doberman pinschers."

"Are you afraid of them?"

"They can be nasty dogs if treated poorly. Or trained to guard."

"Not pinschers. Dogs in general."

Werner hesitates a moment too long. "No. I don't suppose so."

"You're lying."

"It depends on the dog. I was bitten once. Right here." Werner rolls back the cuff of his jacket to reveal four pale scars on his forearm.

"You should be afraid of them. Dogs are animals after all."

"Why are you asking me this, Herr . . . ?"

The American doesn't offer his surname, merely peers at the boy and waits for him to ask the obvious questions.

After an awkward silence the cabin boy continues. "Why do you want to know if I like dogs? And if they scare me?"

"Because there is a dog on this aircraft that I would like you to care for. I'll pay you to do it. But if you're lazy or a coward or cruel I need to know up front. I'd rather not waste my time or money."

"I'm none of those things."

"I didn't think so." He likes the boy. Werner is frank and bright and has just the right amount of confidence to accomplish this task.

"You don't mean the acrobat's dog, do you? Because I doubt he'd like me interfering."

"No. Not that one. There's another dog in the cargo hold that seems to have been forgotten about. I want you to feed it and change the papers in its crate twice a day. I'll pay you ten American dollars to do the job. That way you'll have spending money once we land. Maybe you could buy something for your mother?" The American looks over Werner's shoulder at Irene as she pretends not to watch them. "Or maybe a trinket for Fräulein Doehner?"

Werner's eyes narrow in suspicion. "How do you know what's in the cargo hold? Passengers aren't allowed outside of the passenger areas."

Oh, he likes this kid very much. Werner cleanly ignored the bait and went straight for the jugular. "Neither are cabin boys, from what I hear."

Silence.

"But given the fact that I saw you in the belly of this ship not half an hour ago, I would say that you and I are both people for whom exceptions are made."

"I don't—"

The American holds up a hand to stop him. "No point in lying. I don't care what you were doing. You are clearly ambitious and clever, but those are tools that you should make the most of elsewhere. The only question you need to answer, Herr Franz, is whether or not you would like to make a bit of extra money."

The cabin boy clears his throat. "Of course," he says. "But not if I'll get in trouble for it. I can't afford to lose this job."

"You won't get in trouble. I can promise you that. Simply ensure that the dog is cared for. And if anyone asks what you're doing back there, you can tell them the owner paid you to care for it since he isn't allowed in the cargo hold."

"You own that dog?"

"No. But no one else needs to know that."

Werner considers this proposition for a moment. "What's its name?"

"Owens."

"Is that actually his name?"

"Hell if I know."

"What if it won't answer to Owens? Dogs are smart."

"Trust me. It will answer to anything."

"Why are you doing this? Why pay to care for an animal that isn't yours?"

Sometimes a bit of compassion and decency is reason enough to do something out of the ordinary. This isn't something he will say aloud, however. "That dog doesn't deserve to be abandoned, starved, and left to shit itself."

"I'll do it, then. But you will pay me up front."

The American pulls a ten-dollar bill from his wallet and hands it to Werner. "Agreed."

The boy scrutinizes this windfall for a moment as though to make sure it isn't counterfeit, as though he'd know the difference. Then he tucks it into the small breast pocket of his steward's coat. He gives the American the serious nod of one gentleman conducting business with another.

"Now I'd like to know what we're having for breakfast. I'm starving. And I'm also quite interested to learn everything you know about a certain passenger on board this airship."

"Which passenger?"

He rocks back on his heels, arms crossed, anticipation written into the lines around his mouth. "Leonhard Adelt."

THE NAVIGATOR

Max descends into the control car for his shift and feels the charged atmosphere immediately. He has missed something important. An argument most likely. There's palpable tension in the air. No one makes eye contact or speaks. The officers look like a pack of angry dogs, hackles raised, spines stiff. There's a feral look to Commander Pruss, an aggressive slant to his mouth.

Colonel Erdmann has observation duties this morning, and he has removed himself to the edge of the utility room. He watches, concern evident on his face.

Max sniffs out the situation carefully. "What's wrong?"

Christian Nielsen stands in the navigation room glowering at a set of charts spread on the table. He jabs them with an angry finger. "Headwinds."

"And?"

"We're three hours behind schedule."

It was Max's affinity for logic and order that drew him to navigation in the first place, but it is his capacity for problem-solving and maintaining order that keeps him in this position instead of reaching for command of his own airship. Already his mind is ticking through potential issues, looking for a solution. A loss of this magnitude can easily happen over the course of an entire trip, but for it to happen overnight is highly irregular. Max inspects the instruments on the wall above his desk, looking for the culprit. A broken clock or a malfunctioning triangulation gauge. He even pulls the compass from his pocket to double-check the gauges. But nothing is out of sync.

"Headwinds?" he asks.

"Fifteen knots."

He ponders this for a moment. "Crosswinds?"

Nielsen checks the logbook. "They've stayed around twelve knots, give or take a bit, depending on altitude. But still, we should have crossed the prime meridian at one o'clock. And we didn't get there until three. We've lost another hour since."

"That doesn't make sense," Max says. "It's—"

"Inexcusable," Commander Pruss growls. He stands at the rudder wheel, his back turned, his voice charged with electricity.

So here is the source of the tension, then. Pruss is frustrated, Nielsen is defensive, and everyone else is unwilling to take sides. No matter what might have been spoken between them, the delay cannot be Nielsen's fault. The *Hindenburg* is an aviation marvel but no state-of-the-art technology can defeat Mother Nature. The airship will always be subject to her capricious whims.

"Get us back on course, Max," Pruss says. He dismisses Nielsen with a curt nod.

Nielsen is ready to protest, but Max shakes his head. *No,* the movement says, *it's not worth the trouble you'll make for yourself.* Max is on duty now. He'll fix the problem—it's what he does best after all. If Nielsen is smart he will keep his mouth shut, and Pruss won't remember the incident come nightfall.

Nielsen signs out of the logbook with resignation. Then he salutes Pruss and leaves the control car. There is an immediate shift in the atmosphere, as though Nielsen has taken the strain with him, and as Max assumes his position at the chart, balance is restored.

Max consults his equipment and then traces the ship's course on the chart as he mentally calculates the total air speed and the angle of the wind based on their direction of travel.

He makes a decision. "Commander?"

Max waits for Pruss to turn.

"If we lower altitude fifty feet and alter course two degrees to the south, headwinds will be reduced significantly."

Pruss considers Max's suggestion for a moment—it's for show, as Pruss always defers to Max in this area—then he gives the orders to descend. There is an immediate tug on the airship, like a balloon being pulled forward.

"Well done," Colonel Erdmann says quietly behind him.

Max acknowledges the praise with a slight nod, unnerved at the intensity of Erdmann's gaze and the unasked questions it contains. Then he returns to his duties, feeling rather satisfied with himself. *No, you can't defeat Mother Nature,* he thinks, *but you sure as hell can move out of her way.*

THE JOURNALIST

Gertrud is woken, not so much by light, but by the feeling of being watched. Without opening her eyes she knows that Leonhard's gaze is on her face. Without looking at him she can't tell whether the gaze is amorous or angry, but she can feel its heat nonetheless. Gertrud groans and rolls away, taking the blanket with her. "It's too early. Go back to sleep."

His voice is a warm hum in the near darkness. "Why? When I was so enjoying the surprise of waking to actually find you here."

Damn him. So it's anger, then.

Gertrud shifts onto her back but does not open her eyes. Her scalp hurts. The backs of her eyeballs feel like they are coated with sand. There's fur on her teeth and sleep in her limbs. "That's such a rare thing?"

"Where did you go last night, *Liebchen*?" Leonhard loops an arm around her waist and pulls her against his chest. There is nothing seductive about the gesture. He is locking her in.

"What do you mean?" She won't lie to him exactly, she's never been good at that, but Gertrud feels no guilt about feigning confusion.

"You smell of cigarettes. And booze." He throws the blanket back to expose her rumpled slip. "And last I checked, the only thing you were wearing . . . was me."

She opens her mouth, but Leonhard lays a finger across her lips in warning. He does not like it when she's deceptive. He's giving her a way out.

"And then there's always the fact that when I woke last night you weren't here," he adds.

"Maybe I got cold? Maybe I got up in the middle of the night to use the toilet? *Maybe* I was hungry?"

"Maybe you went looking for trouble because you thought I wouldn't be along to stop you?"

"Does it matter?"

Leonhard gives her a nip on the ear with his teeth. "Of course it does. I am your husband after all."

"Then why didn't you come looking for me if you were so concerned?"

The stateroom is beginning to fill with a pale, silvery light, but they can't see out the window from the angle at which they are lying. "We're six hundred feet in the air. You're afraid of heights. Didn't figure you could get very far."

"I didn't think you'd wake. I'm sorry."

"Clarify that apology, *Liebchen*. Sorry that I woke? That you were reckless? Or that you worried me?"

Gertrud turns to face him. She forces one eye open. "Sorry that you think this is a big deal."

"It is a very big deal. Where did you go?"

"To the bar. I couldn't sleep." The look she gives him suggests that this is his fault, that he'd promised her sleep and didn't deliver on his end of the bargain.

They have spent such a large part of their relationship in some form of playful banter that she is unnerved by the severe crease that forms between his eyes. Leonhard is quite genuinely angry.

"What were you doing? In the bar?"

"Drinking."

"And?"

"Smoking."

"With?"

"Edward Douglas."

"Pray tell, *Liebchen*, who in the *fucking hell* is Edward Douglas?"

Gertrud yawns and stretches her arms behind her head until her palms rest flat against the wall. She pushes against it, and the muscles in her spine begin to protest. "Well, for starters, he's the drunk *Arschloch* who was on the bus yesterday."

"Starters?"

She sits up and folds her legs beneath her. Gertrud pushes her hair away from her face, then crosses her arms over her chest. She does her best to match the harsh expression on Leonhard's face. "He also happens to be the mystery man who ran up the stairs that day in Frankfurt when Herr Goebbels yanked my press card."

Gertrud waits. Leonhard has the squint-eyed look of a man trying hard to remember something just beyond his grasp. After a moment he sits up with a start. "The mustache!"

"It doesn't really suit him, does it?"

"You are a terrifying creature. You know that, right?"

"I like to think I'm simply observant."

Leonhard isn't ready to let her off the hook just yet, however. He sets a gentle hand on each shoulder. "What I'd really like to do right now is shake you so hard your teeth rattle. And I would if I thought for a moment that it would do any good. But I know you better than that. So instead I want you to tell me every single thing you learned about that man. Do you understand? Everything."

"You'll just be disappointed. I don't know much more than you do. Despite my best efforts. He's cagey. And a spectacular liar. He answered my questions, but only just. And in a way that left me with more questions. That bastard had five empty glasses on the table when I got there. And two more by the time the bartender kicked us out at three o'clock, and he wasn't even the least bit drunk. How is that *possible*, Leonhard?"

"Clearly he holds it well."

"No one holds it that well."

"You're using absolutes again. I would have thought life had taught you better by now."

"It's too early to get philosophical."

"This is logic. Not philosophy."

"You want logic? Why the act on the bus yesterday? What could he possibly have gained from that little charade?"

Leonhard isn't a man who smiles often. He isn't jovial. Or histrionic. He often keeps his emotions tucked behind that reserved, precise exterior. So Gertrud is somewhat anxious when a broad, wicked grin stretches across his face. "That is something you'll likely have to puzzle over while you get ready. We're going to breakfast."

"No." She dives back into the covers. Pulls them over her head. "I'm going back to sleep. I'm exhausted."

She can feel the mattress shift beneath her when Leonhard climbs out of bed. And for the briefest moment she actually believes that he will let her sleep. But a second later he yanks the bedding clean off, sheets and all, and drops it to the floor.

"Stop it!"

"Get up."

"No." She flings herself back into the pillows like a petulant child.

There is an edge to his voice now. "You, my dear, are going to get up and make your way to the shower. Then you will dress and put on, not just your makeup, but your best poker face. Because you've been a fool. You have shown your hand. And that man, whoever he might be, now knows ten times more about us than we know about him. We will rectify that today, *Liebchen*. But we will do it together. In a manner that I find appropriate." Leonhard leans across the bed and runs a single calloused thumb across her cheek. "You will get your *Scheiße* together. Starting now."

There are fifteen things that Gertrud wants to say. And for one long, jumbled moment they knock around inside her mind, jockeying for position. Accusations. Profanity. Excuses. Not one, but three Romani hexes she learned from her maternal grandmother. But judging by the look on his face, it's an apology he's looking for, and she cannot find a single one to offer him. So in the end she says nothing. Gertrud is not ready to admit any wrongdoing on her part. And her husband is not ready to accept anything less. An uneasy silence settles between them. After a moment Leonhard lifts a long, cream-colored satin robe from the closet. He holds it out.

"You know," she says, taking a stab at levity, "the best thing about this trip was going to be sleeping in. I can't remember the last time I didn't have to get up early and deal with a child."

"Think about that the next time you crawl into bed smelling like an ashtray. How long has it been since you've smoked? Two years?"

"Almost. It's therapeutic."

"I find it unnerving."

"You used to find it sexy."

"I still do. That's not the point." He shakes the robe, impatient.

So this is how it will be. Fine. Gertrud slides off the bed and lets Leonhard help her into the robe. He secures it high on her breastbone, then ties it at her waist. Leonhard hands her the cosmetic bag and a towel that hangs beside the sink.

Her voice is clipped. "Which dress?"

"The blue one. It matches your eyes. And I've never seen you wear it without every man in the room staring at you."

"I thought you didn't want me to put myself out there?"

"The problem, *Liebchen*, is that you can be such an idiot in the way you go about doing it."

He is done with argument. Leonhard shoos her out the door. "Be in the dining room in thirty minutes," he says. "We're going to make an appearance at seven like the civilized people we are."

"You're not waiting for me?"

He chucks her chin. "Why bother when you're so good at rushing ahead?"

The only people whom Gertrud encounters on her short trip to the shower are two uniformed crew members who discreetly avert their eyes at the sight of her in a dressing gown. Once inside the small room, Gertrud locks the door and hangs her clothing on a series of hooks bolted to the wall. The shower is split in half and separated by a curtain. The walls and floor are covered in clean white tiles. There's a single light overhead and a drain in the floor. Gertrud hangs up her robe and drops her slip to the tiled floor. When she turns the knob she discovers insufficient pressure and tepid water. It rather feels as though she's being pissed on. Gertrud has to make three full rotations before her entire body is wet, and it takes minutes of standing directly beneath the showerhead to saturate her hair. Gertrud finishes her shower with military efficiency, scrubbing at her body with a bar of lavender soap. Shampoo gets in her eyes, and she can't rinse it out before the sting spreads. What little bit of good humor she had left slips away, leaving behind a raw, bristling anger.

It's not until she goes to step over the lip of the shower that she slips and has to steady herself against the wall. At first she thinks there's a sliver of soap near the drain, but when she bends to pick it up she finds a pendant of some sort at the end of a ball chain. It's oval, tarnished, and stamped with raised letters and numbers. Gertrud wipes it against her towel and holds it up to the light so she can read it.

It looks to be a Deutsches Heer identification tag.

The tin is well worn on one side. She runs the pad of her thumb across it to help identify the digits she can't read. There are ten numbered fields on the disk, each containing a bit of pertinent information about the soldier it was issued to. Religious preference: rk for Catholic. Service number: 100991–K-455(-)6(-)8. Blood type: AB. And various vaccinations. Whoever this soldier might be, she now knows almost everything about him but his name. The only thing that Gertrud is certain of as she squints at the tag, trying to make sense of its presence in this place, is that the American had one very much like it in the bar last night. But she has no intention of giving it back.

She is flushed, excited, as she dries and dresses and readies herself for breakfast. Hair and makeup and general grooming are done in the cabin, in record time, and she's buzzing like a live wire by the time she reaches the dining room. Leonhard rises from his seat and comes to greet her as soon as she enters. He is so hell-bent on intercepting her that he doesn't notice the dramatic change in her countenance. He bends low to place a kiss on her cheek. "You smell better."

"Hhhmm. I did think a bit of food would improve your manners."

Leonhard takes her arm and tucks it into the crook of his arm. "Hold it against me all you like. But I need you angry this morning."

"What's that supposed to mean? You provoked me on purpose?"

"Yes." He pulls out her chair and helps her settle into place at the table. Their voices are low. Polite. No one would guess they are hovering on the edge of a quarrel. "For one, you're at your sharpest when you're angry. I've always rather appreciated that about you."

She snaps out her napkin and then presses it smooth across her lap. Gertrud skewers him with her gaze.

"Well, if I'm honest, it also terrifies me a bit. But I can't deny it's sexy."

"Shall I congratulate you on your bravery?"

"No. But I'd appreciate it if you'd let me finish my point."

She waves a hand indicating that he should go ahead.

"Look around, *Liebchen*. What do you see?" He leans an arm across the back of his chair. "I'm rather surprised you hadn't noticed already. You do dislike the man after all."

The American. Holding court. In the promenade beside the dining room. He is clear-eyed and clean shaven, showing no signs of a man who was up half the night drinking. He never looks in their direction, but Gertrud knows he's watching them nonetheless. His body is angled in such a way that the Adelts are right in his peripheral vision. He is surrounded by a small crowd of male passengers. Whatever he says makes them roar with laughter, and Gertrud looks away in disgust. She is offended at the mere suggestion that such a man could be funny.

Leonhard summons one of the dining stewards to their table. His name tag reads SEVERIN KLEIN, and his face reads Aryan poster child. Blond hair. Square jaw. Blue eyes. "Coffee for both of us, please."

She catches Klein's quick surveillance and immediate approval of them. He tips the silver carafe over her mug, and Gertrud begins an elaborate preparation ritual involving so much sugar and cream that Leonhard shakes his head in disgust. She is soon nursing a full cup of ivory coffee and a viscous mood. Klein hasn't been nearly so attentive to the Jewish businessmen seated next to them. Nor was he last night.

"Do you see what we're up against now?" Leonhard asks. It takes her a moment to realize he is not talking about the steward or all that he represents. He's watching the American with that look he gets when there's a puzzle to be solved. "He'll have them believing anything he says before the dishes are cleared. So yes, I made you angry on purpose. And I'll gladly keep you that way so long as you do not, for a moment, forget that there are certain protections your husband can provide. I'd suggest you make good use of them. Even if the thought does chafe your unique sensibilities. It's what I'm here for, damn it."

It's then that she notices Leonhard has placed himself strategically between her and the American. No matter that the man is twenty feet away or out of earshot. It's a small thing, but he has created a buffer between them. Marking his territory as it were. Leonhard is a man after all. And, she must admit, a good one.

"You are right."

It's the closest she will come to offering an apology, and Leonhard knows well enough to take what he can get. He lifts her hand from the tablecloth and kisses it.

The American's audience has grown by a handful as the passengers wait for breakfast to be served. "What is he going on about over there anyway?"

"Funny you should ask, *Liebchen*."

THE AMERICAN

The American has been watching Leonhard Adelt for twenty minutes. The journalist rises from the table and goes to greet his wife. She looks a bit worse for wear, though it appears as though she has at least managed a shower this morning. The tips of each curl hang heavy with moisture against her jaw, and Leonhard escorts her to their table and seats her in the chair farthest away. Once settled, they begin to have a calm but rather intense debate. The American would wager that her husband was not aware of, or in favor of, her little excursion in the middle of the night. He can tell by the stiffness of her spine and the set of her jaw that she is being taken to task for it now.

His attention is drawn to one of the couples sitting near him.

The wife is complaining about the trip, and he has to hide his irritation. Wealthy brats. They expect to be entertained at all times. The press makes it sound as though movie stars and royalty crowd every voyage, and she is vexed to find herself mingling with common businessmen and housewives.

"This isn't the most exciting voyage so far," she says to her husband. She is disappointed. The weather is dreary. And the company more so. The food is decent, but she has had better. The beds are too small and the temperature too cold. "I wish we had been on the Millionaires Flight last year."

"You can keep your millionaires," her husband says. "I just wish we had been on board when it flew over the Olympics. Can you imagine?"

"Heard about that flight, did you?" the American asks. He moves closer. Introduces himself. Learns they are Otto and Elsa Ernst. Retirees. Upper-middle class. Unimportant.

"Everyone heard about it. The pictures were all over the papers. The *Hindenburg* flew right over the stadium."

The American leans toward them and lowers his voice as though telling a secret. "Did you know that Hitler had the Olympic rings emblazoned on the side of this ship just for the occasion?"

"I don't recall that actually." Otto frowns. The memory is lost somewhere in the folds of his mind.

He shrugs. "Most people never noticed them. The swastikas are rather more obvious."

A nervous tremor runs through the small crowd, and the American keeps his smile hidden. The Nazi symbol represents the white elephant in the room, a thing to be avoided in civilized discussion. Ignore it long enough and it will go away. Keep opinions spare and to yourself. And yet he very much enjoys poking the dragon.

He continues. "The Nazis had just finished funding the completion of our good airship here, and, given their proprietary feelings, it only made sense for them to make a showing during the opening ceremonies last year in Berlin. And it was quite impressive. I was there."

"I wanted to go but had to settle for reading about it in the papers," Otto admits.

A carefully worded version, no doubt. That particular event went down in history but not in the way the Führer intended. At the mention of the Olympics several more people wander into the promenade. The results of one particular competition are well-known in Germany, but little publicized. Curious citizens have to get their gossip where they can.

"It was all rather symbolic for him," the American says. "Prophetic even. It was meant to be the event in which his people showed their superiority. All carefully orchestrated, of course. The very motto of the Olympics, the *hendiatris: Citius, Altius, Fortius.* Higher, Faster, Stronger. It was a sign to him. And the rings, of course. Well, that bit took on a religious significance that we will spend decades debating. Mark my words. But what can you expect from a man who bases his worldview on an opera about Norse mythology?"

They are completely lost at this bit of information, and he doesn't bother to enlighten them. All of these people, these *sheep*, will understand their leader soon enough, and they will wish that they didn't. Let them regret it later. Let them wish they had taken a moment to know who Adolf Hitler really is and what he believes. An old prophecy. A burning of the world. Renewal. Perfection. They put the psychopath in power. Let them live with the consequences. He takes a deep breath to control his own trembling fanaticism. The irony isn't lost on him. It takes a zealot to know a zealot. And sometimes it takes one to stop one. He will do what he can. Even if it means the only thing he stops is Hitler's favorite airship.

"The Führer," he says, "didn't just expect a great German sweep of those games; he was certain of it. Hitler's designs were clear—in his mind, at least, if not in the minds of most people who sat in those stands. Germany was superior. Jessie Owens put an end to that, of course."

He finds Werner Franz in the crowd of faces staring at him and acknowledges the unspoken question in his eyes with a nod. The boy's mouth forms into a circle. Oh. The dog.

The serving pantry door swings wide and three stewards step out holding large trays loaded down with steaming plates. Much of the crowd dissipates. The American can't compete with food. Doesn't intend to. Another seed has been planted. He'll let it germinate before he pokes this soil again. Let them eat. Let them revel in their petty luxuries for a moment. He can live with that. Because something is growing beneath the surface. He can see it in the uneasy shift of their eyes while he speaks. Subversion dressed up as storytelling, as entertainment, as gossip. It's easier to swallow that way. He turns to the window, letting the stragglers come to him if they will.

With gray clouds above and gray sea below, and the *Hindenburg* floating smoothly between them, it feels very much as though they are trapped in the space between lid and pan. The few passengers who wander over to the observation window seem greatly disheartened by the sight. They want scenery. Excitement. Perhaps a breaching whale or a passing steamship. Instead they have stillness and conformity. They are restless, and the American will exploit this.

He notes that the Jewish men seated beside the Adelts make quick work of their meal. No coffee refills. No extra toast or marmalade. Slices of cold bacon are pushed to the edge of their plates. He suspects that their steward, Severin Klein, added it to the order out of spite. In less than ten minutes the two men are standing casually beside him at the observation windows. Heads bent. Eyes fixed, but unseeing, on the ocean below. After a moment they introduce themselves as Moritz Feibusch, a food broker from San Francisco, and William Leuchtenberg, an executive in New York City. Clearly they've been talking about what the American has said.

"The Olympic rings are gone now," Moritz says. "I didn't see them when we boarded."

"Of course. Hitler wouldn't very well keep them painted on the side of his airship next to his swastikas after a black man took home four gold medals, would he?"

William is pensive, eyebrows drawn, lips pursed. "Seems a risk to do it in the first place."

"Oh, it makes perfect sense. Picture it if you can. An open arena. Tens of thousands of spectators. The best athletes from every nation on earth. And the Führer standing glorious on the field as the greatest airship in history flies overhead. What do *you* think he was trying to say?"

"That he couldn't lose," Mortiz says, nodding slowly.

"Except he did," William whispers.

"Some would argue it was his prerogative after all. The Nazis supplied the money to finish construction on the airship. So it became their symbol. Their means of propaganda. And once the rings had outlived their usefulness they were removed."

"Hitler is good at removing things that outlive their usefulness," William mutters darkly.

The American seizes this. Manipulates it. He looks around the dining room, his gaze stopping at strategic points, as though fascinated. "And yet here we all are, funding his cause."

"This is travel. Not politics," Moritz says. Clearly the thought makes him uncomfortable.

"No. This," he spins a finger in the air to indicate the entire ship, "is about luxury. And luxury and politics are always bedfellows. Money is power. And power is courted by politics. Why do you think so much time and press went into the Millionaires Flight last year?" He pauses to let his point sink in. "Take the wealthiest men in the world on a ten-hour flight to garner support for a unique aviation dream. Invite Winthrop Aldrich, Nelson Rockefeller, and executives from TWA and Pan American Airways. Convince Standard Oil to supply the diesel and hydrogen. Make sure key portions are broadcast live on NBC radio so millions of listeners can join them vicariously. It was orchestrated. It was political. You know what a flight like that says?" he asks William Leuchtenberg. "That they are willing to support a tyrant financially. You can call it luxury or convenience, if you like. But it's politics nonetheless."

"If what you say is true, then we are all guilty."

"Ah, my friend, therein lies the rub. We're all willing to justify our actions when we need to."

The American looks up to find Gertrud Adelt glaring at him over the rim of her steaming coffee cup. In a different world he might consider the woman an ally. Perhaps if he were on a different mission. Or if her damned curiosity didn't keep getting in the way of his plans. As it stands, however, the American does not want friends or partners. He wants revenge, and he will not allow this brassy troublemaker to distract him from his job.

"So what's the point of this little lecture, then? Guilt?" William Leuchtenberg asks.

After a moment's thought the American finally says, "Enlightenment."

THE STEWARDESS

The cabin boy has a flower in his hand. It's a carnation. Small and pink and nothing special, but he's fiddling with the stem and shifting from foot to foot as though his privates itch. He has the look of a boy who is winding up his courage for some difficult task. And then Emilie understands why. Werner Franz is staring at Irene Doehner, and the girl is pretending not to notice.

As far as children go, the Doehners are not difficult to care for. Irene has her brothers well in hand most of the time, and even when they drift beyond the boundaries of what she can control, a firm word from Emilie reins them in. They are not picky eaters and haven't rejected anything set before them this morning. They have, however, eaten copious amounts of food, mostly bacon, toast, and cheese. They wanted coffee as well, but Emilie put her foot down. No point in asking for trouble. There is only so much energy they can expend in such close quarters, and she has little interest in picking up the pieces of whatever they may break along the way.

Irene looks flushed; the apples of her cheeks are tinged a warm pink against her pale skin. She glances at the cabin boy and then away. Only the most careful observer would notice the wordless flirting between the two.

"You're a kind girl," Emilie says, pulling Irene's attention away from Werner. "Letting your parents sleep in like this."

"Kindness has little to do with it, *Fräulein*. My brothers stayed in my cabin last night. I didn't think it would be right to wake my parents just because they wanted breakfast."

One of the perks of not having a full flight is that there are cabins to spare. It was easy enough to settle Irene in a room of her own yesterday, right across the hall from her parents. And it's no surprise that they took full advantage of the chance for a little privacy. Emilie can't say that she blames them. She doubts they often get a moment to themselves, what with the boys' perpetual antics. A bit like herding cats, looking after those two.

She winks at Irene, causing the girl's face to flame even brighter. "Like I said, a kind girl."

It makes sense now why the boys came to breakfast in yesterday's rumpled clothes. Emilie had passed it off as a quirk unique to male children. They are not known for their reason or their hygiene. These two in particular. There's a stain on Walter's shirt from dinner last night, and little Werner—he has the same name as the cabin boy, good Lord, she'll never keep them straight—seems to have lost three buttons on his shirt. From wrestling, no doubt. She has never seen children who take such delight in roughhousing. They actually fell down the stairs to B-deck last night, landing in a pile of arms and legs and laughter. She had run after them only to find that they were delighted with the ordeal and wanted to do it again. Emilie had made them sit on their hands in the corridor for ten minutes as punishment.

The boys are slowing their ravenous consumption of eggs, and Emilie clears the empty plates from the table. No sooner has she stepped into the serving pantry to send the dishes down the dumb-waiter than she sees Werner Franz drift toward the table. Werner does nothing inappropriate. He does not look at Irene or speak to her. But, from Emilie's perspective, the sleight of hand is clear. The pink carnation now lies where Irene's breakfast dishes once cluttered the table. He hesitates at her side just long enough to see whether his gift will be accepted and is clearly pleased when Irene lifts the flower from the table, sniffs it quickly, and hides it beneath the napkin in her lap. She meets Werner's gaze for one quick second, offering the sort of smile that no girl of fourteen should know how to wield. Emilie is somewhat surprised that Werner can think, much less walk straight afterwards. But he does. Had Emilie not witnessed the exchange she would not know from his appearance that anything of significance had just passed between the teenagers. Werner is smiling, but in the way he often does. It's a grin of pleased servitude. A steward's grin. Damn if that child doesn't have a rather brilliant poker face.

She returns to clear the remaining dishes from the table only to notice that the American has observed the moment as well. He is stretched out in the promenade, feet propped up on a window ledge, hands behind his head, grinning. The American catches her eye and tips his chin toward Werner. He winks as though this is a secret between them. The fact that he includes her in the observation makes her uncomfortable. The fact that he continues to watch her with a sleepy sort of gaze makes her even more so.

Emilie wonders if she should confront Werner. He doesn't need to meddle with Irene. But as he brushes past her and sets the dishes in the dumbwaiter she can't bring herself to say anything. Why shouldn't someone on this ship be happy? It's not like this crush can go anywhere. In two days Werner will return to Frankfurt, and the Doehners will travel on to Mexico City. This will end before it has a chance to begin.

The thought makes her anxious. And not because of Werner. Or Irene. But for herself. Max has discovered her plan, and now she feels vulnerable and defensive. Emilie doesn't realize she is slamming dirty dishes onto the tray until Walter looks up from the table in alarm.

"I didn't break the plate! It was Werner!" he says, trying to hide a shard in his lap.

God bless a guilty conscience. Who knows what he would have done with the sharp piece of china if he had been able to smuggle it out of the dining room.

She extends her hand, and he surrenders the piece. "Werner?"

He crawls out from under the table with the remaining pieces. Emilie counts them just to be sure. They move so quickly, the little hellions. She never saw them break the plate or try to hide it. She had been too distracted watching the fledgling mating dance of the two resident teenagers.

"Never again," she says.

They nod solemnly, and she doesn't believe them for a moment. A smile erupts despite her best efforts to hide it. The look of alarm fades from Walter's face, and she sees how relieved he is not to be the target of her wrath. The child wants to please. Almost as much as he wants to explore and destroy. And she can't help but wonder what it would be like to have a child of her own.

Emilie grimaces. This is the problem with being a widow. She knows exactly what she's missing. There are biological desires that she can do nothing about. She likes children well enough. She has spent the better part of her adult life caring for them, in fact. But she never wanted one of her own—not when Hans was alive. Once the possibility evaporated, however, she found herself consumed with the thought. There is nothing logical to it. She knows the effort it takes to feed and care for the little miscreants. She simply wants a child because she can't have one. So like human nature.

Emilie shakes the thought away. "Come along, children. We'll wait for your parents in the reading room."

They leave the dining room and circle around to the other side of the ship, through the lounge with its mural depicting the routes of the great explorers, toward the small area at the back. It's quieter here, walled off from the lounge, and she settles all three children into aluminum tube chairs with orange upholstery situated around a small table. The springs squeak in protest as the boys rock back and forth.

She hands them postcards and pencils—she wouldn't trust these boys with a pen if her life depended on it. God only knows the damage they could do with permanent ink. Emilie then removes herself a bit to offer them privacy to compose their thoughts. It has become something of a novelty to receive mail written and posted from the *Hindenburg*. A collector's item. *People place value on the strangest things*, Emilie thinks.

Of all the public rooms on board the *Hindenburg*, the reading room is the most subdued. It has the quiet, genteel atmosphere of a library, and the children can feel it, for they settle down within a few minutes. No jostling. No poking one another with pencils or elbows. Here the fabric-covered walls are painted with murals depicting the history of postal delivery, starting with idyllic agrarian settings. Farms. Fields. Livestock. Children playing with sticks. A placid lake. A shallow stream. It speaks of contentment and simplicity. Irene stares at a small cottage with a dreamy smile, and Emilie knows she's painting domestic fantasies in her mind. Emilie wonders if her own romantic yearnings started at such a young age. She thinks back to Frank Becker and his crass invitation in the butcher shop. Perhaps her own desires were not so innocent.

The airship passes through a cloud bank and into the bright sun for the first time that morning. The atmosphere changes in the time it takes Emilie to blink. Warm golden light spills through the observation windows and across the floor. Irene laughs at the change, her voice a delighted explosion of joy. She runs to look out the window, palms pressed against the glass.

"Look!" someone shouts from the promenade. "A rainbow!"

The boys shoot to their feet, scattering writing paraphernalia across the floor, and dart around the wall. Emilie follows behind, wiping pencil shavings from her skirt as she goes. The long, black shadow of the *Hindenburg* dances across the water below, warped by the movement of the waves. And circling the shadow is a 360-degree rainbow. A perfect areola of flaming color. All seven hues present. Emilie stands with the passengers in awe. She has never seen a rainbow like this, only bits and pieces of them broken by cloud or skyline or any myriad number of obstructions. But this is different. This is what every rainbow should be. Perfect. Unbroken. Exquisite. Each color pitched against the mirrored sea behind it. And huge. It must stretch hundreds of feet in diameter. To Emilie it looks like the promise of something better. Something more. She releases a single, reverence-laden breath.

The promenade begins to fill as more passengers enter, drawn by the disturbance. Among them are Herr and Frau Doehner, looking fresh and alert. They hold hands, and Emilie suspects it was a night well spent. Hermann Doehner is a good eight inches taller than his wife, but she makes up for it with girth and force of personality. She's solid rather than pudgy, but doesn't carry herself like a woman who struggles to maintain her figure. Matilde Doehner practically floats across the floor. Whether from a revived sense of passion, a good night's rest, or simple joy at seeing her children, Emilie cannot tell. Regardless, she swoops the boys into her arms, smothering their little blond heads with kisses. Whispering endearments. Irene tucks herself into the crook beneath her father's arm and smiles at him with adoration. Emilie is struck by the joy in this private reunion. A happy family. Two miracles in one day. What are the odds?

Emilie watches the Doehners from a safe distance, reminded of her own isolation. She thinks of the note Max left in his angry scrawl and their argument this morning. Her thin veneer of composure is a sham—this pleasant smile and unperturbed demeanor. On the inside she is a gurgling mass of apprehension and nervous energy. She feels simultaneously caged and exposed. She wants to hide. She wants to run.

Once the excitement has died down, Emilie helps Matilde usher the children back into the reading room while Hermann stays behind to chat with the two Jewish businessmen, their heads bent in whispered conversation. Walter and Werner each select a pencil from a jar on the shelf. They take their time, looking for pencils with new, flat erasers. The boys stand the pencils on end, the erasers set on the smooth, polished aluminum. They squat next to the table, eyes level with its surface, and wait.

"Your legs will tip over before the pencils do," Emilie says.

"Mother told us about this game," Walter says. "She will give a mark to whoever's pencil stays standing longest."

Emilie gives Matilde a questioning glance and gets a smile in return. Clever woman. The elevator operators in the control car never let the airship drift at more than a five-degree angle. Anything more than that will send dishes sliding off the tables. Frau Doehner must know this. She has counted on it, in fact, because she settles into her chair with a satisfied grin. The boys are competitive. They will be at this for some time.

The morning ambles along pleasantly without any further disturbance. Passengers move in and out of the reading room. They scratch missives onto their postcards. Work the crossword puzzle. Read. A few chat quietly in the corner. Irene scribbles frantically at a pile of postcards. Matilde is absorbed in some novel. Emilie can't read the title, but, given the pinking of her cheeks, she guesses that romance is involved. The boys are still at their game, but now they are trying to blow down one another's pencil.

"No cheating," Frau Doehner warns. "I'll not reward cheaters."

They settle down and she returns to her novel. Emilie can see the cover now. *The Age of Innocence.* She has good taste at least. Not that Emilie can judge. There's a worn copy of *Lady Chatterley's Lover*, translated into Italian, hidden beneath her pillow. It's not available in Germany yet, for obvious reasons. She picked up a copy in Rome several years ago, and, given the number of times she has read it, she has easily gotten her money's worth. Good thing Max didn't find *that* last night or they might have had an entirely different sort of evening.

Emilie looks up just as Max enters the reading room. Her cheeks burn hot and she stares at her feet for a moment. His timing is rather suspect. It's as though she has summoned him with her thoughts. He's wearing his cap and an amiable smile. A basket is tucked under one arm. He moves around the room in a counter-clockwise direction, collecting postcards and offering stamps. He's talkative. Cheery. And Emilie realizes that she knows him well enough now to see through the charade. The bags under his eyes and the pinched line of his mouth reveal a hidden misery. A misery that she has caused.

It's too much for her. Emilie quietly takes leave of the Doehner family. She squeezes Matilde's shoulder and tells her that she has a few tasks that must be tended to before lunch. And then she slips from the room when Max is at the farthest point from her.

He's quick when he needs to be. Damn him. And he can't resist a challenge. She knows this about him too. So she is only mildly surprised to hear his voice in the keel corridor, ringing out behind her. She rushes down the stairs.

"We need to talk, Emilie."

She ignores him, walking faster, eyes darting to and fro in search of a place to escape. The kitchen is her only promising option, and she pushes through the door without having any real plan in mind. It's only when she sees Xaver Maier that an idea takes shape. Max will follow her. She's certain of this. He's still angry and he has not yet said his peace.

"What's wrong?" Xaver asks.

Emilie knows she must look crazed. She steps forward just as the heel of Max's hand smashes against the kitchen door, shoving it inward. She reaches Xaver in three bold steps and throws her arms around his neck. His eyes are wide and alarmed but he hesitates for only a second when she leans in for a kiss. She hears a metal bowl clatter to the floor, dropped by one of the assistant chefs. They have an audience. Good. She can put an end to this situation with Max once and for all.

Xaver is nothing if not opportunistic. His arms are around her waist in a moment. Tight. Greedy. But this kiss is nothing like the one she shared with Max the night before. There is no passion. No warmth. Xaver tastes of yeast and cold water and a hint of parsley. Her skin tingles with nothing but shame, and her ears are tuned to the deep, furious hum emanating from Max's chest behind her. And Xaver, being the bastard that he is, slides his hand down several inches from her waist, threatening to cup her backside. She stiffens beneath him and feels his taunting smile against her lips.

This is the worst kiss of her life. Worse even than the one she had shared with Frank Becker in the back room of her father's shop before she dropped him to the floor. She hadn't told Max that part last night, of course. Emilie wasn't *entirely* innocent in the whole affair. But Xaver is smart enough to know what's happening. He doesn't take this farce too far. If nothing else he possesses a healthy amount of self-preservation. Max is watching after all. No doubt confounded. Bristling.

Each second is interminable. She wants nothing more than to pull away and wipe her mouth. But she cannot do so until Max leaves. It's one thing to do this out of spite; it's another thing to own up to her treachery while he's standing there.

And yet he must know. Because he waits. Silent. Furious. Seeing how long she will pretend.

So Emilie goes for cruelty. She lays her palm flat against Xaver's face and lightly plays with his earlobe. He is a man, after all, and she feels him soften beneath her. His kiss takes on a note of sincerity, and he moves one hand up to cradle her skull. She tries to pull away on reflex, but his grip tightens as his fingers wind through her hair.

Only when she hears the door swoosh shut does she pull away. But she can't look at Xaver right away. She's too ashamed.

"I don't know what is happening between you and Zabel, but don't ever do that to me again."

She's insulted. Angry. Irrational. "You didn't like it?"

"I didn't say that. Clearly. Where the hell did you learn to kiss like that anyway? But still. Shit. I thought he'd kill me by the look on his face."

"You kept your eyes *open*?" Emilie hears her words slip out in a horrified hiss. She flinches at the sound.

"That was rather the point, right? Piss off the navigator? Taunt him? It's not like you've ever kissed me before." He peers at her, curious. "So?"

"I was making a point."

"Well done."

"Would you be serious? Please?"

"That's what you were just now? *Serious?* I'd hate to see you act flippant."

In truth, Emilie is serious. Seriously angry. Seriously ashamed. Seriously confused. Yes. All these things.

"Just"—she holds her palm out, silencing him—"I need to think."

"A bit late for that, I'd say. You've just broken Zabel's heart and confused the hell out of me. He'll probably kill me in my sleep." Xaver's toque was knocked askew during her little display, and he sets it back into place. "Listen. Do what you like with your navigator, but leave me out of it, okay? I actually value my life."

THE NAVIGATOR

If Max could breathe he would call out to Emilie. He would tell her to stop kissing the chef. If he could move he would reach out and break Xaver Maier's skinny neck.

Kiss who you like, he had told Emilie yesterday, *as long as I'm the one you like the most.* But he hadn't meant it. Not really. It was a rash comment, an ineffective parry in their ongoing battle. The truth is Max doesn't want to share this woman with anyone else. The heat behind his eyes builds and then explodes into a dozen tiny sparks when Maier slides his hand down Emilie's waist. He would sooner cut that hand off than see it groping her. But the chef is less of a fool than he seems, for he stops a fraction of an inch before violating what scant, undeserved trust Emilie has placed in him.

Maier has the eyes of a bear—small and dark and vengeful. He narrows them as he kisses Emilie, taunting Max. He is uncertain whether Maier enjoys the kiss, but Max is certain the chef enjoys the victory. His lungs burn with the agony of expansion. He has yet to release the breath he drew on entering the kitchen. His nostrils sting. His hands begin to shake with the effort of not reaching out to pull Emilie out of Maier's arms. In some far-off part of his mind a single thought registers: jealousy isn't just something you feel; it can be tasted as well. Sharp. Metallic. Like blood drawn from the inside of a cheek. He lets the breath out with a whoosh.

Scheiße!

There is nothing to do but leave. One step backward. Then another. One more and the door swings shut on its hinges and he's standing in the corridor swallowing bloody spit and a good portion of his pride while he gasps for breath as though he has just been kicked in the *Hoden*. Voices erupt on the other side of the door, an argument, but it's just noise to his ears. Some foreign language of betrayal.

It's almost noon and he has no interest in food or company, but he must do something. So he takes twelve steps down the corridor to the officers' mess. It's a compact room to the left of the kitchen, connected by an opening in the wall used to pass dishes back and forth. Commander Pruss, Captain Lehmann, and Colonel Erdmann are already seated at the far table, looking out the observation windows while two other officers play poker as they wait for lunch. Werner Franz is busy setting the table. Lunchtimes are staggered, the first at 11:30 and the second at 12:30. The cabin boy often wolfs down his own food in the kitchen before or after, depending on the rush.

Max's face must still be filled with alarm because Werner's eyes grow round and he opens his mouth as though to ask what's wrong. Max is still flushed and out of breath, but he decides to pre-empt the conversation. He says the first thing that comes to mind only to regret it seconds later. "Werner went with me to engine gondola two this morning."

The cabin boy is startled, like he's been shot, and the officers assume varying expressions of horror. It takes a moment for Max to register his mistake. And one more to find a course correction.

Werner is frozen in place. His hand trembles a bit, and Max fears he will drop the plate in his hands. Or begin crying. *Just hold it together, kid,* he thinks.

"He was quite brilliant actually." Max tosses his cap onto the table. Smoothes out the dent in his hair left by the snug band, and drops into the nearest seat. "Didn't even flinch when he went down the ladder. I almost pissed myself the first time I did that midflight. The kid's a natural."

This isn't entirely true. Werner had been terrified and made no effort to hide it. But the accolade has its desired effect on the officers. They turn to Werner. Assess him. Max can almost hear them take stock. He's tall. Hardworking. Werner will be broad shouldered in a few years, and clearly he knows how to keep his mouth shut. This is the first anyone has heard of their little adventure. Many young men would have bragged about such an escapade.

And slowly the look on Werner's face changes from betrayal to confusion to understanding.

"I do recall sending you to fetch Zettel for the repair," Pruss says to the cabin boy.

"I misread the note," Werner confesses. He fidgets, barely able to maintain eye contact. "I was in a hurry. But Max fixed the problem."

"The lid on the engine telegraph dial was loose, so the gauge wasn't pressurized. It was a minor fix. I'd guess we won't have any further issues with it."

"A risky thing taking young Werner with you." Pruss pushes his spine back against the padded banquette. He glares at Max with no small amount of displeasure.

Max could explain that the decision had been coerced. That it was Werner's clever form of blackmail that forced his hand. But then he'd also have to explain his quarrel with Emilie. And he is too exposed already, his pride smeared all over the kitchen floor. So he shrugs and takes responsibility for the decision instead. In truth he is contrite—it was a deeply foolish thing to do—so there is no guile in his voice when he says, "I wasn't much older when my commanding officer had me dangling from the *Vogtland* to repair a broken porthole. I was feeling nostalgic this morning and thought I'd test the boy. If a reprimand is to be given I'm the one who deserves it."

Commander Pruss is not satisfied, but he is interested. "So trial by fire, Herr Franz?"

The cabin boy ducks his head. Tries not to grin. "I do feel a bit singed."

He's greeted with laughter and one raucous slap on the back that almost sends the plate shooting right out of his hands and into the wall. He grabs it at the last second and stands tall before the second barrage of laughter. Werner Franz is, for a few short moments, one of the men.

Lunch, when it's served a few moments later, proves to be simple and elegant. Pan-seared chicken crusted with rosemary. Sautéed asparagus. New potatoes with roasted garlic. Yeast rolls served with sweet cream butter. When Werner sets the plate before Max, the navigator considers shoving it aside on principle. This is Maier's meal. And given the events in the kitchen Max would be justified in indulging in a temporary hunger strike. But he's famished. And smart enough to know that what Emilie did was about *him*, not Maier. So he eats, begrudgingly, only to discover that the meal is superb. When his plate is empty he leaves the officers' mess without giving his compliments to the chef.

Max makes a quick detour to deposit the morning's collection of letters and postcards in the mailroom, then checks his watch. There are only a few minutes left in his lunch break, but he doesn't want to return to the control car just yet. He needs to clear his head. Five minutes of silence in his cabin will do the trick.

Wilhelm Balla intercepts him just as he's leaving the mailroom. "*Du siehst schlimm aus,*" he says. "What has Emilie done now?"

Max hasn't seen a mirror since early this morning, so he guesses that Wilhelm's assessment of his appearance is likely correct. His eyes are dry and they sting when he blinks. He nicked himself while shaving, and every time he smiles it feels as though the cut is splitting open on his chin. Best not to smile, then. It's an overrated expression anyway.

He rubs his jaw. "It was stupid of me to think it would ever work."

"Oh." The tendons beside Balla's mouth curve to accommodate the knowing smirk. "So you got your kiss, then?"

"Maybe," is all Max says. He had gotten his kiss and then some.

"And a broken heart to go along with it. So tell me."

No response.

"She's leaving the airship for one of the luxury hotels?"

A glare.

"She's joining a convent?"

He clenches his jaw.

"She's pregnant with another man's baby."

"For God's sake!"

"What? It's not like you're giving me any hints here. I'm a man after all. My mind is base."

"I would think your mind is blank given this lack of creativity."

"She's dying?"

"Just stop," Max says. "It's much worse than any of that."

"Worse than *dying*?"

"Maybe. Almost." The words sound crass and petty to him and he immediately regrets them. He clears his throat. "If she were dying—which she's not—at least she wouldn't be leaving me on purpose."

"*Leaving?*"

He hadn't planned to confide in Balla. This certainly isn't his secret to share. But he needs to talk to someone, and the steward is the closest thing he has to a friend aboard this airship.

"Emilie is immigrating to America."

"She told you this?"

"No. I found papers in her cabin last night."

"You were in her cabin at least. That's progress," Balla says. "When is she leaving? Maybe you'll have time to change her mind."

He looks at his watch. "In a little less than two days, I'd say."

This brings Balla up short. His eyes have a natural almond shape and they narrow even further at this news. "And you discovered this by . . ."

"Accident."

"I take it she isn't pleased that you know?"

"That's an understatement."

"So she had no intention of telling you. That's a problem."

"The problem is that she's *leaving*. That's why I look like hell and feel worse. *Scheiße!*" Max grabs his cap and throws it against the wall.

"You love her."

"Obviously."

"Does she know that?"

"I don't see how she couldn't."

"But have you said it in so many words?"

"Listen," Max says, the rage he felt in the kitchen returning in a hot whoosh, "it's not like she has reciprocated much. Call me a fool, but I can only put myself out there for so long without any encouragement."

"She kissed you, yes?"

"You could say it was the other way around."

"But she responded?"

Max closes his eyes and gives himself five seconds to remember the kiss. "With enthusiasm."

Something occurs to Max. Clearly she has been planning to leave Germany for some time. Her papers were in order. It must have taken several years to save as much as she has. And the plan alone is meticulous. So Emilie was planning to leave Germany long before she ever met him. She's scared enough to leave everyone and everything she has ever known, and he goes and takes the decision as a personal slight. Stupid. Selfish. He's ashamed, and now he's angry with himself as well.

"*Scheiße!*"

"What now?" Wilhelm asks.

"I'm an idiot."

"I've known that for ages."

Max picks up his cap. Dusts it off. Places it back on his head with precision. "I'm going to set things right."

THE AMERICAN

The American has been asleep for almost an hour—one hour only, he won't allow himself more than that—when there is a rap at his cabin door. Four sharp knocks. Hard. Measured. Insistent. He knows immediately that this is the steward, and he is tempted to leave Wilhelm Balla standing out in the corridor. The steward isn't overly fond of him. That much is clear. But neither does he appear to be a social creature, so there must be some legitimate reason for the visit.

The American eases from his berth and opens the door. He tries to look amiable. Alert. When in reality a desperate sort of exhaustion is creeping up his spine. As a young man he could go for days without sleep and sometimes up to a week on a drinking binge and still be able to function at a high level. But over the last day he has been deprived of one and indulged in the other, and he finds that his body is no longer capable of such abuse.

"Pardon me for interrupting your rest, Herr Douglas. But I have a message from Captain Lehmann."

"Oh? How may I be of service to the captain?"

"He has requested the pleasure of your company at dinner tonight."

Interesting. First the commander, now the captain.

He finds the appropriate smile to offer the steward. Surprised. Humbled. Just the right lift to his eyebrows, and his lips curved but closed. No teeth for this smile. "Please assure the captain that I will be honored to join him."

Balla clicks his heels sharply. Nods his head. Turns to leave. The friendships of men are, by and large, less complicated than the friendships of women. They hinge on loyalty, territory, and tolerance. And the best way to get a man to deliver information is to threaten his friend. It's an unfair tactic, to be honest. But he has never been all that interested in fairness.

"Hold on a minute!" he calls after the steward.

Balla returns to the door with a look of strained patience.

"May I ask you a question?"

"Certainly."

"It is, I'm afraid, rather personal and none of my business."

"Then I shall do my best to answer. If I can."

The American feels the weight of his body settling into his joints. He would much rather return to bed than pursue this line of questioning, but he has a hunch it will pay off. The American does not ignore his hunches. It would be a mistake, however, to let the steward see how confident he feels about getting his answer. So he drops his gaze to the floor and shifts from one foot to the other, feigning awkwardness.

"Yes?" Balla is impatient. Irritated.

Good. The American will wring that out of him. He will make the steward reckless.

"Ah, how should I say this? You are good friends with the navigator, yes?"

"There are four navigators aboard this airship. Which one would you be referring to?"

"Zabel, I believe, Max Zabel."

"Yes, Herr Zabel and I are quite well acquainted."

"Then you would be somewhat privy to his personal life?"

He stiffens. "Perhaps."

The American laughs awkwardly. Purposefully. "So you would know whether he is in a romantic relationship?"

The look that flashes across Wilhelm Balla's face is first confusion. Then alarm. Then something that could be either fear or disgust. The American isn't certain which. It's too fleeting.

Balla holds up a hand. "I can assure you that Max is not—"

"That's not what I meant." He is quite pleased to hear the perfect note of surprise and admonition in his voice. He waits a moment to let the steward's face color fully with embarrassment before he continues. "Please, let's do be clear on *that*."

Balla rubs his nose with the back of one finger. "Yes. Of course. Forgive me. What might you have meant, then?"

"Well. Not to put too fine a point on it, but I am rather curious about whether or not Max Zabel is romantically involved with the stewardess. Emilie . . ."

"Imhof," Wilhelm finishes.

"Yes. Miss Imhof. Are the two of them involved?"

The steward opens his mouth slowly. And then reverses the action. This delayed response is all the answer the American needs. The two are clearly dating and trying to hide it from their fellow crew members.

The American is tired of maintaining his drunk and boisterous act. Now he wants to throw the steward off-kilter. He wants information. "I see," he says. "It's not public knowledge?"

"I don't think—"

"Or perhaps it's not official? In all truth I'd much rather that be the case as I'd planned to invite Miss Imhof to dinner once we reach Lakehurst. So you can see how I would rather save myself the embarrassment of rejection if her affections are engaged elsewhere."

He's not keen on the girl, of course. It's been a long time since a woman turned his head for any reason other than physical gratification, and he certainly doesn't need to go to the trouble of setting up a dinner to find that. No. The stewardess is irrelevant. But the American is quite interested in discovering any weaknesses the navigator might have. And learning how to exploit them.

The steward takes his time in answering. When he comes to a decision there is a sharp, conniving slant to his mouth. He chooses his words carefully—one at a time—and in such a manner that they are both loaded and innocuous. "The only thing I am at liberty to say is that the relationship between Max Zabel and Emilie Imhof is . . . *complicated.*"

The American leans into this morsel of information. "Complicated *how*?"

THE STEWARDESS

It is early afternoon and Emilie is in desperate need of coffee. Her one vice. She rarely drinks and has never dabbled in other recreational substances, but she freely admits that coffee is her addiction. It's not something she intends to apologize for, however. Or give up. As far as fixations go, it's rather benign. Quitting gives her a headache. Overindulgence gives her the jitters. So she places herself firmly in the middle, avoiding either extreme. The easiest place to secure a cup would be the kitchen, but she has no interest in facing Xaver—or his questions. So she makes her way to the bar instead. The coffee there isn't as good, falling somewhere between adequate and pitiful, but under the circumstances she doesn't feel that beggars can be choosers.

Schulze has just arrived at his station and is arranging bottles when Emilie knocks on the air-lock door. He greets her with a jovial grin.

"Another patron! And a lovely one at that."

"A boring patron, I'm afraid. And one whose break isn't nearly long enough. So it will be coffee for me, if you don't mind."

"How do you take it?"

"Black."

"Easy enough. Why don't you take a seat in the smoking room while it brews. You'll have it almost to yourself."

Emilie hadn't counted on anyone else being here so early in the day, and she hesitates as the bartender moves to open the interior air-lock door.

"Julius—"

He stops. "No one calls me that."

"It's your name."

"Not the one I go by."

Most of the crew call him by his middle name. Max. But there are far too many Maxes on board to suit her. The same with Werners, Alfreds, Fritzes, Kurts, Wilhelms, Walters, and Ludwigs. When it comes to naming their children, Germans seem to be highly unoriginal. And Emilie, despite her fantastic memory, has a hard time keeping them straight. So to her Schulze has always been Julius.

He offers that broad, generous smile she is so fond of. "You've only room for one Max in your life?"

"Be warned, that's not a name I'm fond of at this particular moment."

Schulze is no fool. "The thing about bartenders," he says as he pulls the smoking room door open, "is that we know when to pry and when to keep our mouths clamped shut. After you."

Emilie has a habit of observing rooms at different times of day. Lighting can alter not only the ambiance but the aesthetics of a space dramatically. At night the smoking room is exotic. Rich. Sensual. But in the afternoon, with natural daylight streaming through the observation windows, it looks rather like a funeral parlor. Dark and somber. Somewhere you would go to whisper in hushed tones while grieving a loss. It fits her mood splendidly.

"Do you smoke?" Schulze asks.

"Afraid not."

"Will you mind if she does?" He points to the pretty journalist who sits at a round table in the middle of the room, one shoe kicked off and her legs crossed at the knees.

"No. I'm quite used to it."

"I'll get your coffee, then."

Rules. There are always so many damned rules to be considered. Technically Emilie is not working at the moment, but she is in uniform. Approaching the journalist as an equal would be inappropriate, but ignoring her would be worse. She hesitates only until the journalist laughs.

"Please, have a seat. I don't bite."

Emilie accepts the invitation with a nod and pulls out a chair at the table. She settles into it with relief. Her feet are tired. Her lower back aches.

"I owe you an apology. I was quite horrid to you yesterday," the journalist says. She extends her hand in official greeting. "Gertrud Adelt. I am, believe it or not, quite pleased to meet you."

"Emilie Imhof." There is nothing limp about Gertrud's shake. She has a man's grip. Confident. Firm. Abrupt. Emilie returns it the way her father taught her. As one professional to another.

"You need not apologize. It's not an easy thing this . . . flying. Most people are uncomfortable with it."

"Are you?"

"Sometimes. When I think about it logically. It doesn't seem as though such a structure has any business floating through the air."

"Ah, but an engineer would say that it makes all the sense in the world. They would cite any number of facts about the lifting power of hydrogen versus the weight of steel. You'd be bored senseless and no less comfortable with the prospect, so I advise that we avoid the exercise entirely."

Emilie can feel her face soften as her smile spreads wide. "I generally do."

"How do you live with it, then, if it makes you uneasy?"

"It only bothers me when I really stop to think about it. Most of the time I stay busy. And it's not so different from any of the ocean liners or hotels I've worked in. Ships sink. Hotels burn. This is a bit more confined, perhaps. And there's not much in the way of fresh air. But the clientele is the same. The same demands on my time."

"I am quite impressed. You are the first woman ever to work aboard an airship. You should be quite proud." Gertrud winks when Emilie raises a questioning eyebrow. "I read the papers."

Emilie *is* proud. "First and only. So far, at least. I do forget that sometimes."

"You've worked on the *Hindenburg* the entire time?"

"Since it was completed. I am one of the original crew."

"Very altruistic of them, hiring a woman for their 'ship of dreams.'"

"No. Just shrewd. Easier to get wealthy men to book passage for their families if a woman is present to help bathe their children and dress their wives."

"I'd hope there isn't too much dressing involved."

Emilie laughs. "There is an occasional corset to be dealt with."

Gertrud draws on the end of her cigarette, then pinches it between two fingers so the lit end points directly at Emilie. "I won't wear them. I'm convinced those things are a form of subjugation. Only men care about hip-to-waist ratio."

She laughs. "I'd have to quit if it became part of my uniform requirements."

"You must have a rather impressive résumé to land such a position."

"I'm fairly sure it's the gaps in my file that interest them more."

"How so?"

"No husband. No children." She gives Gertrud a long, stoic glance. "No distractions."

There is kindness in the gaze that Gertrud returns but no pity, and Emilie is grateful. If there is one thing she cannot stand, it is being pitied. She may end up liking the journalist after all.

"Ah. I see." Gertrud shifts her gaze to the window and some distant point beyond. "I will be the first to admit that children do create something of a weak spot."

"How many do you have?"

"Just one. But he's more than enough to leave me feeling vulnerable on this flight. That's why I was so terrible to you yesterday, you see. We'd just left him behind."

"I'm sorry."

"It's not your fault."

Schulze pushes through the air-lock door carrying a tray filled with various paraphernalia. Two fine china cups and saucers. A silver carafe of steaming coffee. Spoons. Sugar cubes. A small jug of cream.

"I know you prefer your coffee black, Fräulein Imhof. But I thought Frau Adelt might like some coffee as well, and I wasn't sure how she takes it."

They thank him and Gertrud spends a few moments in silence preparing her drink. As it turns out Frau Adelt isn't quite so bold with her coffee as she seems to be in other areas of her life. Before long the journalist's coffee is the color of ivory and loaded with four cubes of sugar.

"I know," Gertrud says, "it's ungodly. Not to mention a little embarrassing. But I've always taken it this way. And from what I can gather, I may as well enjoy it while I can because the whispers have already begun. *Rationing*. Damn these men and their idiotic wars. I hate rationing."

Gertrud doesn't know the half of it. There are parts of Frankfurt where people can no longer buy milk, much less sugar. Coffee itself will soon be a luxury available only to the elite. The stewardess is reminded of this every time she indulges in this comfort.

Emilie's coffee is boiling and bitter and stings the roof of her mouth when she takes her first sip. It's like consuming motor oil right out of the car. She takes another sip. Sighs. She stretches her legs beneath the table—they are too long to cross. Then she makes a mental note to return to her cabin and brush her teeth before resuming her shift. Schulze was a bit enthusiastic when he measured out the coffee.

"I am curious about one thing," Gertrud says. She takes a sip and looks at Emilie over the rim of her cup. Her expression is too pleasant. Contrived.

"What's that?"

"Do you know all the crew members who work aboard this airship?"

Emilie is aware that there is a smooth tone to Gertrud's question. A change in intensity that hasn't been present until now. She's up to something.

"Many of them. Why?"

Gertrud pulls a military identification tag from her pocket and lays it faceup on the table. She scoots it toward Emilie with her finger. "Is there any way you can help me figure out who this belongs to?"

Emilie lifts the chain and dangles it from one finger. She studies the tag. "What makes you think this belongs to one of the crew?"

"Just a hunch."

It's a military identification tag from the First World War. About twenty years old. Emilie runs her finger over the raised letters and numbers on each side of the tag, paying careful attention to the service number: 100991–K-455(-)6(-)8. Emilie's father was in the Deutsches Heer during the First World War. He had a similar tag, and as a child she spent many hours curled on his lap playing with it. The first series of numbers represent a soldier's birth date. The letter is the first letter in his last name. Three numbers to identify his home district. One number to show how many soldiers serving at that time have the same last initial and the same birthday. And then an error-checking number. Germany never prints the name of a soldier on his tag. Never. Regardless, Emilie knows this tag belongs to Ludwig Knorr, chief rigger serving aboard the *Hindenburg*. There are four crew men on this ship whose last name starts with K. Two of them are too young to have been born on October 9, 1891, and the other has never been in the military. That leaves Ludwig.

"Where did you find this?" Emilie asks.

"I came upon it by accident."

"What do you intend to do with it?"

"That depends on who it belongs to. And what you can tell me about him."

Emilie is very careful to manipulate her expression into one of general curiosity without a hint of understanding. She lays the dog tag back on the table. "I have no idea who this belongs to," she says.

THE JOURNALIST

Gertrud knows that the stewardess is lying. Her pretty face is molded into an expression of bored indifference. As far as poker faces go, Emilie's is rather good. Lips closed but not pressed. No crease in the forehead. Hands folded around the coffee cup. Her gaze fixed at a point behind Gertrud's left ear as though she's lost in thought. The conversation evaporates, and each woman takes a moment to sip her coffee. To think. Gertrud taps her cigarette against the ashtray, then puts the Chesterfield to her mouth. They regard one another but do not speak. Gertrud has spent many years learning the art of quiet observation, however, and everyone has a tell. Everyone. It takes a few long seconds for her to find the evidence of Emilie's internal debate: a slow blink. Emilie is consciously delaying her physical movements.

Finally Gertrud asks, "Did you ever think of going into intelligence? You're an excellent liar."

A wry smile bends the corners of Emilie's mouth. She bows her head slightly as though to say *Touché*. "Intelligence? I've been assured, on more than one occasion, that women do not possess such a trait."

Gertrud snorts. "So have I. Though I'd wager that's part of why women make such damned good spies." She has known three, in fact, all of them alarmingly good. But she doesn't share this with the stewardess.

The ground has shifted a bit with Gertrud's challenge and Emilie's admission, so she's a bit less coy with her next response. "It has never made much sense to put my *deficiencies* to work for anyone other than myself."

"I can drink to that." Gertrud lifts her coffee cup in salute and they clink their cups together.

"The crew member who owns that tag. You know who he is."

Emilie gives a noncommittal shrug.

"I need to speak with him."

"Why?"

This is the trouble in Gertrud's line of work. It's rarely clear who she can confide in, and she usually has little time to make her decision. Lying tends to be the best course of action, followed by charm if she's dealing with the opposite sex. But neither of those options will work with Emilie. She's too shrewd. So Gertrud settles on evasion.

"I'm a journalist."

"And I'm a brunette," Emilie counters. The challenge is clear. Tell her something relevant. "Has he done something illegal?"

"Not that I'm aware of."

"Are you writing a story about him?"

"No."

"And yet you're very curious to know who he is?"

"Ridiculously so, yes."

Again, the challenge. "Why?"

Gertrud debates for a moment, then says, "This tag was lately in the possession of a man I do not like or trust."

"Did you steal it?"

"I found it. And I would wager a good deal that the man who had it would like to get it back. However, I'm not inclined to let that happen just yet. Nor am I inclined to let him locate the owner if that can be at all avoided. Which is why I need your help."

Emilie's blink slows again. Her hands grow still on the coffee cup. What is she holding back? Gertrud wonders. More than just a name. She knows this man. She wants to protect him.

"Are you going to return that tag to its owner?" Emilie asks.

Gertrud picks it up and cradles it in her palm. Returns it to her pocket. "Not just yet, if you don't mind."

"Why would I mind?"

"Because I'm a stranger. And a nosey one at that. Given the events of yesterday and our conversation just now, I've not proven myself to be the kindest or most ethical person. Though I would like the record to show that I've been honest. And I think that should count for something."

"I do believe you have been honest," Emilie says. "In the explicit details. Though I do wonder why you've come to me with this."

"Technically I was here first. So you came to me. But to answer your question, this airship is populated by men. A gender I distrust implicitly. I married the only man I've ever been truly fond of."

"As did I."

Gertrud glances at the stewardess's bare ring finger. She senses a story but chooses not to ask. "Then we have that in common, at least."

"You trust me simply because I'm a woman?"

"I am inclined to trust you *more* because of that, yes."

"You don't know women all that well, then."

Gertrud laughs at this. A deep, throaty laugh that draws a smile from the stewardess. "I didn't say I *like* women. I said I tend to trust them at a higher capacity."

The stewardess drains her cup and sets it lightly on the table. "My break is over."

"Emilie?"

"Yes?"

"Why won't you tell me who this tag belongs to?"

"You might be predisposed to trust other women but I am not."

THE NAVIGATOR

The bartender looks up when Max taps on the air-lock door.

"Max! Come in! What can I get for you?"

"I need a quick favor." There's little time left in his break and he needs to be as expedient as possible.

"Anything for you." Schulze secures the air-lock door behind them and gives Max an expectant look.

"What I'm going to ask you is technically against the rules." He sighs. He has been doing a lot of rule breaking on this voyage. "So now is your chance to pretend you didn't hear me. Or that I didn't ask. Whatever you prefer."

The bartender clucks his tongue. "I'm not so easily scared."

Max is committed now. He may as well continue. "I was in France a number of years ago on holiday. I stayed at an inn in a small town by myself. It rained the entire time and I was unspeakably miserable. The trip would have been a total loss if not for a certain kind of brandy produced in Gascony that I drank every evening by a roaring fire. I'm rather ashamed to say that I went through several bottles that week. And while drunkenness and gluttony are not vices I'd normally boast about, I do confess that I've never enjoyed any beverage more."

Schulze is a man of spirits, literally and metaphorically. He can be as moody as any woman, though he tends toward cheerfulness. But it is the spirit that comes corked and bottled that he knows best.

"Brandy, you say?"

"Armagnac, to be precise."

Schulze swirls his finger in the air and turns toward the mirrored shelves behind him. "I knew you were a man of fine taste. It's a fine liquor. Some would say mystical. Vital du Four once claimed that Armagnac has forty therapeutic virtues. I don't recall that healing the lovesick was among them. However, should you suffer from burning eyes, hepatitis, consumption, gout, canker sores, impotence"—he gives Max a skeptical glance at this—"or memory loss, it's certainly the drink for you."

"Would these mystical properties include helping a woman set aside lunacy and think straight?"

"Not even God could do such a thing," Schulze says. "As for myself, I simply prefer the taste, the warmth, and the feeling of invincibility after consuming a bottle." He shifts a few large decanters around on the shelf, then stretches up on his tiptoes. Max Schulze is not a tall man. After a moment he sets a lovely teardrop-shaped bottle on the counter. It is corked and sealed with wax. The liquid inside is the color of stained and polished cedar. "To be fair, the bottles are quite small."

"You have some." Max breathes a sigh of relief.

"The first thing you need to know about me is that I always have some of everything."

"Duly noted." He lifts the bottle. Gives Schulze a questioning glance.

"If you tell anyone I will swear you stole it."

"My lips are sealed." Max slides the bottle into a deep pocket of his trousers. "Might you have two glasses that I could borrow? I will return them first thing in the morning, of course."

Schulze sets a pair of crystal goblets on the counter. "I can respect a man of action."

They both turn at the tapping sound on the smoking room door. Emilie stands on the other side, staring daggers at Max, waiting to be let out.

The bartender is smart enough to say nothing. Schulze escorts Emilie through one air lock and then the other. Her chin is lifted, her unwavering gaze directed at the corridor. She does not speak to Max or look at him. Once she has departed, Schulze steps back behind the bar and laughs. "Good luck. You may need more than one bottle of Armagnac to win her over."

"Do you have more?"

"No."

When Max returns to his cabin, Balla is waiting for him.

"I may have solved your problem," the steward says.

His broad mouth is curved into an unfamiliar smile. The steward is pleased with himself. Max registers this first—it's so unusual to see the man smile—before he can actually make sense of what Balla has just said. Max hears the words, but from a distance. He simply wants to deposit the Armagnac and goblets in his cabin and finish his shift.

"I'm sorry. What was that?"

"Emilie."

"What now?"

"You want her to stay?"

"Of course I do.

"Let's just say it will be very difficult for Emilie to follow through with her plans if she is no longer in possession of her papers."

Max steps around Balla and unlocks his cabin door. He deposits the brandy and goblets next to the sink so he won't break them over the steward's head. He turns slowly. Fists clenched at his side. "What have you done?"

THE JOURNALIST

W ho else have you shown this tag to?" Leonhard asks. The chain lies wadded in the palm of his hand. He pokes it with his finger.

"Only the stewardess."

He is surprised at this. "Why?"

Gertrud thinks for a moment, looking for a way to explain. "There's something about her mind. She seems to remember everything. Names and places. Dates. Insignificant details. They say she's fluent in *seven* languages. Can you imagine?"

"I know exactly what this is," Leonhard says. "But I can't tell you what half of it means. Much less who it belongs to. Why would you think that she could?"

"It was a hunch. Not to mention damned good timing. She showed up in the bar while I was puzzling through it all. And I was right. I know I was. She just wouldn't tell me."

"Don't you think that was an unnecessary risk?"

"We have to do something, Leonhard. I don't know what that American is up to. But it can't be good." She closes his fist around the chain. "This man has to be warned."

"Who would you have me tell? We know nothing! Only the whisper of a threat."

"Tell Captain Lehmann. You're friends. He trusts you."

"We will not speak a word of this to him. Not now."

"So we just keep it to ourselves?"

"What exactly are we keeping, *Liebchen*? A rumor. My God, last I checked that was called discretion."

"What if something happens to the man who owns that tag?"

"So your plan is to run to the captain and babble about this like a crazed goose? You want to figure this out?" He shakes her by the shoulders a bit too roughly, then lays his palms gently on her arms, apologetic. "Yes? Then we use our *minds*, *Liebchen*.

That's our greatest weapon. We learn something useful. Then we speak."

"What about the bomb?"

"We don't know if there is a bomb! This ship has been picked over with a fine-tooth comb."

"But the threats—"

"There are *always* threats, *Liebchen*. They multiply like a venereal disease everywhere Hitler goes. We must learn to maneuver them if we are to survive."

A slow, constricting panic crawls up her throat and tightens around her vocal cords. Gertrud feels as though she can't breathe. She has assumed all this time that Leonhard isn't concerned. That he has simply been frustrated with her wild theories and tired of accommodating her fear of this trip. But she sees now that a deep concern has taken root. His eyes have grown tight. Dark. Leonhard pulls her into his chest. His shirt smells of books and pipe smoke and the faintest traces of his cologne. "We can figure this out."

"But can we do it in time?"

"I hope so."

"I hear the clock ticking, Leonhard."

"This isn't the first time we've worked on deadline. And," he tucks a curl behind her ear, "this time we don't have to mess with the writing itself. Just the investigation. I have always suspected that is your favorite part anyway."

She grins. "I do love *having* written."

"Don't we all."

Gertrud snorts. "Oh, don't lie. You're a purist. You don't struggle with the actual craft the way the rest of us do. You enjoy the construction. I just want the finished product."

He does smile at this. It's true after all. Leonhard very much enjoys the process of writing. In the years that she has known him, Gertrud has never once heard him complain while at work. He's happy to sit in his study and collect his thoughts on paper.

"I do like my job," he concedes.

Gertrud sniffs and raises up onto her toes to look him in the eye.

"Well, it would be easy for me too," she says, "if I had a wife to make my dinner and care for my son and press my trousers."

"You look terrible in trousers."

She smacks his shoulder.

"I look quite nice in trousers, thank you very much. All the men tell me so."

"The men are trying to get *in* your trousers, *Liebchen*, not encourage you to wear them more often."

"Just because you went about it that way . . ."

"As I recall, you were wearing a skirt, and all I had to do was lift it up, like this." Leonhard demonstrates his method and slides his hands along the smooth skin of her outer thigh.

"You are changing the subject."

He buries his face in her neck. "It's a much better subject."

"Really, I don't know what I'm going to do with you. One minute you're lecturing me, the next you're trying to seduce me. Aren't old men supposed to lose interest in sex?"

"I'm not an old man. And men never lose interest in sex."

"You're a great deal older than I am."

"And a good thing too. You wouldn't have been able to keep up with me when I was your age."

"Insatiable?"

"So I was told."

Leonhard has most of her clothing off at this point. "Well, I don't want to hear the sordid details. Nothing before my time, mind you."

"It was just practice, *Liebchen*."

"Ugh. You're not even sorry about it!"

"Well, I *was* married once before, you know."

"I don't want to hear about her either."

The only thing left on Gertrud's body at this point are her under-clothes, and Leonhard tries to dispatch those as well. She steps away from him. Sets her arms on her hips in protest. "We're late for drinks."

He sighs. Pulls a tailored red dress from the closet and hands it to her. "It's not wine I'm thirsty for."

Gertrud takes the dress from him, being careful to stay out of reach. They will never make it to the bar otherwise. "We have work to do."

THE NAVIGATOR

It's two o'clock on the dot, and Christian Nielsen steps into the chart room just as Max's concentration begins to waver. After so many years working aboard ocean liners, and now airships, he finds that his body works to the clock. He has trained himself to operate at an acute level of performance for the exact duration of his shift. But when the clock turns, his mind and body are only too happy to follow.

There are only a few details to make Nielsen aware of, and he goes through the list quickly. "Keep an eye on the engine telegraph dial for gondola two. I had to make an outboard repair this morning."

"You did? Why not Zettel?"

"Don't ask."

"All right. But—"

"We're still fighting strong headwinds," Max interrupts, "and it looks as though they will get stronger overnight. We haven't made up much time today. Less than an hour at most. I've been checking coordinates every fifteen minutes to make sure we stay on course." He taps the chart, drawing Nielsen's eye to the complex grid of lines, a language of longitude and latitude decipherable only to their kind. "If we're not here by midnight"—he points at a specific point on the grid and lowers his voice to a whisper—"I'd suggest you increase that to every ten minutes. Pruss is feeling ... *hostile* at the moment."

Nielsen looks through the door at the rigid form of Commander Pruss, who stands over the elevator man, questioning every small adjustment. The young man looks frayed with the effort of not arguing with Pruss.

"Good luck." Max hands over the logbook and clears his belongings from the navigation desk. Watch. Compass. Pen. He fastens the watch around his wrist and tucks the other items in his pocket. Max goes through his mental checklist: sign out of the logbook, make sure the officers' safe beneath the chart table is locked, verify that all of the navigational instruments are operating correctly.

Nielsen has worked aboard the *Graf Zeppelin*, and he survived a spectacular wrecking of the sailboat *Pinnas*. Yet Max still has to prepare himself to hand over command of his post every night. Nielsen is thorough, attentive, and cautious. Traits every navigator is recruited for. But this small space is Max's territory. His kingdom. And relinquishing control is a battle, especially since he was not able to fully correct the delay. But he has other things to attend to at the moment. He must perform his postmaster duties and he must find Emilie. He has to warn her about what Wilhelm Balla has done.

THE AMERICAN

The American has never been a fan of beef Wellington. It's a meal that tries too hard, not to mention being damned hard to get right. The *Hindenburg*'s chef is clearly adept, for the dish is cooked perfectly. Still the American is unimpressed. He would have preferred a steak and roasted potatoes. A stout beer. A cigar. And if there weren't such a dearth of women in the immediate vicinity, perhaps one of those as well.

"Are you not enjoying your meal, Herr Douglas?" Captain Lehmann asks.

The American slices off a piece of the tenderloin and places it in his mouth, chewing slowly as if savoring it. "It is easily the best beef Wellington I've ever tasted."

"I'm glad to hear it."

National pride can extend to so many bizarre things. Now

that the *Hindenburg* has become irrevocably linked to the Third Reich it seems that serving any meal that falls short would mar the Führer's reputation.

The American and Captain Lehmann have one of the smaller tables to themselves. Tonight's flower is a dahlia the size of a soup bowl. A profusion of orange petals at the end of a long, thick stem. It's quite lovely. But the American can't fathom where they came by such a flower at this time of year. The tables are impeccable. Bright linens. Fine china. Shining silver. The tenderloin is soft enough to cut with a spoon, but the stewards have provided steak knives anyway. The American wonders at his chances of sneaking one into his suit pocket. Perhaps it isn't necessary, but it might come in handy. All is going according to plan so far, but he learned long ago that things can go pear-shaped at any moment. It's always good to be prepared. And armed. He thinks better of pocketing the knife when he notices the smallest Doehner boy watching him from the next table. He relaxes his hand, drawing it away from the knife. No point giving the little rascal any ideas. He will wait for a better opportunity. Hermann and Matilde Doehner are talking in the quiet, lazy drawl common to exhausted parents. Their children chatter and pepper them with questions while they hem and haw, offering noncommittal answers.

"I was surprised to get your invitation," the American says, switching to English so as not to be overheard by his neighbors.

Lehmann adjusts his language to accommodate him with only the slightest sign of irritation. "How so?"

"I fear I did not make a favorable impression on Commander Pruss last night." He pushes the haricots verts to the edge of his plate. Spears one. Eats it without much enthusiasm. It tastes like a plant. Nothing more.

"He did mention your peculiar theories."

"I'm not the only person who holds them."

"Perhaps not. But popularity and truth are not mutually exclusive."

"You don't seem concerned that Pruss and I didn't manage to become friends."

The steward sets a rich German red on the table beside Lehmann. Typical. Lehmann lifts the wineglass. Takes a sip. Nods in appreciation. "I can count on one hand the number of people Commander Pruss calls friend."

"Are you among them?"

"We have mutual goals. That can constitute a friendship."

"Do those goals include protecting this airship and its passengers?"

"Of course."

"I'm very glad to hear it." The American lifts his own wineglass, containing a French white.

Lehmann leans across the table. Lowers his voice. "Is there something I need to know?"

"That depends on how you feel about reciprocation."

"I don't like games, Herr Douglas."

"Neither do I. My preference lies with information."

"What kind of information?"

"A name. Nothing more."

"And you propose an *exchange* of information?"

"I do. A name for a name."

Lehmann pulls away and settles back into his chair. He has the smug look of superiority about him. "What sort of name could you possibly give me that would be of interest?"

The American forces down another bite of beef Wellington, then pushes his plate away. He sets his napkin over the knife, then dabs the corner of his mouth with the bright linen and deftly sets both napkin and knife in his lap. "The name of your crew member who is planning to remain in America."

THE NAVIGATOR

As usual there is only a handful of men in the officers' mess at this hour. Captain Lehmann dines with the other passengers—

never here—then retreats to the bar. This has been his habit on every trip that Max has ever flown with him, whether the captain is on duty or not. So it comes as something of a surprise to see Lehmann enter the room. He leans against the door, arms crossed, chin tipped upward as he listens to the ongoing conversation. The officers are discussing the curious sport of American baseball, and the general consensus seems to be one of indifference and confusion.

"Good evening, Captain." Max salutes. The other officers scramble to do the same.

Lehmann returns the salute and then motions Max forward. "May I have a word with you?"

"Of course," Max says, but he hopes this won't take long. He's hungry. And exhausted. And mostly he wants to deposit today's mail, find Emilie, and retreat to his cabin so they can enjoy the bottle of Armagnac he pilfered from the bar this afternoon. Max spent the better part of the afternoon trying to speak with Emilie, but she avoided him—either leaving the room entirely or ignoring his presence. To get her alone would have required making a scene, and that certainly wouldn't help his cause. In the end their duties drew them apart and he hasn't found another opportunity to make amends.

"After you." Lehmann follows Max from the officers' mess.

Once in the corridor the captain takes off without an explanation, and Max has to increase his pace to match Lehmann's long stride.

"May I ask what this is about?"

"You'll see."

They go straight down the keel corridor, through the passenger quarters, and into the short hallway that houses the domestic crew: cooks, stewards, cabin boy, and bartender. Lehmann stops at the last door on the left and Max pulls back in alarm. Emilie's cabin. Lehmann doesn't knock but rather pulls a key ring from his pocket, unlocks the door, and steps in without announcement or invitation.

"I don't think—"

"I assure you that Fräulein Imhof is not here."

"Still—"

"I am the captain of this ship. This is an official matter. And I need your assistance. Must I ask you again?"

Lehmann is an observer on this flight, so whatever is happening now should be Commander Pruss's responsibility, but Max does not point this out. He swallows hard instead. "No."

"Then by all means, come in."

Emilie has left the room tidy. All of her clothing hangs in the small closet, and only a few personal items are visible. Her toothbrush. A damp washcloth left over the sink edge to dry. A pair of shoes—one of them tipped onto its side—beneath the bed. A comb. Three bobby pins. The room smells of her perfume.

Lehmann closes the door behind them and holds his hands behind his back in an official military gesture. He watches Max but says nothing for a moment.

"What are we doing here?"

"I thought you might like to tell me that."

No. No. No. It takes him a moment to realize that he is shaking his head. Max has to force his body to slow and then stop the movement. "I must confess to a certain amount of confusion," he says.

It's a lie, of course. He knows perfectly well what is happening. Wilhelm told him this afternoon. And to his great shame he wasn't able to warn Emilie in time. Max certainly didn't plan on being a witness to the fallout. And he didn't think it would happen today.

Lehmann sighs. It's an abrupt, disappointed sound. As though he expected better of Max. He looks at the ceiling for a moment, appealing to a higher power for help. But his gaze, when he finally levels it on Max, is cold and shrewd and unforgiving. "I would like you to tell me where you found Fräulein Imhof's papers last night."

"I don't—"

"Yes you do. And I realize that you are rather fond of the girl. But lying is not advisable in this situation."

The door vibrates with a quiet knock. *"Bitte treten Sie ein!"* Lehmann says without looking away from Max.

Wilhelm Balla enters the room looking abashed. He closes the door behind him.

Lehmann waves off the accusation that is building at the base of Max's throat. "Don't worry. Your friend didn't tell me. And I've no interest in listening to him explain to you who he did tell. Or how that knowledge came to me. What I care about at this particular moment is that the two of you knew before I did. There were three links in the chain before it reached me, and I find that . . . disturbing. One of my crew plans to violate her contract and I am the last to know? Do you know what that makes me, *Herren*? A fool. And I'm sure you can guess how much I like being made to look a fool."

Balla has not looked at Max once since he set foot in Emilie's cabin. His gaze shifts between his feet, the doorknob, the cleft in Captain Lehmann's chin, and the wall behind Max's shoulder. He does not speak during this monologue or comment when it's over.

"I asked Herr Balla to join us as a simple means of coercion. Unfair, perhaps. But likely quite effective. I will call him to speak as witness if I find you to be uncooperative, but I'm hoping that will not be necessary. So"—Captain Lehmann smiles, but there's no friendliness in the expression—"I will repeat my earlier question. Would you please show me where you found the documents indicating that Fräulein Imhof plans to leave?"

"Immigrate." The word comes out as a croak. "She intends to immigrate, Captain."

"I see you have discussed this to some degree with her. But she has either misled you as to the legality of her actions or she is ignorant of them—which I highly doubt. She is many things, but ignorant is not one of them. We would not have commissioned her service had that been the case. She is not immigrating. She is leaving."

Max doesn't care about the semantics. Immigrating. Leaving. They both mean the same damn thing. Emilie is leaving him. There's no need to force Lehmann to ask his question a third time, or to involve Balla any further—he will deal with the steward later. So Max takes a single step across the narrow cabin and opens the closet door. "Here," he says, pointing to the pile of neatly folded underclothes at the bottom of the closet. "I found the papers here."

Lehmann leans a few degrees to the left but doesn't touch anything. "It seems they have been moved."

Max does not answer the obvious, unspoken question.

"It is a guess, though I believe it to be accurate, that you are somewhat acquainted with Fräulein Imhof's personal belongings?"

"I would have to argue that."

"You have touched them on at least one occasion?"

"A few of them. Perhaps."

"Then you have a greater familiarity with them than I do. So I will leave it to you to find the papers."

"That is unfair. And uncalled for. If you need to find something, I suggest you summon Emilie."

"You forget yourself, Herr Zabel. Male and female crew members do not address one another by their first names on this airship."

Max does not apologize.

"I will reprimand Fräulein Imhof soon enough. Right now I am commanding you to locate her papers. And I assure you that I am doing this as a courtesy because I know you care for her. And that you will respect her privacy in ways that other men perhaps might not. I can call another officer to conduct the search or you can do it yourself."

Captain Lehmann offers no time limits, no room for argument. Take it or leave it.

Max begins in the closet. He lifts the items carefully, sliding his hands in folds and pockets, finding nothing. The top bunk and the suitcase beneath the bottom berth similarly yield no trace of the documents. He makes careful work of the job as Lehmann and Balla watch. He wants to make sure that they cannot argue about his thoroughness. But soon there is nothing left unsearched in the room except for Emilie's cosmetic case. And searching it seems the greatest violation of her privacy so far. There are things in this case that Max cannot name or describe. Items that he does not know the use for. It has her scent, though, and as he lifts the objects out, one by one, his senses are filled with her. He feels very much as though he is stripping her naked and allowing her to be ogled by strangers. When the case is empty, and the items are piled on the bed, he turns it over and shakes it three times.

Perhaps she didn't place the hidden panel back in firmly, or maybe the movement knocks the panel loose. Regardless, the thin, stiff board falls out, followed by her travel documents and the cash she has saved. Max sees the note he scribbled on the envelope and turns away.

For the first time since entering the room Lehmann touches her effects. He gives the papers a cursory look, just long enough to verify what they are. He reads the message but does not count the money. He simply stacks everything in a pile and holds it in his palm as though balancing a tray.

"You may go, Herr Balla," he says, waving one hand at the steward dismissively.

Balla obeys, quickly and silently.

"Will that be all, Captain?" The tone of Max's question is blunt and angry, bordering on disrespect.

"Almost. If you would follow me, Commander Pruss would like to have a quick word with you as well. Then you are free to go." Lehmann hands him Emilie's papers. "Hold these."

Max is struggling to fit them neatly in the crook of his arm when Lehmann pushes open the door to the officers' mess and reveals Emilie sitting at the plush banquette with Commander Pruss. When she lifts her face he can see that she has been crying. Her gaze settles on what he holds in his arm and a look of acute betrayal sweeps across those light, rust-colored eyes.

THE STEWARDESS

Emilie does not taste her dinner. She would be hard-pressed to say what it is, exactly, that she's eating. She simply cuts and eats and then repeats the process, all the while trying not to stare at Ludwig Knorr, who is seated at the table beside her in the crew's mess. As a rigger, his primary duties include takeoff and landing. Mooring lines and such. Although he's frequently called on to make in-flight repairs all over the ship. He's quite well liked among the crew and thanks to a spectacular midair fix he accomplished on the *Graf Zeppelin* a decade ago he has become a legend among the shipmen. He is revered. Respected. She cannot think of any reason why Gertrud Adelt—or anyone else for that matter—would consider him a threat. Physically he's not much to look at. Middle-aged. Nondescript except for a long, thin mouth that looks bovine when he isn't speaking.

"Can I help you, Fräulein Imhof?"

It takes her a moment to realize that Knorr has spoken to her. He has caught her staring. "Oh. I'm sorry," she says. "Forgive me. I was just thinking."

"It must be a weighty thought to cause such a frown."

A beat and then she says, "I was thinking about my father." The falsehood comes so quickly she is startled. "He died fifteen years ago today." Another lie, God help her.

"I am sorry for your loss."

Well, hell. She's committed now. She may as well follow through. "Thank you. But we lost him long before he died. He was never the same after the war."

Something of a shadow passes over Knorr's face. "It was a terrible time. Many men came home empty."

Emilie tilts her head to the side. It's a gesture intended to show interest, to put him at ease. "You served? How?"

"Flying on the zeppelins mostly. Air raids over England."

The raids were legendary and the casualties—both military and civilian—were numerous. It is a thing about which many men of his generation feel both pride and shame. Her father rarely talked about his time in the Luftwaffe. Emilie isn't sure whether to thank Knorr for his service or apologize. It's a difficult thing, this. Emilie would like to pepper him with more questions, but Commander

Pruss walks into the crew's mess and Knorr jumps to his feet with a salute.

"As you were," Pruss says, scanning the small room. "Ah. Fräulein Imhof. There you are. May I have a word?"

This sort of thing happens occasionally—some delicate matter is confided to the commander and he finds the most discreet steward to deal with it. She'd been in such a position once or twice before and has proved herself quite capable. She likes to think that Commander Pruss regards her highly. So it isn't until he leads her into the officers' mess, seats her in the corner, and asks if she is comfortable that Emilie begins to realize what is happening. They make small talk as they wait and slowly, steadily her heart begins to beat faster. Her eyes burn and fill and she blinks rapidly.

And then Captain Lehmann walks through the door followed by Max.

Lehmann looks at her calmly. "We have an issue, Fräulein."

"Yes," she says, "I can see that."

Her voice is emotionless. Distant. It's the same voice she has used many times in the years since Hans died. It's the voice she calls upon when people ask how she's doing or if she's ready to begin seeing other men. *I'm doing fine,* or, *Not just yet, thank you.* It is the voice of evasion, of self-protection. Disinterest. Yet she is stunned at the pain she's able to hide behind this calm exterior, as though a knife has slid cleanly between her shoulder blades.

Et tu, Brute? The line, so famous, so applicable, flashes across her mind. Max stands in the doorway, his hands filled with her most private, most precious belongings, and she cannot bring herself to look at him. Emilie studies the points of his shirt collar. She is afraid to see an expression of triumph on his face. Of superiority. Even worse, she fears the pity she knows she will find there. She will take anything from Max but pity.

Commander Pruss motions them into the room. "Fräulein Imhof has been keeping me company for the last few minutes. I've been quite interested to hear of her experience on our airship so far. A little over a year, correct?"

"That's right."

"And to think I was rather under the impression that you enjoyed being part of this crew."

"I do," she says.

"And yet we have this." Pruss lifts the papers and the envelope from Max's stiff hands and sets them on the table before her. "Herr Zabel was kind enough to collect them for us."

A sound escapes Max's throat. Something like a mewl. Emilie does not acknowledge it.

"Yes. I'm sure he was," she says.

Commander Pruss begins looking through the documents. "Is there anything you would like to explain?"

"Forgive me, I mean no disrespect, but I doubt explanations would do much good. The papers speak for themselves."

"See," Captain Lehmann says, looking at Max, "I told you she was not ignorant."

"You plan to leave Germany?" Pruss asks.

"I did." She offers him a small shrug and a resigned smile. "I very much doubt that I will be allowed to do so now."

"That would be correct. Though I must inquire as to why you would feel such a compulsion to begin with."

"May I speak frankly?"

"Certainly."

"I have no desire to live through a war. Or to die in one."

Lehmann laughs. "Have you received word of an invasion? I certainly have not."

"I have eyes. And ears."

Emilie can feel Max's gaze burning, probing her face. She will not give him the satisfaction of meeting it.

"What is to be done about this?" Lehmann asks.

"I would assume that I am to be dismissed from my duties, Captain?"

"That would be the obvious answer," he says, "though not the correct one."

She did not expect this. "I can keep my job?"

"It's rather a matter of you *having* to keep your position. We have made something of a fuss over you in the press. Your sudden departure, regardless of the reason, would make the Zeppelin-Reederei look quite inept. So you will keep your position and you will be *delighted* to do so."

This is too easy. She is frightened by the simplicity of the solution. "And when we are not flying? What then?"

There is a note of admiration in Captain Lehmann's voice when he says, "Ah. Not even the slightest bit ignorant." He chooses his next words carefully. "That has yet to be determined. There are others who must be consulted before we will know the answer to that question. I expect there will be discussions when we return to Frankfurt."

There is no need to give her any further warnings. She has no means of escape. "You are dismissed," Commander Pruss says. "I trust you will return to your duties in the morning in a timely fashion."

"Of course," she says, rising from the table. She makes sure her legs are stable before stepping toward the door. *"Guten Abend."*

Max reaches out a hand as she passes him, but she drops her shoulder, evading the touch.

"Emilie." His voice cracks with emotion.

She does not speak to him. She does not look at him. Emilie leaves the officers' mess without ever having once acknowledged his presence. And as far as she is concerned she will never do so again.

DAY THREE

Tomorrow's arrival will be the first of eighteen this summer. Slight interest in the *Hindenburg* is being shown by persons other than naval officers. Arrival and departure of the world's largest lighter-than-air craft on schedule is now taken here as a matter of course.

— *Newspaper report on May 5, 1937*

In all the time that Werner has worked aboard the *Hindenburg* he has never once been late for his shift. He sets an alarm every night but rarely needs it, usually waking on his own minutes before it goes off. This morning is different, however. He jolts awake when his covers are thrown back.

Werner thrashes into a sitting position and looks at the darkened shape of Wilhelm Balla. "What's going on? Am I late? Kubis will kill me!"

He slides off the edge and lands on his feet with a small stagger. The blow that rattles the side of his head knocks him backward even farther. It takes Werner nearly five seconds in his exhausted stupor to realize that Balla has boxed his ear.

"Why did you do that!"

"Be *quiet*."

"But I'm late!"

"You're not late."

"What time is it?"

"Four-twenty."

There are no windows in their cabin—neither of them has the rank for such a luxury—and no lights are on. There's only a lucent strip of illumination leaking beneath the door from the corridor outside. Werner can see dark shapes against darker shadows but no specific details, so the expression on Balla's face is lost to him. He tries to concentrate on the subtext in Balla's voice. Tries to figure out whatever he's missed, the reason he has been yanked out of bed in the middle of the night. He is *tired* of being yanked out of bed in the middle of the night. There is a very short connection between exhaustion and rage for the boy and Werner feels it shuddering now.

"I already shined the shoes."

"I don't care about the shoes."

Werner's anger ignites and he feels the heat behind his eyes. He's glad Balla can't see them in the dark room. "Then why did you pull me out of bed!"

"Hush. Or I will box you again. You like Max Zabel, yes?"

"Of course"—a moment of silent confusion and then—"he's my friend."

"You need to go roust him out of bed and get him to the shower before he loses his job."

Werner's body is alert but his mind is still groggy. "I don't understand."

"Herr Zabel had a terrible evening and decided to console himself with a bottle of very expensive French brandy. I would guess that he is probably unconscious at the moment. He will likely remain in that condition for a good long while unless someone intervenes. This is a problem considering his shift starts in less than two hours and he has a great deal of sobering up to do. So given the circumstances and his current lack of goodwill toward me, it would be best if that someone were you."

Werner looks at Balla's dim shape with the lethargic stare of a child who is trying, and failing, to comprehend. Balla shakes him again. "Do you understand what I've just said?" There is a guilty note to the steward's voice that Werner doesn't understand.

"Yes."

"Prove it."

"Max is drunk and can't wake up. He'll lose his job if he misses his shift."

"Good. Now get dressed. And go wake him up."

"Am I allowed to turn on the light?"

"If you must."

The bulb flashes over them, and Werner buries his face in the crook of his arm so his eyes will have a moment to adjust to the glare. He looks up when he is certain he can do so without squinting.

As Balla bends over the cabin boy in the dim light, Werner thinks he looks much like a stick figure that has been broken in half. "Max will need a shower," Balla says. "You might have to drag him there, and it's best that no one see or hear you. Coffee will make him alert and water will force the alcohol out of his system. Make sure he gets large quantities of both." The steward sets large, pale, frog-like hands on Werner's shoulders and gives him a small shake. "Can you do this?"

"Yes."

Balla shoves something hard and cold into the palm of Werner's hand. "Good. Take this. It's a master cabin key and will get you into Max's room. You will use it this one time only. And you will bring it back to me when your task is done. Understood?"

Again the boy says, "Yes." It's an easy, uncomplicated word, and he doesn't have to summon any energy to find it at this early hour. Werner is certain he has missed something important, namely why this is his responsibility, but he can't order his thoughts well enough to ask the proper questions. So he does the only thing he knows how to do in these kinds of situations. He begins to move. And once he has begun the well-established routine of getting ready for work, muscle memory takes over. He brushes his teeth and combs his hair without thinking, then pulls on his uniform and buttons the steward's jacket. He tucks his flashlight into his belt and straightens his collar.

Wilhelm Balla is snoring in the lower berth before Werner turns off the light and slips out the door, shutting it quietly behind him. The keel corridor is lit by industrial yellow lights at even intervals along the walls and he rushes past them, then beyond the stairs that lead to A-deck. He slows at this point, quieting his footfalls so as not to wake any of the other crew members. He silently passes the radio room—he can hear voices and static within—and then into the short hallway beyond that houses the officers' quarters. Once he has come to a stop in the middle of the corridor, Werner realizes that he does not know which room belongs to Max. Balla never told him. Werner stands in the middle of the hallway, hands on his hips, eyes narrowed, and looks at each door in turn. Being the younger brother is a boon in this particular situation. He has grown accustomed to observation. Max is a junior officer, one of four navigators aboard this ship, so he wouldn't be at the end. Those cabins are reserved for Commander Pruss and Captain Lehmann. So Werner works his way backward, eliminating one cabin at a time as he does a head count of the officers in order of their rank. This leaves him with two cabins, one on either side, farthest from the nose of the ship. Right or left? he wonders. He can't very well go knocking to find out. So Werner does what any inquisitive boy would do: he listens at the door. It takes less than a minute for him to decide on the door to the right. The snores coming from within sound like gravel rolling around a bucket. He turns the knob and finds it locked just as Balla suspected it would be. Werner fingers the key in his pocket but doesn't pull it out until he's certain that all the rooms are quiet and the officers are still asleep within. Because it occurs to him only now that he has been a tremendous fool. He has finally woken up enough to make sense of this situation and to understand the gravity. Getting caught sneaking into an officer's cabin is enough to get him fired if not jailed. And Balla must have known this or he would have performed the task himself. Werner curses his own stupidity.

But he likes Max and feels beholden to him, so he slides the key into the lock and turns it slowly, listening as the tumblers connect with a sharp metallic click. Werner turns the knob and pushes the door inward without a sound. He immediately knows he has found the right cabin by the smell. He claps a hand over his nose and takes a step back.

For two years Werner's brother has apprenticed at the Hof Hotel in Frankfurt as a waiter. The stories that Günter has brought home are equal parts hilarious and informative. High-maintenance diners. Aristocrats. Travelers. Gestapo. Americans—those stories are always the best. But what Werner enjoys the most about Günter's adventures are the impersonations, usually of drunk men. There are fewer of drunk women—whether because that gender is naturally more restrained or is better at holding their liquor, Werner isn't sure. Regardless, his brother staggers around the living room, alternately shouting and mumbling and causing the rest of the family to collapse in hysterics. He tells Werner what the patrons have been drinking and how it makes them act. He has also told a good many stories about how excess booze makes a man smell. And, to tell the truth, Werner has always thought that Günter was embellishing his stories for dramatic effect. Until now. Max Zabel smells like he's been dragged through a swamp, then left to marinate in a rum barrel filled with donkey sweat. Unpleasant does not begin to describe it.

Werner readies himself to begin the task and steps into the room. He shuts the door gently behind him and gets to work. Werner sets the flashlight on the small dressing table and points the beam toward the ceiling. A soft, warm light fills the room, but Max doesn't notice. He's lying facedown on the bunk, spread eagle, still wearing his uniform, with one arm draped over the side. An empty bottle lies on the floor beneath his hand. Werner can see that Max has drooled on the pillow and sweated through his jacket. Now, to wake him without causing a ruckus.

Werner is quite familiar with officers' uniforms at this point in his job and finds all the necessary items of clothing in the small closet beside the sink. Trousers. Shoes. Shirt and jacket and cap. He sets them in a tidy pile on top of the counter and turns back to the navigator. Werner doesn't think Max's underwear is any of his business, but the navigator can't very well go without it, so the boy digs around in a canvas bag at the bottom of the closet until he finds a pair, along with socks, then adds them to the pile.

"Wake up, Max." Werner puts a hand to the navigator's shoulder and shakes him but gets no response. Another shake, much rougher than the first. "Max. Please."

Nothing.

Werner can think of a dozen scenarios he anticipated prior to his first flight. There are so many things that can go wrong on an airship after all. But it never occurred to him that he would find himself in this position. Max looks to be similar in size to Werner's father, and this gives the boy an idea. Ever since his father fell sick, Werner has taken on much of his care. Including getting him to the bathroom. Thankfully his assistance isn't needed once the door is closed, but Werner does have some idea how to get a grown man to his feet. Max will need to be awake first, however. The answer is simple enough, though the navigator will find it highly unpleasant.

Werner fills the brandy bottle with water from the sink and then leans over Max's prone form. He makes sure that most of his body is out of arms' reach should Max strike out, but there's only so much he can do. He tips the bottle over and controls the flow of water so that a thin stream dribbles into Max's ear. It takes a few seconds before the nuisance registers. First Max's head jerks to the side. Werner increases the flow. Max turns his head over completely and exposes his other ear. He mumbles something crass in his sleep. Werner pours the water again, drenching Max's ear and the pillow. And now the best part—the part that Werner has always enjoyed most when he plays this trick on Günter—Max slaps himself. A hard, wet smack against his cheek. Water splats around the berth as Max jerks into a sitting position. Werner can't help but laugh.

The cabin boy isn't sure if he would describe what comes out of Max's mouth as speech exactly, more like a bastard language resembling illiterate German and stuttering laced with profanity. Werner backs away the moment he suspects Max is in control of his limbs. He speaks very quietly.

"You need to wake up, Herr Zabel."

"What?"

"It's Werner and it's really important that you wake up. Right now."

Max follows the sound of the boy's voice, but it's clear that he doesn't see Werner. His eyes are swollen and clenched tight.

"You woke me up."

"I'm trying to, yes."

Max lowers himself onto one elbow and pulls his feet back into the bed. He has every appearance of a man intent on going back to sleep.

"I can't let you do that," Werner says, and throws the bottle at Max.

It glances off the navigator's forehead but has the desired effect of bringing him into a more heightened state of awareness. Rage, to be precise.

"What the *hell* was that?" He's trying to yell but his throat is too hoarse, so the sound comes out like a gurgle.

"A brandy bottle, I believe."

"You hit me?"

"You tried to go back to sleep."

"Wouldn't you?"

"Not if I wanted to keep my job. Which I do. As should you. So it would be really nice if you could stand up so I can help you to the shower."

Werner has always known Max to be shrewd and intelligent and fiercely clever. So it's no surprise that a small light goes off in his mind. It's not enough to register the severity of the situation, but it's a move in the right direction. Max slaps his wrist, looking for his watch. "What time is it?"

"Almost five."

Max slumps at the news, relaxed. "So I'm not late for my shift?"

"Not yet. But you can't go in looking like that. Shower. Coffee. Water. That's what I was told you needed. And in that order."

"Who told you that?"

"Wilhelm Balla."

Werner has never heard such creative insults as what comes out of Max's mouth at the sound of Balla's name.

"Will you let me help you up? I can't drag you all the way to the shower."

Max considers this. Tries to stand. Wobbles badly. "I suppose so," he says.

It's something of a vaudeville act the way that Werner gathers the clothes and flashlight with one hand while keeping his friend vertical with the other, and even more impressive that he is able to get Max out the door and down the hall without falling over. If he'd not had so much practice with his father he would never have been able to pull it off. As it is, however, they barely make it to the shower without toppling over one another or crashing through one of the thin foam board walls.

"In you go," Werner says, with Max draped over his shoulder as if he were a crutch. He gets the navigator situated as upright as possible beneath the shower nozzle, sets the clean clothes in a pile on the other side of the curtain, and turns the water on.

Max yelps and curses and stumbles backwards. The wall stops him from going ass over teakettle, but he swats at his face like a man being attacked by a swarm of bees. He tries to swipe the water out of his eyes but only succeeds in hitting himself.

"The rest is up to you," Werner says. "Your clothes are here and I'll be back in ten minutes. You might want to drink some of that water while you're standing there."

THE AMERICAN

The dog tag is missing. This realization is not new. He first discovered it was gone while at dinner last night with Captain Lehmann. The American had slipped his hand into his pocket, intending to pull it out with dramatic flair and set it on the table. He didn't bother digging around. He could feel that it was gone. So he'd taken a sip of wine instead and allowed his mind the few seconds necessary to find a different course of action. He had given Lehmann the stewardess's name as a boon, an act of good faith. Emilie Imhof. He'd spoken it with all the confidence of an informant, making it seem less like blackmail and more like charity by going first. So magnanimous of him. And in return? Well, his reward would come today. Lehmann had been skeptical, of course, and he wanted to test the American's claim.

The tag is small. And the information engraved on it long since memorized. The American had simply requested pen and paper from Wilhelm Balla—it appears as though he's stuck with the steward for the duration of the flight—then written the information down for Lehmann. He didn't expect the captain to have a memory like his. Lehmann told him it will take a bit of time to collect the data. But he doesn't mind waiting a few hours. It's a reasonable sacrifice so long as he can move closer to his goal. The American's real problem, and the thing that has kept him up half the night, is that the dog tag has fallen into the hands of a stranger. This is an unforgivable error on his part. Not just a miscalculation. A catastrophic mistake. The worst kind of misfortune.

Because the chance to kill the owner of that dog tag is the only reason he agreed to this mission. And he would sooner throw himself out the access hatch, onto the engine rotors, than miss it. But someone has his bartering piece. And if that someone is smart enough to figure out the owner's identity and warn him, then many years of carefully planned revenge will be lost. And that is a scenario that the American simply cannot accept.

He's on his feet pacing now, but he restrains the urge to kick the walls in frustration. The dog tag had been in his pocket at this time yesterday. He'd put it there in the morning, the cool weight of it seeping through his satin pocket liner into his skin, its bulk a necessary irritation. He had heard the small, metallic ping when he dropped his trousers onto the tile floor of the shower.

The American is still wearing yesterday's clothes. He had thrown himself onto the berth fully dressed and lay there most of the night, fits of restless sleep enveloping him as he chased his thoughts in circles, like a mangy dog chewing its own tail. Fretting. Plotting. And the answer only comes to him now because exhaustion has filled the small wells inside his mind, poured itself into the hollows of his bones.

He lost the dog tag in the shower. Of course. Yes. An amateur mistake but there you have it.

He kicks his shoes off and lies back down on the bed. He crosses his hands over his chest and closes his eyes as though mimicking a corpse. The American sees it clearly now in this dream-like state as his limbs relax into the mattress.

He had shaken out his trousers before folding them. Years and years of military training had instilled this habit in him. He never wads his clothes into a ball and throws them in the hamper. He straightens and folds them along their crease lines instead. He sets them in orderly stacks and sends them to the cleaners.

The dog tag could still be in the shower, one part of his brain offers. This voice is the hopeful one, the one he has tried to systematically stomp to death over many years. He listens to it on rare occasions, but this is not one of them. No. The American is certain the dog tag was found. His job is to figure out by whom.

The art of extracting his own memories is something he learned from military interrogators. It was part of his training, albeit small, when they determined his particular gifts would be better used in other areas. His real job—not the one he performs for the advertising agency in Frankfurt—is to have conversations and repeat them to his handlers. He strikes up conversations and asks the right questions to the right people at the right moments. He finds his targets when they are unguarded. When they feel safe. In a bar or on a train or in a department store. He learns their secrets but almost never by force. His betrayals are acute and painful and personal. It's a morally ambiguous career, to be sure, and not one that comes without consequence. But he is two decades in and has long since learned to justify the means and the ends and everything in between. He is not sorry for what he has done or what he is about to do. *Usually it's nothing personal,* he thinks; this is what it takes to save the world.

So the American rewinds his brain and goes back over the day before. He begins in the shower, with that last moment that he had the dog tag, and he creates a mental marker of that moment when he shook out his trousers. He moves forward, one frame at a time, to everything that happened after that. Sneaking back to the cargo area. Watching the navigator and the cabin boy exit the ship. No. There's nothing significant there, so he continues on. Paying the cabin boy to care for the dog. Breakfast. Watching Leonhard Adelt. His mind skitters a bit so he slows and carefully goes through his little monologue before the passengers. Gertrud Adelt entering the dining room. And there, like a flashbulb, he has it: damp curls hanging heavy against her chin. Pink skin warmed by the shower.

Gertrud Adelt was in the shower yesterday morning. Gertrud Adelt has the tag. This certainty comes to him at the exact moment that his mind officially surrenders to sleep. And because it is both a conscious thought and a dream it is tattooed into his memory. It will be his first thought upon waking.

THE NAVIGATOR

Max is almost certain that he has dressed himself correctly. There's a bit of chafing in a couple of areas, but he doesn't see any obvious tags or seams. He checks his collar and runs his fingers down the front of his shirt, counting buttons, making sure everything is lined up correctly. Tying his shoes is problematic. Not because his fingers aren't working properly but because bending over makes him want to die. And dreams vomit. And then drive an ice pick through his eye and out the back of his own skull. All of which would be counterproductive given his current situation. So in the end he has to lean against the wall and lift his foot as high as he can without falling over.

This is demoralizing, he thinks. Nothing so easily renders a man helpless as a ferocious hangover. Max has seen grown men cry for their mothers after waking up from a night of binge drinking. Not that he's experienced this often himself. He is, typically, a man of moderation. But there's something about Emilie that drives him to extremes.

He doesn't remember much about last night. Shutting the door to his cabin. Kicking off his shoes. Bypassing the glass and going straight for the bottle. And that look on her face. He can't get it out of his mind no matter how many times he blinks or rubs his swollen eyes. She hadn't even looked at him. Emilie had simply walked straight past, chin tilted, eyes glassy, mouth set. If he'd had to describe the look in a single word he'd say hatred. She hates him. And can he really blame her? He's a fool. Wilhelm Balla? Why the hell did he share her secret with the steward? Why had he shared it with anyone? Max knew by the look on her face that there was no making this right. And yet Emilie is the least of his problems right now. The navigator is certain that if he can't get his *Scheiße* together this morning, if he can't do a convincing job of hiding his indiscretion, he will face the wrath of Commander Pruss.

His dirty clothes are soaked and wadded in a corner. He'll have to leave them there and send Werner back with a bucket to collect them. There's no way to carry wet clothes back to his cabin.

Werner.

Max needs him. It rankles him that his best chance of recovering from this situation requires the help of a pubescent boy. And this after the lecture he'd given Werner the day before about respect and behaving like a man. Max isn't sure whether he should apologize to the cabin boy or strangle him.

Werner knocks on the door. Opens it. Beckons him out with a wave of his hand. "Follow me," the boy whispers, and leads Max toward the kitchen.

We're making a habit of this, Max thinks. Two mornings in a row Werner has taken it upon himself to interfere. Twice now Max has been fetched from that small tiled room by a boy who doesn't even shave.

Max expected the headache and the dizziness and the cotton mouth. Standing in the shower, fully clothed and deeply exhausted, he had even made peace with the looming nausea. What he hadn't prepared for was the emotional excess brought on by his physically weakened state. Every emotion is visceral, floating right beneath the surface. Anxiety that his secret will be found out. Panic. Paranoia. Fear. And then a profound and complete anger when Werner swings the kitchen door inward and he finds himself staring into the smug face of Xaver Maier.

"Damn," the chef says. "How much did you drink?"

Max can feel himself pull an arm back, ready to knock Maier's head right off his knobby shoulders. But he's moving slowly because Werner leaps up and grabs Max's arm. Drags it down against his side.

"No!" the boy scolds. "We need his help."

He wonders briefly if the chefs have been talking, if Emilie's little spectacle has been rehashed at every opportunity since yesterday afternoon. He wonders if Werner knows, and then he decides that he doesn't care. Max lunges at the chef again.

Werner swats his hand—actually swats his hand—like he's batting away a fly. "Stop," the cabin boy says. "No fighting."

It's an admonition that he must have heard a million times growing up. There's the hint of matronly impatience to the tone, and Max suspects that Werner is mimicking his mother.

Maier looks over the navigator's appearance, eyes settling on Max's collar, and he is certain he must have buttoned something wrong.

"You need coffee," the chef says. "A lot of it."

Werner chimes in, trying to be helpful. "And water. The colder the better. That's what Balla said. Lots of water."

A silver carafe of steaming coffee is on the stainless-steel counter—Maier has been hard at work already—along with a bowl of sugar and a small pitcher of cream. The chef pours Max a cup without asking permission or preference. He offers it, black and piping hot.

Max doesn't take it from Maier's hand.

"Drink."

"Fuck you."

Werner's eyes go round.

"*She* kissed *me*. You saw that much yourself."

"You didn't seem to mind."

"And?" Maier says. "Good grief. I'm a man. I know a pretty woman when I see one. Not that it matters. You're the one she wants. And I don't know what you did to piss her off, but please stop blaming me for it. I don't owe you anything. Certainly not an apology. And I didn't have to get out of bed early to help sober up your sorry ass. Drink the coffee."

Maier hands the coffee cup to Werner and Werner places it in Max's hand. "Why are you doing this?" Max asks.

"Emilie is my friend. She wouldn't want you punished. Thank *her*."

"We aren't exactly on speaking terms at the moment." Max takes a sip and struggles to swallow it. He spits it back into his cup. "Too hot."

"Hold this down and I'll give you one with sugar. Hold that down and I'll give you some cream. Start with water if it's too much. I'm not going to spend my morning mopping up vomit. And learn how to hold your liquor. This is disgraceful."

The concession is demoralizing. He looks at Werner. "Water."

Werner swaps out a glass for the mug in his hand. The water is easier to take than the coffee. Max swishes it around his mouth to warm it up and then swallows. He repeats this process, head tipped back and eyes closed, until half the glass is gone. Then he guzzles.

Max breathes deeply through his nose for several minutes once the water hits his stomach. Yes? No? He's not sure for one long moment whether it's coming back up, but in the end he decides it's going to stay down.

"Coffee," he demands, extending his hand.

He takes one sip and his begrudging respect for Xaver Maier grows by several degrees. The coffee is good. Hot and strong and smooth. He'd prefer it with a bit of sugar and a drop of cream—just enough to cut the shine—but this will do. Max takes several long, measured sips, then stands there, eyes closed, working on the coffee until the mug is empty.

"Sit down," Maier says. He looks at Werner. "Wait a few minutes. Don't give him anything else. I'll cook him something."

Max lays his head on his forearms, mumbles into the fabric of his sleeve: "Not hungry."

"Don't care." Maier turns his back and pulls a skillet from the pan rack hanging above the counter.

A few minutes later the smell of bacon and fried eggs fills the small kitchen.

"The key," Maier says, "to surviving a hangover is to trick the body back into operating like normal. Right now all of your energy is being spent on removing the alcohol from your system. Which is why you're nauseous and addled and sluggish. Your head feels like a wheel of cheese with a chunk broken off. Your eyes have been rubbed with salt. Your throat is scorched. Too much energy is being expended in all the wrong places. It's a waste of body function."

Shut up. Too many words. Max's mental protest does not stop the chef from continuing. He flips an egg in the pan and sprinkles it with salt and cracked pepper.

"I can live at a level near complete intoxication without any-one being the wiser because of three things: salt, coffee, and water. Thus," he says, dumping the food onto one of the white china plates, "bacon and eggs. Eat up."

THE STEWARDESS

Gertrud Adelt is obviously wearing nothing under her satin robe when she opens the cabin door. And even this covering has been hastily pulled over her body. It's tied loosely at her waist, and she clutches the seams together at her throat. Her hair is wild, her eyes squinty, and her husband nowhere to be seen.

"Good morning, Frau Adelt." Emilie's voice is warm and amiable and rises at the end of this last syllable in a note of false pleasantry.

Gertrud squeezes her eyes shut, then blinks several times rap-idly, trying to force away her fatigue. She looks down the corridor in both directions—it's filled with passengers and stewards going about their morning business—and then she looks back at Emilie.

"Why are you here?"

Emilie holds her gaze and speaks slowly, as though to a child. Or an idiot. "It's a quarter past seven. You requested that I stop by at this time to assist you. Have you forgotten?"

Though Emilie does not spend much of her free time around

other women, one thing she does appreciate about her gender is that they can communicate almost entirely with their eyes. Gertrud narrows hers in understanding and says, "Yes. I must have. Do come in."

Once Emilie is in the cabin, Gertrud leans against the door and crosses her arms over her chest. "Why are you *really* here?"

"I got tired of waiting for you in the dining room."

"I'm not an early riser."

"Your husband has already gone through a pot of coffee and a rack of bacon."

"My *husband*," Gertrud says, "agreed to let me sleep in this morning. I find myself rather cross that I did not get to do so."

"You asked for my help yesterday in the bar. I'm prepared to give it."

"In exchange for what?"

"The truth. You tell me why you're looking for the man who owns that dog tag and I will give you his name."

Emilie stands in the middle of the cabin, hands folded below her waist. It is the posture she always maintains when attending to a passenger. On the surface it appears to be one of subservience, but in reality it is a stance of fortitude. She will do what she has to do.

Gertrud circles her now, like a wolf assessing its prey. She looks the stewardess over with those sharp, watchful eyes, searching for a weakness. A clue. She finally stops in front of Emilie. Taps her slender bare foot on the floor. "Something has changed since yesterday."

"I find myself in a rather precarious situation and I'm looking for . . . *options*. I believe you can provide me with one."

The decision came to Emilie immediately upon waking this morning. She learned long ago never to rob herself of sleep, no matter the tragedy or trouble she faced. To Emilie sleep is the solution to every problem. She lets each worry surface in her mind once her head is on the pillow, but she does not try to solve any of them. Emilie thinks of them as tiny spots of light, like those luminous pinpricks that dance in her peripheral vision when she is dizzy. Each concern is a bright spot in her mind. She studies the problems from every angle, acknowledges their presence, waits for them to go dark or brighten. And then she wills her body to sleep, starting at her toes and working her way up, inch by inch, toward her mind. The stewardess learned this skill in the hard, lonely days after her husband died, when she would lie awake at night weeping and worrying, only to be disgusted with herself in the morning, stumbling around in a state beyond anything that could even be described as exhaustion. Now when she faces a troubling issue she sits with it before falling asleep, then passes it off to her subconscious mind to solve. It is a rare morning that she wakes without an answer. Today that single pinprick of light grew and blazed and came barreling into her mind like a meteor.

"Well." Gertrud sits on the bed and crosses her legs. "This is unexpected."

"It has been my experience that the worst things in life usually are."

Gertrud grunts, disdainful. "Please. It's too early for theatrics. Speak plainly. I have a headache."

"I understand that you are a woman who is usually in control, *Frau Adelt*." She stresses the title as a reminder that using it behind this closed door, under these circumstances, is a choice, not an obligation. "But it would be a mistake to assume that is the case with me. I'm not interested in melodrama. Nor do I offer second chances. I am here because I have no other options. We are not friends. We do not engage in witty banter. Tell me what you know or you will not get your name. Is that *plain* enough for you?"

"Quite. Plain." Gertrud's mouth spreads into a wide grin despite the clipped reply.

Emilie expected rage but gets delight instead. What the hell is wrong with this woman?

"Are you sure you don't want to be friends? I imagine we could get into all sorts of trouble."

"I have enough trouble, thank you."

"Alright then," she says with an exaggerated pout. Gertrud pulls the dog tag out of a small jewelry box on the counter and drops it into Emilie's palm. "There is an American passenger on board this airship named Edward Douglas. He's a businessman of some dubious variety. I'd be very interested to know exactly what it is he does. Regardless, I believe that he is on this ship to find the owner of this tag. I doubt very much that his motives are altruistic, and if I had to bet money I'd say they lean toward suspicious."

"You are sure of this?"

"Four months ago my press card was revoked by the fucking Ministry of Propaganda. Oh, don't look so shocked. I'm a grown woman and I've never met a curse word I didn't like. Politeness is a lost cause in my profession." Gertrud returns to her spot on the edge of the bed and tightens the edges of her robe around her bare legs. "Edward Douglas was in the building that day. His office is a floor below, and I did not take it well when they tried to escort me from the building sans press card. That is all beside the point, however."

"So what is your point, then?" Emilie realizes what a relief it is to speak frankly with another person, and a woman at that. It's as though a small bubble of tension has burst in her chest and she can breathe a bit easier. Emilie relaxes into the small chair beside the dressing table. There is no need to guard her expressions or her words for the moment.

"Consider it backstory. Important, but generally left out of the narrative." Gertrud is awake now, albeit reluctantly, and she goes to the sink and splashes cold water on her face. Emilie knows she's thinking, sorting through what she does and doesn't want to share. Finally Gertrud grabs a brush from her cosmetics case and begins working it through her erratic curls. "The night we took off, you were asked to summon a woman from the hangar?"

"Yes. Dorothea Erdmann. Colonel Erdmann's wife."

"Why?"

"He wanted to say good-bye."

"Don't you think it's odd that the family members of all the other passengers and crew members were made to say their farewells at the Hof Hotel? No one was allowed near the airfield. We were bused there under armed guard. And yet Dorothea Erdmann was a stone's throw away in the hangar, at her husband's beck and call."

"He is a very high ranking military official."

"Certainly. I can understand why she was allowed to wait in the hangar and why they made an exception for her. I just don't understand why he insisted on it. Colonel Erdmann did not say a single word to her when she came on board. But he held on to her like a drowning man." She looks at Emilie now and her expression is pointed. "He held on to her like a man who suspected he would never see his wife again."

"I did not stay and watch," Emilie says.

"No. I suppose you wouldn't have." Gertrud glances at her bare hand, and Emilie can see that she is eager to ask questions of a more personal nature. "I'd like to know what capacity he is serving on this voyage. He makes frequent trips to the control car but he's not in uniform. Sometimes he eats with the passengers and other times he's absent—I'm guessing he dines with the crew for those meals. What is he doing here, Emilie?"

"What does this have to do with Edward Douglas?"

"I suspect this has everything to do with him. I suspect Colonel Erdmann is on board this ship to stop whatever it is the American has planned."

THE JOURNALIST

Colonel Erdmann is on board this flight as an observer."

"What does that mean?" Gertrud asks.

"Nothing as exciting as you might think. This ship is state-of-the-art. We're using navigational techniques and weather forecasting technology that are unheard of in the aviation world. Of course the German military has a vested interest. It makes perfect sense that they would want someone on board to watch and learn."

"And that doesn't bother you?"

Emilie snorts. "Did you look at this thing when you drove up? The swastikas are enormous. I work in a Nazi hotel. How could anything bother me more than that?"

The stewardess seems startled at her own words. It is the most honest thing she has said to Gertrud this entire trip. Anyone else would backtrack. Maybe justify the sentiment or explain their loyalty. But Emilie sits a little straighter. She lifts her chin, daring Gertrud to object or show any sign of shock.

"You keep saying you're not interested in friendship, but I think you just proved otherwise."

Emilie sighs. She is weary. "The only thing I'm interested in at this particular moment is self-preservation."

"So tell me the name of the man who owns those dog tags. Tell me what you know about him. Then use the information however you see fit."

"His name is Ludwig Knorr," the stewardess says. It's a fact stated simply and without effect now that they have established a truce. "He's something of a war hero. He flew on a number of air raids over England in the First World War. And then he became an aviation legend about a decade ago during the *Graf Zeppelin*'s first flight to the United States."

"How so?"

"A huge section of fabric tore away from the ship midflight and Ludwig led a spectacular repair mission that saved the *Graf Zeppelin* and everyone on board."

"So he's a mechanic?"

Emilie shakes her head. "No. A rigger. Chief rigger, in fact. He holds the same position here."

"Please forgive my ignorance. But I don't know what a rigger does."

"They handle liftoff and landing. The ropes in particular. Landing lines. That sort of thing. It's a tricky process to bring a ship down level. It's about balance and weight distribution. More than one ship has gone ass over elbows because the riggers miscalculated."

"So what does a rigger do midflight, then?"

Emilie shrugs. "Whatever's needed."

It's a sparse biography, and Gertrud can't think of any reason why Knorr should be singled out by the American. "What else do you know about him? Anything would help."

Gertrud studies Emilie's face while she thinks, but she cannot see any signs that the stewardess is holding anything back.

"He's married. I think he has a couple of children. Girls, maybe. I'm not sure."

"Have you ever spoken with him?"

"This is starting to feel like an interrogation, not an exchange of information."

Gertrud laughs at this. It's true. She has leaned closer. Her voice has reached a higher pitch. Her muscles are wound tight. "I apologize. Subtlety is not one of my gifts." She takes a deep breath and returns to her place on the rumpled bed. Gertrud lays her hands on her lap, palms up—a sign of détente. She tries again, her voice soft and child-like. To her it sounds uncomfortably close to mockery, but Emilie doesn't seem to mind. "Have you ever spoken with him?"

"A handful of times. We don't exactly cross paths often. The riggers don't spend much time in the passenger areas."

There. Gertrud sees Emilie slide back into protective mode. Her face is smooth, a little too relaxed. A little too pleasant. Gertrud presses for more but does her best not to sound threatening in the process. "When was the last time you had a conversation with him?"

Damn it. Emilie pulls back, coiling inward. Her guard is up again. "You are frightening. Has anyone ever told you that?"

"This isn't frightening. Leonhard would call this heightened curiosity. Frightening is when I'm on deadline and every source has dried up and I'm afraid someone else will scoop my story. We can both be thankful those factors are not currently in play." She picks a piece of lint off the bedspread and drops it to the floor. "You've spoken with him on this flight, haven't you?"

"Last night."

"Why?"

"Curiosity. You had shown me the dog tag earlier in the day and there he was, in the crew's mess, at dinner. It seemed too good an opportunity to miss."

"Is that the only time Ludwig Knorr comes in the passenger areas? At dinner?"

Again the hesitation, the internal debate as Emilie struggles with whether or not to confide what she knows. Gertrud decides to preempt the debate with a peace offering.

"There is another reason why Colonel Erdmann is on this flight."

Emilie's face stays expressionless.

"The bomb threats. He believes they are legitimate, that someone might attempt to destroy the *Hindenburg* on this flight." Gertrud leans forward a bit, imploring. "So you see, it's not just that I'm putting my nose where it doesn't belong or that I'm overly curious. I'd get off this damned ship right now if I could. But that's not a choice I can make. So all I'm left with is figuring out what the hell is going on before someone blows us out of the sky." She lifts one trembling hand to illustrate her sincerity.

It's the closest Gertrud will come to begging, and still it takes several long, quiet seconds before Emilie finally speaks.

"There's a poker game," she says. "It takes place in the crew's mess every night after dinner. There are usually only four or five men who play, but Ludwig Knorr is always one of them."

One corner of Gertrud's mouth curls upward in a devious smile. "Are passengers allowed to join?"

"No. Not officially. But in the end, it's poker. The only thing that really matters is what you bring to the table."

This morsel of information settles in Gertrud's mind. Takes root. She knows it is important, can feel it the way she does every good lead, but she does not yet know why. It will come to her. It always does. She stands, ready to usher Emilie out. "Are you satisfied with our exchange of information?"

"I believe so, yes."

"Good," Gertrud says. "I wouldn't exactly say it's been a pleasure, but I am grateful that you came to me. I hope we've formed something of an alliance."

Emilie rises from the chair and wipes her hands across her skirt, as though dusting them off. "You're dismissing me?"

"I prefer to think of it as freeing up your time. You are on the clock after all."

"I can't leave yet."

"You have something left to say?"

"As far as anyone outside this room is concerned, I came here to perform my duties as a stewardess, not the least of which is assisting with the needs of my female passengers."

"And you're under the impression that I need your assistance?" Gertrud turns to the mirror over the sink. The reflection that greets her is alarming.

"I mean no offense, Frau Adelt, but if you leave this room in your current state my reputation will be ruined."

"Fine, then."

Gertrud lowers herself into the chair before the dressing table and submits herself to Emilie's ministrations. Her clothes are selected with care, as are her cosmetics, perfume, and hygiene products. Before long she is dressed and primped. All that's left is to find some way of taming her hair. And, to give Emilie credit, she does try. But the curls and the static are too much even for her considerable skill. After several frustrating attempts to arrange Gertrud's hair into finger waves, Emilie steps back and plants her fists firmly at her waist.

"Do you have a hat?"

THE NAVIGATOR

Once, when Max was a child, his family toured the ruins of Flossenbürg Castle while on vacation in Bavaria. They arrived early in the morning to find the crumbling stone walls shrouded in a fog so dense Max felt as though he could poke it with a stick. They moved slowly through the ruins, holding hands and trying to restrain the terrified laughter that pressed against their lungs—the irrational, frantic hilarity brought on by the sense of looming disaster. Max loved the foreboding that prickled the back of his neck as they picked their way amongst the rubble. Here and there a dark corner stood in sharp relief against the spectral mist, or a stately pine rose up from the gloom sprawled across the castle grounds, but apart from those occasional landmarks he and his family wandered blindly through the vestiges of a great fortress split asunder during the Thirty Years' War. He sensed as though he was present in some bend in time and if he just took the right turn he might be able to step backwards and witness history with his own eyes. A siege. A slaughter. He was transported. Suspended. Sometime later, when the light began to shift and the sun turned warm enough to burn through the gloom, he felt a gnawing disappointment. By midmorning the air was crisp and clean and the magic had dissipated.

That day, however, was the beginning of Max Zabel's love affair with fog. It is the reason that he wakes early and often volunteers for the first shift in any rotation. Max has been known to pray for fog the way some men pray for deliverance. So it is a great irony that today, of all days, should be the one when the airship flies into a swamp-like bank of mist off the coast of Newfoundland. Max has not seen the like since that day at Flossenbürg Castle. They have been drifting through heavy cloud cover since dawn. But this is different. He can feel the shift in air pressure as they pass through sparse clouds and into the wall of coastal fog. The air around him becomes solid. The roar of engines grows muffled, as though someone has stuffed them with cotton. Everything dulls. Max notes the change in atmosphere and the time on his flight log—force of habit—but no one else in the control car pays the transformation any mind. This is a normal part of flying. It just happens to be his *favorite* way to fly. Half-blind and mute. Max does not pretend this is rational or ideal. It's rather dangerous, in fact—if one wants to take it at face value—but thrilling nonetheless.

Pity he can't enjoy it. The remnants of his spectacular hangover are still present, like ball bearings rolling around his skull. If he moves his head too quickly they clang against one another, making him dizzy, making his eyes water and his tongue stick to the roof of his mouth. It's little more than sixty degrees in the control car, but Max is sweating along his lower back, beneath his arms, and across his upper lip as his body works to expel the last traces of alcohol. He wipes his mouth with the back of his hand. Dries his hand on his trousers.

Max is thirsty. But there's little that can be done about that now. It isn't time for his break. He will stay fixed at his station if it kills him. He will not flinch. He will not complain. He will not acknowledge his mistake last night or let it affect his ability to perform his duties today. The other officers must feel the static charge of his determination, for they do not speak to him unless necessary. They avoid eye contact. The gloom outside has permeated the control car and subdued every man on duty.

From where he's standing at his chart table, Max cannot see the rudder wheel at the front of the bridge, though he knows that Helmut Lau is on duty at the moment. He can hear the intermittent calls between Lau, Commander Pruss, and Kurt Bauer, the elevator man, but they recede into background chatter as he watches the instruments on the panel before him. He makes adjustments for altitude and headwinds. Max slips carefully and purposefully into his private zone. This is a world of numbers and precision, a world where you do one thing and there is a specific, predictable outcome. And it is in this moment of deep concentration that he is struck by a thought: it is a pity that he cannot chart the human heart. Were it possible, he would spread Emilie's heart out on the table before him. Smooth out the creases. Measure its latitude and longitude. And then, when he could see the unbroken whole, he would place himself directly in the center. He would draw himself there in red ink. Permanent. That might have been possible before he inadvertently betrayed her trust. But now her papers are confiscated and she is a breath away from being lost to him for good.

Max is broken from this trance by the panicked voice of Kurt Bauer.

"We are only a few kilometers from Cape Race."

"No," Max says, "that's not possible. That would put us . . ." he turns to his chart and flips the pages three at a time. It is one long moment of suspended animation in which Max realizes what has happened. What he has done. And then the *Hindenburg*'s newly installed sonic altimeter begins to beep—two bright chirps with a five-second gap between them—indicating that the ground is rising fast.

"On the cliffs," Bauer finishes for him.

There is a pause in the control car, no more than four seconds, as every man in the room looks at one another and then at the instruments in front of them. Denial. Shock. Fear. These emotions are evident on their faces, tumbling over one another like falling dominoes. When the next chirp sounds they all fly into action. But now the time between alarms is only three seconds.

The device is new and state-of-the-art and has been on board for less than a year. It measures the distance between the control car and the ground, much like the sounding line on a boat, but with the added benefit of an audible warning system that alerts crew when the distance begins to recede quickly.

There is a nervous tremor in Kurt Bauer's voice. "Ground rising at approximately ten feet per second!"

"Bring it up!" Pruss shouts. "Lau, back at the rudder."

Pruss takes two quick steps from where he has been stationed since they flew into fog and hovers over Bauer at the elevator wheel. His eyes are locked on the sonic altimeter, watching the needle climb. "Up. Now!" Pruss commands, and Bauer spins the wheel like a mad pirate at the helm of the ship. Max cannot help but think of Blackbeard and the *Queen Anne's Revenge*, and he feels, in his post-drunken state, that he has been transported to a land of make-believe where pirates take to the skies in flying whales. He is brought back to reality when the nose of the *Hindenburg* tips upward abruptly as the fins at the back of the ship respond and direct the structure to rise. Max can feel the weight of his body shift into his heels as he adjusts his balance.

Two seconds between chirps now.

Then one.

"Faster!" Lehmann orders as the alarm merges into one unbroken, shrill tone indicating that they are flying directly into a landmass.

Max does not realize he has been holding his breath until his lungs begin to burn and the pounding of his heart echoes in his ears. He gasps, pulls in a panicked breath, and holds that one as well.

The screeching alarm continues its metallic warning. Max can feel the sharpness of the sound in his brain, like claws on metal. It is the sound of looming disaster. He watches the elevator wheel spin and waits for the sickening crunch of metal against rock. The officers are coiled, waiting for impact. They can see nothing outside the windows. They can hear nothing but the sonic altimeter. They are blind and deaf and hanging vulnerably beneath the *Hindenburg* in a cage of metal and glass.

THE CABIN BOY

The floor beneath Werner tilts. It's almost imperceptible at first, but after a few seconds he finds that he's leaning forward several degrees to keep his balance, and there is a slight strain along his Achilles tendon, as though he has begun to walk uphill. The airship is lifting at a rapid pace.

He stops in the middle of the catwalk and listens. Werner is fifteen yards from the spiral staircase that connects the keel catwalk to the axial catwalk above, exactly in the middle of the ship. At this distance he can see it shudder against the strain of such a rapid, uneven ascent. All around him the supports and girders begin to groan, low at first, and then deeper as the climb continues. It is the sound of an old man rising from a chair.

Thirty seconds. A minute maybe. He doesn't count, but it can't be longer than that. It's over quickly and the floor levels out beneath him, but it takes another ten seconds before the structure around him ceases to object. There is an echo of metallic tensity, and the gas cells that hold the hydrogen quiver. Then calm. The stillness at the end of a deep breath. But Werner knows something is very wrong. The *Hindenburg* never makes such drastic movements. She is a great lumbering beast, not a jackrabbit. Now the space around him feels different somehow, as though it has lost elasticity.

Only once Werner has started the trek back toward the passenger quarters does he notice that he's been holding the paper bag in his hand so tightly that his fingernails have dug imprints into the heel of his hand. He relaxes his grip on the empty bag, then wads it up. Owens gobbled up all the scraps Werner had taken with him. The dog is a bottomless pit, and Werner is more than a little curious to know who its owner is.

Werner fights the instinct to run. The security door is still far ahead, but rushing will do nothing other than make him clumsy. The last thing he needs is to fall and hurt himself and lose what modicum of respect he has earned.

The cabin boy lengthens each stride and reaches the access door in record time. He swaps out the felt shoes for his loafers and steps back into B-deck, expecting there to be pandemonium. Instead he finds two stewards and a cook's assistant loitering in the corridor between crew cabins. They have the restless look of men who would like to be on a smoke break but can't afford cigarettes. One of them has made a lewd joke—the boy can tell by the color in their cheeks and the coarse laughter—but they do not look troubled about what has just happened. Nor do they share the punch line.

"What are you doing back there?" Severin Klein asks.

He lifts the empty bag. "Feeding the dog."

"I thought that stupid mutt was going to bite me when we boarded it. I'd sooner shoot it than waste my time feeding it breakfast."

"Do you know who it belongs to? Not the white one. The mutt."

"No idea. I didn't check. Why do you care?"

Werner doesn't answer. He simply shrugs and continues down

the corridor. But his adolescent mind has found a puzzle, and, as is typical of boys his age, he is fixated on solving it. He doubts Kubis will let him look at the manifests, but Werner has long since learned that the chief steward cannot be everywhere at once. The manifests are kept in his stateroom, and anyone with a bit of time and a master key can get in to take a look.

THE STEWARDESS

Emilie feels as though she is wound tight, ready to spring. She is a jack-in-the-box, locked inside a floating cage, waiting for disaster. She has grown familiar with calamity over the last decade, but still, this is too much. Bomb threats and confiscated papers. Arguments and intrigue. Every fiber of her body feels keyed up. Tuned in. It is exhausting. If she were at home, away from curious eyes, she would pace the walls and pick at her cuticles. As it stands, however, she forces herself to sit with the Doehner family, to stay relaxed. Amiable. Feet crossed at the ankles. Hands in her lap. Expression languid and unperturbed.

Yet it is this heightened state of awareness that enables her to notice the pencil. It falls, rolls to the edge of the table, and drops to the floor. Emilie stares at it, nearly oblivious to the shoving match that has ensued between Walter and Werner Doehner.

"You owe me five marks!" Walter shouts.

"Liar! It was my turn. You owe *me*!"

They roll on the floor like ferocious little octopi, arms and legs flailing. Something white—teeth maybe—flashes in her peripheral vision. One of them throws a punch, and Matilde Doehner rises with a sigh. She does not raise her voice, merely bends over the children, her fists propped on her ample hips. Emilie can barely hear her over the tumult.

"Stop it. This moment."

Emilie once heard that a whisper is more effective than a scream when dealing with children, and this must be true, for the boys come apart and look at their mother warily.

"Sit on your hands. Both of you. And if you so much as blink before I give you permission . . ."

Matilde Doehner doesn't finish the threat. She doesn't have to. The boys drop to the floor like sacks of grain, their hands covered by their tiny rear ends. Matilde returns to her novel without giving them a second glance.

Matilde didn't see it, Emilie thinks. Neither of the boys touched that pencil. Neither of them breathed on it. It fell on its own.

Emilie rises from her chair, walks to the observation windows, and leans over the glass. The view looks exactly as it has all morning; they are little more than a gray object in a gray mist over an invisible sea. But then something breaks the fog not twenty feet below the observation windows, like the arched back of a breaching whale. But this is dark and solid with a sharp edge and a soft green surface.

A cliff.

Moss.

Granite.

The floor tilts a bit beneath her feet. Emilie takes an involuntary step back and gasps. She turns in a circle, expecting a cry of alarm from the passengers at any moment. But they are all absorbed in their reading or writing. Curled up in chairs. Several of them are napping. A few converse in the low tones of a dreary morning. In seconds the fog has swallowed whatever ground lies beneath them.

A teacup clatters to the floor at Matilde Doehner's feet and she turns her fierce gaze upon her sons. "Ten more minutes on your hands and then you'll clean up every sliver of that broken cup. Do you understand?"

Walter looks wounded. Emilie can tell he wants to argue, to explain that they haven't moved, but the child knows better. He will not cross his mother, not even when he's justified. He nods his head and blinks back a film of tears instead.

Emilie could intervene on his behalf. She ought to. But she doesn't want to alert the passengers to what is happening. All across the reading room she can see items shifting on the tables. A neatly stacked deck of cards spills out like an accordion across the polished wood surface of an end table. A book slides a few inches from the elbow of its owner. She wouldn't feel this movement at all if she weren't standing. She wouldn't see it if she weren't paying attention.

And then it's over as quickly as it began. The floor beneath her levels out and her balance shifts in response. Nothing else moves on the tables. And beneath them she can once again see the faint, glassy reflection of the ocean's surface between strips of cloud. Emilie lays her hand flat on her breastbone, right beneath the clavicle, and takes a deep, calming breath.

For an entire decade Emilie has been left on her own to handle crises. She has long since fallen away from the habit of turning to a man to fix things. She must find the landlord when the pipes burst in her apartment. She must pay the bills. She must read the maps and translate directions when she travels. At first this was a strange burden to bear, an uncomfortable load for a woman who always had a father and then a husband to look after her. But as time has gone on Emilie has grown into this way of living. She has learned to enjoy it. To be proud of herself. So she is alarmed and not a little angry at the thought that fills her mind like a blaring alarm: she has to find Max.

Her feet propel her out of the reading room even as her mind objects. Max betrayed her. She is furious with him. She vowed last night that she would never speak to him again. And Emilie hates this last bit of truth: when it comes to lovers, anger and passion are the same emotion. A kiss is all that separates the two.

Emilie slips into the corridor. There are no emergency alarms blaring. No flickering lights. No sense that danger is near or has recently passed. But she wants an answer nonetheless. She finds Max squatting outside the radio room, head buried in his hands, breathing as though he has just sprinted one hundred yards only to run smack into a brick wall. He's sweating. Trembling. And she can see his pulse hammering staccato in his throat.

"Max?" Emilie kneels next to him, sets her palm lightly on his shoulder. His shirt is damp. "What just happened?"

When he lifts his face Emilie can see the results of another long, hard night in his bloodshot eyes. His voice is ragged when he answers. "I need water. A lot of it."

She's down the corridor and darting around the gangway stairs toward the kitchen before she even stops to consider what she's doing. Too late now. If he needs water she'll get him water, and then she will get her answers. Emilie hasn't spoken to Xaver since the incident yesterday afternoon, so she is irritated to feel the flush of heat in her cheeks when she knocks the kitchen door open with the heel of her hand. Xaver looks at her with trepidation, and then at the door as though expecting Max to follow her in.

"No," he says, holding up one finger. "Not that again."

For one brief moment she is tempted to crack a joke about him not being man enough to handle her, but she decides against it. "I need a pitcher of water. A glass. And a bottle of aspirin wouldn't hurt either—" She can tell Xaver is about to make some smart-ass retort, so she interrupts him. "It's not for me."

His surname might be German, but Emilie has long suspected that Xaver possesses a good bit of French blood. He's dark-haired but light-skinned, slender, and his eyes have that hooded, seductive look the French are so notorious for. Not to mention the fact that he is better in the kitchen than anyone she has ever known.

"I don't recall," he says, waving an arm in exasperation, "that taking orders from you is part of my job description."

Emilie steps around him and lifts a pitcher from the drying rack. She fills it with water from the sink. She picks a glass tumbler—the largest she can find—and reaches up on her tiptoes to retrieve the aspirin from the top shelf in the cabinet. And all the while Xaver glares at her, arms crossed.

"You are too comfortable in my kitchen."

"You love me."

"I tolerate you." There is no animosity in his voice. "Bring it back when you're done. I just lost a pitcher during that near miss. Slid right off the counter and shattered on the floor."

"You saw that?"

"Didn't everyone?"

"No. Thankfully. But I'm going to find out what happened."

Xaver eyes the pitcher tucked into the crook of her arm. "I wouldn't have guessed water would make a good means of bribery."

"Call it a peace offering."

"Oh," he says. "Max." And then, "Don't tell me. I don't want to know."

Max is exactly where she left him, but he's no longer panting. He lifts his face when she stops beside him.

"Can we talk?" she asks.

He pushes off the floor and rises, somewhat unsteadily, to his feet. "Not here. Come with me."

Emilie follows him down the corridor toward the officers' quarters. She has never been in his cabin before but hesitates for only a moment when he holds the door open and nods for her to enter. It's a disaster. The bed is in disarray. An empty liquor bottle is on the floor. Toiletries are strewn across the small dressing table. The closet door hangs open and there is, inexplicably, a bucket filled with wet clothing in the middle of the floor.

Emilie pours him a glass of water and hands it to him.

Max drinks it slowly at first, then tips the tumbler back and drains it. "More. Please."

They repeat this process until he can speak without cotton mouth.

She holds up the bottle. "Aspirin?"

"Yes."

He takes four, then offers her a feeble shrug. "I'm so sorry, Emilie."

It takes her a moment to realize he's talking about her papers and not the near accident. "Why did you do it? I trusted you."

"I didn't." He wipes a bead of sweat from his temple with the back of his hand. "Or at least I didn't mean to. I was angry. And desperate. So I told Wilhelm Balla you were leaving, because I needed to talk to someone, and you sure as hell weren't in the mood. And then he blabbed. I never thought he would. Honestly. I'd have never said a word otherwise. But we'll figure a way out of this mess. You *can* trust me. I promise."

Emilie drops her head. Closes her eyes. "There is no way out of this mess."

"Yes there is. I've been thinking—"

"Stop—"

"You could marry me."

The pronouncement drops between them like a thud. It makes her even sadder, that he would do this for her. That he doesn't know the truth.

"You don't want to marry—"

"Stop telling me what I want!"

"A Jewish woman," she continues, her voice a slow, calm whisper.

Emilie lifts her chin, waiting for him to recoil. Or curse. Or yell. She waits for the accusations and the anger.

Max appears dumbfounded. "You're *Jewish?*"

"Half Jewish."

"Why the bloody hell do you think that would even matter to me?"

She laughs at this. Hard and mirthless. "Don't you dare tell me that being Jewish doesn't *matter* right now."

"Not to me."

"Then you're a fool."

Max places one steady hand on each of her shoulders. He leans in a bit closer. "I need you to listen very carefully. Are you listening?"

She nods.

"You could tell me that you are half ostrich and I would still want to marry you. Is that clear? Do you understand *that*, Emilie Imhof?"

"No," she says. "I don't."

Max slides a hand beneath her collar and lifts the silver chain until the key rests in his palm. "Is it so hard to believe that a German man could want to marry a Jewish woman?"

"That was a long time ago."

"It was yesterday to hear you speak of him."

"Max . . ."

He drops the key back into her blouse and steps away. "You don't have to answer now. God knows I've gotten good at waiting. Just know that this thing you're so worried about does not change my feelings for you."

This conversation—the damn confounding nature of it—has distracted her from why she came to find him in the first place. She takes a deep breath and changes the subject. "What happened a few minutes ago? With the ship?"

Max groans and presses his fingers against his temples. He rubs as though trying to assuage a headache. Emilie guesses this isn't far from the truth.

"It was my fault," he says. "I brought us too close to the coast."

No, it was my fault, Emilie thinks. *I did this to you.* She has brought him to the edge and left him there, teetering. Emilie has never known Max to be careless before. Never known him to miscalculate or lose control or indulge in excess of any kind.

Where Max was all softness and rounded edges a moment ago, he is changing before her eyes. She sees his anger return, accompanied by shame and disappointment. Violent emotions flood his face.

He picks the empty bottle off the floor. "I *let myself* do this. And damn it if I didn't nearly kill us all as a result."

There are a dozen questions she could ask, but Emilie settles on one that covers many subjects at once.

"Do they know?"

It's clear what she means. Do they know you have a hangover? Do they know where you are? Do they know it's your fault? Do they know about what happened last night?

He chooses the safest topic. "No. I don't think so. Anyone could have made that mistake in the fog."

"Except you. You don't make mistakes. Do you, Max?"

"Apparently I do." His grip tightens on the bottle, and Emilie is afraid it will shatter in his palm. Max gently places it in the wastebasket beneath the sink. He turns back to Emilie and his gray eyes are storm clouds. "But I won't let it happen again."

THE NAVIGATOR

Emilie sets the pitcher down on the counter, and the glass beside it. She hands Max the bottle of aspirin. She swallows. Nods. Leaves. Damn it. She thinks he has dismissed her. But his mind is sluggish and stupid, and she's halfway down the corridor before this occurs to him. He won't call after her though. He's been a fool, moping around like a lovesick schoolboy. And look at the price they nearly paid.

There was sadness on her face when she left. But mostly there was resignation, as though she has known all along that he would eventually turn her away. As though her heritage is some Rubicon that he cannot cross. Knowing this complicates things immensely, but only because her confiscated papers threaten to reveal this secret. And to think he was worried about the trouble she would face for trying to leave Germany. The danger she's in now is unspeakable.

This knowledge stokes the frustration burning beneath the surface, and Max drives his fist through the wall beside his bed. The hole is almost perfectly round, and he looks at it in disgust. He will have to pay for those repairs, no doubt. And answer for the damage as well. He would punch himself, if he could, for his own stupidity. How many things has he broken in the span of two days? And there's no time left to fix any of them.

Max is expected back in the control car any moment, but he needs to visit the bathroom first. And he needs to change his damp shirt. Sweat runs in a small stream down the hollow of his spine, and he fears that he smells as bad as he feels. But he's running low on clean clothes, and he must make sure he has enough for the return trip. There likely won't be time to have anything laundered before they leave Lakehurst tomorrow evening.

His trousers, jackets, and two clean shirts hang neatly in the closet, right where he unpacked them when he boarded. And at the bottom of the closet is a small duffel bag filled with personal items. Socks. Underwear. Wallet and travel papers and a bit of money in case their leave in New Jersey stretches to a few hours. The bag also contains his holster and gun and extra bullets. All of the ship's officers are issued weapons, but only the commander and first officer wear them on duty. They make the passengers nervous and they're something of a security risk.

The duffel bag is in the same place where he had left it when he boarded in Frankfurt. Nothing immediately seems out of place. However, he distinctly remembers zipping it all the way. At the moment, the zipper hangs open an inch. He frowns at the bag. Max is fastidious. Always has been. He buttons his shirt to the top. He tucks his trouser pockets in every morning to make sure no lining is visible. He double knots his shoes. And he always closes a zipper. Always.

Max leans into his closet and takes a closer look at the bag. He opens it. Digs around for a minute out of curiosity. And then he steps back with a violent oath. His underwear is folded neatly in a sailor's roll. His socks are tucked into one another as always. His undershirts folded in thirds. But the leather holster that holds his Luger is empty. No gun. No bullets.

THE AMERICAN

I thought I would find you here." The American pulls out a chair at the corner table in the smoking room where Gertrud Adelt and her husband are seated.

She stiffens. Peers at him suspiciously beneath the brim of her red felt hat. The color brings out the natural scarlet tint of her lips, makes her look as though she's bloodthirsty. "I didn't realize you were looking for me."

"You couldn't have."

"Then perhaps I am a bit dismayed at being so easily found."

Leonhard lays a hand on hers in warning. She smiles tightly. Takes a sip of her cocktail.

"It's a small ship. There are only so many places one can go." The American shrugs out of his jacket and hangs it on the back of his chair. He doesn't ask permission to join them. He simply settles into his place and looks at Gertrud expectantly. Leonhard glowers beside her. Protective. Territorial. Angry at not having been greeted or addressed.

"By all means," Leonhard says, "join us."

Schulze arrives, as is his habit, only a moment after the American has settled into his seat. "Can I get you something to drink, Herr Douglas?"

The American looks at Gertrud's champagne glass and the mimosa that is already half drained. And then at the wine balanced in Leonhard's right hand. Sauvignon blanc, if he had to guess. He doesn't seem the type to go for Riesling.

Leonhard sees the question in his gaze and lifts the glass a few inches. "Gewürztraminer, in case you're wondering. It's quite good."

The American waits a beat, then looks at the bar steward. "Nothing for me, thanks. It's a bit early to be hitting the bottle. I just thought I'd visit with my friends for a few moments."

Schulze tactfully ignores the tension that spikes the air around the table. "Let me know if you change your mind."

"I am curious," Leonhard says once the steward has retreated through the air lock, "what would prompt you to use the word *friend* in describing our new acquaintanceship? I have seen you a handful of times and spoken with you never."

"Oh. I beg your pardon. I was referring to your wife."

"My *wife* is your friend?"

"I assumed so. Given that she has something that belongs to me. That's a really *friendly* liberty. Wouldn't you say?"

There are any number of ways to gain the advantage in a situation, but the American has his favorites: a surprise attack or an unexpected silence. Given that he wants the Adelts to be startled into revealing what they know, silence isn't the optimal choice. This first salvo has the desired effect. Both Leonhard and his wife are disconcerted, instantly on the defensive.

Leonhard sets down his glass.

Gertrud picks hers up. Sips. Swallows. Arranges her face—as women are wont to do—for battle.

So predictable, the American thinks, *so easily baited*.

Leonhard is as still as a statue.

Gertrud is practically quivering with the suppressed desire to lunge across the table and throttle him.

"I'm certain I don't know what you mean," she finally says.

"I'm certain you do."

"I hope you are able to explain your presumption, Herr Douglas. I confess that I'm not currently in a good humor, and this game—or whatever it is—is doing little to improve my mood," Leonhard says, draping an arm across Gertrud's back. He cups the ball of her shoulder with his palm. The move is not protective. It's proactive. His fingers spread wide, and the tips press lightly into the thin fabric of her dress. He is restraining her.

Gertrud has rallied from the surprise. Her grin is sly. "I have nothing that belongs to you."

He dismisses this argument with a wave of his hand. "Semantics. Let's not be juvenile. You have an item that was recently in my care."

"I'd question how well you were caring for this item if you've lost it."

Again, the American thinks the best tactic here would be aggression, not caution. He settles into his chair as though settling into a foxhole.

"I have lost many things in my thirty-eight years. I lost my first tooth in the driveway of my parents' house. Bloody mess that was too. My brother knocked it out. I lost my first library book three months later when I fell off a rotten log and into a pond. Again, my brother's fault. He pushed me in while I was reading *The Wind in the Willows*. I lost my first school race to that same brother, the dirty cheater. He was six years older and thought it his moral obligation to teach me humility. A number of years later I lost my virginity in a brothel in France. My brother thought it a sad fate for a man to die never having been with a woman, and since he had no control over whether I'd get cut to pieces by machine gun fire he did what he could and ensured that I had a bit of worldly experience before I stepped on the battlefield. I don't remember the girl's name, but I do remember my brother laughing until he pissed himself when I stumbled around the next morning in a drunken haze fretting over whether or not I'd just acquired syphilis. I didn't, in case you're wondering. The whores in France were uncharacteristically hygienic that year. But the worst loss of my life thus far has been the death of my brother. He was lying in a hospital in Coventry at the end of the Great War, recovering from shrapnel wounds, when a German zeppelin flew overhead and dropped a handful of artillery shells. That's the kind of loss that stays with a man. Not an idiotic dog tag. But that tag is the answer to an eighteen-year search for the man who dropped those artillery shells. So, if you don't mind, I'd like to have it back. I would like to find that man and forgive him so I can lay to rest this god-awful burden I've carried for almost two decades."

There are many things that the American is not good at. The list could stretch for miles. And at the very tattered end would be a single word: forgiveness. But people want to believe good of others. They long for things like hope and reconciliation and redemption. They tout those virtues. Write about them. Press them on their children. But it's hard for a man to stay alive as long as the American has if he's prone to such sympathetic notions. He will forgive the man who killed his brother only after he has put a bullet in his skull.

The American can see Gertrud sorting through a variety of possible responses. It's as though they are laid out on a flat space in her mind and she's shuffling through them, looking for something appropriate. He can detect a glimmer of doubt. She wants to believe him. But she knows better. And though his story is true she has no way of being certain. In the end she picks a response that is relatively benign.

"You don't know his name?"

No condolences. No indication of belief. Simply a question. A salvo.

The American grins. "The note of surprise in your voice leads me to believe that you do."

"Yes." Gertrud looks at Leonhard and they engage in that most mystifying of communications, an entire conversation spoken entirely with body language. A lifted eyebrow. A pursed lip. Unbroken eye contact. A slight nod of the head. There is no way for him to know how they reach the conclusion they do. But after several seconds of intense, silent argument, Gertrud turns to him and says, "The dog tag was issued to a man named Ludwig Knorr."

"And you know this how?"

A smug grin. "I never reveal a source."

Her message is clear. She knows who the American is looking for. She can warn him if she likes. And she has spoken about this issue with at least one other person. Clever girl. She's creating a safety net. But there is little way of knowing whether the name she has given him is accurate. No matter, he will find out soon enough from Captain Lehmann.

Now that the majority of passengers are growing bored, the smoking room begins to fill. Schulze opens the air lock to admit Colonel Erdmann and the American heiress, Margaret Mather. They come immediately to the Adelts' table.

"I was just telling Fräulein Mather," Erdmann says to Gertrud, "that she would do well to meet you." He has the wild, desperate look of a man eager to rid himself of chatty female company. "You have so much in common."

Ovaries at most, the American thinks. And possibly not even that much. Gertrud Adelt may be of the gentler sex, but she has bigger brass balls than most men he knows. He can't think of two women who have less in common.

Gertrud extends a slender hand in greeting. "Do join us . . ."

"Margaret."

"Wonderful to meet you, Margaret. We were just having a fascinating conversation with your countryman here." Her voice turns to syrup. "He's quite a passionate man." A vicious pause. "And single, I might add."

Leonhard chokes back a laugh. Clears his throat. Takes a hearty sip of his Gewürztraminer, then settles into the banquette to watch his wife at work.

Colonel Erdmann is no fool. He mumbles an apology and makes a hasty retreat from the bar. For her part Margaret Mather turns curious, hungry eyes on the American. He knows better than to underestimate the appetites of a wealthy spinster. For the first time since entering the bar, he finds himself on the defensive. Margaret stands there expectantly, and it occurs to him several seconds too late that he ought to pull out her chair. He rises to his feet and does so reluctantly..

"I had dinner with this gentleman on our first night, but I'm afraid I still don't know his name."

"Most people don't," Gertrud says. "He's *very* secretive about it."

"I can't imagine why. A name's a name, after all."

This is why he hates women. They're just too damn coy. Enough of this. "It has been lovely chatting." He pushes his chair against the table. "And though I wish I could stay I'm afraid that I cannot."

"Is your gout acting up again?" Gertrud looks at Margaret and adds, "He has terrible gout," with such convincing concern that he is almost tempted to believe he suffers from the condition.

Margaret Mather looks at him with a combination of pity and disgust, her interest waning immediately. Gout is, apparently, a plebeian affliction for which she has little sympathy.

"Yes." He clears his throat. "It is, in fact. I think I'll go lie down for a bit before lunch."

"Rest up," Leonhard says. "I'd be most interested in continuing our conversation later."

Retreat is a painful thing. The American gathers his coat, straightens his tie, and leaves the bar without a backward glance. Gertrud Adelt is no doubt perched at her table with an expression of triumph, but he doesn't care to give her another small victory by acknowledging it.

The American steps into the corridor. Captain Lehmann is five paces away and barreling toward him like a freight train. He pulls up just in time to avoid a collision.

"Ah," Lehmann says, "I've been looking for you."

"You have the name?"

The captain looks over his shoulder and then down the corridor. "I do."

"And?"

"Wouldn't you rather discuss this over a drink? Or in privacy, if nothing else?"

"No. I would like the thing I came for. And then I would like to retire to my cabin. I've had all the company I can tolerate this morning."

Be blunt, his commanding officer used to tell him; *it's the best way of disarming a threat.*

Captain Lehmann looks relieved rather than offended. "Very well, then. The man you're looking for is Heinrich Kubis, my chief steward. Whatever business you have with him will need to wait until we land. He stays busy and I don't need him distracted."

"Of course. Thank you for the information."

And then Lehmann is gone, back to the control car and his observation duties, but the American stays where he is, unmoving in the corridor. His mind spins, countermoves and contingencies crashing against one another, fighting for dominance. He is confused. Frustrated. The American is trying to find a course of action when Joseph Späh rounds the corner with Hermann Doehner. What he really wants is to take the acrobat into the belly of the ship and see if he can, in fact, climb anything. But he doesn't. Instead, he drops to one knee and pretends to tie his shoes. He gives the men a cordial greeting as they pass and lets them walk away. That part of his plan will have to wait.

Heinrich Kubis. Ludwig Knorr. The chief steward. The chief rigger. He has just been lied to—either by Captain Lehmann or by Gertrud Adelt, but he can't be sure which. Perhaps both. That would be worse. That would make him angry. And when the American gets angry, people tend to suffer as a result.

THE JOURNALIST

Leonhard shuts the door to their cabin and tosses his suit coat on the bed. "*Gout?* Of all the diseases at your disposal you went with gout? If it had been up to me I would have given him herpes." He clenches his jaw. Growls a bit at the back of his throat. "He *is* a herpes. Big. Festering. Pustule of a man."

Her voice is high and tight when she answers. "It was the first thing that came to mind."

His eyes narrow. He can hear the frantic note at the edge of each clipped syllable. "What's wrong?"

"Nothing."

"You're a terrible liar."

"People keep saying that. It's not true. I happen to be an excellent liar."

"No. You're just really good at diversion. Tell me what's wrong."

"I'm fine."

"Your hands are trembling."

Shit, she thinks, *that's the second time today*. Gertrud raises her hands to eye level and dispassionately studies the tremor running through her fingers. She is good at holding things together. She doesn't let circumstances get to her, damn it. Gertrud has, through force of will, taught herself to stand in a maelstrom and function at a high level. But this is too much. She's beginning to crack. "How long have we been on this ship?"

"A little less than forty-eight hours."

"It feels like it's getting smaller. Like it's closing in on us." She presses two fingers into the hollow of her clavicle. "*Scheiße!* I want off this damned thing. I want to go *home.*"

"There's nowhere to go but down at the moment, I'm afraid."

"That's not funny."

"I wasn't going for humor, *Liebchen.*" He crosses the room and points out the observation windows. "We are six hundred feet in the air at some godforsaken point over the North Atlantic. Nothing out there but icebergs." He leans over the window. Looks down. "And a few whales."

Gertrud joins him at the window. There are more than a few whales below. An entire pod — fifteen or twenty maybe, she can't tell from this height — is swimming west, right below them. They have the slow, loping movements of great animals moving at leisure. She has seen elephants travel that way in Africa. A quiet, dignified assurance that they rule their territory. That they face no threat. Gertrud is no expert on marine life, but if she had to wager she would guess the whales are humpbacks. But only because she catches the occasional glimpse of their broad, silver bellies when they breach. They look like children in a wading pool, splashing and jumping, and she can't help but wonder if whales laugh. And if they do, what must that colossal joy sound like beneath the waves? And then Gertrud is weeping, because the very thought of laughter reminds her of Egon and her heart cannot shut out the memory of his laughter. She is afraid she will never hear it again.

Leonhard pulls her to his chest and lets her wring herself out. He might have more than twenty years of life experience on her, but he is no different from any other man in that the thing he fears most is a woman's grief. She knows this about her husband and does her best to spare him, but the dam is broken and she cannot hold back the flood. Gertrud heaves and sobs into the crook of his shoulder. He pulls off her hat and tosses it onto the bed. He runs his fingers through the tangled mass of her hair. He shushes her. Wraps his arms tighter.

Leonhard's shirt is soaked by the time she pulls away, but Gertrud feels a great deal better. Once she is composed he places the hat gently back on her head.

She twists her face into a pout. "That bad?"

"You are beautiful, *Liebchen*, but today your hair is opinionated."

Gertrud looks in the mirror and adjusts the brim so that it's slanted across her forehead. She tucks a frizzy curl behind one ear. "The stewardess made me wear it."

"I fear I've lived to see the end of days if my wife has become a woman who cries spontaneously and takes orders from other women."

"At least hell hasn't frozen over."

"Never going to happen," he says, lifting one eyebrow. "Unless you decide to become the spokesman for wifely submission."

Even Gertrud has to laugh at this. "Don't get your hopes up."

"Since when do you need help dressing in the morning? I can see that heiress summoning Fräulein Imhof, but you? No. What are you up to?"

"Believe it or not, I am not the most conniving person on this airship."

"Truly, the end of days."

"Emilie came to me. She has gotten herself in some sort of trouble and wanted to exchange information."

Leonhard groans and sits down hard on the bed. "And what did this exchange cost us?"

"That American's name. Edward Douglas."

"For?"

She lifts the dog tag from her jewelry box and tosses it to him. "Ludwig Knorr."

"So you told the American his real name? I did wonder if you'd made it up." Leonhard inspects the tag as though searching for clues. "Is that it? She gave you nothing more than a name?"

"Oh, do give me a bit more credit than that. Ludwig Knorr is the chief rigger aboard this airship. He's a war hero. Aaaand"— Gertrud draws this out until she's certain she has Leonhard's full attention—"he plays poker with a few other men in the crew's mess every night."

God, I love my husband, she thinks. Gertrud does not even have to explain her plan. Leonhard can sniff it from five feet away. He turns the dog tag over in his palm and then looks at her, his smile devious and unnerving. "The American wants to find this man."

"He does."

"I do wonder," Leonhard says, holding up the tag by its chain so that it hangs at eye level, "what would happen if they were in the same room together? What might we learn at such a moment?"

"I have been wondering the same thing myself."

Leonhard unbuttons his wet, wrinkled shirt and replaces it with a clean one from the narrow closet. "*Liebchen,* I think it's time we went to lunch."

"You're quite sexy when you get that calculating look in your eye."

Leonhard kisses her beneath the ear. "I learned from the best."

"Darling, that's a skill you perfected long before I was even born."

He laughs. "Who says I was talking about you?"

"Do not," she holds up one finger, "tell me her name if you value the few, short years you have left."

Gertrud takes his arm and they arrive for lunch, only to find that the stewards have rearranged everything to form one long table down the center of the dining room. No more congregating in small groups. The passengers will now be forced to eat together.

"This is new."

"We thought it would be more festive," Wilhelm Balla says as he pulls out a chair for Gertrud at the end of the table. "This is usually the point in the trip when everyone begins to get restless, so we thought we'd change things around a bit. Make it feel more like a banquet. A celebration."

Leonhard sits down beside his wife. Places a warm, rough hand on her knee. She leans into him and waits to see how this new arrangement will change the atmosphere.

It has been only two days, but the passengers have easily fallen into the rhythm of the ship. The others begin arriving within moments. They are delighted with the adjustment and take their places at the table, chattering happily as their glasses are filled with wine—a nice, sparkling Lambrusco.

Gertrud is not surprised when the American sits down directly across from her. She *would* have been surprised had he chosen not to antagonize her. No matter. She will enjoy her lunch and she will get the upper hand. Let the bastard flail around for all she cares.

"You know," Gertrud says, looking straight at him, "I don't believe you've said what it is exactly that you do in Frankfurt, Herr Douglas."

He doesn't miss a beat, doesn't try to be evasive. "I am the director of European operations for the McCann Erickson company."

"I see. Other than having a fancy title and dubious office space, what does that entail? In layman's terms."

The American breaks a breadstick in half, spreads a piece of soft La Tur cheese across its warm center, then dips it in a ramekin of dark, syrupy balsamic reduction. He takes a moment to enjoy this bite before answering.

"If I must simplify, I'd say that I am an advertising executive. I use a wide range of international contacts to get wealthy Europeans to invest in marketing campaigns."

His answer sounds rote, like something memorized from a marketing pamphlet. Gertrud lifts the goblet in her hand and takes a sip of the Lambrusco. She thinks for a moment, resting her bottom lip against the cut-glass rim. The bubbles tickle her nose and the glass is cool against her fingers. "My father always said that advertising is the job in which otherwise noble men learn to lie for a living."

"I would of course beg to differ," he says. "And I'd also argue that advertising is what pays for those newspapers you write for. As a matter of fact, you could even make the case that people like me ensure that people like you have a job."

Leonhard's hand has remained on her knee since they sat down, but instead of tracing lazy, seductive circles on her bare skin, his fingers tighten now in warning.

Gertrud laughs. But it's forced, and she can hear the false note in her voice. "That is where you're mistaken, Herr Douglas. No one would pay a single mark for a paper filled with advertisements. They pay for the news. It's the clutter they tolerate."

The breadsticks are hot and flaky, and the American dusts off his tie after taking another bite. He considers. "I am loathe to think that, despite our biased positions, we might actually need one another. Without me there is no outlet to print the news. And without you there is no forum to shill for my clients."

"We're not bedfellows."

Leonhard takes of bite of his breadstick, so she can't hear his muted response, but it sounds like a cheerful profanity followed by, *Over my dead body.*

The food, as always, is a marvel. Once the bread plates are cleared, watercress salad with peeled grapes, marcona almonds, and *verjus* vinaigrette is set before them. This is followed in short order by fried oysters smothered in a sauce *gribiche*—a concoction of wine, shallots, and fresh herbs. Gertrud tries not to moan as she plucks them delicately from the tines of her fork. Judging by the look of those seated around her, everyone is in a similar state of bliss. Amazing how a good meal can lift the spirits of so many people at once. Even the Doehner children, seated beside them, are happy, their little backs straight, napkins laid smooth on their laps. This isn't the sort of food she would think to feed children, but they are eating it without complaint. Egon has not yet progressed to the sorts of food that don't need to be mashed with a fork first. Gertrud is overcome by a quiet moment of guilt and terror when she realizes that Egon could get his first tooth while they are gone. That he might chew something in her absence. How many milestones will she miss because of this accursed trip? All of them, if she cannot get to the heart of this threat.

Irene Doehner is seated immediately at Gertrud's left and she notices that the girl mimics her movements. Tries to hold her fork the same way. Lifts her glass—Gertrud assumes it is filled with sparkling grape juice—with the same three fingers. Pats the corners of her mouth instead of wiping it with her napkin.

After several moments Gertrud can no longer resist commenting. "I'm a terrible influence, young lady. You should find a better role model." She points at Margaret Mather, seated at the far end of the table. The heiress is dignified even in the simple act of eating. "Like her. She's quite elegant."

Irene's back stiffens. "I think *you* are pretty. And smart. Papa says you're a journalist. Is that like a novelist? That's what I want to be when I grow up."

"Very different, in fact. I'm not allowed to make things up. I'm only allowed to write the facts."

"I think making stuff up would be more fun."

"So do I."

"So why not do that instead?"

It's a good question, one Leonhard has asked often enough. "I suppose, when it comes down to it, I'm quite good at finding the truth. And my mother always taught me to find the thing I'm good at and stick with it."

"If I followed that advice I'd be a nursemaid for the rest of my life. The only thing I'm really good at right now is making sure my brothers don't kill themselves out of pure stupidity."

"There's nothing wrong with being a nursemaid."

"Do you have one?"

"What makes you think I have children?"

"You look sad. Only someone who has left a child at home could be sad on an adventure like this."

It is a knife in the heart. Gertrud gives Irene an appraising look. Reassesses the girl. Perhaps not so silly after all. Observant. "No," she says. "I don't have a nursemaid."

Irene gives a stiff nod as though this makes her point exactly, thank you very much.

"Don't worry. You're still young. You have plenty of time to figure out what you're good at."

"I *hate* when people say that."

"Hating something doesn't make it less true."

Irene rolls her eyes at this, in the way that only an adolescent girl can. It takes every bit of Gertrud's self-control not to laugh at her. Such a pity, the arrogance of youth. And wasted too. She'd love to have a bit more of her own former bravado back. Gertrud has an unsettling suspicion that she'll need every ounce she can muster in the coming hours.

Gertrud turns back to her lunch and lets the current of conversation drift on without her. But after a few moments, Leonhard tugs on the white sleeve of Wilhelm Balla's steward's jacket. The tone of his voice suggests a desire for discretion, and Gertrud sees the American turn toward Moritz Feibusch so that his shoulder, and therefore his ear, is angled toward Leonhard. The bastard is listening. As always.

"Might I have a word with you?" her husband asks the steward.

Balla bends at the waist and tilts his ear toward Leonhard.

"I've heard that there is a poker game that takes place in the evenings on board this ship."

"I don't go in for games of chance myself, Herr Adelt."

It's a nonanswer if ever Gertrud heard one.

"But there is a game?"

"I believe," the steward says, cautiously, "that a few of the crew members gather for such a game after their shift. In the crew's mess. But passengers are not allowed in areas reserved for the crew."

Leonhard purses his mouth. Thinks for a moment. "Do you suppose these gentlemen could be persuaded to move their game to an area where passengers *are* allowed? Say, the promenade? Or the smoking room?"

"A good solution, no doubt, but I'm afraid that the crew is prohibited from gambling with the passengers. Poor taste, we're told."

"I see." Leonhard tucks a bill into Wilhelm Balla's hand. "If the rules should happen to change, do let me know."

"Of course, *mein Herr. Danke schön.*" The steward clears their plates and ambles off.

"What was that about?" she hisses.

Leonhard squeezes her knee and nods, just a fraction of an inch, toward the American. He doesn't bother to lower his voice. "We'll discuss it later, *Liebchen.*"

Lunch is wrapped up with linzer cookies sprinkled with powdered sugar and filled with a spiced raspberry jam. The chef has added a touch of black pepper to the jam—Gertrud can taste it amidst the nutmeg and cloves—and the result is stunning. She eats hers slowly, savoring each bite, sad when the plate is empty.

The passengers are full and happy and quite content to push their chairs back and swap stories as long as the stewards are willing to keep their goblets filled. All of them except for the American. He is stiff and tense and excuses himself from the table at the first opportunity.

"Where do you think he's off to?" Gertrud asks.

"If I had to put money on it, I'd say he's got poker on his mind."

THE CABIN BOY

Werner cracks the door open an inch and peers into the small antechamber outside Heinrich Kubis's cabin to make sure it's empty. Once he's certain that the coast is clear he steps out of the room, shuts the door behind him, then wiggles the doorknob to make sure it's locked. Kubis is the only steward who gets a cabin to himself. *Not that anyone would want to bunk with him*, Werner thinks; the man has neither a pulse nor a sense of humor. But he does have privacy and access to the ship's manifest, and that is something Werner very much wants to see. The results of his little investigation have left Werner bewildered, however.

The chief steward has the first stateroom on B-deck. The location enables him to better serve the wealthiest passengers. The room is accessed by a door that leads into a small antechamber off the keel corridor. Lunch is almost over and Kubis could come through the door at any moment, so Werner wants to put as much distance as he can between himself and the cabin before anyone discovers what he has done.

The antechamber is little more than the size of a closet and is lined entirely on one wall with shelves holding wicker baskets, brushes, and shoe polish. It smells of perfectionism. Werner opens the door to the corridor and walks directly into the broad chest of Max Zabel.

"What are you doing in there?" the navigator asks.

"Shoes!" The word comes out higher and squeakier than he'd like. But at least the lie was prepared in advance. He clears his throat. "I came to check on the shoes. It's my break, and I thought I'd get a head start polishing them so I wouldn't have to do it tonight. Kubis keeps shunting the job off on me."

Max sets a large, heavy hand on the bony point of Werner's shoulder. He bends down six inches so he can speak directly into Werner's ear.

"You were in Kubis's cabin."

"No—"

"Don't. You'll save yourself a great deal of trouble if you can refrain from lying. I was just in that antechamber. And you were in the cabin. The only way this situation can go well for you is if you choose to tell me the truth right now."

It's a quarter to three, and Werner doesn't have much time left on his afternoon break. He gets thirty minutes in the afternoon once his first shift ends at 2:30. Yesterday he spent it napping in his cabin after being up half the night shining shoes for Kubis. He has sacrificed the sleep today in order to satisfy his curiosity. It's a choice he regrets now, looking up into the navigator's angry gaze.

Max gives his shoulder an abrupt shake. "Why?"

"The manifest!" he squeaks.

"What about it?"

"I wanted to see who owns the dog."

"That *Schwachkopf* Joseph Späh owns the dog. Everyone knows that. He turned the boarding process into a fiasco."

"No. The other dog."

Max takes a step back at this. He tilts his head to the side. "There are two?"

"They're both in the cargo area."

"How do you know what's stored in the cargo area?"

Werner blanches at this but decides it's best to tell Max everything. "The American passenger. I don't know his name."

"What about him?"

"He paid me to feed the dog. No one has been doing it, and it's a sad mess back there."

"Why was the American in the cargo hold?"

"I don't know," Werner hedges. "But he knows about the dog." He pauses, afraid to say the next thing.

"What?"

"He saw us yesterday. When we went out the hatch."

"He said that?"

"He said that he wouldn't tell anyone we were back there if I agreed to feed the dog. He said he'd give me ten dollars, American money."

Max snorts. "I hope you got it up front."

"I did. I'm going to buy my mother something when we get to Lakehurst."

Werner can't tell whether Max is angry or disappointed. But Max steps away and tucks his hands into his pockets. It's the look he gets when he's thinking about something. Finally he says, "Come with me."

"I have to get back to work."

"This won't take long. Five minutes at most."

Werner follows Max down the keel corridor, around the gangway stairs, and toward the officers' quarters. He stops in front of his own cabin. "Open it." When Werner hesitates Max says, "I know you have a key. You got in this morning. What I don't know is where you *got* the key. You've been making good use of it though."

Werner pulls the key from his pocket and holds it lightly in his palm. "Balla gave it to me."

Max steps aside. Motions toward the door. "After you."

Werner lets himself in and Max follows behind, shutting the door. "I'll take that, if you don't mind. I'm sure Balla will be needing it back."

Good riddance, Werner thinks, but he says nothing aloud. The key has felt like a ten-pound weight in his pocket all day. He has been aware of it even when he hasn't used it. "Why did you bring me here?"

Max opens his closet and pulls out an olive drab duffel bag and sets it on the floor.

"I'm sorry I went through your things. But I didn't have a choice. I had to get you up. And you had to be dressed."

"Listen, *kleiner Bube*, I don't care about my socks or my underwear. I want to know why you took my gun and what you did with it."

"I didn't—"

"Don't lie to me."

"I'm not lying! I swear!" Werner hates it when his voice rises and cracks and sounds like a girl's. He hates that he can't control when and where it happens. But his heart is hammering, and his breath is short, and he is terrified that he has stumbled into some kind of trouble that he doesn't understand. "I never saw a gun. It was dark and I found your clothes. That's it." An entire litany of curse words flies into Werner's mind, but he doesn't say them. He's crying. *Stupid boy*, he thinks, *you look like a baby*. So he wipes his nose and stands as straight as he can. "I didn't know you had a gun. I didn't take it. I *promise*."

He isn't sure whether Max believes him, but the navigator relaxes. He puts a hand on Werner's shoulder. "You have to think. Was it there? Did you *see* it?"

"I don't remember. I don't think it was. But I can't be sure. It was dark."

Max gives him a gentle shake. "This is important."

"I didn't see a gun."

"Damn it!" Max rips his cap off and throws it across the room. He yanks on his hair until it's standing on end in clumps. "Someone took it."

A thought occurs to Werner and with it comes a flutter of unease. "I can help you find it."

"How the hell are you going to do that?"

He hesitates, then nods at Max's clenched fist. "That key will get me into any cabin on this ship."

Max unclenches his fingers and looks at the key as if it is some piece of incriminating evidence. "That would be wrong."

Werner doesn't argue. He just waits. This decision is Max's to make. The navigator ponders for so long that Werner worries he will miss the start of his next shift. But finally Max hands him the key. "Don't get caught," he says.

The cabin boy is muttering assurances, backing toward the door, when Max stops him. "Wait. You never told me who brought the other dog on board."

Werner blinks at him for a moment, confused. "You did," he says.

THE NAVIGATOR

I don't have a dog."

"There's one in the cargo hold listed under your name."

Max glares at the boy. "You've read my name wrong before." Something on Werner's face wavers. Uncertainty perhaps. "You *can* read, can't you?"

"Of course I can read!"

"And you are certain, *absolutely* certain, you read my name?"

"Yes. Three times. Just to make sure."

Werner is like a puppy standing there wagging his tail, waiting for a pat on the head, some morsel of approval. Max believes him. He has never known Werner to lie. To omit information, yes. And to evade, yes. But the boy is not a liar. Max needs time to think, time to sort through what this means. Why would someone put his name on that manifest? "Go back to work," he says, "but I want to talk to you tonight, after your shift."

Max can tell that Werner wants to ask him something but is too afraid. He takes a guess at what is worrying him. "Don't worry, I won't tell anyone. Besides, I need your help."

Werner holds up the key. "And this?"

"Do what you can. But don't let anyone see you."

"Balla will want it back."

"Then give it to him. Don't argue. And don't let on that you know anything."

Max watches him hurry down the corridor and around the corner. He's due back on duty in a few minutes, but there's something he needs to check first. The mailroom is only a few yards from the officers' quarters, and all the keys are on a hook at his belt. His room key. The key that opens the radio room. One for the mailroom. One for the officers' safe in the control car. And a small pewter skeleton key for the lockbox. He used it that first night when he placed the brown paper package in the lockbox, and he holds it between thumb and forefinger now.

The owner of the package is trustworthy. Respected. Formidable. And, when Max looks up, he appears before him, as though summoned by guilt or magic or kismet. Regardless of the cause, Colonel Erdmann pushes open the radio room door just as Max reaches for the knob. Erdmann has been there, as he is most mornings, quietly observing. Taking notes. There is no reason to suspect his sudden appearance. And yet Max does. Especially when Erdmann steps into the hall and shuts the radio room door behind him. He clears his throat and scans the empty corridor.

"I trust that the package I placed in your care is still safe, Herr Zabel?"

Max nods, mute. A toxic, unholy fear begins to bloom in his chest.

"Good. You will receive the rest of your payment once we arrive in Lakehurst."

THE STEWARDESS

They are unhappy because there is nothing left to do, Emilie thinks. The passengers have reached that point in the trip where cabin fever has set in. It is late afternoon, on the last full day of travel, and there is a stifled feeling in the air. A thickness. These men and women have seen and done everything. There are no more rooms to explore—at least no rooms where they are allowed. The newness has worn off, as has the exuberance. They are tired of one another and tired of the doting crew, though, if pressed, they would argue that the service could be better. They are tired of coffee and pastries and card games and the dissatisfied droning of their peers. They wish the piano hadn't been removed last year—it would be nice to have a little music. They wish the sun would come out. They want to be in New York. Fifteen hours. That's all they should have left until arrival. But that time has been lengthened now, a seemingly interminable age to these fatigued travelers. They are angry about the ever-increasing flight delays. Angry they won't be on their way to some new grand adventure tomorrow morning.

For Emilie the remaining hours cannot pass quickly enough. She sits in the promenade with Matilde Doehner and her children. Irene is crying her way through a difficult cross-stitch pattern. She has pricked her finger three times, and a tissue lies wadded in her lap in anticipation of a fourth. It's the frustration more than anything else that has the girl in tears. She wants to get it right but can't. Emilie can sympathize with this. She has spent the majority of her life feeling the same way.

"Would it help if I held the hoop? That way you'd have both

hands free," Emilie says. Helping Irene gives her something to do. It's a way to forget her anxiety of what will happen when they land.

Irene looks up at her, embarrassed to be caught with tears dripping off the end of her nose. Emilie wipes them away with her apron and receives a smile in exchange.

"I don't know. Maybe. It's this stupid flower. It's supposed to be a tulip but it looks more like a bloodstain. It's gross."

Emilie wants to reassure her that the small bouquet of red, yellow, and blue flowers is pretty, but it's not. It looks as though a cat has gotten hold of three balls of yarn while high on catnip. The cross-stitch is a disaster. It cannot be salvaged. Emilie pries the hoop from Irene's tense fist and drops to her knees before the girl. She holds the hoop steady and urges Irene to continue.

When Irene's hand has stopped shaking in anger, Emilie leans forward and whispers, "Can I tell you a secret?"

The girl nods.

"I don't know how to cross-stitch. So you're already better than I am."

It's only a small thing, but to a girl of fourteen, being superior to a grown woman in any area is a very big deal. Irene sniffs, lifts her chin, and turns her attention back to the hoop. "Your mother really should have taught you."

Emilie suppresses the urge to laugh. It feels good, this sudden mirth, but she shows nothing more than a twitching smile. The stewardess has long since mastered the art of restraint. One day Irene Doehner will learn that restraint trumps superiority every time. But the poor girl has many years to go before she will be open to such a lesson.

After several long moments Emilie can sense that Matilde Doehner is watching her. When she looks up, the mother winks and mutters something about herculean efforts and the patience of saints. It feels good to be part of this small domestic scene.

Little Werner chooses this moment to roll out of his chair and flop around on the carpet like a dying bird. "I'm bored!" he begins to squawk over and over again. Emilie has to admit that his thin, piercing voice is eerily avian. His siblings, however, do not see the humor in his actions. Walter kicks him and tells him to shut up. Irene begs her mother to make him stop.

"Werner," Matilde says, her voice low, almost disinterested, "get control of yourself."

Perhaps the children have run out of coping skills as well, because the boy decides to test his mother. He continues thrashing around, arms and legs akimbo. "Bored, bored, bored. So bored!"

Matilde sighs. "Irene, go get your father."

Before Emilie can draw her next breath, Werner is on his feet begging and pleading and promising to behave.

"You made your choice," his mother says. "Sit on your hands and wait."

Hermann Doehner isn't all that tall for a man, but he has a kind and handsome face. He is mostly bald, but his blue eyes and dark brows make up for this. He enters the promenade, hands on hips. Lips pressed together. Irene trails behind him, trying not to look triumphant.

"Come with me," Hermann says.

Little Werner shakes his head. "I don't want to."

He leans over his son. Whispers. "I expect better of you."

Hermann sets a hand on Werner's shoulder and smiles at his wife. It's a look that says boys will be boys. But it also says that he will take care of this and she needn't trouble herself. He plants a kiss on Matilde's forehead, looks at Emilie, then says to his wife, "Have you asked her yet?"

"I was just getting to that."

"If she says no we'll blame it on this little rascal." Hermann leads a white-faced Werner out of the room.

Matilde watches her husband go with a calculating expression but doesn't explain his comment. Instead she says, "Just think, this time tomorrow we will be touring New York City. Hermann has booked us a suite at the Astor Hotel in Times Square. I hear they have copper bathtubs and room service. We're only in New York for two days, but we'll be going to Carnegie Hall and Broadway and the Central Park Zoo. On Saturday we're boarding an ocean liner for Havana where we'll have a week on the beach. Palm trees and pineapple juice. Can you imagine?"

No. Emilie cannot. But she smiles politely anyway.

"It's one day from Havana to the port in Veracruz. Plus another day or so to travel inland, and then it's Mexico City and home to our cool, tiled house and windows that don't need glass, only shutters. We have a terrace and a garden and fifteen banana trees in the yard. There is no winter in Mexico, did you know that? It is warm and beautiful all year long."

"It sounds absolutely lovely."

If Emilie had been paying attention she would have realized that Matilde has been working up to this all along. "You could come with us, you know?"

A long, uncertain pause. "I beg your pardon?"

"You're very good with the children. They like you."

"I'm afraid I don't understand."

"It was Hermann's idea. Not that I oppose, mind you. But it's just the way businessmen think. Acquiring assets and such."

She understands now, or at least she thinks she does, but Emilie wants Matilde to spell it out because she is tired of false hope. "What are you asking?"

"I'm offering you a job, Fräulein Imhof. We would like you to come to Mexico with us and be our governess."

Her response is cautious. "I have a job."

"Not one you like, if you don't mind me saying. We can give you a better life. Something stable. A little luxury—that never hurt anyone. Hermann has already promised he will pay you twice what you're making here. And"—she holds up one palm to stop whatever rebuttal Emilie is preparing—"we can help you with the trouble you're in."

"How could you possibly know about that?"

She shrugs, as though it's obvious. "There are no secrets on board an airship like this. You of all people should know that."

Emilie wants to reach out and grab the lifeline that has been offered to her. She wants Matilde to tell her everything, to help her believe that this could be possible. But she is afraid of having one more precious thing ripped away. She knows firsthand that hope deferred makes the heart sick.

Emilie adds this offer to her list of possible scenarios. She weighs it against Max's proposal and what little she knows of the American's shadowy machinations. Gertrud has told her very little of the latter, but what Emilie does know leaves her feeling uneasy. She is startled by how very tempted she is to accept the Doehners' offer. Emilie considers the possibility, but no matter how she tries to imagine a new start in Mexico, she cannot reconcile it with the reality of her situation. Lehmann and Pruss will never let her off this ship.

Matilde could have been a diplomat. She could have been anything really, so great is her skill with people. She doesn't rush Emilie, or try to persuade her. She simply offers the patient, indulgent smile so often graced on her children, the one that encourages them to make the right decision. "Think about it," she says.

THE AMERICAN

The American has a theory about small men. They are exhibitionists. He has never known a small man to be quiet. Or humble. They are never farmers or dentists. They need to be seen. Every small man he has ever known is loud and gregarious. They become entertainers or jockeys or soldiers. Musicians. Actors. Take up reckless jobs or ones that draw attention to themselves. Occasionally you'll find one who becomes a surgeon, but only because this heroism causes him to be adored by others. Small men are tense and wiry. They spring when they walk. They notice everything around them. They have opinions and make them known. The American has heard the arguments about such men feeling inferior and overcompensating with theatrics. He thinks this is bullshit. It is, he believes, a simple matter of having more heart than body to contain it. Given the choice he'd go into a foxhole with a small man over a giant any day. He has found them to be indestructible. And, if honest, he would admit that such men are small targets. That's always a plus in his profession.

"Twenty dollars says you can't do it." The American stops and tilts his head back to stare at the cruciform bracing directly above them.

"I was in jail once," Joseph Späh says. "Some nameless town on the Austrian border. Spent three days in the cell for public intoxication. I didn't much enjoy it, and if you don't mind I'd rather not repeat the process. The food's terrible in jail. So is the company."

The acrobat barely comes to his shoulder, so it's impossible not to look down at him. The American drifts back a few steps so it's not as obvious. Small men don't tend to appreciate the reminder. "Who's going to see you?" The American spreads his arms, spins on the empty walkway to illustrate the point.

The keel catwalk is empty in both directions. Passengers and crew are at dinner. It's the last night of the flight. Everyone is otherwise occupied. They are killing time. Waiting for bed. Because tomorrow they will be flying over New York City, and then things will finally get interesting. Everyone on board this ship is thinking about what they are going to do when they land. The American is thinking about what must happen in the next few precious hours.

"Do you know what would happen if they caught me climbing that? Do you know what they would think?"

"That the infamous Joseph Späh is worth the ticket price."

This is too much for the acrobat's ego. Few men can withstand such blatant stroking. "I will tell them that you dared me," he says. He points a finger but already it's halfhearted. The idea is planted. "That you paid me."

"You'd have to be caught first, and that isn't going to happen. Let me tell you a secret." The American lowers his voice, makes it conspiratorial. "People don't look up. Not at the clouds or the cobwebs in the corners of the ceiling. They don't look at tree branches or gutters. Want to stay hidden? Start climbing."

This isn't entirely true, of course. But it's what Späh wants to hear. He's experiencing withdrawal. He needs to perform. The man hasn't heard applause in at least three days. He hasn't been able to sit still for hours. It's a wonder he hasn't broken into song or started tap-dancing on the tables yet.

"If I go to jail, you go to jail." He slips out of his suit coat and hands it to the American.

"Fear not, I'm good behind bars." Good at getting what he wants. Good at making sure his throat doesn't get cut in the middle of the night.

Späh doesn't stretch or roll up his shirtsleeves. He simply leaps. Had he not witnessed it himself, the American would never have believed that such a short man could get so far off the ground. But he squats, coils, and springs. He is four feet in the air before the American can blink. It's like watching a monkey or a squirrel or a lemur—one of those creatures with a preternatural sense of balance. He bends, flips, swings up the cruciform bracing, leaping from beam to beam. He doesn't make it look easy; he makes it look like destiny. As if humans ought to abandon their time as dirt dwellers and take to the sky. As if Späh might actually throw himself off, sprout wings, and fly.

For the first time since meeting the strange little acrobat, the American feels a twinge of jealousy. Späh is halfway up now, just below the axial catwalk, and he slows, lifts his head up to make sure the way up is clear, then continues the ascent. The American assumed that Späh would do the minimum necessary to prove that he could climb the girders. But he has proven he can climb whatever the bloody hell he wants. The American concedes a begrudging respect.

It is 135 feet from the base of the *Hindenburg* to its highest point. And Joseph Späh climbs all sixteen stories with such ease that he appears bored. And there, at the very top, he leans out at a near ninety-degree angle and waves. Then because he's a damn showoff he reaches out and lays a hand on one of the hydrogen gas cells. Maybe to say, *Here I am and I've conquered this bastard.* Or, most likely, just because he can. But that single intimate touch gives the American an idea. He feels another piece of his plan snap into place.

Späh comes down just as easily—perhaps more so—and the American steps aside to give him room to land. He takes a bow. "Well?"

"Impressive."

"I was going for spectacular."

"Hungry for applause?" He hands Späh his jacket and the plate loaded with dinner scraps, then turns toward the cargo area where Ulla is waiting for her dinner.

"Recognition. There's a big difference."

No, the American thinks, *there is only the matter of motive.* The *why* behind our actions. He will make sure that Joseph Späh gets recognition for what he has just done. But it won't be in a way the acrobat likes or will even be aware of. At some point tonight when he relaxes with the other passengers in the lounge or the bar, the American will mention this tremendous feat, that gentle touch on the gas cell, and they will remember these details later. They will repeat them. They just won't remember how they came by this knowledge.

The art of disinformation lies in placing suspicion elsewhere. Leave a trail of breadcrumbs that lead nowhere. Create a distraction. Provide reasonable doubt. Coerce a man into performing an acrobatic feat when he feels safe and unseen, and then make sure others know he is capable of the act. Slowly, subtly, constantly cast suspicion on everyone but yourself. Do this and there will be so many questions, so many possibilities, that no one will ever connect the dots.

THE JOURNALIST

As Leonhard sets the Maybach 12 onto the lacquered table in front of Captain Lehmann, the frosted glass immediately begins to sweat. He pulls out a chair for Gertrud first, directly across from the captain, then settles in beside her.

Lehmann raises the glass in toast, takes a sip, and says, "To what do I owe this honor?"

"We need to talk," Leonhard says.

Gertrud scrapes a bit of frost from her glass with a thumbnail. She listens. They agreed on this earlier. She will listen. Nothing more. Leonhard and the captain have known each other for over twenty years and have developed a legitimate friendship in the course of co-writing Lehmann's biography. Lehmann does not know Gertrud at all, and he will not appreciate any contribution she could make to this particular conversation.

Lehmann's biography—simply titled *Zeppelin*—has done well in Germany, and all signs suggest it will be a hit in America as well when it is released next month. Leonhard has earned Lehmann's trust the old-fashioned way, with time and consistency. Yet Gertrud itches to interrogate the captain anyway. She has questions and she wants answers, but she has promised Leonhard that she will chew on her tongue if necessary.

"What do we need to talk about?" Lehmann asks.

Leonhard rests his elbows on the table. "The American passenger on board this flight."

"Which one? There are many."

"Edward Douglas." Leonhard says the name slowly and watches Lehmann's face for any sign of duplicity.

"Ah. That one. I suspected as much."

"Do explain."

"Edward Douglas is something of an anomaly."

"You know him?"

"I know of him. He works for an American advertising company in Frankfurt. His paperwork checks out. According to our sources he is going home to visit family, a mother and four brothers, to be precise. We have no official reason to suspect his actions or his passage on board this trip."

Leonhard tries very hard not to pounce on this information. Gertrud can see him tensing beside her, putting pieces together in his mind.

"And yet?" he asks.

"We are monitoring him."

Leonhard laughs this off. "You're monitoring everyone."

Lehmann doesn't deny it. He simply glances at Gertrud, offers a patronizing smile, and turns back to Leonhard. So that's how it is. Lehmann will not speak freely in her presence. Fine. Gertrud isn't a fool. Leonhard can get the job done. He has been prying information out of sources since before she was born.

Gertrud yawns and stretches, then lays a hand on Leonhard's arm. "If you don't mind, I think I'll join the ladies in the reading room. I'd like to finish my book."

Leonhard is not fooled by her doe-eyed look. A smile twitches at the corner of his mouth. He winks at Lehmann and says, "Do excuse my wife."

Both men rise from the table, and Lehmann hands her the Maybach 12. "Good evening, Frau Adelt. Don't forget your drink."

Gertrud walks from the smoking room with an exaggerated, feminine sway, but once she's alone in the corridor she tips her glass back and drinks the Maybach 12 in two long gulps. Then she wipes her mouth with the back of her hand and swears.

THE CABIN BOY

Werner watches the last of the crew finish dinner and stack their plates in the middle of the table. He pulls out his pocket watch. Frowns. He holds it to his ear to make sure it's still working. Sure enough, the steady *tick-tick-tick* sounds within. The watch is correct. It's only eight o'clock but everyone is done with dinner. They normally linger, dragging out each free moment until their duties resume. But tonight the crew's mess has emptied early. He gathers the dishes and carries them into the kitchen. The sink is his for fifteen minutes—Xaver's routine will only allow for a short interruption—so the cabin boy makes quick work of the delicate china. Werner returns to the crew's mess to put the dishes away and wipe down the tables. He sweeps. Checks the chairs and banquettes for crumbs and sticky patches, then declares the job complete. This gives him a moment to pause as he does a quick calculation. He now has half an hour of free time. A rare luxury.

Last year the *Hindenburg* carried a Blüthner baby grand piano in the lounge. It was custom-made to comply with flight requirements—weighing a mere 397 pounds—and instead of the standard wood shell was covered with yellow pig skin. While on break Werner would linger in the lounge listening to passengers play ragtime on the piano. He liked the raucous music and the gregarious singing that accompanied it. He misses it. Had it been up to him, he would have kept the piano. But the powers that be decided that the few hundred pounds of weight could be better used to store cargo. Freight brings a profit; pianos do not. So there is no music on this flight and, as a result, Werner thinks the atmosphere is too somber. He heads toward the lounge anyway. There's no telling what the passengers will be up to, and there's a good chance he'll find some form of entertainment. A card game. Or perhaps a bit of storytelling. There are a number of Americans on board. They always seem to have the most outrageous stories. And a curious sense of humor.

Later tonight, when he finally crawls into bed, he will wonder if Irene Doehner lingered on the stairs because she was waiting for him. But now he only thinks that he is pleased to see her. That the gangway stairs are his favorite spot on the ship because he has the habit of running into her here. She is sitting halfway up the steps, a mess of needlepoint on her lap. She looks frustrated. And then delighted when she sees him. Irene rises to her feet, and he notes that there is nothing awkward about the motion. She is simply standing where a moment before she was sitting.

He offers a shy smile, and she returns it with one of her own. Werner nods, polite. "Pardon me, *Fräulein.*"

He tries to step around her, but she says, "Wait."

He never expected a kiss. Werner would have been happy with smiles and a handful of flirtatious glances. Had he been particularly bold, he would have orchestrated a way for his hand to touch hers just once during the flight. So when Irene sets her mouth at the corner of his and presses in with her small, soft lips he nearly falls backward down the stairs. It doesn't last more than a second or two, but to him time freezes and every bit of the sensation comes rushing into his mind. He records everything, as though taking notes for a paper at school. The way her hair brushes against his ear. The way she smells of soap—nice and clean and with the faintest tang of lye. The warmth of her mouth. The buzzing of his blood as it rushes through his ears. He has been kissed. It is a shock and a wonder.

One of Irene's front teeth is slightly crooked. He can see this when she pulls away and her smile grows wider. She is delighted by his surprise.

"Thank you," she says, "for the flower. I kept it. I have it pressed inside a book."

Werner is dumbfounded. He has lost all capacity for speech. *Say something, you Dummkopf,* he thinks. Finally, after an aching silence, he says, "I will bring you another one tomorrow."

He isn't sure if his voice cracks or squeaks or if he has even said this out loud until Irene laughs.

"I will look for it."

The poor boy has no idea what to do next. Is he supposed to stay and talk to her? Should he return the kiss? Should he jump and whoop and holler and run around like he has scored the winning kick in *Fußball*? He has spent a lot of time talking with his brother about girls. He has even had a few conversations with his father.

But no one has bothered to tell him what happens after a moment like this. And when he realizes that he is staring at Irene, mute and dumb, he does the only thing he can think to do: he laughs as well—high and bright and too close to a giggle for his liking—then runs up the stairs.

Werner takes them two at a time and arrives at the top with a wild bound. *The wattage on my face must be blinding,* he thinks. And he is half-blinded himself because it takes him a second or two to see Gertrud Adelt studying him. She has witnessed the entire thing.

THE JOURNALIST

The cabin boy looks as though he has been struck by lightning. But the second he sees her, his expression of delight drains away and is replaced by terror. Werner freezes at the top of the stairs, mouth open. It takes Gertrud only a moment to realize that she can play this to her advantage. She holds up one finger—silence—until Irene's retreating back disappears below. It's not fair, but what's the point of being intimidating if she doesn't exercise the skill every once in a while? And it's not like he will be permanently harmed by what she's about to do. Just startled. And really, when dealing with teenage boys, it's best to keep them off balance.

"Are you trying to get that girl in trouble?" she demands.

Werner flinches, and she has to stuff her guilt behind an impassive expression.

"No."

"So what are you playing at, then?"

"Nothing! I . . . she kissed *me.*"

"You've been flirting with her. You gave her a flower."

The circulatory system of the adolescent male is superior to that of all other humans. There is no other explanation for the ferocious color that fills his cheeks. Adults simply cannot get that red. Gertrud isn't sure if the boy is going to cry or faint, so as an act of mercy she places one calming hand on his shoulder. Gives him a gentle pat.

"Please don't—"

"I won't tell—"

"Oh, thank God!"

"I won't tell," she repeats, slower this time, "if you will do me one small favor."

He may only be fourteen, but he is smart and cautious, and he frowns at her now, suspicious. "What sort of favor?"

"The kind where you do what I tell you, no questions asked."

"I don't—"

"The alternative," she says, "is that I go to Irene Doehner's father—he's just around that corner, on the promenade—and tell him that his daughter is kissing cabin boys in the corridors. That she is keeping and pressing flowers that have been given to her. That young boys can't be trusted, and that he ought to keep a better eye on his daughter so she doesn't get taken advantage of. What do you think a man like Hermann Doehner would think of such things?"

Werner is quick and shrewd and thinks well on his feet. "So you would have me exchange one trouble for another?"

"If I wanted to get you in trouble I wouldn't bother trying to negotiate. If you are as clever as I suspect you are, you will find no danger in this task."

"And if not?"

Gertrud ponders this for a moment. "Then we will both find ourselves in a very difficult predicament. Does that sound fair enough to you?"

"It all depends on the task, I suppose."

THE STEWARDESS

When Emilie was hired by the Deutsche Zeppelin-Reederei in September of 1936, the company sent out a press release and a number of photographs, one of which showed Emilie bathing a young girl in a child-size tub. At first glance it appears that both Emilie and her young charge are on the *Hindenburg* and that the picture is a candid snapshot of her work life. Germany was fascinated by the world's first airship stewardess, after all. And her employment on this ship is a milestone for women. Emilie thinks of that photo at some point during every flight. Not because she accomplished something no other woman ever has, but because she badly wishes there was a bathtub on the *Hindenburg*. The photo was staged, of course. There is only the one shower, and it's not the most practical place for bathing children. Yet the Doehner boys have gone from smelling rangy to smelling ripe, and their mother has ordered them to shower. She has brought Emilie along to assist. Once they're inside the small room, and the boys are shrieking and splashing beneath the spray, Emilie realizes that Matilde is also creating space for them to speak without being heard.

"You have questions, I suppose?" Matilde crosses her arms over her chest—how she does this with such large breasts Emilie can't fathom—and looks at her expectantly.

"I wouldn't call them questions."

"Doubts?"

"Fears." Emilie collects Walter's trousers from the floor and folds them neatly. She sets them on the bench and then does the same with Werner's. "How did you know about my situation?"

She shrugs. "It didn't take much sleuthing, I'm afraid. We overheard something at dinner last night. They were speaking English at the table next to us. Hermann is better at it than I am, but it comes with the territory. We travel a lot. We speak a number of languages, though not so many as you, I suspect."

Emilie turns her attention back to the dirty clothes. She folds each item slowly. She doesn't want to seem too eager. "Who was speaking in English?"

"Captain Lehmann and that strange American fellow."

"What did they say about me?"

"Lehmann didn't say much, to be honest. But the American wanted to make an exchange."

"Of?"

"Names. The name of someone on board the ship for the name of a crew member planning to remain in America."

"And he gave my name?"

"He did."

Emilie thinks of the dog tag. "Did Captain Lehmann offer a name as well?"

"No. He did not. The American scribbled something on a napkin and when the captain read it he said he would get back to him with the name."

Emilie tries to keep her voice from sounding frantic. "Anything else?"

"That was it. But it's enough. When we got back to the cabin, Hermann suggested we offer you the job. We need a governess, and you want to leave Germany—at least you haven't denied it."

"You would offer a job to a woman you barely know?"

"No." She swats the suggestion away. "We would poach the world's first airship stewardess from the Nazis. A woman who speaks a number of languages. How many exactly?"

"Seven fluently. I'm passable in three others."

"Ten languages! Amazing. That's a rare gift. So you see, our interest is not just in needing help with our children, but in tutoring them as well. We show you the world; you help Irene, Werner, and Walter learn to navigate it. I think that's a fair trade."

"It's not that simple. Captain Lehmann knows I was planning to leave. I've been reprimanded. My papers have been confiscated." She looks at Matilde. "They won't let me off the ship when we land."

"Is that what you're worried about?"

"It's plenty. I will be under house arrest."

Matilde waves this off as if they were discussing the difficulties in negotiating a restrictive curfew. "That's not a problem." She peeks around the curtain and hands each boy a washcloth and a bar of soap. "Clean all of your parts. Especially the ones you can't see. You have five minutes."

"They are wonderful children. And I would love to care for them. But I'm afraid I don't share your optimism about my situation."

"So what is your alternative?"

"Return to Germany and continue my work with the Zeppelin-Reederei." She does not mention Max or his proposal. That is too private, and she will not share it with Matilde Doehner. Not yet, anyway.

Matilde thinks about this for a moment and then changes tactics. "Do you know what my husband does for a living?"

"No."

Matilde laughs. "Neither do I, if I'm being honest. Not the particulars, at any rate. But what I can tell you is that he is the general manager of Beick, Félix y Compañía, a wholesale drug company based in Mexico City. They dabble in a variety of pharmaceuticals but primarily focus on vaccines. According to his visa, Hermann was just in Germany to organize an affiliate company in Hamburg. Our visas stated that we accompanied him as dependents."

Emilie squints. "Are you telling me that was not the case?"

"It was a partial truth. One of Hermann's chemists went missing a number of months ago. The trip was a convenient excuse to find him."

There are a dozen questions that Emilie could ask at this point, but she gets the impression that Matilde is more interested in completing her story, so she waits silently for her to continue.

"This chemist is a good friend of ours. A kind man. Practically a genius, if you want to know the truth. Generous. Charming." Matilde pulls two towels from the canvas bag at her feet. "His name is David Rothstein. He is Jewish. And he is an outspoken critic of Adolf Hitler."

"Oh." Emilie sees what Frau Doehner is getting at.

"That is the Germany you are returning to. A place where brilliant minds are persecuted because they happen to be of an unpopular race."

Emilie can't be sure whether or not Matilde suspects her heritage. But if nothing else the woman does have an uncanny sense of the political situation at home.

"Listen, your offer is tempting. Please don't get me wrong. I simply don't see how it can possibly work."

Again Matilde seems unperturbed. "Have you ever gone out in public with children, *Fräulein?* Gotten off an ocean liner or an airship?"

Emilie shakes her head.

"Have you ever taken them shopping or walked down the street with three of them in tow? Gone into a bank or a grocery store or a park with a pack of bickering children?"

It's an interesting question, but Emilie can't see how it pertains, and she isn't sure if Matilde is trying to rub salt into what she perceives as an open wound. "No. I haven't."

"You really should try it sometime. It's a fascinating experiment." Matilde lifts two towels from the bench and shakes them out. "No matter how lovely or striking a woman is, when she goes out in public with children she becomes invisible. I once saw Luise Rainer standing at a bus stop in Düsseldorf—that was her hometown you know, she made it famous—next to a set of twins. They weren't even hers. And she was dressed like a movie star. Thirteen men got on that bus and seven got off. Not one of them looked in her direction. Why? Because two children sat at her feet. This is a reality for every woman who bears a child. I was put out to pasture the day Irene was born. Children are the perfect camouflage."

"And you are offering your children as camouflage?"

"Tomorrow when we land, things will be hectic. We will be late.

Some passengers will be in a rush, others excited. The crew will be busy. There will be crowds awaiting our arrival. You will wear one of my dresses—"

"I'm a good deal taller than you are."

"Then you wear your skirt and my blouse. My hat. You walk out on the arm of my husband—"

"I'm taller than he is as well—"

"Then slouch—"

"But—"

"You will have my children at your side, and no one will see you. That is a guarantee."

"And you?"

"I will wait in the cabin and exit a few moments after you do. I will find a crowd. Place myself in the center. Then I will meet you at the car on the airfield. And then we will be gone. You will come to New York with us. Cuba. Mexico. Before long Germany will be a distant memory."

Emilie wants this. She does. And yet her heart twists a bit at the idea. She forces Max's face from her mind. "Someone will see. If not when they bring the luggage, then sooner. It will never work."

Matilde pushes the curtain aside. She turns off the shower and drapes a towel over each son, then sniffs both little blond heads to make sure they have properly followed her instructions. Matilde does not argue with Emilie as she attempts to dry them off. But the boys are ticklish and squirmy and she abandons the exercise after a few seconds. The boys fling water droplets from their hair and giggle as they try to pull dry clothes onto wet bodies. Matilde checks them carefully before sending them from the bathroom with a pat on their bottoms.

"Do give me more credit than that, *Fräulein*," she says. "You wouldn't be the first person I've smuggled out of a country. I am very, very good at it. Just ask David Rothstein."

THE AMERICAN

I t is close to midnight, and the crew's mess is empty except for five tired souls. Four of them have recently ended their shifts, and the fifth is breaking the rules by being there. But then again, the American has never been one for following the rules. Nor is he the sort of man who will ignore a poker game once he knows it exists. They hadn't intended to let him stay—he could tell that much by the look on their faces when he'd walked in twenty minutes ago—but he had given them reason to set the rules aside. Margaret Mather's diamond solitaire ring. He had dropped it on the table and let it bounce and skitter to a stop. It looked like a small fortune there in the middle of that pile of dingy marks. The chief steward pulled out a chair and personally invited the American to join them.

"There's more where that came from."

"Dare I ask how you acquired such a bauble? I will deeply regret my invitation if you say it was won at poker." It was a halfhearted attempt to be threatening. But Kubis is married and the American could see that he had plans for the ring already.

"It was part of my divorce settlement. I'd planned to sell it along with some other items when I get to New York. I certainly don't have a use for them anymore. But I'd just as soon try my luck with them tonight." He'd looked up then, met each man glance for glance. "As long as you don't mind. I have cash as well. If you prefer."

Not a single man at the table objected. Chairs were scooted over. Elbows tucked in. Welcomes muttered. They dealt him in.

He looks at the five cards in his hand now—shit every one of them—but doesn't let on. "Pass," he says, and throws a mark into the pot. The others were at the game for almost an hour before he got here. They're already warmed up, clued in to one another. He will have to catch up fast. It shouldn't be hard. Poker is a game uniquely suited to his particular abilities.

Of the four other men seated at this table Heinrich Kubis is the easiest to read. He tries to keep a neutral expression. But he's working so hard at masking his face that he forgets the rest of his body. He leans forward when his cards are good but droops to the left, into the armrest, when they're bad. He's constantly shifting in his chair, trying to get comfortable.

Xaver Maier wants to smoke. He would be far more comfortable playing this game in the corner of a seedy tavern where he could smoke and drink and run the table than in this regimented airship. So he twitches. He pulls at his mouth and taps his cards on the table—but only when he thinks he can win. If he thinks losing is likely he lays the cards in his lap and waits.

August Deutschle is the American's strongest competition. This is a man who knows how to gamble. He's comfortable with the idea of losing money and feels certain he'll win it back. He's the one who raises the stakes on each round, pushing the others a bit further than they are comfortable with. He doesn't bluff often but likes to call out others when they do.

And then there is Ludwig Knorr. He makes the American nervous. Ludwig is a big man, and the cards look small in his broad, scarred hands—like he's playing with a child's deck. He has an unnerving way of never making eye contact, even when he answers a question directly. He hedges. Holds back. Hides his cards and his emotions. It's a good thing he's not a particularly good poker player or he would be very dangerous.

In the last twenty years the American has learned that men can keep only one secret at a time. And while these men are protecting their cards, all of their thoughts and energy are bent toward that one goal. They want to win the pot of money on the table. Each of them has something in mind that he will spend it on. Some debt he will pay off. Some girl he will seduce. So all of them are paying little attention to the conversation at the table, the questions that are asked, or the answers that are given.

Gertrud Adelt told the American that the dog tag belonged to Ludwig Knorr. But Captain Lehmann said it is Heinrich Kubis's. One of these men was on a zeppelin that dropped bombs over

Coventry in 1918, and there is only one way to find out which it was.

"How long have you gentlemen been flying?" the American asks.

Kubis is the first to answer. "Since 1912. I catered on the airship *Schwaben*. First air steward in history."

The chef groans. "He never misses an opportunity to remind us. Shut up about it already. You've made history. We get it. *You're special.*"

"And you?" the American asks. He puts a card down. Takes another.

He shrugs. "Four years. I started on the *Graf Zeppelin*."

"Rookie," Ludwig Knorr says with a grunt.

"Old man," replies Kubis.

"Old enough to be your father."

"My father is better looking."

They go around the table like this. Swapping cards and insults. Adding money to the pile. Telling their zeppelin stories.

"Just a year and a half for me," August Deutschle says.

Xaver snorts. "Baby."

"I'm older than you."

"You're still drinking from your mother's tit."

"I like your mother's tits better."

This makes the American think of his brother and how his mother laments that boys are like dogs—how they do things in a pack that they would never do by themselves. Age has no bearing on this truth. Especially given the fact that boys never really grow up. They simply age. There is something about male camaraderie that lends itself to insults. You will never see men who dislike each other trading jabs like this without drawing blood. But friends can be bitterly cruel and end up loving each other more. It's about wit and laughter and one-upmanship with men. Insults become terms of endearment. This is the thing that the American misses most about the military.

"I've got the most seniority," Ludwig Knorr says, stating a simple fact.

Again the groan. Xaver tosses a coin in the pile. "As usual."

"Took my first flight in '06. But that was a balloon. I've been on zeppelins since 1912."

"You've all got me beat, I'm afraid," the American says. "Six months ago for me. On the *Graf Zeppelin*. I like this ship better. But given the choice I'd prefer to do my traveling on the ground."

Ludwig tries to hide the disdain in his voice. "Afraid of heights?"

"Only when falling." The American arranges his cards. He's ready to call. "I just prefer to be on the ground when disaster strikes. Easier to tuck and roll."

Knorr narrows his eyes. "So the military, then?"

"For a short while, 1918 mostly. France. You?"

"For most of my life. All of the Great War." He doesn't look up. This is sensitive territory. Two men at the same table who were on opposite sides of the same conflict. Ludwig Knorr pulls further into himself. He sheds the visage of good humor. He becomes a soldier again before the American's eyes.

He looks at Heinrich Kubis but asks the entire table, "Anyone else?"

"No," Kubis says.

Maier and Deutschle shake their heads. The American can see this from his peripheral vision.

"Good," he says, laying his cards facedown on the table. Four of a kind. Tens and the ace of spades. "I call."

He is about to collect his winnings when Ludwig lays his cards down with a cold smile. A straight flush. Hearts. The American watches as Margaret Mather's ring is stuffed inside the chief rigger's coat pocket.

The American has found his target—Ludwig Knorr—but there is, strangely, little satisfaction in having done so. Captain Lehmann lied to him. It is certain the captain does not trust him, and with good reason. But why protect one man only to endanger another? He has to concentrate, to heighten his intuition. He studies them, and the answer soon becomes clear. Heinrich Kubis is innocuous. Arrogant, yes. But he is no threat, and he is almost always surrounded by other people. Lehmann knows this. Ludwig Knorr, on the other hand, is a different kind of man entirely. Lehmann took a calculated risk with his deception, hoping to distract the American. No matter. Tomorrow he will kill Ludwig Knorr. And then he will destroy the *Hindenburg*.

THE CABIN BOY

Werner Franz crouches outside the swinging door that leads from the kitchen into the crew's mess. It's past midnight and the American has been in there for long enough that Werner is starting to feel stiff and cramped in this position. That is his task: spy on the American. Frau Adelt wants to know whom he speaks to and what he says. She wants to know where he sits in the room. The journalist was very clear about these things, but when he asked why she was so interested he was told it was none of his business.

The boy knows nothing of poker, although he hears it's not all that different from chess in that it requires a straight face and a good bit of strategy. But his father has always told him that chess is a thinking man's game and that he's raising Werner to be a thinking man, not one who relies on the luck of the draw. So that's how they spend their time together when he is home. Sitting at the kitchen table beside the fire escape, discussing the merits of the Sicilian Defense over the Alekhine Defense. The Queen's Gambit. The English Opening. The Stonewall Attack. They rehearse the moves, pieces in hand, eyes on the board, the name of each play and the name of each piece suggesting arcane military tactics. And he wonders if the men in the kitchen have names for their own moves. Is it just a bluff? Or a blindman's bluff? A fold? Or a Folded Hat? Is there room for such creativity in a game of chance, or does a man simply rely on his own luck and powers of subterfuge?

As he listens, conversation moves to flying, how long each man has served aboard the *Hindenburg*, and then on to military service.

This topic of conversation seems to interest the American more than the others. He is very curious about Ludwig Knorr and the time he spent flying over England during the Great War.

The American has not won a game yet. Or is it a hand? Werner isn't sure. Regardless, they've dealt the cards a number of times, and the American has come up short on all of them. However, he suspects that is about to change because he lost something valuable in the last hand and now he tosses something heavy and metallic into the middle of the table that sends coins scattering in all directions. The other men gasp. Someone whistles.

"I told you I had more," the American says.

"That confident, are you?" This sounds like Heinrich Kubis.

The American. "My wife had a thick neck. That never looked good on her anyway."

So a necklace, then. The American is betting jewelry. No wonder they let him in the game. Werner tried to get in a game once, but all he had to bet was the five marks he'd earned as a tip the day before, and the men had sent him scuttling out the door. He suspects they wouldn't let him play because the entire crew knows he works to help support his family and none of them wants to be responsible for any damage his brother and parents would suffer because of a loss. Most of them are rough and dirty men, but they are honorable. And many of them have wives and children of their own at home. They know what it's like to come up short for the month, and how bitter it is when their own stupidity is at fault.

Around the table they go, betting, raising, folding. Two players leave the game in disgust. Eventually the American calls. Cards slap the table. Someone curses. The American has kept his necklace and everything else along with it. Werner does his best to remember these details so he can report them to Gertrud Adelt.

More money goes in the pot. Cards are dealt again. The men swap war stories. And the American wins again. Only now Werner isn't paying attention. He is fascinated. He rarely hears of battlefields and brothels when they know he is within earshot, so he misses the signal that the American is calling it quits for the night. He hears the footsteps but doesn't have time to scramble away. Before he can get to his feet, Werner is knocked backward by the door. He doesn't grunt or call out when he lands hard on his tailbone, so his presence goes undetected by the crew in the other room. They hover over the table, looking at new cards, trying to recover their losses. As the door swings shut, the American bends low over Werner's crouched form, murder in his eyes.

DAY FOUR

THURSDAY, MAY 6, 1937 — 5:35 A.M., EASTERN STANDARD TIME

THE EASTERN COAST OF THE UNITED STATES NEAR PORTLAND, MAINE

13 hours and 50 minutes until the explosion

I rated the Zeppelin much lower as a weapon of war than almost anyone else. I believed that this enormous bladder of combustible and explosive gas would prove to be easily destructible.

—*Winston S. Churchill, First Lord of the Admiralty*

D o you think he believed you?" Gertrud asks. Their stateroom is dark—nothing more than a suggestion of light coming from the westward-facing windows—and filled with pre-dawn quiet. Her voice sounds like an intrusion. But she knows Leonhard is awake, has been for at least an hour, because he's tracing tiny circles around the knobs of her spine. Slowly. Methodically. From her tailbone to the base of her skull, he does not miss one vertebra.

She can feel his answer from where she lies across his chest—a shake of the head. "No, *Liebchen*," he says. "I do not."

There's no need to explain her question. He knows well enough what she means. And he's angry with himself for falling into such a neatly laid trap. Of course there's no way the two of them could have figured out the owner of the dog tag on their own. And Leonhard's nonchalant explanation about the deductive skills of journalists did nothing to convince Captain Lehmann last night in the bar. He knows that Leonhard lied to him, and that leaves them at a disadvantage. They talked for over an hour and, when pressed, Leonhard had been forced to tell Lehmann their suspicions regarding the American and his interest in Ludwig Knorr. He had, thankfully, left out Emilie's part in their discovery.

Gertrud burrows deeper into the warmth of Leonhard's bare arm. "Thank you for protecting her."

"Never give up a source, right?" He murmurs it against her hair.

"She's a friend," Gertrud says, and then amends her comment, "for my part, at least."

"I didn't think you made friends."

"End of days."

He laughs at this and rolls her over so she's lying on her back, pinned to the mattress by the weight of his body. "What am I going to do with you?"

"Take me *home*."

It's the closest she will come to begging, and he flinches at the desperate note in her voice. "I'm trying."

"We seem to be going in the opposite direction."

"No way out but through, *Liebchen*. You want to go home to Egon? Home is through Lakehurst and then New York, and then this godforsaken book tour. We miss a single one of those steps and we won't have a son to go home to."

Leonhard has never said the words so plainly, though she has known the truth of them for some time.

"Is that what Goebbels told you?"

"That and more."

The breath catches in her throat. "I'm so sorry. I caused this trouble."

"No. You were just a handy excuse. *I* have co-written a book about German aviation and the Nazis' recent grasp for power. *I* have become a public figure now that the book will be published internationally. *I* have put this target on our backs."

"I certainly didn't help things."

"No. But you made them a hell of a lot more interesting."

Leonhard moves across her body, tucking his head into the crook of her neck, as though protecting her from an assailant. "I am sorry, *Liebchen*."

The mood is heavy, too much for Gertrud. She tickles him in the ribs until he curses and slides away.

"You can't help yourself. You've been making mischief with your words since the beginning. I'd be rather disappointed if you stopped now."

"So mischief is what you want?" He slides a hand over her bare hip, down her thigh.

"Tempting." Gertrud yawns. "But at this particular moment I'd rather have sleep."

"Come home to me, then." Leonhard loops an arm around her and pulls her into his chest as he whispers their pet saying. The first time they made love, Leonhard told her that having her in his arms felt like being home. And so now every time he wants her near him he asks her to come home. And she obediently backs herself into the warmth of his broad chest. As Gertrud sinks a few degrees toward unconsciousness, a single question tugs at her mind.

"What do we do about the American? Lehmann listened to you. But he's stalling. We both know that."

Leonhard lies there, silent for a moment. Then he pulls the blanket high over their bare shoulders. "First we rest. Then we bide our time and get off this damned airship when it lands tomorrow. With any luck we won't have to do a thing about the American. We've planted the seed with Lehmann. He can take it from here."

"And the cabin boy?"

"What about him?"

"He never came back last night."

Leonhard's voice is heavy with sleep. "Look for him in the morning. See what he learned."

And so she drifts toward that blissful void known as sleep. And as she goes she thinks of Werner. How she needs to find him. She thinks of the peculiar absurdity of the adolescent male. She thinks of boys. Boys and brothers. Something about brothers. One or four or what was it? Some inconsistency she has heard. And then the thought has slipped from her and her frantic mind is suspended in temporary peace.

THE NAVIGATOR

Max drops into the control car exactly twenty-five minutes early for his shift. It's not like him, and Christian Nielsen squints in his direction, his tired eyes pinched at the corners, suspicious.

"Couldn't sleep," Max says as he makes his way into the chart room. He stands beside the window, hands crammed deep into his pockets, and surveys the landscape for nearly five minutes before something obvious occurs to him. "That isn't New Jersey."

"Maine," Nielsen says.

"We should be over New Jersey." Max looks at the clock above the chart table. "We're supposed to land this morning."

"More headwinds," Nielsen says by way of explanation. "Pruss just radioed Lakehurst to let them know they should expect us around four this afternoon. Hopefully we can make up some time now that we're over land. But if so, it won't be much."

Commander Pruss is at the helm, looking out the front windows of the control car into the early morning gloom. The persistent cloud cover that has plagued the entire trip is present here as well—but with a more sinister look. Pruss doesn't comment on the delay or greet Max. He simply stands there, hands on the rudder wheel, glaring out into the mist, daring the weather to turn adverse. They can't afford to lose any more time.

They've been fighting headwinds since the first night, but this is an even more significant delay than he expected. Max assumed they were five or six hours behind schedule, but not—he looks at the clock again to double-check his mental calculations—ten.

"How?" he asks Nielsen.

"The jet stream picked up east of Nova Scotia. There was a block of low pressure offshore, and when we flew into it we lost a lot of speed."

It's amazing what can happen while a man sleeps. While Max tossed and turned in his cabin not twenty feet away, the ship practically ground to a halt without his knowing. Two, maybe three hours of sleep is all he got. But he has a plan now, and that's more than he had yesterday.

Max doesn't answer Nielsen. He's afraid his voice will betray relief. He feared he wouldn't have time to do the thing he needs to do, but this fortuitous delay has blown his plan wide open and given him the gift of unexpected time. Perhaps he is not doomed after all.

Nielsen's shift is almost over, and he looks like a man with his mind bent on breakfast. Max cannot help but feel a certain amount of glee at the realization that Xaver Maier will be forced to cook a number of unexpected meals today. He makes a mental note to stop by the kitchen at some point and gloat.

When Werner announces the arrival of coffee a few minutes later, it's Max who goes to fetch the tray. And if the cabin boy is surprised to see him in the control car so early he doesn't let on. But neither does he make eye contact. Something about the boy doesn't look right.

"What's wrong?" Max asks.

Werner shakes his head. "Nothing."

He lowers his voice to a near whisper. "Look at me and say that."

Werner's eyes are clear, and he doesn't appear to be injured. His uniform is crisp and clean. His hair parted. But there is no light in his eyes. "I'm fine," he says. But he meets Max's curious gaze with reserve.

"I don't believe you."

Werner hesitates, then sighs. "You weren't there last night when I came back to your cabin. You told me to come back. I waited as long as I could."

The boy's voice sounds hurt and accusing, and Max feels a stab of guilt. "I'm sorry, I—"

Werner pulls back from the hatch a few inches. Whispers. "There's something I need to tell you." But when Max leans forward, curious, Werner nods toward Commander Pruss at the helm. "Not now."

THE AMERICAN

Breakfast! For the bitches!" Joseph Späh thrusts a plate into the American's face.

"I beg your pardon?"

"Oh, come off it. You're not a prude. And that is a perfectly correct reference for female dogs. Dogs which, I might add, are waiting to be fed."

"Ulla is female. Owens is not. Therefore your plural usage is *incorrect.*"

"Owens?"

"We have to call him something."

"Not something stupid." The American looks at him with disdain, so Späh feigns an expression of mock supplication and a bad English accent. "My good fellow, would you care to accompany me to feed the *hounds?*"

Werner Franz has most likely fed the dog already, but the American isn't about to tell Späh. "Might as well," he finally says. "It's not like I have anything else to do."

It's a familiar ritual by now. The American follows Späh through the security door and down the keel catwalk. The little acrobat looks wistfully at the cruciform bracing as they pass underneath. He tells the American that with a little practice he could make a real spectacle out of that climb. They are discussing the merits of such a display when a man moves toward them from the access walkway that leads to the first engine gondola.

"What are you doing here?"

The voice is hard and deep and commanding. It is the voice of Ludwig Knorr.

"The same thing I've done twice a day every day since this ship departed Frankfurt." Späh takes a dramatic bow. "Feeding my dog."

"Passengers aren't allowed in this part of the ship." He looks at the American and receives a disinterested shrug in return.

"Tell that to every crewman who has seen me traverse this stretch of catwalk for the last three days."

If Späh has been intercepted on his solo trips he has not mentioned it to the American. Most likely he's bluffing.

Knorr is unconvinced. "Names."

"Joseph Späh and"—he looks at the American—"I don't know his name. No one does. But he answers to Asshole in a pinch."

"Not your names, your—"

"Right. You meant the dogs. Ulla and Owens. The latter is the dumbest name I've ever heard for a dog. But it's what we've come to expect from Asshole here."

"Listen, *Arschmade*, I meant the crewmen. I want the names of the men who let you back here."

"I didn't ask. And I wouldn't remember anyway. There are so many of you. And you all look alike in your boring gray uniforms."

The American does his best not to laugh. Späh is quick and clever. He has a rapier wit and the perfect timing of a man who is accustomed to heckling. He enjoys the game immensely. However, the banter is a nuisance to the chief rigger, and he raises a hand to silence the little man.

"I will take you to the cargo hold." Knorr glares at each of them in turn. "And then escort you back to the passengers' quarters."

Knorr leads the way with the air of a martyr, watching while the dogs are fed and their messes cleaned, standing apart from them, inconvenienced and determined to let them know. The American hadn't intended to actually participate in this ritual, and he finds it distasteful. Dogs are not hygienic creatures. The way they eat and the way they defecate and clean themselves repulses him—Owens in particular with the little clods of shit clumped around his ass. But the American is keenly aware of Ludwig Knorr's curious gaze, so he plays the part.

They are almost done when Werner Franz enters the cargo room door holding a paper bag filled with scraps. He eyes the men in turns—Späh and Knorr first, but upon seeing the American he cannot disguise his fear. The American gives him an almost imperceptible shake of the head. *Don't say a word*, the look commands.

"Why are you here?" Knorr demands.

He points an unsteady hand at the wicker cage. "To feed the dog."

Owens sees Werner and begins to leap around, pushing his nose through the narrow slats, begging for attention. *Stupid, pathetic creature and his easily bought affections*, the American thinks. When Werner offers his hand the dog licks it with devotion.

Knorr watches this display of affection for a moment. "*Why?*"

It's a direct question from a superior, and the American cannot blame the boy for answering truthfully.

"I was paid to do so."

Knorr's voice drops lower. Curious. "By whom?"

There is no hesitancy in Werner's voice when he answers. He has chosen his course and committed to it. "Him."

Knorr's full curiosity turns to the American now. "It seems you have a habit of being where you do not belong."

The poker game. The cargo hold. Knorr's curiosity turns to suspicion in an instant.

"It is a long flight and I am easily bored."

"Is that dog yours?" Knorr asks.

He pauses, just long enough to choose the lie. But he speaks it plainly and confidently when he does. "Yes."

Knorr doesn't believe him. That much is clear. But he doesn't argue while Werner and Späh are staring at the two of them with open astonishment.

"It is ugly," he says and then turns to the cabin boy. "Finish what you're doing and then escort these men back to the passengers' quarters. They are not to come back again while this ship is in the air. Understood?"

"Yes."

And Knorr is gone, walking back into the belly of the ship. The American watches his retreating back until the cargo hold door swings shut again. He allows himself the brief fantasy of driving a knife between those shoulder blades.

"What was that?" Späh asks.

"That," he answers, "is a complication."

THE NAVIGATOR

1:55 p.m. — five hours and thirty minutes until the explosion

Max fiddles with the key ring clipped to his belt. Making up his mind. Summoning courage. Fumbling for a plausible excuse should he be caught. And, he must admit, getting caught is the most likely scenario because Commander Pruss is standing ten feet away at the helm, arguing about the delay with Colonel Erdmann in barely hushed tones. They have not quite reached the point of gesticulation, but neither of them is happy. If Max is going to go through with this he must do it now.

Whatever fool decided that *Faint heart never won fair lady* clearly was not in possession of a pulse. Max can feel his blood pounding in his ears as he tucks the key to the officers' safe into his palm. He can feel the cool weight of it against his skin like an indictment, a flagrant violation of protocol.

Max leans over the chart table, his forearms on the polished wood surface, as though studying something. In the end it's easy. Max drops his right arm. He slides the key into the lock and turns it. The safe door swings outward a few inches without so much as a squeak, and Max only has to lean over a bit more to grab the manila envelope that Pruss took from Emilie's cabin. There is no digging around the safe to make sure he has picked up the right thing. It is empty apart from this, and his fingers fumble only a little as he pulls the packet from the safe and slides it beneath his logbook. Locking the safe is harder now that Max's hand is sweating. He holds his breath as he struggles to make sure the tumblers lock. He's trying too hard. Forcing the key. Applying too much pressure. He lets go and stands back. Flexes his hand. When he dares a glance into the bridge, he sees that Helmut Lau has taken Commander Pruss's place at the helm while Erdmann stares through the front windows as though willing the distance to lessen.

"Is something wrong?"

Pruss stands in the door between the bridge and the chart room looking at Max with narrowed eyes.

Everything is wrong. Every damn possible thing. Max doesn't break eye contact with Pruss, but in his peripheral vision he can see the key sticking out from the lock. It seems as obvious to him as a corpse lying in the middle of an empty room. A blinking arrow pointing to his guilt. And a corner of Emilie's envelope is visible beneath the black leather logbook. It may as well be blood on the table for all the attention it draws to itself.

Have I answered? Max thinks. Shit. He's not sure.

"No," he says. "There's nothing wrong."

"Why are you holding your wrist?"

And so he is. Damn it. Max's left hand is clamped around his right wrist while he continues to flex his fingers self-consciously.

Again, he takes too long to respond. His answer is a single word, the only explanation he can summon under Pruss's intimidating stare. "Tendonitis."

Whether or not Pruss believes him, Max can't tell.

"If it's giving you trouble, go to the kitchen and ice it when your shift is over. There won't be time to have it seen to when we land. We'll need to get in the air as soon as possible for the return flight." Pruss lowers his eyes to Max's collar, and Max fears that there must be a sweat ring there because the commander adds, "We won't be staying for return laundry service either."

Assuming that he actually had tendonitis, Max doubts that Xaver Maier would relinquish so much as one cube of his precious ice to aid him. He says none of this to Pruss, however. He simply nods and says, "I'll see to it." Then he drops his hand to his side as though to prove it feels better already.

Pruss looks away briefly as another navigator descends the ladder into the utility room to take Max's place for the next shift. Max takes the opportunity to duck down and pull the key discreetly from the lock. Then he drops to his knee and tucks the key into the side of his shoe. He pulls the knot on an already loosened shoelace and ties it again. When he straightens, Pruss has moved back into the bridge.

Max never counted the money Emilie had stashed away, but it must be a decent sum because the envelope is thick and he has trouble tucking it between his dress shirt and the waistband at the small of his back. He pulls his jacket down to cover it, and feels as though everyone must notice the obvious bulk at his waist. He greets the officers who arrive for second shift and hopes the guilt isn't evident on his face. As Max climbs the ladder into the radio room he waits for the damning signal that he has been caught. A shout. A command. His name yelled loudly and sharply like the report of a rifle. But it does not come, and Max ascends the ladder as calmly as possible, up and out and down the corridor.

He goes immediately to his cabin and places Emilie's documents at the bottom of his closet, beneath his duffel bag. They will land in a few hours and he doesn't have long to finish this task. But first he needs to find Werner.

THE CABIN BOY

3:00 p.m. — four hours and twenty-five minutes until the explosion

Werner Franz is in the officers' mess preparing for afternoon coffee break when the New York City skyline rises into view. It's such a sudden change in landscape that he is startled. For the last several hours they have been floating over fields and forests and small ambling towns that dwindle and melt into the countryside. Winding roads, often gravel, that loop and switch back and then disappear altogether into pine scrubs or sandy beaches.

The Big Apple. It's a puzzling nickname, but the boy likes the way it sounds when he says it in English. *The Big Apple.* A combination of hard letters and smooth syllables. However, based on what he can see from the window of the crew's mess, there couldn't be an actual apple tree in all of New York. Not with its ribbons of concrete and towers of steel. It is the largest, most dazzling thing that Werner has ever seen. There appears to be no end, and from this height it feels as though civilization is a great gaping maw that is ready to swallow everything whole.

They fly in along the coast and then up the Hudson River toward the docks. For three days they've flown over the Atlantic, but this is a different sort of ocean, no less formidable and teaming with life, but consisting entirely of skyscrapers as far as the eye can see. The entire horizon is filled with buildings that stretch to impossible heights, their plate-glass windows winking in the sporadic sunlight. It is as though New York is pushing the storm clouds away just for them, doing what it does best: putting on a show. Werner can see the elevated trains rattling along their tracks and the streetcars below guided by straight lines and electric cables. Buses. Vehicles. Taxicabs—a shocking yellow even from this height. And everywhere there are crowds of people moving in swarms as though by telepathy. To Werner they look like ants rushing from their hills, off to conquer a fallen crumb. Occasionally he sees a train rise from its hole beneath the ground and sprout to the surface like an earthworm tunneling toward the light.

On previous flights the *Hindenburg* has flown down the center of the city and made sure passengers could see the major landmarks. But it has never taken its time as it does now. Whether to make up for the frustrating delay or to give the passengers their money's worth, Werner isn't sure. Regardless, the airship turns and makes a great, lazy loop around the city. They fly so near and so low over the Empire State Building that he can wave to tourists on the observation deck. If anyone else were in the crew's mess he wouldn't risk the scolding, but he is alone and feeling brave, so Werner slides the window panel aside and presses his chest against the sill. He leans out and waves madly to the delighted little figures below, watching as a handful take pictures of the ship. The cabin boy wonders if he will be in those pictures. If they will make the paper. If he will ever see them. He doesn't have long to ponder the idea, however, because he hears voices in the corridor outside and snaps the window shut again.

Max enters the mess with Christian Nielsen and Kurt Bauer. They join him at the window. It is gratifying, this bit of company. Werner is glad that even seasoned airmen are compelled by the sight. It makes him feel less juvenile.

The *Hindenburg* turns again and glides to the very foot of Manhattan, and there, rising from her pedestal in the water, is the Statue of Liberty.

"It looks like a porcelain figure, don't you think?" he asks Max.

"I've never really noticed before, but yes, I suppose it does. To be honest, it's the green that has always confused me. I had imagined her to be white—like marble—before I saw her for the first time."

This is not Werner's country nor his landmark, but there is something inspiring about the statue nonetheless. A sort of defiance that appeals to his adolescent mind. Werner idly wonders if he could pluck her up and take her home as a souvenir. Would liberty spread to his own homeland if he did? Would it be the peculiar American brand? So loud and brash and unapologetic? Would the Gestapo patrol the streets of Frankfurt and her citizens cower behind closed doors if she were standing on the shores of his country? How tempting to reach down and grasp her outstretched hand. How tempting to find out.

Christian Nielsen, however, appears entirely unimpressed with Lady Liberty. "The French are so sentimental. What a stupid gift."

"He's only saying that because his ex-wife is French," Max says to Werner. He's trying not to laugh. "She left him for a more *sentimental* man."

The *Hindenburg* turns again, back up the East River this time, then away from the city. Werner looks up to find Max Zabel watching him with a peculiar expression.

"What?"

"It's different from the air. Most people will never get to experience it the way you just have. It's breathtaking. But you might not like it so much if you were down there in the crowds and noise and grime."

"Maybe," Werner says. "But I'd like the chance to find out for myself. One day."

Nielsen and Bauer eventually get bored with the sight and leave the crew's mess. They are humming with expectant energy, eager to do something during these last hours on board the airship.

While Werner watches them go, Max holds up one finger. Wait, that finger says, and when the room is empty he sits at the booth and motions Werner to join him.

"I'm sorry about last night."

"What happened?"

"I was talking to Kubis."

"About what?"

"The dog."

Werner is stricken at this admission. Every threat that Kubis has made returns to him now.

"Don't worry," Max says. "I didn't tell him that you saw the manifest. I was just poking around, trying to figure out what he knows. I told him the crew has been complaining about the dogs. The noise and the smell. I asked if he knew whose they are. He was sure one belongs to the acrobat. But he didn't know about the other dog."

"So why bother asking?"

"I wanted to make him curious. He'll check the manifest, and when he sees my name he'll know the paperwork has been tampered with. And then he'll come to me. It's his job on the line over this, not mine. And if I know Kubis at all, the first thing he will do is cover his ass."

"Why do you think the dog is listed as yours?"

"I don't know. But I want to find out." Max taps two fingernails on the table in rapid succession. They sound like castanets. He goes on like this for several moments but he doesn't share his thoughts with Werner.

The cabin boy knows that adults keep their secrets. And this airship abounds with them. The journalist had found him before lunch and interrogated him about the poker game the night before. He told her all that he could remember about the American and the questions he asked. He told her about getting caught, and she seemed contrite at the danger she placed him in. Werner doesn't understand what she's after, but he knows that all of these things are related somehow. He just can't piece them together. He doesn't understand the bigger picture.

The silence stretches on for so long that Werner finally says, "I didn't find it."

The gun. He doesn't mention this out loud. And Max doesn't need him to clarify. It's simply understood.

"Did you look in any of the rooms?"

"No. Balla took the key back not long after I left your room."

Werner is about to apologize, but Max holds up his hand. "Don't worry about it. It was wrong of me to let you try."

"I did learn something yesterday, though." Max waits for him to continue and Werner thinks for a minute, trying to get the order of events straight. "That woman, the journalist, made me go to the kitchen last night to spy for her—"

"Made?" Max interrupts.

"She blackmailed me." He shrugs as though this should be obvious.

"How?" Max asks, his knuckles white as he grips the table. "Did she have something to blackmail you with?"

This is the second time in as many days that Werner has found himself dealing with the issue of blackmail, and he knows that Max has less patience for it now than he did the first time. Werner shrinks back several inches and forces himself not to cover his ears. He's afraid Max will box them at any moment.

"Irene Doehner kissed me yesterday, and the journalist saw, and she said she would tell Irene's father if I didn't do what she asked." The words tumble out in one long string. Werner doesn't stop to catch his breath until he has dumped the entire confession right in front of Max.

The navigator raises one eyebrow in disbelief. "*She* kissed *you?*"

Werner crosses his arms over his chest and slouches against the booth. "Yes. Is it that much of a surprise?"

Max laughs. "Yes."

So he's not angry, then, just surprised.

"For the record," Max adds, "I would have done the same thing if I were you. But I am curious what she had you spy on."

"The poker game in the crew's mess."

"Why?"

"The American joined the game last night even though he's not supposed to. But they let him in because he had money and some expensive jewelry. She wanted me to listen to everything he said and did. She wanted all the details."

"And did you tell her these details?"

"Yes."

Max groans and sinks into his seat. "Good grief, Werner. You get into more trouble than any boy I've ever met."

"Don't worry," Werner says, and it's his turn to have a mischievous grin. "The American didn't find out why I was there."

"Oh?"

"I go to the kitchen every night to fetch Kubis after I shine the shoes. I told the American they never let me join the game, but I wanted to listen anyway. He let me go."

"Just like that?"

"Well, he walked me back to my cabin—no doubt to make sure I didn't run off and talk to anyone. But he didn't bother me after that."

Max leans across the table, curious now. "What exactly did you learn, Werner?"

Just as he's about to tell Max about the American and the poker game, the conversations, betting, and the distinct interest in Ludwig Knorr, Commander Pruss walks into the crew's mess.

"Coffee," the commander tells Werner. "Cream, no sugar."

The cabin boy leaps up to obey this order, and Pruss takes his place at the table. He drops his cap onto the lacquered wood surface and says, "We have a problem."

Werner thinks Max's face betrays a look of fear, but the expression is gone in a blink.

"How so?" Max asks.

Pruss cracks the knuckles on his left hand. "We're going to land much later than expected."

THE STEWARDESS

3:45 p.m.—three hours and forty minutes until the explosion

The Doehner boys are on their hands and knees in the middle of the lounge chasing their small motorized truck around the floor. Margaret Mather has emptied her coin purse onto the table and divided it between them. They are using this unexpected source of funds to make bets on whether the truck will drive in a straight line and whether they will have to wind it a second time before it reaches the far wall. Little Werner, ever optimistic, has wagered in favor of both, and it looks like he will be out two marks as a result. The car jerks and sputters, and it veers off-center toward a table leg. Emilie can hear the small gears grinding, and three bright sparks shoot out from the wheel wells and dissipate immediately. The boys are delighted. They cheer and collapse onto the carpet in laughter. For her part, Margaret Mather sits to the side, hands folded in her lap, looking the part of a generous benefactor.

Matilde Doehner watches her sons with resignation. "Men will bet on anything," she says. "Even the miniature ones. Horse races. Car races. Games. Politics. How far they can pee. It's why this world is going to hell—men and their stupid wagers."

Walter wins the bet when the truck stops with a sudden jolt.

They set new terms, up the ante—there are three marks on the line this time—and he winds up the truck again. This time the sparks begin immediately.

"Stop that! Give it here!"

Heinrich Kubis strides toward the boys and all eyes in the lounge turn to him. Walter and Werner freeze immediately. They know authority when they hear it. Matilde sits straight in her chair, gaze swiveling between her children and the chief steward. She isn't sure whether they have done something wrong and therefore need to be punished or whether they are being threatened and therefore need to be protected.

Kubis scoops the car off the floor and stops the motor. He shakes it at the children and then turns to Emilie, furious. "Sparks! How could you let them play with something that *sparks*? Have you forgotten where we are?" He sticks the little tin truck in her face.

Emilie has been so distracted by her situation, by Max's proposal and Matilde's offer, that she never stopped to think what the sparks could mean in an airship lifted by combustible hydrogen.

"You're right. It's my fault. I wasn't paying attention," she says.

Already Matilde feels she needs to defend Emilie. She doesn't stand. She doesn't apologize. Or speak at all, for that matter. She simply holds out her hand, palm up, with a question in her eyes. Will Kubis return the car? The choice is his, and she intends to let him make it publicly. Frau Doehner is quite aware that she has an audience.

Kubis stiffens in anger. He moves his hand, effectively hiding the car behind his back. He sniffs. "I will return this when we land. Not a moment before. The risk is too great."

Matilde watches him leave, the corners of her mouth twisted in triumph. When the lounge occupants have returned to their business she leans close to Emilie and whispers, "We fly on a Nazi airship, but our greatest threat comes from a child's toy?"

"It depends on how you define a threat," Emilie says.

Margaret Mather, bored with the game, moves to the observation windows to stand beside Irene. The girl is wearing a blue dress with pleats and a scoop neck. It is quite pretty. It brings out the cornflower in her eyes and accents the slight curves on her slender body. The dress makes her look older than fourteen. Emilie suspects Irene has chosen this dress to catch the cabin boy's eye—not that she needs to try hard for that. He can hardly keep his eyes off her as it is. Of the three Doehner children, Emilie fears that Irene will be the most difficult to look after.

The stewardess likes the girl. She sees much of her former self in that sly, pretty face. Emilie can't help but find Irene rather entertaining. And the idea of watching her continue to grow and mature and become her own woman is appealing.

"Do you see that?" Margaret Mather taps the window with one neatly rounded fingernail, then points at something beneath them. She speaks in German for Irene's benefit.

"Yes," the girl says, "what is it?"

"Princeton University."

"It looks lovely."

"Oh, it is! You should see it from the ground. All the ivy and the stonework and the gardens."

"Did you go to school there?"

Margaret laughs at this. "Me? No. You forget that young ladies are not permitted to attend Princeton."

"At all?" Irene asks.

"No."

Emilie is humored by the look of consternation on Irene's face. The girl takes in Margaret's polished form. "But . . ."

"What?"

"You're rich."

The assumption is simple. Naïve. Entitled. And from the corner of her eye Emilie sees Matilde shake her head. Irene is quite intelligent, but clearly her education has been lacking.

"There are things that money cannot buy, young lady. A forward-thinking father is one of them." Margaret sets a gentle hand on Irene's shoulder. "Having one is a privilege you should not take for granted."

"How do you know so much about Princeton if you didn't go there?"

"My brother is one of their art and architecture professors."

"Really?"

"Yes. I've come home to visit him for the summer."

Emilie watches Irene's face change. She sees the resolve drop like a curtain falling across a window. "I will go to university," she declares, then turns to her mother. "Can I go, Mama?"

There is humor in Matilde's voice. But there is also pride. "It's a bit early for that, don't you think?"

Irene shifts those imperious blue eyes back to Margaret Mather. "How do I get into university?"

Margaret stifles a grin. "Learning English would be a good place to start. As a matter of fact, learn as many languages as you can. Study. Observe. Learn to communicate intelligently—both with your voice and in print."

Matilde gives Emilie a pointed look as if to say: *See, my daughter's dreams depend on you.*

Emilie sighs. Irene is pointing at things on the ground below and having Margaret tell her the English names. She repeats the words carefully, her mind already set on learning this strange new language. It seems possible, this life she's being offered. Appealing even. There is no threat to her life and very little to her heart. Why shouldn't she leave? Why shouldn't she build a life for herself apart from ghosts and dictators? Emilie watches Irene Doehner make her first stubborn attempts to learn a new language, and she pushes the thought of Max from her mind.

Emilie looks at Matilde and nods. "Very well, then."

THE NAVIGATOR

4:00 p.m. — three hours and twenty-five minutes until the explosion

The light at four o'clock in the afternoon is different from that of any other time of day. Max feels that this is true even now, with the sun blotted out by storm clouds. He would prefer a cobalt sky filled with golden light, of course. This never-ending gray-upon-gray does nothing to lighten his mood, and yet he must admit the sky is oddly beautiful. But it's a savage beauty, and it makes him uneasy. The clouds are heavy-bottomed, dark and churning, with the low roll of thunder threatening violence.

The crew is restless. They want this ship on the ground. The passengers are restless. They want to be off the *Hindenburg* and on their way. But six hundred feet is a long way to descend safely when the weather turns unstable. His shift ended two hours ago, but he has come back to the control car to assist with landing.

Max can see the struggle play out on Commander Pruss's face. His gaze is on neither the sky nor the soil, but straight ahead at that midpoint on the horizon where the two meet. They all hope the path is clearer ahead and that by some miracle they will be able to land, but things are not looking good. Pruss leans forward, tense. His jaw is clenched. His eyes, not tight but wide and round, are unblinking.

The airship glides over the New Jersey Pine Barrens, dotted by the occasional flat scrub oak, and begins its initial approach toward Lakehurst. The enormous bulk of Hangar No. 1 dwarfs everything else in the vicinity. Max notes that the landing crew has not assembled on the field. A bad sign. There are spectators and a handful of reporters—he can see the tiny pop of flashbulbs—but the great hangar doors are closed. And then the telegraph machine sends out a series of abrasive little chirps in the radio room above. Max doesn't wait for the order. He goes to retrieve the message and then understands why the landing crew has not assembled.

He hands it to Commander Pruss, who reads it aloud: "Wind gusts now twenty-five knots."

Max can feel the faintest drag of the ship as the crew struggles to keep it from bearing port side. It has not begun to rain. And though the sky threatens lightning, it has yet to manifest. But Pruss will not be able to land the ship. Not now, at any rate. Not with this wind.

The commander's shoulders drop, just an inch, and his body uncoils from the strain of determination. A sigh. A muttered curse. "Head southeastward," he finally says, "toward the coast. We will wait out the storm."

THE AMERICAN

4:15 p.m. — three hours and ten minutes until the explosion

Where are we going? Why aren't we landing?" What little hair Moritz Feibusch has sits on the top of his scalp in an unruly pile that he has twisted into something resembling a Brillo pad.

It is an odd camaraderie the American has formed with the two Jewish businessmen. They seek him out whenever the passengers congregate in groups. They join him at meals. They speak with him, as though speaking with a friend. The American is not used to being liked. It makes him uncomfortable.

"We can't land in a storm," the American says. And then, "What have you done to your hair?"

Feibusch lays his palm on the tangled nest. Laughs. "It's a bad habit. I tug my hair when I'm nervous."

"You've been twirling your hair like a schoolgirl for the last ten minutes. It's disturbing," William Leuchtenberg says.

The American wanders away, leaving the men to their good-natured jabs. He had not counted on the delay. He had not counted on the headwinds over the North Atlantic or the fact that the *Hindenburg* itself would not cooperate with him. When he sat in his office in Frankfurt all those months ago reading the telegram and considering, *really* considering, this opportunity and all it would mean for his life and his career, for the chance at revenge, he had never once taken into account that the airship would arrive twelve hours late, that there would be virtually no time between landing and the next takeoff. He has killed an innocent man—a fellow American—just for the chance to kill Ludwig Knorr. So the thought of abandoning his mission feels untenable. Wasteful. He could always dispatch Knorr and leave his primary orders unfulfilled, but that leaves the Nazi government in possession of the largest, most technically advanced airship in history. It leaves them in a position of worldwide aviation dominance. He may be a small, petty man hell-bent on personal vengeance, but he is also a zealot. He *believes* in this cause. So there is nothing left to do now but keep himself occupied. He must think. He must sort through all the available options and find the one—there has to be *one*—that enables him to accomplish what he came on board to do.

The American wanders through the passenger areas with restless energy. He creates a pattern without giving it much thought. The smoking room and then the bar. He chats with the passengers and then Schulze. He orders a gin and tonic but doesn't drink it all. He ambles off with it in his hand, then leaves it two-thirds full on the first flat surface he can find. Next comes the dining room and the promenade. He drifts among the tables, initiating conversation, provoking arguments. He approaches this task as though he is conversational carbonation, forcing air and livelihood into the dialogue. But he's quick to abandon the banter once it flares to life. He moves on to the lounge. The reading room. The observation deck. These areas are last. He finds them tedious. This is where the women and children are gathered, fretting over needlepoint and romance novels. But, still, he cannot afford to linger in any place for too long, so he adds these rooms to the rotation, then starts over, making sure to avoid Feibusch and Leuchtenberg on the second rotation. He does not want friends. Friends complicate things.

For now he will stay busy. He will keep his mind sharp. And when the moment is right he will make his move.

THE NAVIGATOR

6:00 p.m. — one hour and twenty-five minutes until the explosion

Max settles into his favorite booth in the crew's mess as the *Hindenburg* flies low over Asbury Park, New Jersey. He can see the boardwalk directly beneath them and the small forms of lovers strolling hand in hand on this warm May evening. Some crane their necks and wave. Others whistle. A child jumps up and down, ecstatic, and Max can see a small dog spinning in circles, barking at them madly. For one short moment Max is captivated by the picturesque scene and grateful for his place in it. Then he presses back into his seat and feels the uncomfortable bulk of the envelope and he remembers what he must do. He has fetched the documents from his room, and he feels the weight of them like an anchor lashed to his waist.

But first, dinner.

Max has had so few opportunities to feel superior to Xaver Maier in the last seventy-two hours that he indulges the lesser side of his character now, grinning with delight as the chef pushes the swinging door open and drops a tray of finger sandwiches onto the table.

"Not a word," Maier says.

Max doesn't have to say anything. He simply plucks a roast beef sandwich from the tray and bites off a corner. The bread is fresh, the beef is perfectly seasoned, and the creamy horseradish sauce is perfect. It's hard to hate a man who cooks so well, but Max gives it his best effort anyway. He won't soon forget the image of Maier kissing Emilie.

In the end Max can't resist. "Do you think she will remember your name? This girl who's waiting for you?" Max asks as the chef stares longingly out the window. "Or does she even know it?"

Maier is known for making the most of their short leaves in New Jersey and for the lecherous grin he wears when reporting for duty again. But this delay has ensured that the chef will not make whatever appointment he has been looking forward to. Max experiences no small amount of satisfaction in this. Maier glares at him like a fractious child and returns to the kitchen with a huff. He sends one of the assistant chefs to bring the platters of fruit and cheese into the crew's mess in his stead. It seems that Maier has had quite enough of the navigator.

Max turns from the window as Werner rushes through the door, a couple of minutes late. His cheeks are flushed and his eyes are bright as he begins pulling plates and silverware from the cabinet to serve the crew. He loads a plate for Max without asking his preference and sets it in front of him, avoiding eye contact. Max is about to ask the boy why he's blushing, but the door opens then and a handful of riggers enter. Max doesn't want to embarrass Werner. Ludwig Knorr ruffles Werner's hair, and the cabin boy turns away to serve them.

It seems to Max that Werner is euphoric. So it's the girl, then. They've kissed again or done something equally stupid. He just hopes that whatever the boy is doing goes unnoticed by her parents as well as the officers. It would not go well for Werner if he were caught fraternizing with the daughter of a wealthy passenger. He makes a mental note to scold the boy later.

Max adjusts the envelope at his waist before pushing his plate away. He beckons Werner over with a hand.

"Have you seen Emilie?" Max asks. "I need to have a word with her."

"She was headed up to A-deck a few minutes ago. Probably going to start tidying the cabins for the return trip."

"Thank you."

Max checks the clock above the door. It's 6:30 now. He doesn't have much time.

He finds Emilie on A-deck stepping out of a passenger cabin. She closes the door behind her, holding a bundle in her arms. It appears to be a pillowcase stuffed with dirty linens. She jumps, startled, when she sees Max. He searches her face, looking for any hint of pleasure or hope or relief. But her expression is carefully guarded, so he must do this with no encouragement from her.

"I have something for you," he says.

Emilie tilts her head a bit in surprise but says nothing.

"Consider this my apology—for everything—and the only way I have of proving that I do love you." He pauses. "Please don't let that word scare you. *Scheiße*. I can see that I've scared you. Oh, well. Too late now. It's the truth. I love you. And I hope this proves it."

Max reaches behind him and pulls the now-crumpled envelope from his waistband. He can see his own handwriting and the message he had written for her a couple of days ago. *You should have told me sooner.* He still believes that. Believes that knowing Emilie's plans would have changed everything. But the decision is hers to make now. Max holds the envelope out to her, an offering.

Her voice trembles. "Where did you find that?"

"I didn't find it. I stole it. From the officers' safe in the control car while Commander Pruss was standing ten feet away. And if that doesn't show you that I'm an irredeemable fool, nothing will."

Max takes a step forward and she doesn't flinch, so he takes another. And another. He is only a foot away, and he slowly raises his hand to the bundle she holds in her hands. He doesn't break eye contact with her as he spreads wide the mouth of the pillow case and tucks the envelope inside with whatever else she has in there.

He leans close to her ear. Whispers, "You can leave if you want. I won't stop you. The choice is yours, as it should be. But if you decide to stay, I will be here, Emilie. I will be here for you. I will keep you safe." A thought occurs to him and he laughs. "You might have to wait for *me* to get out of prison, of course, if they find out I took those papers. But it changes nothing on my end."

"Thank you." Emilie hugs the bundle to her chest, and he sees that she is blinking fast, trying to force a storm of sudden tears into submission. "I don't deserve this."

"You deserve much more."

She shakes her head in argument, but Max raises his hand and lays it on her cheek to stop the movement. He strokes her face with his thumb. And he looks deep into the rust color of her eyes as he leans in for the kiss he has been imagining for the last two hours.

"I love you." It is a whisper against her lips. "Whatever happens, do not forget that."

Max kisses her in the middle of the hallway, the bundle pressed between them, not caring who sees. If this is to be the last time he kisses Emilie Imhof, he will make sure it is a kiss worth remembering. He can feel the hand that holds her bundle pressed against his chest, and he hopes she can feel the frantic, hopeful beating of his heart. It takes a moment, but her other hand rises to his arm, his shoulder, and then slides up his neck. When she moves her fingers to play with his earlobe he allows himself a small moan of pleasure. Max locks Emilie against him with one arm around her waist and one hand at the back of her neck. He drinks her in. He consumes her with his kiss, and she surrenders completely to it.

He is almost past the point of having any sense at all when he hears his name being called lightly from behind.

"Max."

He ignores it at first.

"Max!"

Finally, reluctantly, he pulls away just enough to turn his head and see the stunned, blushing face of Werner Franz who is standing to his left.

"What?" His voice is filled with gravel and passion.

"We've been cleared to land. You're needed in the control car."

Max pulls Emilie close. He buries his face in the hair behind her ear, then allows himself the luxury of begging just this once. "Stay with me," he whispers.

THE STEWARDESS

6:45 p.m. — forty minutes until the explosion

She owes Max an answer.

This is all she can think of as he walks away, hands tucked in his pockets. His kiss still warm on her lips. His plea echoing in her ear. Emilie lays three fingers across her mouth. A prayer. An apology.

She can envision two different versions of her future. One is certain and thrilling, filled with adventure and borrowed wealth and a loneliness that the Doehner family, lovely though they are, cannot fill. And the other contains Max. Max and a million unanswerable questions. But it also contains passion and love. Companionship. Lurking danger. Both options are impossible. And yet she must choose.

The *Hindenburg* will land in less than an hour and the passengers will disperse. The next departure is still scheduled for later that night, and the crew members will have no time to leave the ship. There will be no trips to New York or dalliances in Lakehurst. No time to sleep or even rest. There will be no time to let her subconscious mind sort out this mess. She will have to make the decision, and she will have to live with the consequences.

She checks her watch. Ten minutes. That's all the time she has to spare for this task. Best to get it over with before she can change her mind.

Emilie descends to her cabin on B-deck and places the pillowcase with Matilde's clothing and the newly returned documents on the bed. A pen. An envelope. One sheet of paper. She sets these things flat on her writing desk. Emilie Imhof, stewardess, widow, brokenhearted woman, picks up the pen with her hand and begins to write, her left wrist bent at an awkward angle, her fingers clenching at the first stroke of ink.

Max.

His name and three more words—*I am sorry*—before her hand begins to tremble. She drops the pen and flexes her fingers. Summons every ounce of courage. And then she continues. Two short paragraphs. Her answer. Her reasons. Her heart splattered on the clean page, as bold and plain as the ink itself. It will have to be enough. She does not have time nor heart for more than what she has written.

Emilie folds the letter in thirds and slides it into the envelope. She seals it and writes his name on the front. Then she goes in search of Kurt Schönherr.

Like Max, he has been called to the control car for landing, and she finds him entering the radio room.

"Kurt!"

"Fräulein." He nods his head. Smiles. The older man has always been kind to her. Always respectful. "How can I help you?"

"I need you to do something for me."

He turns his wrist. Glances at his watch.

"Please," she says before he can argue. "I wouldn't ask if it wasn't important."

"What do you need?"

"Do you still have your mailroom keys?"

A hesitant nod. "I do."

She pulls the letter from her pocket. Holds it out to him. "Will you put this in the lockbox? For Max. Please?"

"I can take it to him in the control car. He's there now." Kurt takes the letter from her hands and holds it between two fingers the way he would a cigarette or a playing card.

Emilie smiles, sad and winsome. "He asked me to send my answer by post."

Kurt appraises her with keen, sharp eyes. "Then we wouldn't want to disappoint him, would we?"

Too late for that. She doesn't say it out loud, but he can see the sadness in her eyes. "Very well, then," he says, and Emilie watches him step across the hall and enter the mailroom.

THE AMERICAN

6:55 p.m. — thirty minutes until the explosion

The stewards pass around trays of finger sandwiches, cheese, and fresh fruit while the passengers hover beside the windows watching Lakehurst come into view once again. They see the mooring mast first, its black triangular form rising above the airfield like a crane, and then the arched form of Hangar No. 1. Members of the ground hover at the edge of the landing circle, waiting to secure the lines.

The American is hungry, but he doesn't eat. He likes the hollow feeling in his stomach, this base, human craving. He savors it. Focuses on it. Denies himself the ability to meet it as his thoughts, so erratic all day, finally begin to settle and focus into a single point of action. It is time to kill Ludwig Knorr.

The American would have preferred his original plan. He would have preferred to wait in his cabin in the dark recess beneath the berth, letting the ship empty and lie quiet through the long day-time hours. He would have preferred to find the chief rigger in the belly of the ship and dispatch him quietly. To hide the body and then send a spark hurtling into this giant, combustible bag. It would have been better for things to play out like that. He would have truly enjoyed watching the airship burn to ash.

But the airship is late, and it will not sit in this New Jersey field over- night. It will not lie empty for hours. He doesn't have the luxury of time. He must adapt. The American leaves the other passengers at the window, then winds his way around the corner, down the gangway stairs, into the keel corridor, and to his cabin. He does not spare a glance at the window but goes straight to his berth and pulls the green canvas bag from where he has kept it hidden for the last three and a half days.

He lifts the pistol and checks the clip. Seven bullets. He will need only one. The Luger of a *Hindenburg* officer. That's what he requested. The mechanics of delivering it were rather complicated, he suspects. He was told only that the Gestapo would inspect the ship prior to liftoff as part of security measures due to the bomb threats, and that one of those men had been paid to locate a gun and place it in this cabin. He knows nothing of motives or payments involved. All men have secrets they want kept. All men have pressure points. And he doesn't care how his employers persuaded or bribed that young Gestapo officer to comply. He provided the gun and the American has it now. He tucks it into his waistband. He straightens his jacket. He pulls the door open.

Captain Lehmann stands before him, accompanied by an officer so young and clean-shaven the American doubts he has finished puberty.

"Herr Douglas." A nod, not the least bit polite.

"Captain."

"May I have a word with you?"

It takes every ounce of self-control for the American not to shoot the captain or his companion. He cannot afford this delay. "Can it wait a few moments? I'd like to watch the landing."

Lehmann smiles. "You'll need to do so from your room, I'm afraid. You have a window after all. A luxury most of the passengers don't enjoy."

A bristling anger begins to heat his blood. He flexes his fingers. Struggles to stay calm. "I don't understand."

"We've had complaints from the crew that you have been wandering into areas of the ship that are prohibited to passengers. We will need to look into these accusations. And until the matter can be cleared up you will remain here."

"You are placing me under . . . what? House arrest?"

Lehmann surveys the small room and, upon seeing nothing out of place, replies, "*Arrest* is a strong word."

"*Arrest* is the word used for detaining a man against his will."

"Ah. I see you're familiar with the process at least. Then this should be easy. I have ordered Captain Ziegler here to wait outside your cabin until my return."

Ziegler rests the heel of one hand on the pistol at his waist. It's the first time the American has seen any of the officers armed since the ship left Frankfurt. The captain tries to look menacing, but the threat is lost on the American.

"Is he going to *shoot* me if I leave?"

Lehmann shrugs, as though leaving that possibility entirely up to him. "I'd rather that it not come to that."

The American pauses, recalculates. "May I know the name of the man who has accused me of this behavior?"

"I think you know his name already. You've had a very keen interest in him during the entire flight. And that is something I plan on discussing with you as well. When I return."

THE CABIN BOY

7:03 p.m. — twenty-two minutes until the explosion

The naval air station in Lakehurst, New Jersey, is surrounded by empty fields and dotted with scrub brush, patches of grass, and bright, colorful pinpricks that Werner guesses to be wildflowers. And there, on a dirt path, are two young boys peddling beneath the airship on their bicycles. The frantic pumping of their arms and legs looks comical from above. But they wave and whoop, trying desperately to keep up with the *Hindenburg* as it loops around the massive airfield, getting into position. Like much of the population of Lakehurst, the boys have come to watch the landing.

In moments the children are out of sight, and Werner turns back to his work, eager to get the crew's mess clean so he can go watch the landing on A-deck with the passengers. He blushes, even though the room is empty and no one can see him, as he imagines the delight on Irene Doehner's face when the airship lands. He knows it's silly and he knows he will never see the girl again after today, but Werner wants to witness her awe. It's how he wants to remember the first girl who ever kissed him.

THE NAVIGATOR

7:10 p.m. — fifteen minutes until the explosion

Pruss hands the telegraph to Max. It reads: CONDITIONS DEFINITELY IMPROVED RECOMMEND EARLIEST POSSIBLE LANDING.

"Give the signal for landing," Pruss says, and a few seconds later Max cringes as the discordant blast of the air horn rips through the air. His eyes twitch at the sound.

Max wonders at Colonel Erdmann's absence. He would have thought that the man would be so eager to get off this airship that he would not miss the ritual. But he is nowhere to be seen. He assumes they will discuss the package later.

The storm has abated and they are now traveling through an insignificant misting rain. The sky is not as dark, the wind has decreased. Max feels confident that they will be able to get the ship on the ground this time.

"Weigh off," Pruss orders, and the crew begins the familiar routine of valving the gas to lower their altitude.

The wind is still rougher than they are comfortable with, so Pruss has them circle north and then west of the airfield in a series of tight figure-eight turns. Max feels the strain of the airship as the floor beneath him shudders in response. Pruss is in a hurry to take advantage of this short window of opportunity, so they make another abrupt left turn at full speed, and Max can hear the engines reverse—a slow, grinding whir and then a rapid popping—as the *Hindenburg* shudders and slows. They loop over the airfield once more and the mooring mast rises up beside them.

"Final approach!" Pruss bellows. There's no need to yell, but it's his habit, and they are all accustomed to it by now.

"We're a thousand kilograms stern heavy, Commander," Bauer says. Unlike most of the crew inside the control car, his eyes are not on the ground below but fixed to an instrument in front of him where a needle wavers right of center.

"Empty the ballasts at stern," Pruss answers.

Bauer pulls the toggle, waits a few seconds as the instrument registers an insignificant change, then pulls it again. He holds the lever for a count of five as water from the ballast bags at the rear of the ship cascades onto the ground below. He shakes his head. Looks at Pruss. "We're still tail heavy."

Pruss glowers. "Drop another five hundred kilos."

The crowd of spectators gathered on the field below are slightly portside and downwind of the airship. Max sees the tiny, dark forms stiffen in shock as the water drenches them.

Bauer shakes his head. "Sorry, Commander, we're still out of trim."

"Call the kitchen. Order six crew men into the bow for counterbalance."

THE AMERICAN

7:15 p.m. — ten minutes until the explosion

The landing signal sounds with a raucous blast. A minute, maybe two, he's been staring at the closed door, recalculating. He could kill the guard outside. It wouldn't be difficult. But the likelihood of being seen or caught is high. And he's only one man among a crew of more than sixty. Count in the male passengers—he's not worried about the females—and the odds are ninety to one. Even he can't beat that.

Damn it.

There is a moment when the American is certain he has failed. It is such a new sensation that he cannot properly name the emotion that assaults him. Disappointment? No, that's not strong enough. Anger? No. Not that either. He settles on grief because this emotion, this feeling, this assault on his senses is the same thing he felt the day his brother died in that hospital in Coventry.

His brother. He will not miss the chance to avenge his brother.

The American is pointing the revolver at the cabin door, in the approximate location he guesses the guard's right kidney to be, when another option occurs to him.

The steak knife.

He presses hard on one of the foam-board walls to test this new possibility.

It could work.

He locks the door.

The ship is descending and there is no time to second-guess himself, so he slips into action. The American pulls the steak knife from where he left it beneath his mattress, then he shimmies beneath the berth, his stomach pressed to the floor and his arms stretched out in front of him. He sets the knifepoint against wall and pushes with a quick thrust. The blade slides easily through the foam, down to the hilt. The American begins to saw a straight, deep line through the wall he shares with Heinrich Kubis. Once punctured, the foam board cuts easily. He tears a strip of fabric away. Shoves it aside, and continues to carve an opening in the wall.

Within a minute he has cut a square two feet wide—as much as he can remove between the duralumin posts that frame the walls. It will have to be enough. He goes to work on the foam board on the steward's side of the room, cutting more quickly now, motivated. The sawing, ripping sound is loud to his ears, but Ziegler outside does not cry out in alarm or attempt to enter.

The American does not wait. He is through the hole and out from under the bed and standing in the middle of Heinrich Kubis's room in a matter of seconds. The knife goes into his pocket, and he dusts the foam particles from his clothing. Takes a deep breath. Steps into the antechamber. Opens the door. Scans the hallway.

The officer assigned to watch his room grumbles in German, hidden around the corner. Stomping his feet impatiently. Irritated at having to babysit.

The American leaves him without another thought. He's at the gangway stairs and around the corner in three seconds. He passes someone in the keel corridor but doesn't pause to acknowledge them. The security door is fifty feet ahead. He walks faster.

Forty feet.

Thirty feet.

Twenty.

Ten.

He leans his shoulder against the door and pushes into the great, yawing body cavity of the *Hindenburg*.

There is no roar of engines, only the distant, echoing voices of men as they shout orders back and forth, orchestrating the intimate dance of water ballasts and gas valves and rudder fins. He sees men dotted around the structure at their stations and begins to run toward the crew quarters near the cargo hold, his feet pounding the keel catwalk. The noise, loud and rumbling, draws shouts from above, but he does not look up to see who might be watching him from above on the axial catwalk. He does not stop. He rushes forward, determined.

He finds Ludwig Knorr standing on the catwalk between the crew quarters and the cargo hold, looking up. His hands are on his hips and his chin is turned so high the American can see the tendons in his neck stretch tight. Knorr stares at the hydrogen cell directly above them with such intent that he does not even register the American's presence. And now he understands why. There is a hole in the gasbag—perhaps the size of a melon—and the material around it is fluttering as the hydrogen escapes. There is a slight whining sound, like air being let out of a balloon. One of the duralumin girders holding the gas cell in place has snapped, and a narrow rod of metal has punctured the cell.

Ludwig Knorr is trembling.

The American pulls the pistol from his waistband and points it directly at the chief rigger. Only when he cocks the hammer does Knorr turn around and look at him. The American has thought of this moment for almost twenty years. He has planned for it. Dreamed of it. But he underestimated the feeling of total satisfaction he would experience as realization flickers in Knorr's eyes.

The rigger's voice is hoarse with panic. "What are you doing, Herr Douglas?"

"I really wish people would stop calling me that. It's not my name." The American is deeply satisfied by the look of profound confusion on Knorr's face. "Edward Douglas is dead, has been since the morning we departed Frankfurt. I took his papers. I took his ticket. And I took his spot on this flight. His body will never be found. My employers made sure of that."

Knorr says nothing, merely stares at him in horror.

"If it makes you feel better, I didn't enjoy killing him. He was a good man. I liked working with him."

The American has drawn a paycheck from the McCann Erickson company for well over a year, but that isn't who he works for. Not really. He doesn't bother explaining this to Ludwig Knorr, however.

The rigger returns his gaze to the gun. He speaks slowly. "Why are you doing this?"

"Revenge."

"I have done nothing to you."

"I didn't expect you to remember. It was eighteen years ago. And you were little more than a boy, just like my brother. And it was a war. Some would even call your actions heroic." The American steadies his hand. "No. I didn't expect you to remember. But I do. That's enough."

Hydrogen does not have an odor. It is colorless and tasteless. And the American cannot feel it entering his lungs, filling the little pockets and membranes with each rise and fall of his chest. It spreads around him like an invisible, deadly fog. He does not care.

Ludwig Knorr raises his hands, palms out, in surrender. His eyes flicker from the American to the hole in the gas cell. "Please don't," he says. "You will kill us all."

"I wonder, did you think of death when you dropped bombs on that hospital in Coventry? Did you care that men were dying below? That those who survived the actual blast were left to rot beneath the rubble for days?"

He can see it on Knorr's face. Panic. Desperation. Bewilderment. The poor bastard doesn't remember that flight over England. He has probably never thought of it again. To the American this is unforgivable. He has killed many men in his life, but he always looked at them when he did so, and he never forgot them afterward. Never. Not the first one decades ago and not Edward Douglas three days ago. He lives with the memory of each frightened face. Their fear and confusion is a burden he must carry.

"If you kill a man you should remember it," the American says.

"Are you even paying attention?" Knorr waves at the gas cell. He's no longer a soldier. He's only a man. And he is deranged with fear, screaming. "If you fire that thing you will kill everyone on this ship!"

"If that's what it takes."

The American doesn't realize how committed he is until the words are out of his mouth. There are two reasons he came on board this airship: to avenge his brother's death and to destroy the *Hindenburg*. Nazi Germany cannot be the world's aviation leader. Not if he has the ability to stop them. The world's largest, most luxuriant, most technologically advanced aircraft is emblazoned with swastikas and funded by Adolf Hitler? This is untenable.

Yes, he would have preferred his original plan. He would have preferred to burn the airship once it was moored at Lakehurst. But the landing is twelve hours late and he has no choice now. The collateral damage will be higher than expected, but not total. There is a chance that some will survive. But not him. No. For him this ends today. It ends right now.

The American pulls the trigger.

The last thing he sees is the muzzle flash. A long strip of flame—pure, clean, white, and searing hot—that shoots from the end of the pistol and then ignites the air itself. The combustion is almost beautiful. And then he is blind. He breathes once—a single gasp of surprise—and his lungs are filled with liquid flame.

He feels nothing else. Hears nothing else. Sees nothing else. The American is simply consumed.

*

The slug tears from the muzzle. It is a molten, flaming chunk of lead, a comet streaking through this small, gas-filled universe, its tail growing larger and more destructive as it goes. The fireball builds and then roars upward through the gas cells, igniting everything in its path.

Outside, a single member of the ground crew sees a glimpse of flame licking the great silver spine of the airship. A phosphorescent blue blaze known as Saint Elmo's fire. This is the last visible trace of the bullet as it rips from the Hindenburg's body, its ascent slowing, and then stopping altogether. The bullet falls unseen. It lands in the grass unnoticed. It will never be found.

Because now every horror-stricken eye has turned to the great burning airship.

THE NAVIGATOR

Max Zabel sighs with relief—the hardest part of landing is over—and then he feels an almost imperceptible shudder. It

is different from the normal shifts and tugs that accompany landing. The convulsion in the floor beneath him is not right. It is not
normal. Something has gone very wrong.

Max looks up. He's not certain anyone else has felt it. But the
expressions on his fellow crewmen's faces show that they have, in
fact, noticed the tremor. There is a pause. A shudder. Then a singular, unending vibration that he can feel first in the soles of his feet
and then throughout his entire body. The control car shakes with
it. Rattles. Hums. Glass convulses in its frame. There's a buzzing,
spinning ghost of a noise at first that morphs into something far
more terrifying within seconds. The palms of Max's hands tingle
with the reverberation as he presses them into the windowsill. And
then he hears the thing he doesn't realize he has been waiting for:
a muffled explosion.

THE JOURNALIST

The ground is so close Gertrud can almost touch it. Sixty feet
below and a startling green from the May rain. Leonhard grabs
her hand and squeezes it reassuringly as they lean over the observation windows in the starboard lounge.

"Almost there," he whispers, and she lets out a long, calming
breath. Her desire to be on the ground once again is profound,
almost reckless.

The ground crew runs onto the field below them to grab the
landing lines, and she can feel a slight tug as the ship goes taut.
The ground begins to rise, faster now. And it is then that she turns
to her husband with relief and gratitude. She is confused for one
second when he does not return the smile but rather straightens
and then steps away from the window, pulling her with him.

Gertrud is about to ask what is wrong, but the ship has gone
unnaturally quiet, as though holding its breath. She can sense the

terror coiling in her husband's body. It's written there in his eyes, and when his hand tightens on her she feels the dread herself.

It's a moment, nothing more, that they stand there frozen. But it's enough.

There is a dull report behind them, no louder than the sound of a beer bottle being opened or a paper bag behind popped. The noise comes from behind, somewhere in the bowels of the ship.

And then chaos.

THE STEWARDESS

Emilie lays the borrowed clothes on Matilde Doehner's bed. She cannot wear them. She cannot go with the family to Mexico. She cannot leave Max. Emilie has known this all along, somewhere deep down. But she is afraid of what it means to love again. This surrendering of her heart and the vulnerability it requires of her is so much harder the second time around. It was easy when she was young and innocent, when she had never been broken. Now she knows what it is to suffer loss. Now she knows what it means to have her heart ripped from her soul. To be dislocated.

And this time she chooses, knowing that it could happen again. Emilie chooses Max. What is faith if not this? Matilde will be disappointed, of course. But she is a woman. And she will understand.

Having made her decision, Emilie is at peace. She reaches for the door and something shifts. She sees her own trembling but she isn't afraid. She isn't shaking. This quiver comes not from within but from without. Everything trembles. The walls. The floor. Her own body. She feels it in the air and in the balls of her feet. It rises up and through her.

She feels herself lifted. Thrown. Catapulted backward into the hard edge of the berth. Emilie hears her head hit with a crack so loud her teeth throb. She feels the flair of pain at her scalp, along her hairline. She feels it acutely, and then she's slipping into darkness. Then there is silence. There is nothing.

THE CABIN BOY

Werner sets the last plate in the cabinet above the banquette and steps back with a triumphant grin. But this feeling is gone before he has taken a step toward the door. Werner Franz is rendered a child quickly and completely when he hears the explosion. He is frightened by what he hopes—in the single moment he has left for hope—is a crack of thunder.

And then the air surrounding Werner splinters. It isn't just the floor or the walls or some shudder within the structure like yesterday morning on the catwalk. It sounds as though the *Hindenburg* is tearing itself apart at the seams. The cupboard doors fly open and all the dishes that Werner so carefully washed and dried and put away only moments ago come sliding out and crash to the floor, where they shatter into wicked little pieces. He stands there, mute and dumb and bewildered, even as the floor tilts away behind him. To Werner, the explosion sounds like breaking glass. It will sound like that for as long as he has the capacity to remember it.

He is broken out of this stupor when the *Hindenburg* drops again sharply aft and he falls onto his haunches. Werner is aware of the broken china sliding across the floor toward him. He is aware of the raging, popping, explosive sounds that come from all directions now. And the screams—some distant and some in the next room—but the only thing the cabin boy can focus on is the door. It never occurs to him that he could go out the window. His only thought is of getting through the door. So he crawls and scrambles across the linoleum, grabbing onto table legs for balance and support. Once he has regained his balance, Werner throws himself toward the door, then down the corridor until he's through the security threshold and into the ship's cavity. The walkway is empty and, in the time it takes him to blink once, he understands why. A colossal, roiling fireball is rushing toward him, consuming everything in its wake.

THE JOURNALIST

The floor drops out from underneath them. First Leonhard and then Gertrud is hurled against the far wall. She can hear a woman scream in a cabin on the other side, a hard thump, and then nothing. The air rushes from Leonhard's lungs, and his rib cage heaves with a thin whistling sound. Gertrud is pinned to the wall by one of his arms as chairs, dishes, and fellow passengers tumble toward them. She can feel her husband thrashing beside her, trying to cover her body with his own. To protect her.

"Leonhard," she breathes his name and nods toward the window where blooming clouds of flame have filled the sky. "It's on fire."

THE NAVIGATOR

Max does not see the fire at first. He notices the glow of it lighting the ground and the clouds and the eyes of the men who stare out the window beside him. But he takes no more than one breath before he sees it in the air around him as well. Everywhere. The sky is lit with it. And then all is chaos. Max knows that the other officers are screaming, cursing, and shouting orders, but he can do nothing but stand beside the window in awe.

The sky is liquid gold.

The sky is death.

He might have stayed there, gazing into his own doom, but the stern drops suddenly, pulling him backward. Max throws out his hands to catch himself on the rear wall of the navigation room as the ship tilts upward, until he is pressed flat against the wall, supported by his hands, as though lying on the floor.

Bedlam.

A man rolls past him shrieking and smashes against the rear wall of the control car. Bauer? He isn't sure. The contents previously on his chart table slide off and fly toward his face. He whips his head to the side just in time to avoid his nose being broken by the heavy leather-bound logbook. Pencils, pens, and instruments rain down around him and still the airship tilts ever upward.

So far the only thing he has heard are the panicked screams of his fellow crew members. But now the fire roars to life and becomes a ravenous beast consuming all other sound. It is hard to breathe. The air around him is ripped away, sucked toward the hungry flames.

Something snaps. Metallic and brittle. And then the bow drops and the ship is level for one protracted moment. The *Hindenburg's* spine has broken in half.

Max hears Commander Pruss bellow over the cacophony. A single word, "Jump!" and Max scrambles to obey.

THE JOURNALIST

There is a man beside Gertrud, but she cannot see his face. He is praying madly, frantically in German as the ship convulses around them. People scream. Colonel Erdmann loses his grip on the windowsill and slides away. Something flies through the air. A coffee cup? There's the smell of smoke and a strange ripping sound. A child bawls—the two Doehner boys hold on to the leg of a table, their little legs dangling in the air as their sister reaches for them. Gertrud's mind registers each of these things in turn, but it isn't until she sees the look of abject horror on Matilde Doehner's face that she has a cognizant thought of her own. This maternal fear strikes something deep and instinctual inside of her, and it rips through her soul like a prayer. *Oh God*, Gertrud thinks, *please let it end quickly.*

THE CABIN BOY

Werner windmills madly away from the fire as it thunders through the hydrogen cells above him. Roaring. Consuming. Eviscerating. It is not so much heat that he feels but an incineration of the air itself. His mouth is dry from the wild gulps of air he swallows in his attempt to flee.

Something snaps. There's a deafening metallic crunch and the ship's hull crashes to the ground. Werner is knocked off his feet. Thrown to his hands and knees. He tips forward, onto his chest, and slides toward the flames. He can do nothing but grab one of the ropes that line each side of the keel corridor to slow his descent into hell.

THE NAVIGATOR

Max struggles onto the chart table but has little control over where his body goes as the room jerks and trembles and tilts around him. He is a pebble inside a can, tossed around at the whim of a belligerent child. Finally he kneels near the window, shoving the glass aside with fingers that are stiff with fear. The ground is twenty feet below—maybe fifteen—he can't accurately measure the distance with the fire and the smoke and the screams blurring his senses.

Max means to jump feetfirst, to control his fall, but the tail of the airship hits the ground and the control car jerks sideways. He goes out the window in a frantic tumble, his foot catching on the sill and his arms splayed. He tries to scream, but a scream requires breath and his lungs are filled with smoke; all he can see is the burning, coiling mass of searing grass and the fleeing ground crew. There is no one to catch him. There is nothing to break his fall. Max drops headfirst into the inferno below.

THE CABIN BOY

Werner Franz prepares to be consumed. He can feel the heat now, so close that it singes his hair. He can smell the burning fabric and melting steel. His fingernails are hot. The boy closes his eyes. He wants to be a man, but he cannot find the courage to watch himself die.

But it is not fire that washes over him. It is water. And it is cold. It takes his breath away. The cabin boy gasps and sputters and cranes his neck to see a torrent rushing from the water ballast above the walkway forty feet in front of him. The impact of the ship hitting the ground has knocked it loose from its moorings, and the contents are cascading over the boy and down the walkway.

Sudden deliverance and bone-chilling cold return Werner to his senses, and he looks around frantically for a means of escape. There is only one option: go out the provisioning hatch to his right. Werner does not trust his trembling legs to carry him, so he crawls the six feet and kicks at the latch with the heel of his boot.

THE JOURNALIST

There is fire in the lounge. It licks the walls. It rakes its tongue across the floor. The flames are a liquid, spilling thing, and Gertrud feels the heat of it in her eyes as it crawls toward them. Dryness. Burning. A shudder that runs the length of the ship, pitching the floor forward and almost level again. This threat is all Leonhard needs to gain his composure.

"Through the windows!" It's not a scream or a shout but an order roared so loudly that every person in the lounge looks at him, blinks, and then scrambles toward the row of observation windows.

Leonhard drags her. Four long steps and they are at the glass and Leonhard shoves it aside. She can feel him bend beside her, one arm already looping beneath her knees. He plans to throw her out the window. But she sees Matilde Doehner wrestling her boys toward the window alone, as she reaches for her daughter with one hand. Irene stands there, stupefied, screaming for her father over and over and over until the crazed pitch of her voice rises above that of snapping metal and shattered glass. It is the sound of a breaking heart, and the look on Matilde's face alone could destroy Gertrud.

She wriggles out of Leonhard's arms. "We need to help them."

They have to get out of the ship. She can see that written on his face. This might be their only chance. The windows are crowded with people waiting to jump, shoving one another out of the way. Smoke swirls across the floor in boiling waves and Gertrud can no longer see her shoes. Her ankles. Her calves.

The children are not hers, but they are children, no less innocent than Egon, and she cannot leave them to the fire any more than she would be able to leave her own son.

"Clear the window," she tells Leonhard, then runs back to Matilde Doehner.

THE NAVIGATOR

Max hits the ground—whether by miracle or willpower he isn't sure—roughly on his feet. But the impact sends him staggering forward wildly and he crashes onto his hands and knees, then farther forward onto his chin. He is stunned. His head is ringing. There is blood in his mouth and grass in his nose. He has bitten his tongue and the side of his cheek. He tastes iron and dread. With his arms pinned beneath him and his kneecaps throbbing, he can turn his head only a few inches to the side to see the entire flaming mass of the airship falling all around him. On top of him.

Max pitches forward. Rolls. Stumbles to his knees and then his feet, despite the fact that forty different places on his body are protesting the sudden movement.

He runs. And just as he does he can feel the middle of the ship hit the ground behind him. Sparks fall in a shower on his hair and his jacket and the toes of his shoes. One of them burns a deep black hole into the back of his hand. He feels it. He ignores it. He runs.

And then the ship does the impossible. It rebounds, driven back into the air a dozen or more feet by the impact of the landing wheel crashing into the ground. It is the only thing that stopped the structure from coming down on top of him. That extra twist he gave to lock the wheel in place. His thoroughness has given him the chance to stumble out from beneath the flaming debris.

Max's foot hits fresh soil and then the airship descends a second time. It shatters into ochre and flame.

THE CABIN BOY

Werner kicks at the provisioning hatch with water dripping in his eyes even as everything around him is obliterated by flames. The flat, inset door is four feet wide and four feet long and Werner is afraid to touch the handle and burn his bare hand, so he kicks and kicks until it unlatches. The hatch swings upward three inches and he forces it the rest of the way open with his foot.

The cabin boy slides forward on his stomach and looks over the edge to find that the ground is rising toward him rapidly. Ten feet. He takes a deep breath and scrambles into a crouched position at the lip of the opening. Five feet.

He jumps.

Werner hits the ground at the same time as the airship, and he is certain that it will crush him. There is an explosion of sparks. The sickening, shattering crunch of metal. The sound of a structure collapsing upon itself.

But then the ship rebounds upward, bizarrely, miraculously off the forward landing wheel, and Werner sees a path forward beneath the wreckage.

He runs.

THE JOURNALIST

Walter Doehner is heavier than he looks. He screams and reaches for his mother, so Gertrud drags him bodily to the window. He thrashes, arms and legs flailing in terror. Matilde is right behind her, little Werner tucked beneath one arm like a bag of oats.

"Thank you," she whispers, huffing behind Gertrud. "I can't carry them both."

And then Matilde screams for Irene, begs her to follow, but the girl is walking backward, away from the windows, searching for her father, calling his name.

The fire is everywhere. It touches everything, and Gertrud looks down at Walter to see a line of flame trace its way across his cheek toward his hair. The boy is on fire. His shirt. The tips of his shoes. A patch of hair. A tear drips from the end of his nose and is evaporated by the flame that eats his face.

All reason is lost to Gertrud then. She throws the boy at her husband and Leonhard catches him by his collar. Like a cat. Like some sort of feral animal. With one arm he holds the small boy over the open window and simply drops him. Walter Doehner vanishes from sight, his screams fading as he falls.

It is much harder to get little Werner through the window. He's frightened and fighting hard to stay with his mother. When Leonhard picks him up like an invalid and throws him at the window, the child bounces off, splayed across the casement like a starfish.

There is sadness and gentleness in Leonhard's deep voice when he looks at the boy and says, "I'm sorry."

Gertrud's husband sets a huge, strong hand on each side of the boy's waist and pushes. Like a peg in a hole, he pops through. And then he too is gone.

"Irene!" Matilde shouts, but her daughter is nowhere to be seen. The three of them are the only people left in the lounge, and they can barely speak or breathe or cry with the smoke billowing and churning around them. The hem of Gertrud's dress is on fire and she is slapping at it madly. A part of her registers that the skin on the palm of her right hand begins to hum in pain.

"Irene!"

Gertrud wonders how Matilde does it, how she goes out the window without Irene. How she chooses her sons over her daughter. But she does. Gertrud blinks and Matilde is scrambling over the windowsill, her feet dangling, and then with a wounded cry that has nothing to do with fire or pain or burning, she drops to the ground below.

Leonhard reaches for Gertrud. He will not wait any longer. But the ship hits the ground and they are knocked apart, thrown to their hands and knees. Chairs slide and topple and join together in a giant knot between them. Leonhard reaches for her. Calls her name with such a note of fear that her heart stumbles in response

He is closer to the window than she is. He could jump. He *should* jump.

Gertrud reaches for him. "Please don't leave me."

THE STEWARDESS

Emilie opens her eyes. She blinks. She sees nothing but red and smells nothing but smoke. Something wet and warm drips down her forehead and into her eyes, and she realizes that her scalp is bleeding. She wipes the back of her hand across her face. Wipes the blood out of her eyes.

Emilie hears a deep groan and realizes it's coming from her. She rolls to her side. Coughs. There is so much smoke in the room and it is so hot and she can't order the frantic bursts of thought that ricochet inside her skull. Emilie tries to remember where she is and what's happening. Matilde Doehner's cabin. Something is very wrong. Something happened and she is hurt and she needs to get out of this room, but she can't remember why or how. And then . . .

Oh.

An explosion.

Emilie raises herself onto her hands and knees. She crawls forward.

THE JOURNALIST

I could never leave you," Leonhard says.

He flings chairs out of the way. She hears this, barely, over the roar of the fire, and then his arm is around her waist like a steel cable and they are loping toward the window. He does not release his grip as they scramble over the edge or even as they hover there for a moment, their legs dangling into space. It is only when they drop into smoke and emptiness that she feels his grip on her waist relax, and only then because he does not want to fall on top of her.

The drop is no more than ten feet, but she has no way of preparing for the impact with so much smoke obscuring her vision.

She hits the ground leaning forward with her legs slightly bent and she's pitched forward, unable to break her fall. The impact knocks the air from her lungs. Gertrud lies there, stunned, the side of her face mashed into earth that is strangely damp and cool. Leonhard's feet come into view, and then his hand is at her waistband, yanking her up. But she still can't breathe. Her lips tingle and her eyes burn. There is a scratch on her cheek, and it feels as though she's holding a hot coal in the palm of her right hand. She looks at it, confused, and sees angry red blisters where she beat out the fire on her hemline.

Gertrud feels a bright, clean thread of air entering her lungs and she gasps for it more greedily. Leonhard pulls her forward without an ounce of gentleness. He is almost brutal in his desperation to get out from beneath the burning airship. They run through the obstacle course of debris, fallen girders, flaming furniture, a charred body—she looks away from this—hunks of wreckage and objects so twisted by fire and the impact of the wreck that she cannot even identify them.

They run.

But not fast enough.

Gertrud feels the sparks on her shoulders and in her scalp. She looks up to see an inferno settling down on top of them.

THE NAVIGATOR

Max runs aft. Aft. Aft. He veers around the blazing purgatory toward the passenger decks. Emilie. That is all he can think of. Her name is scorched into his mind. He must find Emilie. He must. He will.

The base of the airship is on the ground and tilting badly, but that does not stop him from throwing his shoulder against the first section of glass that he can find. He expects it to shatter or explode or lacerate his arm, but it does none of these things. The glass leading into the observation deck beside the dining room simply crumbles and he finds himself staring up into the faces of two men and two women. Shell-shocked faces. Almost blank. None of these faces belong to Emilie, but he reaches his arms out nonetheless, pulls the people from the wreckage, shoves them forward. Away.

And then he hears the screams, pitched into the highest key possible by dread. The screams are his. He is calling her name.

"Emilie!"

THE STEWARDESS

Emilie hears Max calling her name. She hears the fear and the desperation, and it becomes her compass. Her true north. She turns, searching for it.

She cannot stand.

She cannot see.

She cannot breathe.

But she can hear him. She can hear him calling to her, and it is enough. Emilie crawls forward into the dark, swirling, strangling smoke.

Max.

Max.

Max.

She isn't sure if she says his name out loud. If it is a whisper or a shout. But she calls it. From her heart if from nowhere else.

Hands, knees, one in front of the other. Emilie moves toward him.

"Max."

THE CABIN BOY

Werner is alive. Wet and freezing and shaking so badly that he drops to the ground in an uncoordinated heap. But he is alive. He squeezes his eyes shut and waits for the pain. Because it is inevitable.

One minute. He can feel the heat of the burning ship rolling off the field.

Three minutes. This is when the screams really begin to bother him. Screams from within the ship. He can hear the terror and fear and pain of men caught in the flames. But there is something worse about the screams coming from every direction across the field. The spectators can do nothing but watch in horror as their friends and loved ones are consumed within the *Hindenburg*. They are watching people die. And they will live to remember it.

Five minutes.

He feels nothing more than a scratch on the palm of his hand where he caught himself. It's not deep. But it stings. And this pain—insignificant though it is—is the thing that roots him to reality. It is the thing that convinces him that he isn't dead.

THE JOURNALIST

Leonhard shoves her. A ruthless thrust to her back that sends Gertrud stumbling forward with a grunt and a curse. Her limbs sprawl and she hits the ground so hard that her vision blurs. The last thing she sees before the *Hindenburg* collapses and explodes into a cloud of sparks is Leonhard lying beside her in a heap of elbows and knees bent at unnatural angles.

They lie ten feet from a girder that glows so red she fears it will melt and the metal will spread toward them. Leonhard reaches out. Grabs her hand and gives it a tender squeeze. But pain rockets through her and she pulls away.

"You're hurt." Leonhard is on his knees now, inspecting the raw flesh of her palm.

"It's not that bad."

"It's not good, *Liebchen*."

A high-pitched keening begins somewhere near them as they scramble to their feet. A form stands in the flames on the other side of the structure, waving madly. Begging. A *man*, she thinks, *desperate to find his way out of the inferno*. She is frozen at the sound of his screams. Terrified. Appalled. But something wakens in Leonhard and he lurches forward with a demon-like urge toward self-destruction, like a moth driven into the flame.

It is Gertrud's turn to save her husband. She calls to him once, twice. She begs him to stop, but he is compelled by the burning figure. Gertrud grabs his arm, her fingernails digging into the bare skin of his forearm, and she throws her weight backward, nearly sitting on the ground before she stops his forward momentum.

"No." Her command is loud and clear and final. She will not let him go.

Leonhard stops and looks at her, startled. He reluctantly allows himself to be dragged away, the screams still ringing from a dozen places within the ship. Men. Women. Gertrud chooses not to think of Irene Doehner as they stumble away.

THE NAVIGATOR

Max can't see anyone else inside the ship. Everything is consumed by flames. So he stumbles backward. Catches his heel on some plant with deep, sprawling roots.

"Fuck-bloody-fucking-hell-shit-damn-sonavabitch." It's a prayer.

It's a litany. It's the cry of a heart that has found itself in hell and is begging God, not for release, but for the chance to free another.

"Where is she?"

"Where is she?"

"Where is she?"

He repeats this over and over and over as he stumbles away again, toward the control car. He hadn't even bothered to see if anyone remained there. He has simply run after her.

The control car is illumined by raging flames, and when he stretches onto the balls of his feet to look inside he finds it empty. To the bow, then, and around the other side. This is what he intends. There are twelve men in the bow of the ship. *No*, he thinks, *there were twelve men*. None could have survived. The nose of the ship is completely incinerated. Rescuers carry a man, a body, still burning, from the blackened hull. He can smell the scorched flesh. The burnt hair. He can hear the gurgling, final groans of a man who did not die quickly enough.

Max Zabel vomits onto his shoes.

Then he breathes in the stench and hurls himself forward again. He circles the fiery mass to the starboard side. Flames press against the window. He sees the silhouette of a hand pressed against the glass and then it clenches and falls.

He moves toward it but someone—nameless and faceless, there might be two because each of his arms is clamped into a vise-like grip—drags him away. Drags him kicking and screaming and cursing and bellowing the only single coherent word that he knows right now.

"Emilie!"

THE CABIN BOY

Werner is on his feet. He isn't sure when he stood or even how he made the decision to do so, but he's away from the wreckage, watching the flames as bile rises in his throat. He doesn't want to witness any more, but he can't seem to turn away.

"What are you doing?"

The voice is harsh and familiar. When a large, heavy hand clamps onto his shoulder he knows who it belongs to: Heinrich Kubis.

Werner turns a dazed and dirty face to the chief steward. The man has never been one to offer pity, but he does so now. Fear has softened him.

"Why are you standing here?" he shouts. "Get away!"

Kubis shoves Werner to get him moving, but the boy, exhausted and confused, goes in the wrong direction. He stumbles into the blanket of low-hanging smoke, toward the blazing wreck instead of away from it.

"Get off the field, you idiot! You'll die!" The words are English, and Werner only catches half of them in the commotion.

His English is limited, and under the circumstances he can't think of the right words to respond to the soldier who has risen out of the smoke. Not with the heat and noise and this man trying to drag him away from the ship.

So finally Werner digs his heels into the ground and points at the fire, then back at himself. "*Ich bin der cabin-boy vom* Hindenburg!" And again, louder this time. "*Ich bin der cabin-boy vom* Hindenburg!"

The soldier takes in his grubby uniform and then lets go, speechless. Then he claps Werner on the shoulder and calls out to the men around them, "Hey! This is the cabin boy!"

Werner is swarmed by young American soldiers who pat him and hug him and shake his hand. They ask him questions he can't answer. They congratulate him on making it out alive, as if his surviving was up to him and not a matter of providence and stupid luck.

The first soldier is the only one to notice that Werner is soaked to the skin and shivering. He takes off his coat and wraps it tightly around the boy. The coat is six inches too long in the sleeves and hangs to the middle of the boy's thighs, but the warmth is a gift. Werner feels his muscles uncoil. His teeth stop chattering.

Werner Franz stands with these strangers and watches the *Hindenburg* burn.

After several minutes, a familiar face wanders into view. Wilhelm Balla. He's limping slightly but doesn't seem to be hurt otherwise. Werner has never been so glad to see the sour-faced steward, especially when Balla wraps a protective arm around his shoulders and leads him away.

"Come on, son," Balla says, "there's nothing more we can do here."

The last thing Werner Franz sees as he leaves the airfield is the pristine form of Xaver Maier standing near the wreck, his white jacket as clean as though it has just been laundered. Not a smudge anywhere on him. The only thing missing is his toque. Maier doesn't look amazed or afraid or sad. He looks lost, as though for the first time in his entire life he isn't sure what to do.

Werner watches as the chef dips two fingers into the breast pocket of his coat and pulls a cigarette from the pack he keeps there at all times. Xaver tips the end of his cigarette into a burning pile of rubble, then puts it to his lips and inhales. The chef walks away, nonchalant, having once again found his bearings.

THE JOURNALIST

Gertrud can feel the heat of the fire only in her palm but she can smell it everywhere: in the smoke and the wisps of burnt hair that drift toward her nose. She can smell the bodies. She can smell urine and vomit on the stumbling forms she and Leonhard pass in the field. Gertrud can smell the despair.

A man in a white Panama hat—so startling and clean compared to everything around him—appears to sprout from the ground in front of them.

"This way!" he yells and grabs Leonhard's sleeve.

This bizarre, pristine stranger leads them toward a limousine that idles at the edge of the field. The car was meant to ferry the passengers from the landing area to the hangar, but it's being used as an ambulance instead.

The man opens the car door and motions them to get inside, but a wild, desperate voice screams at him from within.

"There's no more room in here! Go away!" It is female. German. Deranged.

Gertrud braves one glance and sees Matilde Doehner crouched in the otherwise empty vehicle, a badly burned son tucked beneath each arm. She is a fierce, feral lioness protecting her children.

THE NAVIGATOR

Hangar No. 1, the closest structure to the wreck, has been set up as a makeshift infirmary. It was a spontaneous decision made by whatever rescuer pulled the first broken body from the airship. A matter of practicality. Less distance to drag, carry, pull the wounded.

No, Max thinks, as he limps toward the hangar, *not everyone within is wounded.* That word implies survival. And he knows that some of the people he has seen being carted through the wide, gaping doors no longer exist on this side of eternity.

Max does not know how long he sat there in the field. He only knows that it was damp, because of either the rain or the water ballasts, and that he couldn't move or think or function. He simply sat, hunched over, head lolling to the side as the ship consumed itself.

No one should have survived. And yet here they are, wandering around like scattered sheep after a storm. Passengers. Crew members. Ground crew. Reporters. Spectators. All here in the field together. All of them disoriented. All of them horrified. And there are cars zooming about. Not just military jeeps but civilian cars as well, ferrying the survivors hither and yon. Who the hell can tell where anyone is in this mess?

Max has never had to think about setting one foot in front of the other before. He has never had to give his body specific, simple instructions. But he does now. And it seems an age before he reaches the hangar and stumbles inside.

Someone yells for help, then wraps a blanket around his shoulders. Asks a series of nonsensical questions in English. Who cares what year it is or what his name is or who the president is?

"Where is Emilie?" He croaks the question out. Coughs.

The overly talkative, curious stranger shoves a cup of water into his hands. Urges him to drink. And he does, marveling at the miraculous properties of water. The coolness. The wetness. The perfect satiating *waterness* of it.

It takes only a moment for the stranger to assess that the worst damage Max has suffered is shock. He's led to a cot that immediately collapses the moment he puts his weight on it. He's yanked to his feet, as though this is his error and not the fault of poor assembly. He wanders away while the man tries to make the cot sturdy enough to hold his weight.

The hangar is huge, almost twice the size of the *Hindenburg*, and is filled with cots and bedrolls and people shouting, wandering through its cavernous belly. People lie everywhere. Others stand in groups talking in hushed whispers. Doctors call for help. Nurses rush from one victim to the next, substituting busyness for help because really, there is nothing that can be done for most of them.

Max picks an end—it doesn't matter which one—and begins to work his way down the row of cots. He stops. Looks. Searches the ruined faces. And at every bedside he asks one question: "Emilie?"

THE JOURNALIST

It's a hangar. She knows that much. And it has been turned into an infirmary. There are people sprawled across cots and on the floor. There are people running around and shouting directions. A handful of young, fresh-faced girls in white nurse uniforms look on, horror-stricken.

Someone has found a chair for Gertrud and she sits still and quiet, watching Colonel Erdmann dying at her feet. Leonhard has gone to get help for her hand, but she has lost sight of him. A priest stands ten feet away giving last rites to a crew member. The priest has been going down the line, attending these men by order of who is closest to dying.

"My shoes are too tight," Erdmann says.

His skin is singed black in patches. Portions of his clothing are burned off and others are melted to his skin.

"My shoes are too tight." He says it again, and Gertrud realizes that he is speaking to her. His single functioning eye is fixed on her, and she can no more refuse him than she could leave the Doehner boys behind.

Gertrud slides off the chair and onto her knees. The concrete floor is hard and cool and oddly soothing. She carefully unties the colonel's boots and slips them off. She pulls off his socks as well and lays her hands on his feet to comfort him. They are the only part of his body not covered with lethal burns. He trembles a bit at her touch but does not complain.

"Dorothea." It's the barest whisper of a word.

The priest drops to his knees beside her. "You are a kind woman."

When Erdmann sees him he begins to speak frantically, but Gertrud notices that he has slipped into a rare dialect unknown to the American priest. But the priest hesitates for only a moment. He does not let on as the colonel gives his final confession, but rather bends low and receives the words with mercy. The priest whispers comfort into dying ears.

Only God understands him now, Gertrud thinks.

Soon the words have stopped and he is still. The priest straightens with a weary look and searches the row of patients for the next to die. He ambles away, leaving Gertrud alone with the body of a man she barely knows.

THE CABIN BOY

The airfield is dotted with hangars of various shapes and sizes, all of them dwarfed by Hangar No. 1. It's a glorified garage, large enough to house the biggest of zeppelins in the event of a storm, but this is not where Wilhelm Balla leads Werner.

"You don't want to go in there," Balla says, steering him away. "That's where they're taking the bodies."

He takes the boy instead to a low-hanging, rectangular structure that looks to Werner like a barracks. Wilhelm explains to the older gentleman who greets them, in English, who Werner is and why he's soaking wet. At the first sign of comprehension Balla hands the cabin boy over to the ministrations of this stranger and leaves. The stone-faced steward does not offer a single look or word of farewell, but Werner understands now, after all this time and after what has just happened, that it is because, once summoned, Balla has no capacity to control his emotions. The solution for him is simply to not give in to them at all.

"Come with me," the old man says.

Werner follows, too tired to object, through the hangar, down a hall, and into a small living quarters where an old woman sits at a table with a stricken expression. The man hands him over to the care of his wife, speaking so rapidly that most of the words are lost to Werner. And then he too is gone, slipping out the door to help where he can.

The woman pulls a bundle of clothing out of a closet and sets it carefully in his arms but he can barely lift it. Werner's arms feel as though they are weighed down with lead. And then she takes him back through the building to a long, narrow room filled with bunk beds. He changes into the dry clothes once she's gone, then sinks into the nearest bed. He grabs the heavy woolen blanket and rolls to his side. And then the boy is gone, lost to sleep and grief and trauma before his eyes have fully closed.

THE JOURNALIST

The skin has blistered off Gertrud's right palm, leaving the exposed flesh red and weeping. She cannot close her hand. She can't focus on anything apart from the burning fire still cradled in her palm. It is as though her entire body has drawn inward to that one spot. She feels nothing else.

Her fingers are splayed open on her lap, her gaze still fixed on them when a young medic arrives.

"Are you badly hurt?" he asks.

"No." She lifts her hand an inch and inclines it toward him. "Just this."

He is remarkably gentle for such a large man. He lifts her hand in one of his own, pulling it close to his face. "It's a bad burn. But it's clean. I can wrap it and give you morphine for the pain, but time will have to do the rest."

The medic pulls a syringe the size of a bicycle pump from the bag at his feet and she recoils.

"Don't worry. It won't hurt once the medicine hits your bloodstream."

"No morphine. I've misplaced my husband, and he won't be able to find me if I'm lying here asleep." The medic gives her such a look of pity that she rolls her eyes. "Oh, good grief. Leonhard's *alive*. He just wandered off."

"Of course he is." The medic pats her shoulder in pity and begins to clean her hand.

Gertrud cranes her neck in search of Leonhard instead. It's a bad habit of her husband's, this wandering off. She has often accused him of being part Aborigine because of his penchant for going on walkabout. Sometimes he's gone for hours. Other times it's no more than a few minutes. Leonhard insists it's his way of finding time to think, to sort through a problem. But problem or not, Gertrud is getting increasingly upset about his absence.

When the medic finishes cleaning her hand and wrapping it in gauze she thanks him and slips off the table. It takes some effort but she finally locates Leonhard in a small room at the back of the hangar with Captain Lehmann. The captain is sitting on a table—*like a child*, she thinks—dabbing at his burns with a wad of gauze. Every few seconds he dips the gauze in a tin of picric acid, then braces himself before applying it to his skin. The medicine is astringent—the very smell burns her nose. She can't imagine how Lehmann manages to use it on such terrible wounds. Leonhard solemnly bears witness to the gruesome ritual. He does not speak to the captain or touch him, but Gertrud knows his presence is a comfort.

After several more moments, the wounds on Lehmann's chest and thighs are all covered with the fatty-looking yellow salve, and he turns pleading, apologetic eyes on Leonhard.

He is looking for absolution, Gertrud thinks.

Leonhard bends his head down so that his cheek rests against the captain's. It is the closest he can come to giving his friend a reassuring embrace.

"What happened?" Leonhard asks.

Lehmann has the blank-faced expression of a man given over to shock. He offers a shrug and even that small movement pains him. Lehmann winces, pulling air through his teeth. Gertrud can see him searching for an answer, something, anything that makes sense. "*Blitzschlag,*" he finally says, and then doubles over in a fit of coughing. It sounds liquid and raw. She cringes at the sound.

Blitzschlag.

Lightning.

Leonhard's shoulders begin to quiver, and Gertrud eases away from the door. He is not a man who weeps easily, and he would be furious to know she has witnessed this quiet, intimate moment between friends. There is only one thing she can do to help, so she goes in search of her medic. She finds him on the other side of the hangar, covering a body in what appears to be a wool blanket. The hand that slips out from underneath is decidedly delicate and feminine. He tucks it back under the blanket and looks at Gertrud with a detached expression known only to those who have witnessed disaster and then been called upon to tend the carnage.

"Did you find your husband?"

"I did. Do you still have the morphine?"

"Yes. Are you in pain?"

Gertrud swallows. Clears her throat. "I am. But it's not for me."

She leads the young medic to Captain Lehmann and watches from the door as he receives the ghastly needle with gratitude.

THE NAVIGATOR

It is hours after the crash. Night has fallen. Portions of the ship still glow in the field even though the ground crew has tried their best to douse it with water hoses. Lights blare across the airfield. Jeeps race back and forth as military personnel gather and disperse and respond to orders. Max has circled the hangar at least four times, but he can't be certain if he has been to every bed. People won't stay still. They keep moving. They wander off. Even the patients stand and walk away. They sit. They move from a blanket on the floor to a cot against the wall, and hell if he knows whom he has spoken to and whom he hasn't.

Max knows it's a flawed search method, but it's the only one he has. He would continue with it straight until dawn if he didn't feel the firm grip of Xaver Maier's hand on his jacket sleeve.

Max looks at the chef in wonder. "You're alive."

He grins sadly. "I'm not so easy to get rid of."

"What do you want?"

Maier pulls at his sleeve. "You need to come with me."

"I can't. I have to find Emilie."

"That's what I'm trying to tell you. We found her."

The chef has turned before Max can search his face for clues. He doesn't know whether Maier's eyes are filled with relief or sadness or pity. He knows nothing. He simply follows him through Hangar No. 1 and out into the night.

THE JOURNALIST

Gertrud Adelt turns in her seat to take one last look at the *Hindenburg*. It is well after dark, but the airfield is lit up like a macabre circus. Floodlights illuminate the wreckage, and parts of the ship still glow menacing and red. The fabric covering has burned completely away, leaving the gruesome skeleton. As men pick through the rubble their shadows are cast long across the field by the harsh lights. They look like carrion birds picking at a carcass.

The driver glances at Gertrud in the rearview mirror. He does not bother to hide his concern. "Where should I take you?"

Leonhard has laid himself across the backseat, his head in her lap, and she rests her good hand upon his forehead. He hasn't breathed easily since the wreck, but the wheezing started to grow worse an hour ago and the coughing began shortly afterward. A slow, pained gurgle emanates from his chest now.

"To a hospital," Gertrud says. "Quickly."

The car maneuvers its way across the airfield and then through the cordon, bouncing through every rut and track and pothole along the way. Gertrud holds Leonhard's head steady on her lap. She listens to his shallow breathing. Within minutes they are on the highway heading toward Toms River and Lakehurst is nothing but a strange and lurid glow behind them.

THE CABIN BOY

The sun has been up for hours when Werner finally wakes. He hasn't moved all night, hasn't even rolled out of fetal position, and his right arm is rubbery and asleep. The strange clothes he's wearing are clean and dry—it takes him a moment to remember where they came from—but he can smell smoke in his hair and on his skin. Everything comes back to Werner. He drops his face into his hands and takes a few deep, shuddering breaths between his splayed fingers.

When he lifts his head again he sees that the barracks are empty. Every bunk but his has been made, the blankets are stretched smooth and tucked tightly beneath the mattress. The air is still and warm, but he can hear muted shouts and the rumble of machinery outside. He doesn't want to leave his bunk a mess, so he pulls the covers as snug as he can.

The cabin boy steps blinking into the sunlight. The airfield looks different during the day. The clouds are gone, the sky is crisp, and the wreckage sprawls before him, unavoidable. Werner does not understand why the airship looks larger than it ever did, now that it is burned and broken. But it does, lying there stretched beside the mooring mast.

He is still standing there staring at the *Hindenburg* sometime later when a hand rests on his shoulders. Wilhelm Balla passes him a newspaper and says, "Telegram your parents. Tell them you're not dead."

The front page shows the airship falling and consumed by flames. The headline screams: HINDENBURG BURNS IN LAKE-HURST CRASH: 21 KNOWN DEAD, 12 MISSING; 64 ESCAPE. All eight columns are devoted to the tragedy, and one of them lists the names of known fatalities. The last name reads: Werner Franz, cabin boy.

It is a strange thing to see yourself pronounced dead while you are still in possession of a beating heart.

"Where?" Werner asks, but his voice cracks so he clears his throat and tries again. "Where can I send a telegram?"

"The office in Hangar No. 1."

The boy doesn't move immediately. He's staring at the paper still grasped in his hands—hands, he notes, that do not tremble at all.

"Why do they think I'm dead?"

"Probably because they couldn't find you last night." Balla waves an arm around the chaotic scene.

Werner feels ashamed. He didn't mean to cause anyone to worry. Especially his parents. "I was sleeping." The admission feels juvenile.

Something ripples across Balla's usually impassive face. A stray, unguarded emotion. Compassion. His eyes soften and he lays a comforting hand upon the boy's head. "As well you should have."

THE NAVIGATOR

Stiff. Cold. Devoid of all emotion and thought and logic. This is Max as he sits beside Emilie's still form. She has been laid straight on the cot, arms at her side, her head turned slightly to the left. Covered with a thick wool blanket. He has not seen what lies beneath. He has been told he does not want to. And yet he sits here, as he has the entire night, his eyes fixed upon her chest, willing it to rise and fall beneath her shroud.

It has not.

It will not.

He knows this somewhere, in the deeper parts of his mind, but he won't admit it to himself yet.

Because he can hardly breathe himself.

Max Zabel does not move from her side. He cannot move at all.

He marks the passage of time by the sun at his feet. The rectangular patch from the window far above his head has moved three feet when someone drops the lockbox beside the cot. Later he will remember that it must have been last year's postmaster, Kurt Schönherr, because a key is pressed into his hand as well. He squeezes Max's shoulder and then leaves. There are no words to fix this, and the helmsman is smart enough not to try.

Max looks at the lockbox, charred but perfectly intact, and then at the key in his palm. The part of his mind that controls thought and reason and choice wakes up and pushes aside the instinct he has been surviving on for the last nine hours. He looks up. He sees people going about their work. The smell of smoke and disaster still hangs heavy in the air, but something else is present as well: spring. The hangar doors are open and a southerly breeze brings an occasional breath of fresh-cut grass and warm pine. Max turns his face to the light and breathes deeply and long through his nose.

Emilie was pronounced dead last night, but she was only positively identified an hour ago. He had held out hope, of course, that he had been keeping vigil over the wrong woman. That there was some mistake. That Emilie was simply on another part of the airfield, asleep or unconscious. But in the end it was Xaver Maier who took his last shred of hope and ground it to dust. Max had not even known that Emilie had fillings in her teeth. But the chef did, and the medical examiner confirmed the size and location that Maier described to him. And all the while Max sat beside her, his gaze on her still form, and prayed for a miracle that would never come.

So far Maier is the only one who has been brave enough to acknowledge his grief, and this one small gesture enables Max to forgive the chef.

"I am so sorry," Maier said when the medical examiner pulled the blanket back over Emilie's body.

That's all he said. And yet it was enough. Max nodded at him, and then the chef was gone, puffing away at his damned cigarette, leaving Max alone to say his final good-byes.

It is the lockbox that finally draws his attention away from Emilie. The burned chunk of metal and its contents give him something to do, something to focus on besides the black hole of his grief.

Max reaches out one trembling hand and lays it on top of the blanket, cupping the side of Emilie's face. She is still beneath his touch. She is gone. Max rises slowly from the chair beside her, his body groaning in protest as joints and muscles stretch beyond the point of comfort.

"I love you," he says, then chokes back a sob when she does not answer.

Max stoops to lift the lockbox from the floor, wincing at the twinge in his back, then tucks it under one arm. A pause, short and filled with yearning beside the cot where Emilie lies, and then he turns toward the hangar door and limps out into the sunlight.

The sight that greets him on the field is surprising. It is orderly. It is controlled. The images of death and carnage from the night before have been replaced by order and discipline. The airship is there, of course, but the smoke and fire and screams are gone. As are the spectators—they have been cordoned off, a mile away at the outer edge of the base. Crewmen and soldiers pick through the wreckage, like scavengers, looking for clues, for souvenirs. But not survivors. That hope is long past.

Max grabs a passing naval officer by the sleeve. He has to order his rusted mind to search for the words in English. Finally they come. "A quiet room."

The young man is busy and impatient. "Why?"

He lifts the lockbox. "The mail. I have a job to do."

"Right. Okay. This way." He leads Max toward one of the smaller hangars where survivors gathered the night before. It's mostly empty now. The healthy passengers have fled and only a handful of the *Hindenburg*'s crew loiter about.

"Max!" As always Werner's voice is bright, his expression wide open.

"I need a room. To sort the mail." He clears his throat. "And something to drink."

"Have you eaten yet?"

Max has no idea what he looks like, but it must be alarming. Werner's eyes rove over his uniform in amazement. The boy is too polite to comment.

"This way. There's an office at the back where they keep the telegraph machine."

Werner leads him to the small windowless room and helps him lift the lockbox onto the table. "Do you want a shower first? A change of clothes?"

"No. That can wait. I need to do this now."

He *has* to do it now. This is his anchor.

The door closes with a soft click, and Max sits at the table beneath the single hanging lightbulb. He opens his palm and studies the key.

The lockbox opens easily and Max pulls out the package that Colonel Erdmann paid him to keep. It is addressed to his wife, Dorothea, and the very way he has written her name—the gentle, sloping letters—suggests an adoration that makes Max wince.

He will not open the package, but his curiosity is aroused. He gives it a gentle shake, then presses his ear against the brown paper wrapping. Within he can hear the faint chimes of a music box, a few random notes let loose by the movement. Erdmann could have given his wife this gift in Frankfurt when he'd had her paged. But no, he had waited. And Max believes he had done so purposefully. This was to be a gift she would receive in the event of his death. A farewell. He slides the package carefully to the side, incapable of sorting through his emotions.

Erdmann's is the only package in the box. The rest are letters and postcards. He pulls them out and places them in two large stacks to be counted. There are 358, but this is not something he will be able to say with any degree of certainty for at least an hour. Because he has counted half of the first stack when he finds the letter.

There is no stamp. No address—return or otherwise. Just one name written hastily in black ink.

Max.

His own name. And he recognizes Emilie's direct handwriting.

The letters blur before his eyes, and frantic blinking does nothing to clear his vision. He lays the envelope on the table and presses it down with a trembling hand.

Max Zabel drops his head to the table and weeps.

THE CABIN BOY

Werner won't back away from the cordoned-off wreckage despite orders from the gruff soldier. The man can't be much older than Werner, but he's had the fear of God put in him and he won't let Werner near the airship. American soldiers stand at regular intervals guarding what's left of the *Hindenburg*. They hadn't moved quickly enough the night before, so spectators made off with bits of the ship and various objects. Now they don't know if important clues were lost. Commander Pruss blames this on the Lakehurst leadership. They blame it on him. Tension sweeps through both ranks, and the finger-pointing and the whispering have already begun.

In theory Werner could move down the line and try his luck with the next soldier, but he doesn't see the point. The base commander has given him permission to search for his grandfather's pocket watch, and he intends to do just that.

"My name is Werner Franz—"

"I don't care who you are," the soldier says but then hesitates when he notes the heavy German accent.

"—And I'm cabin boy on this ship." Werner chooses words that he knows. Simple, clear words. He speaks them loudly. With confidence. "Rosendahl gave me permission."

He doesn't break eye contact and he doesn't betray any emotion. The soldier looks uncertain, but Werner stands there, hands clasped in front of him, waiting. He'll go back and get it in writing if he has to.

"Let him through, Frank!" someone shouts from twenty feet away. "That's the kid I told you about last night."

Werner turns to see the soldier who had so kindly lent him a coat. He waves a greeting and then ducks under the rope before anyone else has a chance to object.

The ship has burned its mark into the field; a patch of scorched earth the exact length and width of the *Hindenburg*. Werner stands at the edge, unsure how to enter. It's only when he catches a glimpse of Max picking his way through rubble at the rear of the ship that Werner finds the courage to step in.

He goes first to where the officers' mess was located. Even with nothing left but ashes and blistered metal, he finds the place by instinct, making turns where corridors would have been, imagining the steps down to B-deck. Werner knows the pocket watch could not be here, but he doesn't think he'll get another chance to look around. Besides, he wants to find a souvenir if he can. Perhaps a bit of the fine china on which he used to serve meals to the officers. He wants proof—something he can hold on to with his own hands— that he was on the *Hindenburg* and that he survived. Seeing his name in print this morning has made him fear his own mortality. But it has also made him proud of his service.

There is nothing left of the officers' mess. Not a dish. Not a table. Nothing but bits of broken metal and melted glass. So he moves on toward the crew quarters and the room he shared with Wilhelm Balla. He has a sinking feeling in his heart that the watch has been lost forever. How will he explain that to his father and his grandfather? They gave the watch to him, not Günter. He should have taken better care of it.

Werner is mentally berating himself when he steps through what is left of the doorway to his cabin. The fabric-covered walls, the carpet, the beds have all been burnt to ash. But he sees a glimpse of what used to be the closet. He kicks at it with his foot and it crumbles further, revealing the corner of a burlap bag. Hope trembles in his chest. Werner squats to pick through the bag. Bits of burned clothing and the heel of a shoe are all that's left. Or at least he thinks so until his fingers touch the unmistakable links of chain.

He lifts his grandfather's pocket watch from the ruins with the tip of one dirty finger. He sits back on his rear end, right in a pile of ashes, astonished. Had he been forced to wager, he would have said the watch was lost. Yet here it is, cradled in the palm of his hand, its survival as improbable as his own.

Werner sets the watch in his pocket and dusts the soot from his pants. He isn't certain what to do with himself now that he has no duties to perform. The officers and crew members who survived are either in the infirmary or meeting with the base commander to figure out what happened, *how* this could possibly have happened, and what they will do about it now. There is no place for Werner, so he wanders away from the wreckage, circling it aimlessly.

He has seen the small clumps of flowers, but it's not until the toe of his boot catches one for the third time and he stumbles forward that he stops and looks at them. The petals are small, but they are bright and open and they smell like spring.

Werner Franz has something to do after all.

He picks a messy handful of the white starbursts and jogs back to the main office where he left the newspaper earlier that day. He scans the list of names more thoroughly this time now that the shock has worn off. He finds the one he's looking for and reads it three times, just to make sure. He sounds out the letters carefully, using the tricks that his mother taught him.

It is not a pleasant task but Werner will keep his promise. He finds Irene Doehner laid out beside her father, arms crossed over her chest, a blanket laid across her body. Their names are written on cardboard signs at the base of their cots. There are almost three dozen bodies in the room, and hers is the smallest of them. Werner does not see her mother or her brothers, either on the cots or anywhere else, and he wonders where they might be. He wonders, but he doesn't go in search of them to offer his condolences because his business is with Irene alone.

"I told you that I would bring you flowers today," Werner whispers over her still, slender form. He lays them on her chest, then presses the heels of his hands into his eyes and rubs. The tears spill around them. Down his cheeks. Over his chin. Werner stands beside the body of Irene Doehner and cries until his throat is dry and his nose is red.

THE NAVIGATOR

Twenty-four hours ago Max was kissing Emilie for the last time and now he's standing inside the burnt skeleton of the *Hindenburg*. The sight is confounding. This is the ship he has lived in every day for almost two years, but it's only an echo of the ship he knew. The bones are here but the flesh is gone. The shape is broken. Twisted. Warped by heat and impact. And yet he knows exactly where he is. The axial catwalk is usually forty feet in the air and hangs directly over the keel catwalk. But they lie parallel on the ground now, and Max stands between them, hands in the pockets of a borrowed U.S. Navy petty officer's uniform. It's the best they could do on short notice, and judging by the uneasy glances he has received for the last three hours, they're eager for his clothes to be laundered and returned.

The fire started here, somewhere in the vicinity of gas cell number four. That's what the witnesses on the ground reported to Pruss. Now that Lakehurst is swarming with reporters and cameras and gawkers, the crew will be called upon to give an answer. There is a rumor, though he can't believe it is true, that the explosion was recorded and broadcast over the radio and that the entire wreck was filmed for a newsreel. They are saying this disaster made history.

The questions are coming from all directions. Why? How? No one knows. Not yet. But Max is here, picking through the rubble like every other crew member who can stand without crutches, in an effort to give his commanding officers an answer to these questions.

Airships crash sometimes. And they've been torn apart by storms, but Max has never heard of one exploding for no reason. During battle, yes. But the *Hindenburg* wasn't taking fire and it wasn't under duress—the strain of their near miss off Newfoundland and again during landing might have torn a gas cell, but still, there would need to be a spark to ignite the hydrogen. It couldn't have been lightning. That happens often enough. And the ship was built to withstand it. He can think of no plausible explanation for how the ship exploded. So he looks for one instead.

For an hour Max searches the rubble, at times focusing on the larger, twisted skeleton for clues, and then digging through the ash itself. The wicker cages that held the dogs are gone but he finds a collar—little more than burnt leather and a melted nameplate that reads ULLA. There are charred bones as well, but he can't bear to look at them, so he walks away.

Max misses the object at first. It appears to be nothing more than a lump of blackened metal caught on the twisted girders at the rear of the ship. But something catches in his mind and he turns to look at it again. Bends lower. He nudges it with the toe of his shoe and it slides loose, clatters across the metal, and comes to a stop three inches from his foot.

It is a pistol. A Luger. He knows the shape of this gun because he owns one himself. Or he did until it was taken from his cabin. He doesn't have to check the serial number stamped on the side to know that this is his weapon. With a detached calm, Max opens the chamber and counts the bullets inside. One round is missing. A single shot. He has seen muzzle flash on countless firing ranges. It's not just a spark, but a small bolt of flame large enough to ignite an airship carrying two hundred thousand cubic meters of combustible hydrogen.

Max Zabel stares at the weapon in his hand with the stupid, horrified expression of a man who is slowly coming to a terrible conclusion. The gun issued to him brought down the *Hindenburg*.

U.S. Commerce Department Board of Inquiry

Hindenburg Accident Hearings

May 19, 1937

Naval Air Station, Main Hangar, Lakehurst, New Jersey

Though sabotage could have produced the phenomena observed in the fire that destroyed the *Hindenburg*, there is still in my opinion no convincing evidence of a plot, either Communist or Nazi inspired. The one indisputable fact in the disaster is that the *Hindenburg* burned because she was inflated with hydrogen.

—*Douglas H. Robinson*, Giants in the Sky: A History of the Rigid Airship

Max has decided on his lie, but in the end it doesn't matter. The Board of Inquiry is not interested in the people who traveled on board the *Hindenburg*—the quarrels and plans, the passions or the duplicities. They are interested in gas valves and bracing wires and stub keels. They are interested in technicalities. The Board of Inquiry wants to know if the tight turns the airship took in its second approach toward Lakehurst resulted in structural damage that punctured the gas cells. They want to know if everyone on board followed protocol. The committee of experts gathered to investigate the disaster is focused on mechanics. They spend a good bit of time talking about lightning strikes and static electricity. An hour is spent discussing wind speeds. Another twenty minutes on mooring lines.

Max Zabel sits in his wooden chair before a room full of people and carefully explains how he lowered the forward landing wheel.

He tells them how strong headwinds delayed the trip by twelve hours over the journey of three and a half days, how the first landing attempt was thwarted by storms.

He is never asked about tensions between the passengers or secrets kept. He is never probed about his relationship with Emilie or the confiscation of her travel papers. He is not called on to account for his missing pistol or why his name was listed on the manifest as the owner of the second dog. Nor does he volunteer any of this information.

The German and American aviation experts gathered at Lakehurst are here to absolve themselves of blame. They are concerned only with things that do not matter. They are each determined to acquit their own countries. The one great success of the Board of Inquiry is that they agree on a single thing: they agree that they do not know why the airship crashed, only that it did. Only that its massive, combustible stores of hydrogen are at fault.

Sabotage is mentioned, of course. It has to be. But there is no *proof*. And while this might not be a court of law, they still require an eyewitness. A weapon. A motive. And none of these things is readily available, so the possibility of malicious intent is cast aside before it can be seriously considered. The results of this great raucous investigation are inconclusive. And that answer is more than good enough for both countries.

THE CABIN BOY

May 22, 1937, aboard the steamship Europa, *6:05 a.m.*

Werner Franz has forgotten that today is his fifteenth birthday. He sees this reminder written on a cardboard sign in the hands of Xaver Maier when he enters the steamship's elegant dining hall. He stands in the doorway as a small group of surviving stewards and kitchen crew members let out a chorus of raucous shouts and whistles. Most of his fellow crew members cluster near the chef, but a handful linger at the door, waiting for him to enter. Waiting to slap him on the back. Xaver steps away from the small round table to reveal a birthday cake.

The chef shrugs when he sees Werner's stunned expression. "They let me use the kitchen."

"You made that?" Werner asks.

There is something mischievous in Xaver's smirk. He tries to hide it by drawing on the lit cigarette in his hand. "It's a big day."

Even though they are on board the *Europa* as passengers, Werner cannot shake the habit of rising early and reporting for duty. The others have teased him about this for days, but Werner can't help it. He doesn't know what to do with himself anymore. He doesn't know how to let others serve his meals or make his bed. Nor does he enjoy this languid rocking pace at sea. It makes him nauseous. He is restless and out of sorts. So he sticks with the comfort of long-established routine. Yet this is the first time any of the crew has joined him in the dining room so early. He has gotten used to eating alone. Werner finds that he is so grateful for the company that he has to twist his face so they won't see him cry. The sight of his friends and this gift is so overwhelming that he can allow only one delighted smile, a small nod, and then he stares at his shoes. It is too much.

He is wondering how to get control of these erratic feelings when suddenly there is a frigid torrent rushing down his shirt and into his trousers, followed by the sound of splashing water. Werner gasps, eyes squeezed shut, arms out, mouth open. When he tries to yelp he chokes on ice water. The water keeps coming, and he can hear laughter and cheering. He tries to speak but coughs instead. He stands there, before his fellow crew members, dripping wet. Werner shakes his floppy hair and water splatters across the plush carpet.

The cabin boy is frozen in place, dripping from head to toe, staring at Xaver Maier, who laughs so hard he has to steady himself against the table. "You look like a drowned cat."

Werner spits a mouthful of water into his hand. "What did you do that for?"

"It was my idea." The boy turns slowly at the stern voice of Heinrich Kubis. The chief steward holds an empty bucket in one hand and a towel in the other. "Congratulations, Herr Franz, you have just crossed the line."

A sailor's baptism can take many forms—most of them far more cruel than what Werner experienced—but they all have one thing in common: a new sailor is initiated upon crossing the equator for the first time. It's a sign that he can handle a long journey, that he is accepted by his peers. Werner has heard the stories often enough, but he never thought that he would experience the ritual.

"But we didn't cross the equator," Werner argues.

He has never seen the chief steward smile before. Under different circumstances he might mistake it for a wince.

"Perhaps not," Kubis says. "But today we land in Bremershaven and this voyage will be complete. You have carried yourself like a man. You deserve to be recognized." He looks directly at Werner and when he speaks again his voice is filled with sincerity. "You have passed your probationary period, Werner. Would you like a permanent position with the Zeppelin-Reederei?"

He is confused. "But the ship is gone."

Kubis appears unconcerned. "They will find a place for you."

"You mean I still have a job?"

"Not just any job." Kubis pulls a telegram from his pocket and hands it to Werner. "You have been invited to become a steward on the *Graf Zeppelin*. By Captain Hans von Schiller himself."

Hope, that small fluttering thing, beats against his rib cage. Werner has been mourning the loss of his job as deeply as he has mourned his friends. He did not know how much he loved flying until he set foot on the damp, rocking deck of the *Europa*. Every day on board the steamship has been a small, acute death for him.

Werner takes the telegram from Kubis and reads it for himself. Slowly. Carefully. If he struggles over a word or two he does not let on. He stands there for a moment letting the invitation sink in. Werner is no longer a cabin boy. He is a steward.

Heinrich Kubis grabs Werner's hand and shakes it with a firm, confident grip. Man to man. "They are expecting your response this morning. But first you should have some cake."

THE NAVIGATOR

July 24, 1937, Hauptfriedhof cemetery, Frankfurt, 7:25 p.m.

This is not a place where people linger. The cemetery is so filled with shadows and sorrow that Max finds himself alone, as he has every other evening he has come to visit Emilie's grave. This is a place that whispers of loss if you listen closely. And if you linger beneath the sprawling branches or walk among the worn headstones, you will be lured into an otherworldly trance. This frightens most people and they hasten away the moment their tears and flowers have been laid upon the ground. But Max knows that if you resist the instinct to run you will find something lovely here. You will find peace. And he craves that more than company these days.

Max sits beside Emilie, his shoulder pressed against the smooth granite of her headstone, watching the sun sink above a copse of spruce trees that have turned beryl and fragrant in the summer heat. In this gathering dusk the light has a spectral quality, a shimmering goldenness that is breathtaking. Humbling, even. The beauty of this silent, reverent place lifts the shell of numbness that Max has carried since the wreck. His body aches, desperate for Emilie's phantom touch, the way she tugged his earlobe between thumb and forefinger when they kissed. Her cool hand at the base of his neck. Her laughter. Anything. Everything. Max misses the entirety of her. So he participates in this aching, visceral ritual. It is a cruelty he inflicts upon himself, the pulling of a scab from an aging wound, one he picks constantly to keep her near.

Her memory returns, hovers at his side as he prepares to read the letter again. Max can almost see her gliding through this verdant place, the beautiful woman who could have been his wife, now nothing more than ghost and memory. He can almost hear the sound of her laughter, can almost feel the warmth of her hand. This vision of Emilie evaporates as quickly as it came, but emotions follow immediately in its wake. They come first as pain—there are so many and they are so intense—but he closes his eyes and lets them wash over him. Soon they turn to other things. Sadness. Joy. Loneliness. Anger. Hope. Regret. Guilt. Love—this is the hardest to bear, and he bends beneath its weight. Max receives the emotions one by one, and when the wave has subsided he looks to the sky again. He breathes.

It took him weeks to understand that he asked Emilie to do the impossible. He wanted her to let go of her husband's memory. To accept that he was dead. To move on. It was a foolish thing to expect. He knows that now. Her death proved that. There is no moving on from this kind of loss.

It was Emilie's letter, however, that began the work of patching him back together. Max is shattered. He may always be. But he finally has the answer he wanted, and that is enough for today. Tomorrow. A lifetime perhaps. Max has memorized the words, but he reads them every evening at 7:25 anyway. It is the moment when the fire broke out, the moment when he lost Emilie. He unfolds the letter and turns his back to the setting sun so he will have light to read.

Max,

I'm so sorry I don't have the courage to say this in person. But I imagine you sitting somewhere in one of those straight-backed chairs that you prefer, spectacles on the end of your nose (yes, I realize you don't wear spectacles but this is my fantasy, so you must suffer through as I see it), sifting letters and sorting them into piles. I imagine you lifting this one from the stack. To be honest, I hope that your breath catches in your throat or that your heart beats a little faster. And I know it has taken me ages to come to that conclusion. But you must forgive me. My heart isn't whole. It has been broken and badly put back together. Yet the truth is that I want you to lean forward a bit when you see your name in my handwriting. I want that. And it's only now that I realize I need it as well. I need you.

So my answer is yes. It's that simple. Yes, you can have my heart, all that's left of it, at any rate. There's a part of me that will always belong to Hans. There is nothing I can do about that. But it's a part of me that lived a long time ago and now resides in distant shadow. All that I am today is yours. My heart is no great prize. I am scared and selfish and years away from being young. But I will be waiting for you on our return flight. Please come find me any day or night or anytime that you are not guiding us home with your strong and sure hands. In the meantime wear this. It's not the key to my heart—we are too old for sentimental gestures—but it is proof that I trust you with it.

Yes, I will be your wife if you will still have me.

Emilie

The first time Max read the letter he didn't have the courage to take her necklace from the envelope. But he wears it now, tucked beneath his uniform. Emilie gave him everything she was capable of giving. More than he deserves. He has the letter and he has her key. And now he is the one who will hold memories and mourn her loss. Max will carry her the way that she carried her first husband. She will be the beautiful, painful wound that will never entirely heal.

THE JOURNALIST

August 10, 1937, Frankfurt, Germany, 9:15 a.m.

Gertrud steps into her own kitchen. It is filled with morning light, and the windows are open. A bee buzzes at the screen. She can hear the neighbors talking about road conditions and rationing. Leonhard is still in the driveway, pulling bags from the car. He calls to them and they answer back, but he sounds older since the wreck. There is a coarseness in his voice that wasn't there before. This trip aged him, and for the first time since they married he looks two decades older than her.

Gertrud's mother sits at the kitchen table sipping a cup of tea, her focus on the morning paper and its blaring headlines. There, in black and white, is a photo of the *Hindenburg* in all its blazing, horrific glory. Gertrud blanches at the sight. It has been months and she still can't look at the pictures or read the articles.

She stands there for a moment waiting for the absurd panic to subside. She listens. Waits. And then, when she is certain that she can speak without her voice trembling, she says, "Mother," and to her ears she sounds like a child.

"You're home!"

"Where is he?"

Her mother rises from the table and reaches for her. She wraps Gertrud in warmth and comfort and then speaks slowly into her ear, "There is something I need to tell you."

Gertrud grabs the counter for support and her mother realizes her mistake. "Egon is fine," she says in a rush. "Absolutely fine. You can go to him in a moment. But you must know something first."

"What?" Leonhard stands at the kitchen door now, a suitcase under each arm.

Her mother places a finger over her lips and nods toward the neighbor's house. They are quiet now. Listening, perhaps.

"The Gestapo," her mother mouths the words.

Leonhard sets the bags down carefully. He pushes them away with his foot. "What about them?"

"The crash has been all over the news for months. And they are concerned."

They lean toward one another like the legs on a stool, their whispers no louder than the bees at the screen.

"Why?" Gertrud asks.

"They have visited several times. The Ministry of Propaganda is worried that you have been telling a version of events that they do not approve of."

"We have been in America for months!"

"That is exactly the point. They could not control what you said or who you spoke with. Know that they are watching. They are listening. They came here three times while you were gone, asking the same questions in different ways." She shakes Gertrud's shoulders. "You have no friends. Do you understand? None. You have me. And you have each other. That is all."

"It is enough." Leonhard lays his hand across the small of Gertrud's back. He kisses her temple lightly. "Go to him, *Liebchen.*"

It has been months since she has walked through the rooms of this home, but her feet carry her around the corner, down the hall, and to the doorway of Egon's room. She hears him before she sees him. Hears him laughing and chattering to himself.

Gertrud's heart is loud and tight within her chest. She stops two feet from the door and listens. She drinks in that glorious sound. And then she steps forward.

The windows in Egon's room stretch from floor to ceiling, and he stands before one, his back to her, watching a butterfly on the bush outside. He is mesmerized. Delighted. Her son wears only a cloth diaper. The light catches his hair. It is curlier than when they left. Longer. It is soft and molten, like caramel, and she longs to loop one of those lazy curls around her finger.

Leonhard rests his chin on her shoulder. They watch their son for a moment and then he whispers in her ear, "Go on. Don't be afraid."

"What if he has forgotten me?"

"You are a silly thing, *Liebchen*. No man could forget you."

The tears come and she has to swallow them. She has to breathe. She has to compose herself. Gertrud drops to her knees in the doorway.

"Egon."

The boy jumps, then turns around. For one second the blankness on his face confirms her fear. He is afraid. He will cry. But no, he is only startled. His small, pink lip trembles for a moment, and then his face is transformed into joy. Nothing but pure, breathtaking joy. He has four teeth now. His dimples are deeper, his eyes are bluer, and he can walk.

Egon Adelt grins with unabashed delight, raises his arms, and takes three triumphant steps toward his mother before dropping into a frantic crawl. He knows her. He comes to her. And she scoops him up, overcome. Gertrud inhales the clean smell of him. The powder and the sweetness of his skin. She laughs and she weeps as Leonhard folds his arms around them both.

They are home.

They said it was an uneventful flight. This phrase is repeated countless times in the hundreds of pages of eyewitness testimony compiled by the Commerce Department Board of Inquiry. Leonhard Adelt, a German journalist, later wrote, "Our trip on the *Hindenburg* in May was the most uneventful journey I ever undertook in an airship." In November 1937 the American heiress Margaret Mather wrote an article for *Harper's* in which she described the trip with such banality that one has to wonder why the passengers didn't sleep the entire time.

An uneventful flight.

But here's the problem: I don't believe them. Ninety-seven people traveled on a floating luxury hotel for three days over the Atlantic Ocean. The events that took place on board might not have been explosive—at least not until the end—but I doubt they were *uneventful*. I've taken enough transatlantic flights to know you can't place that many people in such a small space for any length of time and not have tension brewing beneath the surface. But if you're going to call bullshit on historical events, you'd best have a good theory to offer as an alternative. This novel is my attempt at a theory. It is the result of my short-term love affair with that spectacular moment in history. I hope that you will humor me. And I hope you enjoy the ride.

I've long been familiar with the iconic photos of the *Hindenburg*'s destruction and with Herb Morrison's famous exclamation, "Oh, the humanity!" But until I began researching this book, I couldn't tell you the name of a single person on board the airship. Thirty-six people lost their lives when the *Hindenburg* exploded over Lakehurst, New Jersey, and I wanted to know who they were.

In writing *Flight of Dreams* I was determined to use the real people who were on that last ill-fated flight. I was determined that I would not change their fate—even when it broke my heart (which it did many times during the month when I wrote of the disaster itself). If they survived in real life, they survived in this novel. If they died in real life, they died in this novel.

But since I was writing about real people, I needed help. We're talking about men and women who lived and died almost eighty years ago. Most of them were not famous. No biographies were written about them. No articles. By and large, history remembers them with only the occasional anecdote or footnote. Which is why Patrick Russell's Web site, www.facesofthehindenburg.blogspot.com, was such a godsend. He has spent years compiling extensive biographical information on every passenger and crew member on that last flight. Every article is filled with fascinating minutiae about them. Among many things, I learned from Mr. Russell that Gertrud Adelt's press card had recently been revoked by the Nazis, that Werner Franz's grandfather gave him a pocket watch, that Max Zabel had recently taken over as postmaster, that the American worked in the same building as Hitler's Ministry of Propaganda, and that Emilie Imhof was the only woman ever to work aboard a zeppelin. To me, these seemingly insignificant things—when studied and sifted and rearranged—became the spine of this story. Tiny true things made bigger and more relevant when added together.

I confess that prior to writing this novel I knew absolutely nothing about zeppelins. And why would I? The reign of airships ended on May 6, 1937, in that New Jersey field. It was the first disaster of that scale ever to be recorded on film. And while it was not broadcast live, as we've often been told, it was played on air later that night. And then played repeatedly on every newsreel in every theater around much of the world afterward. Today zeppelins are the stuff of fantasy and steampunk. But they were highly functional engineering marvels at the time. And to re-create those three and a half days in midair I needed to become a pseudo-expert on airship travel and construction. Dan Grossman's Web site, www.airships .net, and Rick Archbold's book *Hindenburg: An Illustrated History* provided everything I needed to know about the engineering and operation of the *Hindenburg*. I endeavored to faithfully portray the airship—its strengths and weaknesses, its peculiar quirks—and consulted these resources daily while working on *Flight of Dreams*. However, my primary focus has been, and always will be, the people on board. So any mistakes with the airship itself—how it was designed and how it functioned—are entirely mine. I offer my advance apologies to any students of airship history who find fault with my fictional rendering of the *Hindenburg*.

Some of the events, conversations, meals, and rivalries described in this book really happened. But most of them, to the best of my knowledge, did not. Having done my research and committed to writing about the real people on board, there came a point when I had to tell my own story. My version of the events. What I believe *could have happened*, not necessarily what did happen. Because none of us will ever truly know what occurred on board or why the *Hindenburg* exploded. And believe me, people have tried to find these answers for almost eighty years. Theories abound—I did my best to give a nod to each of them—but facts are hard to come by. It was this mystery that drew me to the story in the first place. The fact that we do not know what happened. The fact that we will *never* know. I built this story within those blank, unknown spaces.

My job was to find a plausible explanation for the spark. The *Hindenburg* burned in thirty-four seconds. Half of one minute. That is mind-boggling if you think about it. And all that we truly know is that it burned so quickly because of a combination of hydrogen and thermite (a huge thanks to *MythBusters* and their countless experiments for answering that long-standing question). But no one has ever been able to say for certain what ignited the hydrogen. I know there are a myriad of possible technical, mechanical, and meteorological causes for that spark. But when my turn came to tell this story, I wanted the catalyst to be human.

That said, much of what happens here is pure fiction. I took all the known disparate details, from the dogs on board to the mail drop over Cologne, and wove them together in a way that made sense to me. I claim to have no special knowledge. I simply wanted to find a good story and then tell it in a way that would bring these people and their journey to life for you. And in so doing I am deeply aware that I have written about people who really lived. I have assumed things about them. I have put words in their mouths. I have made them do things—sometimes noble and sometimes despicable—that they likely never did in real life. That is the risk I took, and it is sobering to say the least. I know from experience how the loved ones of real people may read a fictionalized account of an event and then feel compelled to contact the writer. So I did my best to be honest and honorable on these pages.

In some instances dialogue and phrases were taken directly from written accounts and interviews of *Hindenburg* survivors. A few examples include the incident with Joseph Späh and his arrival at the airfield, both the ruckus he caused and the soldier's examination of his daughter's doll. Leonhard Adelt said the ship was "a gray object in a gray mist, over an invisible sea." I took the liberty of using his words in a scene with Emilie Imhof. The near crash off the coast of Newfoundland actually occurred during a flight to Lakehurst in 1936. Gertrud's trouble with the customs officer in Frankfurt was an event that in reality happened to Margaret Mather. Werner Franz's dramatic escape from the airship—although seemingly unbelievable—unfolded exactly as written here and has been described in numerous places over the years. In the end I wanted the passengers' thoughts and words and experiences to permeate this novel. It is about them, after all, and to portray this flight as they saw it was important to me. Again, my primary sources of research—in particular *Hindenburg: An Illustrated History* and www.facesofthehindenburg.blogspot.com—helped tremendously in my search for specific details of their experiences, escapes, and tragic deaths.

It bears repeating that this book is *fiction*. But it is my fiction, and I am desperately proud of this story. I hope you come to love this book the way I do. And I hope you remember these men and women. Because they deserve to be remembered.

ACKNOWLEDGMENTS

"'Thank you' is the best prayer anyone could say."

—*Alice Walker*

Thank you. Simple words, really, but so hard to get right. Especially for someone who trades in words for a living. But I will do my best and I ask that you bear with me for a moment while I extol those who helped make this book a reality.

Literary agents don't come better than Elisabeth Weed. She is brilliant. Kind. Patient. Funny. And she never makes me feel stupid when I call her with stupid questions. I have worked with her for almost four years and can't imagine navigating the choppy waters of publishing without her. She has been a friend and life preserver and a constant encouragement. Her assistant, Dana Murphy, is lovely and helpful and I'd steal her away in a skinny minute. Jenny Meyer handles foreign rights and I suspect she moonlights as a superhero. *Thank you.*

My amazing editor, Melissa Danaczko, is a godsend. Sometimes I think we have the same brain because there's no other way to explain how she *gets* me and my stories and my random, guarded writing process. She knows when to give me free rein and when to rein me in. I've never met another person who can wield a red pen with such wisdom and precision. I mean it quite sincerely when I say that this book would not exist without her. If not for her redirection, I would have gone with another idea and *Flight of Dreams* would have never been. *Thank you.*

Blake Leyers is my first reader and early editor. And for this I apologize because she sees my stories when they bear a greater resemblance to steaming piles of manure than soon-to-be books. Yet she never fails to tell me what I've done right and help me see what I've done wrong. She was to this novel what guardrails are to a careening vehicle. I'm so grateful she kept it from flying off the edge. *Thank you.*

Marybeth Whalen is the sort of friend every woman should have. She came into my life seven years ago and made it better with her wit and loyalty and dogged encouragement. She invited me to join her on a wild experiment called She Reads, and I don't think either of us will ever be the same—nor would we want to be. She celebrates with me. She listens to me bleat. And she texts me ten times a day with things that either make me laugh or cry. Some of them I can't repeat in public. *Thank you.*

JT Ellison and Paige Crutcher have been two of the best things about moving back to Nashville. I never expected new friends. Yet these two burst into my world with their laughter and *queso* and f-bombs, and my life is all the richer for it. I'm so grateful for our lunch dates and yoga sessions and story dissection. I couldn't do this without you. *Thank you.*

The publishing wizards at Doubleday never cease to amaze me. I am so incredibly thankful for SuperTodd Doughty (the best publicist I've ever known or worked with), Judy Jacoby (marketer extraordinaire), Margo Shickmanter (editorial assistant), John Fontana (cover designer), Bill Thomas (publisher and all-around champion), Nora Reichard (production editor), Maggie Carr (copy editor), and Benjamin Hamilton (German-language proofreader). The Random House sales team (especially Cathy Calvert, Ann Kingman, Stacie Carlini, Emily Bates, Lynn Kovach, Beth Koehler, Beth Meister, James Kimball, Janet Cook, Ruth Liebmann, David Weller, and Jason Gobble) are kinder to me than I deserve. *Thank you.*

Additional thanks go to Abby Belbeck, Rocko Beezlenut, Dian Belbeck, Jannell Barefoot, Tayler Storrs, Michael Easley, Kaylee Storrs, Emily Allison, Kristee Mays, River Jordan, Joy Jordan-Lake, DeeAnn Blackburn, Shelby Rawson, the She Reads blog network, and the amazing women who teach my children so I can write for six hours a day. For your friendship, your service, your leadership, your love, your mentoring, your truth speaking, your diligence, your encouragement, your presence in my life, *thank you.*

My husband, Ashley, has known and loved me for sixteen years. He is the green-eyed, dimpled, Texan miracle I behold every day. And if I never experience another miracle for the rest of my life, he will be enough. For listening to me when he'd rather have silence, for making coffee when I can't wake up, for making lunches and taking the early shift with carpool, for being my best friend, my lover, my safe place, *thank you.*

The Wild Rumpus (London, Parker, Marshall, and Riggs) is the part of my heart that walks around outside of my body. Seeing them grow and mature and learn and risk is the greatest privilege of my life. For this honor, I *thank you.*

I once heard that to be a Christian simply means that I am a beggar showing other beggars where to find bread. It is the truest thing I know. I am a beggar. And to the Giver of Bread, I say *thank You.*

And finally, dear reader, for taking a chance on me and on this novel, I *thank you.*

ALSO BY

ARIEL LAWHON

I WAS ANASTASIA

Russia, July 17, 1918: Under direct orders from Vladimir
Lenin, Bolshevik secret police force Anastasia Romanov and
her family into a damp basement, where they face a mer-
ciless firing squad. None survive. At least that is what the
executioners have always claimed. Germany, February 17,
1920: A young woman bearing an uncanny resemblance to
Anastasia Romanov is pulled shivering from a canal and
is taken to the hospital, where an examination reveals that
her body is riddled with countless horrific scars. As rumors
begin to circulate through European society that the young-
est Romanov daughter has survived, old enemies and new
threats are awakened. This thrilling saga is every bit as moving and momentous as it is harrowing and twisted.

Fiction

THE WIFE, THE MAID, AND THE MISTRESS

One summer night in 1930, Judge Joseph Crater steps into a
New York City cab and is never heard from again. Behind this
great man are three women, each with her own tale to tell:
Stella, his fashionable wife, the picture of propriety; Maria,
their steadfast maid, indebted to the judge; and Ritzi, his
showgirl mistress, willing to seize any chance to break out of
the chorus line. As the twisted truth emerges, Ariel Lawhon's
debut mystery novel tantalizingly reimagines a scandalous
murder mystery that rocked the nation.

Fiction

ANCHOR BOOKS
Available wherever books are sold.
www.anchorbooks.com

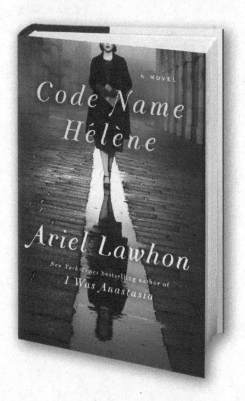